A
FORGERY
OF
ROSES

Books by Jessica S. Olson
available from Inkyard Press

Sing Me Forgotten
A Forgery of Roses

A FORGERY OF ROSES

JESSICA S. OLSON

inkyard
PRESS

If you purchased this book without a cover you should be aware
that this book is stolen property. It was reported as "unsold and
destroyed" to the publisher, and neither the author nor the
publisher has received any payment for this "stripped book."

Recycling programs
for this product may
not exist in your area.

ISBN-13: 978-1-335-42919-3

A Forgery of Roses

First published in 2022. This edition published in 2023.

Copyright © 2022 by Jessica Olson

All rights reserved. No part of this book may be used or reproduced in any manner
whatsoever without written permission except in the case of brief quotations
embodied in critical articles and reviews.

This is a work of fiction. Names, characters, places and incidents are either the
product of the author's imagination or are used fictitiously. Any resemblance to
actual persons, living or dead, businesses, companies, events or locales is entirely
coincidental.

For questions and comments about the quality of this book, please contact us
at CustomerService@Harlequin.com.

Inkyard Press
22 Adelaide St. West, 41st Floor
Toronto, Ontario M5H 4E3, Canada
www.InkyardPress.com

Printed in U.S.A.

For those who fear what they cannot control.

I

When ladyroses burn, they bleed.

"A symbol of life," Mother used to say when we would bend over the smoke together.

But now, as I hold flame to stem, as I watch hungry, glowing embers devour leaves and thorns, as floral perfume curdles to ribbons of soot in my nose, I know she was wrong. For when the fire reaches the petals, they shrivel, curling as though in pain. And then they melt. Great fat rubies dribbling over my fingers and smattering into my bowl like gore.

Mother called it beautiful. But now that she and Father have gone, all I see is death.

Gritting my teeth, I tear my gaze from the slow trickle of red and try to steady the quake of my movements as I drop the scorched ladyrose stems into the trash bin and blow out my candle. Crossing to a pot of water I've got heating over the fire in the corner, I tip the bowl of ladyrose drippings in.

As soon as it hits the water, the rose blood fans out, a spiderweb of shimmering scarlet veins crawling through the pot until the whole thing clouds like it's full of sparkling garnet dust. I dip a spoon into the mixture and stir. It bubbles, smokes, and blackens.

Closing my eyes, I breathe in the sharp, cloying scent. Mother used to come home every day smelling like this—her clothes, her hair, her skin. With my head thick in a fog of exhaustion, it's easy to allow myself to imagine she's here next to me, chatting happily about how mixing burnt umber with ultramarine blue makes a far superior black than the tube of flat paint many artists purchase at the store. "It creates a more eye-catching hue," I can almost hear her say. "Make the shadows breathe, Myra."

From across the studio, the piercing laugh of my employer, portrait artist Elsie Moore, breaks through my thoughts, and I sigh as the echo of Mother's voice fades from my mind.

How long will it be before I forget what that sounded like?

Forcing away thoughts of Mother, I continue stirring the contents of my pot. Another few minutes, and it should be ready to remove from the heat, cover, and set in a cool place to coagulate. Three days hence, the bubbling charcoal syrup will thicken into a clear jellylike substance that I'll then transfer into tubes to stock alongside Elsie's paints, solvents, and brushes. Ladyrose gel. A painting medium I both revere and fear.

I toss the spoon into the sink and wrap a towel around the pot. Then I hoist it to the counter beneath the window to cool and drape a cloth over its top. Satisfied, I turn to my next task of the morning: a bouquet of dirty brushes waiting to be cleaned. As I unscrew the cap from a bottle of turpentine, I let my gaze wander to where Elsie's putting the finishing touches on a portrait of Mrs. Ramos across the room. Cadmium bright paints, eye-catching phthalo hues, and quinacridone details swirl together like smoke on Elsie's canvas. She holds her brushes with a steady hand, chattering animatedly to Mrs. Ramos without a care in the world.

What would it be like to paint so freely? To wield a brush without the threat of magic commandeering the portrait? To give in to the high of pure creation?

Painting used to be like that for me, back before my powers sparked to life a few years ago. In those days, there was no greater ecstasy than the promise of a blank canvas and a palette full of colors. Before magic, painting *was* magic.

The memory of it is enough to make me weep.

I press the bristles of a filbert brush against the coil at the bottom of the jar of turpentine to loosen the oils, but when Elsie gasps, I glance back up.

"No!" She presses a dramatic hand to her heart. "Wilburt Jr.? What does he have?"

Mrs. Ramos, sitting daintily on a settee in a pale pink dress, nods, her mouth twisted in a frown. "The papers don't say. I think it could be pneumonia, though. It's been going around this year. Mrs. Potsworth down the street passed away from a nasty case of it not last week!"

I frown. The only Wilburt Jr. they can possibly be talking about is the governor's son. A tall, strikingly handsome boy around my age whom I've only ever glimpsed at Lalverton city events.

Pursing my lips, I set aside the turpentine and dunk the brushes into the sink. Soap bubbles in my palm as I work it through the bristles, and I stare absently out the window at the snow swirling in the street and the passersby kicking through muddy slush on the sidewalk. I fall into a rhythm, imagining I'm back at the flat my family used to live in downtown. Mother is at my side in front of the kitchen sink, scrubbing burnt sienna out from underneath her fingernails. Father bustles in through the door, arms laden with bowls of leftover soups from his restaurant. My little sister, Lucy, rushes at him, asking if her pet frog can have the lobster bisque. *You know it's his favorite, Pa!*

"Myra?" Elsie says behind me, and I jump, dropping the brushes, which hit the bottom of the basin with a faint series of *plinks.*

"Ms. Moore!" I say, looking back to where she was chatting with Mrs. Ramos earlier. I catch sight of the curly haired woman tugging a coat over her dress as she heads out the door. "You scared me."

Elsie chuckles, thunking down another cupful of dirty brushes. "An ox could sneak up on you, dear. You spend too much time in your head." She turns her back to me and gestures at the buttons down her spine. "Help me off with my smock, please."

I obey. Sweat glistens on the back of her neck, dampening the gray curls that have escaped her tight bun.

"I know it's not my place to ask questions," the old woman continues, patting at her hair, "but…are you sleeping? How's Lucy?"

I paste on a neutral expression and slide the smock from Elsie's shoulders. "The same."

She sighs. "I do wish I could help."

The words are like a backhanded blow. I wonder what Mother would think if she heard them. Whether Father would scoff in that indignant way of his at the blatant lie.

I stare at my feet to keep from glancing at the fat amethysts drooping from Elsie's soft white earlobes, the glitter of half a dozen gold chains around her neck, or the bulbous gems on her gnarled fingers. Any one of those sold to a jeweler would fetch the money Lucy and I need, but three months ago when I came begging Elsie for the help she claims she wishes she could give me, she balked at the idea. Said it would do me no favors to hand me a reward I didn't earn.

I knew before I even asked her that she would say no. If

there's anything life has taught me, it's that I can't count on anyone but my sister. We're all each other has. And, in the past, that would have been enough. But with Lucy's illness having taken a turn for the worse and our funds being too meager to afford the medical care she needs, Elsie's patronizing words about "wishing she could help" make me want to scream.

"How was Mrs. Ramos?" I ask a bit too brightly as I fold the smock into a tidy little square and set it on a pile of linens I plan to wash tomorrow.

Elsie draws the back of her hand across her brow. "She's doing well, I think. Her son is visiting this week."

"The senator?"

"Yes. He took her to see Governor Harris's public address yesterday." Her expression sours.

"And?" I ask, not sure if I want to hear any more.

"She said the governor went on for at least five minutes berating Lalverton citizens for buying paintings and thus making light of the Holy Artist's divinity." She huffs. "That man is never going to let it go, is he?"

I groan. "When is he going to remember he's not a priest and that people's worship is not actually his concern?"

"He also said allowing secular art to become such a thriving business is the reason so many painters have gone missing. He apparently thinks it's a sign that the Artist is displeased."

I hiss through my teeth.

Painters have been disappearing one by one over the past year, starting with my mother, and yet the governor—the man whose duty it is to protect Lalverton—has done nothing. No major investigations, no questions asked.

Because we are the scum of the earth to him. Worse, even.

It's nothing I haven't heard before. I used to be forced to stand by as pompous worshippers spit on my mother, accusing her of desecrating the Artist by painting for profit. I watched others cross the street when they passed Elsie's studio, as though merely being in the presence of such heresy could taint their souls.

As the years have trickled by, though, the disdain seems to have eased up a bit. Only the most devout hold painters like Elsie and Mother in such contempt. The majority of people don't seem to mind what we do, and in recent months, portraiture has become quite popular in Lalverton.

But anytime Governor Harris goes on one of his burn-all-the-studios-to-the-ground rampages, my heart sinks.

I want to be a painter, just like Mother was—*is*—but it seems that particular life will always come with a healthy measure of judgment and disgust.

Elsie drops her voice to a whisper. "My bet—and don't you dare repeat this to a soul, dear—is that the governor is exterminating us one by one himself. Wiping us out like stink bugs under his boot."

A jolt zaps through my body.

Elsie registers my expression. "I'm sorry," she says quickly. "I should not have—"

"It's fine," I say, my voice a pitch too high as the image of my parents under Governor Harris's boot, twitching like a pair of dead insects, makes my stomach churn.

"Besides—" Elsie flounders for words "—the fact that your father is among the missing is a testament to the fact that it's not only painters, right?" She gives a nervous chuckle, as if such a statement should comfort me.

I stare at her.

The bell on the front door tinkles.

"Mr. Markleton!" Elsie almost shouts, diving across the room toward the short, balding merchant in the doorway in her hurry to get away from me. "Right on time, as usual!" Her voice fills the air with exaggerated cheeriness. "Come, come!" She weaves among easels stacked with paintings in varying stages of completion and directs Mr. Markleton to a cushy settee in front of one of the backdrops that line the far wall.

"Brought along this—I know how you love to keep up on the Lalverton gossip," he says with a smile, offering Elsie a rolled-up newspaper.

"Oh, yes! I heard about Governor Harris's son." She nods at me to take the paper. "But I did want to read the story myself. Thank you for bringing it along."

Mr. Markleton gives me a friendly wink as I carry the newspaper to the back table. Elsie's careless words about the missing people, about my parents, echo ceaselessly in my head, and I try to catch my breath as a wave of nausea rolls through me.

Elsie means well, I know that. She's always had a knack for speaking before she thinks.

And it's not like I could ever forget my parents are missing anyway. My whole world unraveled when they vanished, and it's only gotten harder the past few months as our bank accounts have emptied. We can scarcely afford food and rent, let alone the medical care Lucy needs now that her illness has worsened.

We had our whole lives planned out. I was to attend the Lalverton Conservatory for Music and the Arts when I turned eighteen next spring, just like Mother. I would graduate with highest marks, just like Mother. Then I would open my own studio, just like Mother did here with Elsie.

Lucy, who was only twelve when our parents disappeared, was already on track to be accepted into some of the most prestigious biology programs in the country. She planned to change the world with her discoveries. Improve the environment and save endangered animals.

But now, those plans are nothing more than dreams from another life. A memory of wishes that will never come true. I've spent the past several months painting portraits until dawn to build up a portfolio in hopes of securing one of the full-ride scholarships the conservatory offers, but...well. Thanks to my magic's interference, my portfolio is meager at best. I have a better chance at winning a scholarship to the moon.

Maybe my dreams were foolish anyway. Keeping my power from being discovered in a place like the conservatory would have been difficult. I don't know how Mother managed it.

Rubbing a fist over my aching eyes, I glance down at the newspaper in my hands. A black-and-white photograph of a square-jawed man smiles kindly back at me from the front page. Why do I recognize him?

I unfurl the paper and read the article.

> **The body of Frederick Bennett, who was reported missing eight years ago, was discovered in the cellar of Roderick Lowell's home last week.**

My fists tighten on the paper, crinkling it. Of course I know his face. Frederick Bennett's somber eyes have stared out from missing-person posters all over the city since I was nine years old. Mother told me she knew him from the conservatory and always wondered if he was a Prodigy like her. When he disappeared, she said she hoped he hadn't been kidnapped and coerced into using his magic for someone cruel and desperate.

With unease stinging in my gut, I read on.

> Autopsy reports reveal that the cause of death was starvation, though many lacerations, bruises, and broken bones were observed. Extensive scarring on his back and arms was noted, as well.
>
> Lowell, a prominent stockholder in Lalverton, has declined to respond to inquiries and is being held for questioning at the Lalverton Police Station.

A roaring fills my ears, and I stumble back several steps before sinking into Elsie's chair.

The report doesn't say the word "Prodigy," but it doesn't have to.

Prodigy magic, which flows through my body just as it did through Mother's, gives an artist the ability to alter human and animal bodies with their paintings, and it is considered by the Church to be even more of an abomination than normal portrait work. According to scripture, my very existence is a defilement of the power of our god, the Great Artist. Prodigies like us have been persecuted by the pious and captured by the greedy since the dawn of time. My head is full of the stories Mother told from her history books, the ones in which entire nations banded together to force a Prodigy to do their bidding. Where the holy priests burned them at the stake to cleanse the world of what they believed to be sinful imitation of the Artist.

As centuries have passed, the number of Prodigies in the world has dwindled—though whether it's because their genetic lines have been killed off or because the ones who have survived have kept their powers hidden like Mother, it's hard to say. With men like Governor Harris in charge of regions across the world, men willing to falsify charges in order to get Prodigies locked up in the name of "purifying" their streets, there's no telling how many of us are out there, hiding.

All I know is that someone found out what Mother was, and then she and Father vanished.

Just like Frederick Bennett.

A flicker of orange flashes in the corner of my eye from the front window, and I glance up from the paper. A small red-haired woman stands outside the studio entrance with a tiny white dog in a sparkling collar tucked under one arm. She nudges the door open, sending the bell above it tinkling once again. A swirl of snow twists into the room as she slips inside, and I stifle a gasp when I catch sight of her face.

Mrs. Adelia Harris, wife to the merciless governor set on

destroying every art studio in town, meets my gaze with a cold, hard stare. I tighten my grip on the newspaper.

With her husband's reelection campaign in full swing, her son in a sickbed, and her belief that portrait art is a sin of the vilest degree, what could she possibly want with us?

Elsie catches sight of her and leaps to her feet with a gasp, knocking over her stool, which clangs against the tile.

"Hello." Mrs. Harris's voice is quiet. Lethal. "I'd like to get a portrait done."

2

Mrs. Harris's face is almost as familiar to me as my own. She features in every photo of the governor I've ever seen, smiling primly at his side, looking on as her husband shakes hands with notable government officials or cuts ribbons for new constructions. Like some kind of maestro directing the scene, a puppeteer enthralling an audience of her own making.

Yet as she stands here before me, she looks markedly different from the version of her I've seen in the papers. Several strawberry wisps of hair trail around the sides of her face, which is drawn and pale. Grayish circles ring her eyes, and the stain usually applied to her lips is missing. She scans the studio, her gaze flitting among the portraits like she's afraid of them. Like they might come to life. But the set of her jaw is fierce, and her posture is rigid.

Elsie rights the fallen stool, cheeks pink, and smooths her hair. "Mrs. Harris! To what do I owe the honor?"

Mrs. Harris steps forward, her heels clacking on the tile

floor. She presses a hand against her dog's fluffy head and kneads the space between its ears. "I'd like to have a portrait done," she repeats.

"I'm terribly sorry, but I'm booked out for the rest of the week," Elsie says, her hands as twitchy as my own—whatever this woman wants with us, it can't be good. "But if you'd like to set up an appointment for later on, I might be able to work you in."

"No, no. I…" Mrs. Harris pauses, still rubbing the poor animal's head with her knuckles. "I need it done today. A private session."

"I assure you, I would love nothing more than to do a portrait for you, ma'am," Elsie says. "But I'm afraid I'm thoroughly swamped."

"I see." Mrs. Harris's mouth twists.

What if she and her husband are looking for a reason to close us down? Some trumped-up charge to put us out of shop? The longer we allow her to stay here observing us, the more opportunities she may have to find something she could accuse us of. Though refusing her service might prove just as fatal to our business in the long run, given her social influence. If there's one thing I've heard about the Harris family, it's that they get their way. Always.

Mrs. Harris cocks her head in my direction, meeting my gaze. Leaping to my feet, I toss the newspaper onto the counter and resume scrubbing Elsie's brushes, the back of my neck burning. But I keep my ears trained on the conversation.

"If you simply cannot wait…" Elsie's words are slow and careful. She's obviously come to the same conclusion as I—that kicking the woman out because we're afraid of her might only further incite the governor's hatred. She wrings her hands. "Perhaps we could arrange for my assistant, Myra Whitlock, to do the portrait?"

I freeze, gaping at Elsie.

"Your assistant?" Mrs. Harris chews on the words like they taste foul.

"Yes." Elsie layers on a thick sweetness to her voice to make up for what the governor's wife obviously took as an insult. "Myra is extremely accomplished. I would not suggest this as an option if I weren't absolutely certain of her capabilities as an artist. I've trained her myself."

"I don't know." Mrs. Harris finally stops massaging the dog's head and shifts the animal's position against her hip. "I had really hoped for a private session with *you*."

I'm still staring at Elsie, my mind racing, heart pounding. She isn't lying; I am capable, but my magic has gotten so out of hand lately I'm not sure if I could get through a whole sitting without giving myself away. And if there's one thing that could get us shut down, it's if Governor Harris gets wind that there's a Prodigy in his city. I wouldn't last the night.

My whole body has gone clammy and rigid.

Lucy's face flashes across my mind, and I force myself to breathe.

However dangerous it might be, doing a commissioned portrait would mean bonus pay over my hourly rate. Artist knows Lucy and I need those funds.

Mrs. Harris glances between me and Elsie for a moment longer before taking a deep breath. "I suppose."

My heart leaps into my throat as I set the dirty brushes aside. Forcing my mouth into what I hope is a professional smile, I step around the sink and cross to her, wiping my palms on my apron. "Good morning, Mrs. Harris."

I extend a hand for her to shake. Her glove is damp, and her eyes are still trained on Elsie, who has moved back to the corner with Mr. Markleton.

"Now, what sort of portrait were you looking for?" I ask, my nerves jangling like coins.

"Portrait?" Mrs. Harris blinks at me as though just remembering I'm here even though we're still shaking hands. "Oh, of course. Right." She releases me and adjusts her dog's collar, which, now that I'm up close, I can see is encrusted with hundreds of tiny gems—maybe diamonds?—that twinkle in the white light streaming in from the front windows. "Would you do a painting of Peony?"

"Peony?"

She holds up her dog, which blinks large, round eyes at me. "My puppy. She's quite a placid thing. She'll hold very still."

"Of course." I lead Mrs. Harris to the wall of backdrops and gesture for her to choose one, trying not to let the nervous tremors in my arms show.

Mrs. Harris selects the mauve-based backdrop near the front of the store and sets her dog on a velvet pillow. "Have you been working for Ms. Moore for very long?" she asks as I cross to the shelves on the adjacent wall and retrieve a palette, a canvas, and an easel. She speaks in a light tone, but I see in the way the tendons tense in her jaw and the careful, slow manner she glances from me to Elsie that this question is much more important to her than small talk.

"I've only officially been working here about a year." Hoping that admission won't make Mrs. Harris change her mind, I rush on. "But my mother was joint owner of the studio before that. I've studied with Elsie since I was a child."

Mrs. Harris smooths back Peony's whiskers. "So you must know her methods well."

"Her methods?" I frown. "I suppose so, yes."

The hollows of her cheeks are deep, and sweat dots her brow. Could she be ill? Maybe she's caught whatever it is that ails her son. My mind runs through a list of illnesses and their symptoms. Consumption? No, I didn't notice an increased temperature when I shook her hand, though she was wearing gloves, so it's hard to say. But she hasn't coughed once. The lack of a fever also means it is unlikely to be influenza. Perhaps anemia?

Lucy would be able to figure out what it is if she were here. My brilliant sister with biology and chemistry knowledge running through her like blood.

I squeeze out globs of my customary array of colors onto my palette—alizarin crimson, phthalocyanine blue, cadmium yellow, raw umber, burnt sienna, and titanium white. Mrs. Harris peppers me with question after question about Elsie. What sort of paintings does she do? How many per week? Does she have any interesting techniques? The way Mrs. Harris phrases the inquiries is breezy, like she doesn't care, but she fires them off one after the other like an interrogation.

As the conversation continues, I clench my teeth. What happens if one of my answers isn't good enough for her? What if I mess up? Even if she doesn't discover I'm a Prodigy, if something I say gives the governor a reason to shut down Elsie's studio, I'll be out of a job.

I catch sight of a rust-colored stain on the dog's left front ankle. I set aside my palette, cross to the animal, and crouch to get a closer look.

Mrs. Harris continues her questioning without pause, and I mutter my responses as I study the dog's leg. It looks like Peony got a scrape of some kind.

Damn it.

Before I've even returned to my canvas, the icy cold itch of my magic has pulsed to life in my fingertips. By the time I've retrieved my palette, it's prickling into my palms.

I close my eyes and force a deep breath.

Just *one* painting to enjoy the high of creating, the euphoria of pure art. That's all I wanted.

Artist *damn* it.

"How soon will the portrait be finished?" Mrs. Harris asks.

I blink up at her, rubbing my hands together in an attempt to quell the magic snapping under my skin. "Oil paintings are done in layers. I'll block out the basic shapes first in what's called the underpainting. Second comes the shadows, the lean darks, and then I'll work up to the medium tones. At that point, I'll come back in to refine the details and highlights with the fattiest oils. But it'll be necessary to let each layer dry as I go."

"How long will that take?"

"Well, since each layer needs to dry before I can move on to the next one, a portrait like this will likely take several days."

Mrs. Harris glances over at Elsie again and licks those thin, terse lips of hers. "I've heard Ms. Moore uses ladyrose gel as a medium sometimes to do rapid-dry paintings. Is that true?"

Mediums are substances that can be mixed into the paints to alter their textures and drying times, and there are dozens of different kinds. Ladyrose gel is rarely used precisely because it makes the paint dry so quickly. I glance at the pot squatting on the counter under the window and grit my teeth. I hate working with ladyrose gel—it makes it much more difficult to control my magic.

But if Mrs. Harris wants it, I'm going to have to deal with it.

"Yes, I think we have some, though it does come at an additional fifteen percent cost," I say, getting to my feet, trying to keep my voice steady even as trepidation makes my head whirl. "If I use that, we should be able to finish by suppertime."

Mrs. Harris's thin lips spread into a prim smile. "Cost is not an issue."

"Very well."

I manage not to stumble as I retreat to the back room and locate one of our last tubes of the medium even though my heartbeat is roaring in my ears with every step.

It's said that when the Artist painted His life-crowning masterpiece, an illustration of a vast world of green and blue, He turned to His lover, the Dear Lady, and noticed Her weeping. When He asked why She cried, She said, "I've never before seen such beauty. It ails me to know it is not real."

So the Artist turned to His painting and pressed His fingertips to its surface. Our world was birthed from His canvas that day. The Dear Lady's tears continued to fall, but they became tears of joy, and as they scattered upon the newborn land, tiny crimson flowers unfurled from the soil.

Ladyrose gel is typically used for holy rites and ceremonies. Employing it as a painting medium is considered by many as one of the ultimate desecrations against the Artist. Though Prodigy magic can be wielded with or without ladyrose gel, our powers are said to be at their strongest when paired with it.

I carry the tube of gel as though I'm transporting a lethal animal. My hands quake, and I can scarcely breathe.

Should I not have admitted we use the medium? As the governor and his wife are some of the most devout people I've ever heard of, the mere act of a portrait artist owning ladyrose gel—let alone using it as a medium—could probably be enough to earn their eternal hatred and disgust.

I try not to let the fear and panic show on my face as I reenter the front room. I've already told her about the gel. There's no going back now.

My magic flickers even colder in such close proximity to the gel, leeching warmth from my palms and even up into my wrists until I'm shivering. I swallow, trying to push it away.

Mother always told me not to fear my magic, to embrace it

and trust it. For though the Church may teach that the very existence of Prodigies is sacrilege, Mother used to say we were the Artist's elect, the children to whom He bequeathed a tiny measure of His infinite power. His most beloved.

But how can I trust my magic when all it's ever done is fight my control?

I return to Mrs. Harris and her dog and squeeze a small dollop of the gel onto my palette, scraping my knife back and forth to mix it with each of the colors in turn. It renders their texture glossy and malleable.

Taking a deep breath, I lean closer to the portrait and begin painting, trying to quell the way my magic dances like pins and needles under my skin.

Artist help me.

3

Hours pass. Midday sun puddles on the floor, reflecting amber shafts of light across my canvas. The bells of Old Sawthorne, the massive clock tower downtown, echo in the distance, making the glittering dust motes in the air quiver. Gripping a dozen brushes in my left hand, trailing one along the portrait with my right, I grit my teeth against the cold of magic blooming in my hands.

Not now. Not today. Not in front of the governor's wife.

Mrs. Harris's questions die away as the afternoon wears on, and she sits by the window, twisting her lace gloves around her fingers and staring through the ice crackling on the glass. The shadows of people in the street outside flicker across her face, and as the seconds tick by, her features grow more drawn, her color more pallid. I find myself wondering once again whether she has contracted whatever illness it is that ails her son.

But it is impossible to dwell on that for long. The itch in my fingers has intensified to a buzz, trailing all the way up to my elbows now. My magic has always had a mind of its own. Like an animal champing at the bit, waiting for me to let down my guard.

Setting my jaw, I do my best to ignore it.

I paint Mrs. Harris's miniature poodle as I see her, with a slight bloody tinge to the fur on her leg. A chill blooms at the base of my skull as I start on the portrait's finishing touches, my magic's signal that it's ready. I swallow hard and give a single shake of my head.

First you render the subject as it is, Mother always said. *Your power will tell you when you've gotten it right. Once the oils are dry, layer on top of it the way you wish the subject to be...*

No. I grip my brush and focus on getting the coal color of Peony's snout right.

There will be no altering reality today. No healing that cut.

I force myself to think of Frederick Bennett. Of Mother.

But even as I do, other thoughts wheedle through my mind. It wouldn't be so great of an indiscretion to heal the cut, would it? Not really. The chances that Mrs. Harris would notice are minuscule. It's just a simple blemish.

The itch creeps up my biceps now, and the cold in my skull prickles. My magic snaps and fizzes, little sparks of lightning setting my hair on end.

Would it be so terrible if I fixed the animal's wound? It's such a small thing...

No. I shake my head, trying to clear out the tingle spreading downward from my skull, creeping through my body, reaching out to meet the twin sensation in my hand and arm.

It would be dangerous to use my magic at all, but in front of the governor's wife? On her very own portrait? I might as well tell her what I am and have her turn me over to her husband right now.

But no matter how I try to will it away, that blasted itch continues, so strong now my hands are shaking visibly and smudging the painting. I pin my tongue between my teeth and force them still, leaning closer to the canvas to fix the illustration.

Sweat dampens the back of my dress.

The buzz of magic hums in my ears, inaudible to everyone else but so loud to me it overpowers every other sound. The electric ice in my system crowds out all sensation. There is nothing but my power. Nothing but the need to wield my paintbrush the way it wants.

I squeeze my eyes shut, shake out my hands, roll my shoulders.

But nothing helps.

I cannot do this.

Maybe I could appease my magic a bit without actually using it. If I just paint over the wound in the portrait, render the change in oils, it might be enough to dull the yearning so I can finish this piece without losing control. And as long as I don't wield my power to make that alteration reality, everything should be all right.

Besides, Mrs. Harris probably wouldn't want me to include the scratch on her dog's leg in the portrait anyway. She seems like the type of woman who keeps things impeccable and clean. A crimson-brown scab on her beloved white dog's coat would not be something she'd want to immortalize in oils on her wall.

So I give in slightly to the forbidden part of me that urges me to erase blemishes, to alter noses and eye shapes, to heal small wounds like this, and I sort through the brushes in my left hand until I find the one I've been using for the dog's white coat. Taking a steadying breath, I sweep a layer of paint over the injury in the image. With careful brushstrokes, I perfect the lay of the hairs with varying shades of white and gray until it looks like the rest of Peony's coat. Once I'm satisfied, I sit back on my stool and let out a slow breath.

The electricity in my palms has dulled enough to be bearable. I set down my brush. "I think that'll do it."

The dog perks up to Mrs. Harris clapping her hands, and it hops off the cushion to tramp over to her feet. It favors its right side, hobbling ever so slightly because of the scrape on its leg.

As I watch the little animal, an image of Lucy flashes across my mind. She would adore this puppy—she's always had a thing for animals. I can just imagine the way she'll scold me later if I tell her about it. *You didn't heal the poor baby? What's the use of having magic if you're going to keep it to yourself?* She will scowl at me like I was the cause of Peony's wound, turn to her pet frog, and cluck her tongue like I'm the world's greatest disappointment.

I almost laugh out loud at the image of her rolling her eyes, but when Peony barks again, pulling me back to reality, my mirth fades.

Imaginary Lucy has a point, though. My magic only makes mostly meaningless changes to appearances, like altering hair colors or lengthening eyelashes. As far as healing goes, I'm capable of remedying only small injuries. Superficial things, like scrapes or broken limbs. But even though the changes it can make seem insignificant in the grand scheme of things, it has certainly made a nuisance of itself since it showed up when I was fourteen, buzzing like a swarm of bees inside my head every time I paint.

For weeks I've been trying to keep my magic at bay, to force it out of my body, out of my art, to pretend it doesn't exist. But now, for once, it could do something good. I could let it out, find release, and help the puppy in the process. And as long as I'm discreet when I do it, everything should be okay.

This wound is small, and it could be gone in an instant.

The painting is already done, the image of the injury buried under a layer of titanium white. It wouldn't even be difficult.

Healing typically requires that I understand how the injury was sustained, but animals are always much easier to alter than humans. For such a small cut, a simple guess would probably be enough for my magic to work. Peony was likely getting into a bit of mischief around the grounds of the Harris's mansion, Rose Manor.

I mop the back of my hand over my eyes.

I cannot build a suitable portfolio for the conservatory. I cannot provide for myself or my sister. I cannot bring my parents back. I've failed at so many things in the past year. The weight of all those failures is crushing the life out of me.

Finally I'm faced with something I could actually *do*. Something within my control when so much has been so utterly out of control for almost a year.

I can't change our financial situation. I can't erase the fact that magic has ruined what once was a joy for me. But I *can* mend this wound.

No. This is ludicrous. I cannot risk it, no matter how convincing my power may be. There is too much at stake.

And yet…

Magic sings in my body, bright columns of color and light pulsing inside my fingertips through my heart to that tingling place at the base of my skull.

"Let me have this," I whisper to the Artist, tightening my hands into fists. "Let me have one moment of success. Let me do this *one thing* right."

And so, even with Mother's warnings jangling as loud as Old Sawthorne's bells in my head, I settle a shaking hand against the painting. Imagining the dog sniffing in places where she shouldn't—maybe under a rosebush or at the base of an iron fence post—I close my eyes, letting that pulse of ice bleed outward, filling my whole body with snapping sparks.

In my mind's eye, the painting under my hand comes to life. The whites and grays and pinks morph and twist. I peek an eye open, making sure the real painting remains unchanged and that Mrs. Harris is still distracted with feeding Peony a treat. Satisfied, I let the eyelid drop once more and focus in on the complex network of tiny threads taking shape under my palm.

These hairlike fibers are called sevren, and they snake just beneath the skin in every animal and human in the world. The connective fibers that bind the soul to the physical form, they're born from each person or animal's emotional perception of their bodies. The more emotionally significant a physical feature is to that person or animal, the tighter and denser the bonds become.

In order to alter these physical traits, my magic has to unravel and sever the applicable sevren, and it can do so only if I have a strong understanding of the significance that trait has for the person. The more emotionally altering it is, the thicker and tighter the weave of the sevren becomes, and the more difficult it is for my magic to detangle.

As I focus on the dog's sevren, my magic rears its head, lunging toward the thickest knot of threads in Peony's system—her heart.

I clamp it down tight.

We will do this my *way*, I tell it. Channeling all of the control I have to keep the current contained, I focus in on the dog's wrist, trailing my fingers over the small snarl of sevren humming there. Holding my breath, I let the tiniest spark of magic out, guiding it through my fingertips to the knot.

Dodging another glance at Mrs. Harris to make sure she isn't watching, I allow the singing of power inside of me to build until all I can hear is the buzz of electricity. It compounds, swelling until my whole body is shivering with it.

And then all at once it releases. The itch in my hands subsides, and a sharp ache blossoms in my left wrist. A quick slice of pain as my body takes on the sensation of the dog's wound. My sevren have adopted the threads I unraveled from the animal's leg, so I'll experience her pain for a time. Luckily, because the dog's sevren are foreign to my system, the sensation won't be permanent. My body will soon absorb the soul-threads, and the pain will disappear.

Opening my eyes, I glance down at the place where my arm feels as though it's been cut. The skin is smooth and unharmed. I run a thumb over it and glance up at Mrs. Harris, who is rifling in her purse. It is always shocking to me that the magic that seems so loud and bright to me is invisible to everyone else. Mrs. Harris hasn't noticed a thing.

I let out a relieved sigh.

No more humming in my hands, no more icy prickles up my arm.

Praise the Artist.

Peony darts for the window, barking shrilly at someone outside, her gait suddenly balanced again, her limp gone. The fur at her ankle is white and tufty like the rest of her.

A small smile tugs at my lips. Artist, it feels good to do something right for once.

But even as pride warms the fingers that were chilled by magic seconds ago, trepidation curdles in my gut.

I can only pray no one notices what I just did.

4

I finish up the last of my tasks and exit Elsie's studio at seven o'clock. Though it's still early, winter clouds have thickened the sky, and it droops black as night, scraping its bulbous belly along chimneys and gables. Wind howls through the alleys, whipping the hair back from my face, slapping my cheeks and making my eyes stream.

I lean into the gusts and head south, in the direction of the Lawrence River, where the markets stock products I can actually afford. The closer I get to the small flat where Lucy and I live, smack in the center of the sooty factory district on Lawrence's banks, the louder the streets become. People spill from inns and taverns, laughing sloppily, singing at the tops of their lungs. Children dressed in rags clamber up the sides of dumpsters to forage for supper.

I leap sideways as a woman slops the contents of a chamber pot out of a window overhead.

Unlike downtown Lalverton, with its glowing clock tower and ornate buildings, its scrubbed cobblestones and people in clean-pressed clothes, the factory district reeks of fish, smoke, and sewage. Human waste clogs the gutters, trash litters the streets, and the people I pass look as though they haven't bathed in weeks.

Lucy and I have lived here for only a few months—just since we ran out of funds and were kicked out of our parents' flat near Old Sawthorne where we grew up—but I don't think I'll ever get used to the clamor and filth, the slurred curses of the drunks lying in the muck on the streets, or the squalling of hungry infants that's as constant as breathing.

I clutch my purse tight inside my jacket and glare at anyone who glances twice at me. The only way to keep from being pickpocketed in this part of Lalverton is to be alert and assertive and keep your hands on your money at all times.

The extra weight of the bonus for completing Mrs. Harris's commission heaped in with my day's wages steadies me as I slip into the sputtering lantern light of a small market shop. I purchase a stale hunk of bread and a handful of bruised persimmons, pausing at the front desk to pick up a few bottles of medicine for my sister before slipping farther along the street to the bait-and-tackle shop to purchase a container of dead crickets for Lucy's pet frog.

Ducking back into the night, I crunch through the slush to the corner bookshop.

I have just enough money left.

"Evening, Miss Whitlock," a voice calls from the register.

"Ernest! Good to see you," I reply, kicking the door shut behind me. The rasp of the wind cuts to silence. Something moves in the corner of my eye outside the window, and I whirl to see what it was.

But only ice purls in the grayish glow of the street gaslights.

"Everything all right?" Ernest asks.

"Fine," I say, frowning as I turn away from the window.

"Why don't you leave your groceries here with me so you can have your hands free?" His smile wrinkles his brown cheeks. The silver hairs of his mustache quiver, and his eyes sparkle behind half-moon spectacles.

"I think I have enough for the one I've been eyeing," I tell him. "Seven golds, isn't it? Lucy's going to be so excited."

He nods. "Would you like me to get it for you?"

"No, thank you, I'll manage." I shuffle among the book-shelves, savoring the intoxicating scent of glue and leather, of fresh pages and ink. Winding my way to the biology section, I run my fingertips along the spines of the medical texts until I locate the thick tome.

Lucy's been working on a special project studying the pollution in the Lawrence River and its effects on local wildlife for months, drafting up data to present to the Lalverton Humane Society, and recently she's decided to include a section on how detrimental the water toxicity is for the citizens of Lalverton, as well. I came across this book while browsing last week and haven't been able to stop thinking about it since. And while the seven golds it'll cost to purchase the book might be better put toward our rent or food expenses, a massive, comprehensive book like this would give her something to work with on days when trudging through the snow to the library is too much.

Gently, I slide the text from the shelf. Its title is embossed in gold with thick, stark lettering. *Encyclopedia of Human Anatomy: Ailments, Injuries, and Environmental Response.* If this doesn't have the kind of data she needs for her project, I don't know what will.

I heft it to the register.

A flash of movement catches my eye near the front window once more, and I pause, squinting to see through the glass as the hairs rise on the back of my neck.

Again, nothing.

My stomach ties itself in knots as I turn back to Ernest, tugging my coin pouch from my belt and dumping the requisite seven coins onto the counter.

Only thirty remain. Just enough to compensate Lucy's nurse.

Ernest scoops up the money. "Don't tell me you'll stop coming around now?"

"Of course not." I load the bags into my arms. "You know how much I love books."

"A love for books is the best indicator of a curious mind." Ernest shuffles over to hold the door open for me.

"I'll see you soon." I nod goodbye as I pass him and step out into the snowy wind. The door snaps shut behind me.

"Miss Whitlock," someone says. It's a prim, regal voice. Female and familiar.

I peek around my sack of groceries and catch sight of Mrs. Harris, her face washed pale by the gaslights, a pile of curls the color of blood clotted like a scab atop her head.

Panic wraps a fist around my heart.

"G-good evening, Mrs. Harris?" My greeting lilts upward at the end as though it's a question. A pair of umber-colored horses paw at the icy cobblestones behind her, a polished black carriage harnessed to their backs.

Mrs. Harris gestures toward the cab. "Would you mind stepping inside? I have something I'd like to discuss."

With the lamp pooling its light on her cheekbones, shadows curdle in the space below her brows, making her look like one of the skulls illustrated in the book I just purchased. All I can see of her eyes is a pair of tiny glimmers watching me from the darkness.

Panic crawls through my limbs, turning my hands clammy. Cold, wet fingers slick down my spine. I force myself to breathe through my nose even as the frigid air burns my nostrils.

Could Mother's disappearance have been something like this? A sleek coach on a forgotten corner that night almost a year ago?

I cast about for an excuse, but my thoughts are frostbitten with fear.

"I have a proposition for you. It comes with a significant payment." Mrs. Harris's voice is so low I almost don't hear it over the wind creaking through the wooden sign above the bookshop and the loud laughter of the people spilling out of the tavern across the street.

My ears perk up at the word *payment*. The Harrises have been the governing family of the city for generations, and they've got the wealth to match it. If Mrs. Harris is using the word "significant" to describe the payment she's offering, I can't imagine what kind of astronomical number might be attached.

But what sort of proposition?

I wet my lips. "I…" My heart rattles as though trying to escape my rib cage. Does it matter what the proposition entails? Maybe whatever Mrs. Harris is offering would finally be enough to get us out of this part of town, enough to afford a doctor for Lucy, enough for her to enroll in those advanced biology programs and for me to have a chance at attending the conservatory.

And even if it's not as much money as all that, it could be a start.

"All right," I manage, my voice splintering on the wind.

Mrs. Harris leads me to the carriage. The driver hops down to open the door and helps me maneuver my armload of goods inside.

The interior of the cab smells of expensive leather and red

wine. The seats are smooth and clean, and a small lantern rests in a sconce on the wall, illuminating padded walls a midnight crimson as deep and dark as ladyrose petals.

Mrs. Harris regards me for a long moment with those sunken eyes before speaking. "You healed my dog."

The four words bludgeon me as though they're made of ice.

"I don't know what you mean," I say, forcing my tone to stay airy and light.

"You are a Prodigy."

Either she's here to take me to prison on trumped-up charges, or she wants to blackmail me. I think of the illustrations in Mother's history books of Prodigies chained to easels and forced to paint, bowing under the angry glares of burly men with knives at their belts. I think of Frederick Bennett, emaciated, bruised, and broken, tortured into doing Lowell's bidding.

How could I have been so foolish?

I smooth my skirt to keep my hands from shaking. "P-Prodigy?"

"Don't look so frightened, dear. I have no intention of harming you." She reaches out her hand and settles it on my knee in what I'm sure she means to be a calming gesture, but every muscle in my body tenses to flee.

My mind fills with memories of the week before Mother went missing. How she came home with fear in her eyes, whispering to Father that someone had come to the studio. Someone who'd seemed to know what she was.

It couldn't have been a coincidence that she vanished days later.

The nights that followed were long and Joyless. Images flash across my mind one by one. Teams of policemen combing the streets of Lalverton. Lucy clinging to me as we wept and prayed and wept some more. Father's face growing wan and waxy until the evening he left to look for her and never returned.

It feels as though the bottom of the carriage has fallen away to reveal a gaping maw waiting to swallow me.

Mrs. Harris levels me with a steady gaze. "I have a fairly delicate situation on my hands, and I'm offering you half a million gold pieces if you are able to do what I ask."

My jaw drops, and blood roars in my ears. "Half a..." I can't even say the words. It's more money than I've ever dared dream of. It would be enough for Lucy and me to move out of our crumbling apartment and reassemble our lives. Lucy could get a new microscope, textbooks and experimental supplies, and maybe even a typewriter for her proposal to the Humane Society. We'd be able to find a doctor to help her and buy whatever medications she needs, too. I could quit my job and have the time to figure out my magic problem so I could paint real portraits, put together my portfolio for the conservatory. I'd actually be able to afford the tuition.

We could both have a shot at our dreams.

"What is it you'd like me to do?" My voice comes out barely more than a rasp.

"I'm sure you're well aware of how precarious my husband's safety and position can be during times such as this, what with the election on the horizon," she says. "He is under extreme stress, and his opponents are looking for any possible way to cut him down. Every move he makes is scrutinized and criticized." She pauses. "As such, you are not to speak of what I am about to say to anyone. If I discover that word has gotten out, whether from your mouth or anyone else's, be assured that it *won't* go unnoticed."

Mrs. Harris's threat hangs in the air between us, razor-sharp.

"I won't tell anyone," I say.

"Swear it."

I clear my throat. "I swear on the Holy Artist and His Dear Lady that I will not disclose anything of our conversation to anyone."

Mrs. Harris's lips press into a grimace that, cast in a dance of lantern light, looks almost wolfish. Hungry. "Very good."

Unease thickens in my stomach, but I wait for her to go on, barely daring to breathe.

"Have you seen the papers today?" she asks, folding her hands in her lap. Pearl earrings glow milky white like bones on either side of her face, twitching with every word she utters.

"I saw that your son has contracted some sort of sickness," I say. "Is he doing all right?"

"My son is not ill."

"No?"

"No." Her eyes glimmer like pond-slick moons. "Wilburt Harris Jr. is dead."

5

gape at the governor's wife. "Dead?" I repeat. "How?" And what does that have to do with me?

"A nasty accident," Mrs. Harris says, her voice fracturing on the last word. "He fell from his balcony this morning."

I think of how Wilburt looked at his father's most recent public address. Handsome, with a spill of auburn hair above his left eyebrow and thick freckles across cheekbones sharp enough to cut stone.

And now he's dead.

"I'd like you to use your magic to restore him to life," Mrs. Harris says, tears gathering like beads on her eyelashes.

I blink. "I beg your pardon?"

She repeats her statement, but my mind is whirling.

Use my power to bring someone back from the dead? Is that even possible?

I was extremely lucky that my mother was such a brilliant Prodigy. She taught me everything she knew. But it's not like there's a textbook of Prodigy magic out there or a school I can attend to learn the exact depth and reach of my capabilities. Prodigy powers, while believed to be genetic, are incredibly rare, skipping sometimes dozens of generations. There just isn't much general knowledge that I can draw from.

Even if it *is* theoretically possible to resurrect a dead person, whether I am capable of doing it is another thing altogether. The most I've been able to achieve has been clearing away blemishes or small cuts and bruises, though I did once manage to mend my ankle when I broke it three years ago. But it's easy to alter my own body—I know intimately how it came to be the way it is. *My* sevren are not a mystery to my power.

When working with other people, though, things get a lot more complicated and begin bordering on impossible. Big changes require an expansive knowledge about the inner workings of the human body and the person's sevren, and physical traits that have deeply affected the person's experience of what it means to be alive and how they experience the world forge complex sevren knots that simply cannot be undone. Besides, those aspects of a person's body are not the kinds of things a Prodigy should ever try to meddle with anyway, even if it were possible. And while Will's death wasn't a permanent condition that he experienced long enough for his soul to forge tight bonds with it, reversing it is certainly going to be more difficult than mending a broken bone or getting rid of a pimple.

The ache from Peony's injury still throbs in my wrist, though now that it has been a few hours, the sensation has begun to fade. That was just a small change. Mother said that big alterations have much stronger, longer-lasting effects. What kinds of injuries did Wilburt sustain when he fell from the balcony? Fractures? Internal bleeding? Crushed lungs? I swallow. Even if I somehow manage whatever she is asking of me, it will be extraordinarily painful for me to do so.

Luckily, though, I only feel the *sensations* of the injuries I heal. I would not actually bleed, and, in this case, I wouldn't die. But I'm not sure I am too keen on feeling what it's like.

"I know what I'm asking you is not insignificant," Mrs. Harris says quietly, as though reading my mind, still watching me with those glassy eyes.

"I'm not sure it's actually possible," I say. "I can see fixing the injuries, but breathing life back where it has gone? I don't know."

Mrs. Harris takes a deep breath and lets it out in a small stream that fogs up the window next to her. One of the tears shuddering on her lashes drops onto her cheek, and she brushes it away. "He's my boy. Won't you please try?"

And for a moment, I see past the hard, stern exterior of the woman before me to the broken person beneath. The one whose hands are shaking in spite of her fierce glare. The one whose tears burn as hot as mine did when I lost my own family.

I frown, twisting the ring on my thumb. It's my father's first wedding band—the one he wore when he and Mother got married. Back before he put on weight and had to get a new one. It's the only thing of value I haven't sold since he and Mother disappeared. I squeeze it, begging Father to hear me from wherever he is, to give me the answers. Is Mrs. Harris simply a heartbroken mother mourning the loss of her only child? Or is she the villain my instincts tell me she is?

But no answers come.

A small chiming sound makes us both jump. Mrs. Harris pulls a watch from her breast pocket, clearing her throat as she inspects the time. The sudden shift pulls me from my thoughts. "I hate to rush you," she says, her voice stern and cold once more, "but time is a luxury we do not have. Every moment we waste is a moment longer that my son's body lies dead in my home. We've obtained a special ladyrose potion from the

North that slows the process of decomposition, but I'm afraid it cannot hold it off forever. Once the rot sets in, I doubt even the most accomplished Prodigy in the world would be able to reverse the damage. You will have to complete the task within the next four days. If that time arrives and you have not succeeded, we will be forced to bring in the embalmer and announce to the world that he has passed."

Every word she speaks warbles as though strummed from brittle violin strings.

"I will send a coach to retrieve you at midnight." She sniffs, tipping her head slightly as though she means to look put together and in control, but there are cracks in the image. The moisture on her lashes, the quiver in her lip, the way her words come out quiet and quick, as if she's afraid her voice might break. "That gives you precisely three and a half hours. Go home. Pack. Get your things in order. Be ready and waiting in front of your building at that time. You will be escorted to Rose Manor, and you will get to work immediately."

I take a deep breath. The money she's offering could mean everything to Lucy and me. But at what cost? The governor hates Prodigies. He's hurt, imprisoned, and even killed them before. How much good could really come of me willingly crawling into the bear's den?

"And," I hedge, "if I say no?"

Her eyes flash. "No?" The word rings cold and cruel.

I tighten my grip on Father's ring.

Mrs. Harris leans in so close the scent of her lilac perfume crawls into my nose "I did not have to offer you money," she says, her voice barely above a whisper. "You do recognize that, don't you, child? We both know what it means to be a Prodigy in this country."

I swallow, my mouth suddenly dry. Her eyes bore into mine, holding my gaze captive so I cannot blink, cannot breathe.

"I am kind," she continues, "and I am generous. I'm offering to treat you as an employee, offering to pay you for your work. But I don't need to, do I?" She raises one slender brow. "If you are so ungrateful as to refuse my offer, I cannot be responsible for who might discover your secret." She leans in even closer. "Do I make myself absolutely clear?"

My heart is pounding so hard in my throat I might choke on it. "Y-yes, ma'am."

"Good girl."

I keep twisting my ring, panic making me dizzy. "But... but what if I try and am not successful?"

Mrs. Harris leans back into her seat, fingering the massive golden brooch at her throat. "Funny, that secret of yours. It makes for a fine bargaining piece, doesn't it? I think that alone should be enough to motivate you." She pauses, eyes glittering. "If I were you, I would try *very* hard to be successful. I have many friends whose views on Prodigies are more extreme even than my husband's. I would hate for them to discover you are one, wouldn't you?"

I give the tiniest nod.

"My driver will see you at midnight," she says, opening the door. Cold air whips inside and sets my teeth chattering.

"Thank you," I manage, getting to my feet and gathering my things. My legs feel like they've forgotten entirely how to stand, and they sway as I struggle to keep my balance.

"I'll see you soon, Miss Whitlock."

6

I sprint down the street, coat flapping behind me in the wind. Tears sting in my eyes, and anger and fear battle in my chest so I can scarcely breathe.

Why couldn't my magic have let me be for once?

Why does it have to exist at all?

And what will happen to Lucy when I fail?

Our apartment building crouches like an ogre at the end of a dirt road. Crooked chimneys jut from its roof like bits of spine, and cracked windows glare as I approach.

I dash inside and mount the crumbling stairs to the sixth floor.

Ava, Lucy's nurse, is upon me as soon as I open my apartment door.

"I'm sorry I'm late," I say, sliding my bags onto the table. I unbutton my coat and drape it over a wooden chair missing its leg.

Ava's lips thin, but she does not chastise me the way I probably deserve. I upend my purse over her palm, and the last of my coins drop into it.

She pockets the money without a word. Though she is only maybe thirty years old, her hair is woven through with strands of silver. She's told me before of the three young children at her apartment across the street. They're probably waiting for her now.

"Actually…" I clear my throat. "Something has come up. A commission from the governor."

Ava's brows rise, and she pauses with her cloak half on.

"They are sending a coach to retrieve me at midnight, and I'll be gone for four days."

"And you'd like me to stay here with Lucy for that time?"

I pull my gloves off and knot them between my hands. "I-I'll give you a bonus?"

My stomach clenches. I shouldn't be promising her more money. The likelihood of me coming back with anything at all is null. And missing four days of pay from Elsie will make it impossible to make the rent payment, let alone scrounge up extra for the nurse.

But what choice do I have?

Ava sighs. "Midnight, you say? I suppose I could make it work. But I will need that bonus. Fifteen percent."

I swallow and force a smile as the back of my neck heats. "I promise."

Mother would be ashamed of me for lying.

"How was she today?" I change the subject, nodding toward the small bed in the corner and the slumbering girl nestled in sheets littered with her customary array of papers full of notes, graphs, and diagrams.

Ava follows my gaze. "No improvements, I'm afraid."

I make to cross toward her, but Ava grasps my elbow. "She needs a doctor."

"I know." I mop a hand across my face. "I'm doing my best."

Ava's frown deepens. "Are you sleeping?"

I make a noncommittal noise in my throat.

"You're of no use to anyone—least of all Lucy—if you fall ill, too. You need to take care of yourself."

Tears burn in the corners of my eyes, but I blink them away and nod.

Ava pulls on her cap. "I'll be back at midnight."

"Thank you," I murmur as she departs.

Taking a deep breath, I cross to the bed and perch on its edge. "Lucy?" I say in a voice much too cheery for all of the tumult and fear in my chest. "Hey, I'm home from work."

Lucy shifts, opening her eyes. The blankets are tangled around her limbs, and her dark hair is plastered to her face. I tuck it behind her ears and smile when her gaze focuses on mine.

"How are you doing?" I ask.

She wraps her arms around her middle, hunching forward and wincing. "I need the chamber pot again."

I cross to the hearth where Ava must have boiled water to clean it out not too long ago and carry it back to the bed. For the thousandth time, I long for the lovely toilets we used to have when Mother and Father were here.

Lucy deserves so much better than this.

She pushes herself out of bed, and I try not to gape. Somehow, impossibly, she seems even thinner than she was this morning. A lump of tears aches in my throat as I take in the way her nightgown hangs off her bony frame, the way the color of her hair has gone dull and her skin sallow.

No thirteen-year-old should ever have to suffer in this way.

I turn away to give her privacy and knuckle my fists across my eyes. I want to cry, want to sob, want to gather her up in my arms and shout obscenities at the sky, at the Artist and His Dear Lady who have abandoned us like our parents did.

"All done." Lucy clambers back into bed, and I take the chamber pot to dump and clean, trying not to look at the blood and mucus clinging to the cracks in the porcelain.

When I've finished, I return to the bed and slide in next to Lucy. She sorts through the pages on her bed, stacking them neatly.

"Were you able to get much done today?" I ask.

Her mouth twists as she nods. "Some. Mostly work on my pollution initiative. Ava and I took Georgie for a walk to get some samples from the Lawrence." She nods at a line of bottles next to the tank where George, her pet frog, lies slumbering on a rock.

"I bet George liked getting out into the fresh air."

"Yes, he did. He gets to be such a crotchety old man if I keep him inside too much." She reaches out a hand to pat the side of the tank fondly. "But I still love you, Georgie."

I lean over her and pluck up one of the vials she collected at the river, inspecting the murky, ink-like water inside. Lucy's been working on her Lawrence River project since she found George on its banks two years ago. He was injured and tangled in some sort of twine. Finding him helpless like that ignited a fire in her, who even at eleven was already so brilliant in the sciences that her schoolteachers were sending home brochures for college programs. Lucy took the frog in and nursed him back to health, and she has been studying the devastating effects the city's pollution has had on the river's wildlife ever since. With this recent flare-up of her illness, however, her research has been forced to slow down quite a bit.

"I was going to do some more work when I got home, but..." She sighs, rubbing her knuckles against her eyes. "I didn't have enough juice."

"Ah," I say.

For her birthday this summer, I splurged and bought a small bushel of oranges, which we squeezed into glasses and pretended was the real, gourmet orange juice our father used to make. As we sat at the table, acting like the drink wasn't sour and pulpy, we got talking about how her illness had come to affect her life. She explained to me that her energy reserves were like that glass of yellow juice. Every action of daily life—getting out of bed, bathing, dressing, doing research—siphoned juice away. Once the glass was empty, no matter how much she had left she needed to do or how much she'd hoped to get done, her body needed to rest. To refill the glass. If she tried to push beyond that, it could knock her out for days. Even weeks.

Lucy grimaces at me. "I ran into Marie and Beth while we were out."

"Oh? And how were they?" Marie and Beth have been Lucy's best friends for years, though it's been a few months since I last saw them around.

"They were on some kind of outing for Marie's birthday," Lucy says, and her eyes glitter. She sniffs. "Apparently they don't think I'm worth an invitation anymore."

"What?"

She hugs her arms around her middle, squeezing her eyes shut. "When I asked why they didn't invite me, Marie said they figured I would say no, so they didn't bother. As if I'm choosing to be sick. As if the reason I didn't go to Beth's spring tea was because I couldn't be bothered and not because I was afraid I might vomit on her mother's sofa." Her voice breaks.

"Oh, Luce." I wrap my arms around her, and she buries her face against my neck.

"Is it so terrible of me to want an invitation, even if I'm unable to go?"

I shake my head, combing my fingers through her hair. "Of course not."

"You know what else Beth said? She said, 'You aren't as fun anymore, and Marie wanted to have a good time.'" A sob chokes out of her lips, and her shoulders shake. "It's like they think I'm lazy or something."

An inferno rages in my chest. I squeeze her tighter, blinking away my own tears. "They're wrong, Lucy. You are the most fun person I know, and you sure as hell aren't lazy. I'd like to see Marie or Beth work half as hard as you."

"But I don't *want* to have to work hard just to live my life. I want to go to the tea parties and the birthday outings and have fun like them." She mops her eyes with her sleeve.

I press a kiss to her forehead as the blood under my skin boils. The things I wish I could say to those girls. To their mothers. I grit my teeth and tighten my arms around my sister, wishing I could protect her from every hurt, every ache, every unkind word. "I know, Luce. I know."

She rolls over and tugs her food diary out from under her stack of Lawrence River Pollution Initiative papers and hands it to me. "The only new development I recorded in here today is that oatmeal seemed to sit okay in my stomach. I kept it down anyway."

"That's good news." I take the notebook from her and flip through it. Food logs, graphs, and lists of symptoms are mapped out carefully on each page. Ever since she first started getting digestive flare-ups years ago, she's taken to documenting every food she eats and every manifestation of the illness, as scientific with managing her health as she is about her biology projects. Thanks to her research, she's been able to minimize flare-ups by being careful to avoid foods that seemed to trigger worse symptoms, like dairy and fatty meats and legumes. And that worked, for a while. The flare-ups would subside after a few days, and they never got debilitating, so Mother and Father chalked it up to having a sensitive stomach.

But three months ago, this new flare-up began, and no diet changes or rest or any of the other things that used to help have made any effect. It's only gotten worse.

"I don't want to talk about it anymore," she says, leaning against me. "Tell me about your day."

"Well, uh... I got to do a real portrait today. For a client."

"Who?"

"Adelia Harris."

Lucy raises her head to stare at me, mouth dropping open in a small O. "The governor's wife?"

"The very one."

She squeals. "What was she like? Was she fashionable? What was she wearing?"

I settle in and give up all of the details of Mrs. Harris's visit to the studio, watching nighttime shadows chase themselves across the sagging, water-stained ceiling. I don't mention the visit afterward in the carriage, though. Lucy and I are in such a warm, comfortable cocoon now, wrapped up here in our tiny pocket of the world. I'm not ready to let in the cold just yet.

But as I speak, Mrs. Harris's voice replays over and over in my head. *If I were you, I would try very hard to be successful.*

I can't let myself hope. But...

What if I did somehow manage to bring Wilburt Jr. back to life? What if I return home four days from now with half a million golds?

I lean closer to Lucy, letting myself consider it for a moment.

For so long we've been surviving day-to-day. Praying for release, but not ever finding it.

Maybe this is the Artist's way of answering those prayers. Maybe He's giving us this chance to look forward to a tomorrow that isn't dreary and painful. Maybe we'll finally be able to build a future. Live our lives.

Lucy eventually drifts off to sleep with her fingertips smudged against the frog tank's side. I press my lips to her forehead, squeezing my eyes shut, and stroke her hair, remembering how she used to let me tie it up in pretty ribbons to go to fancy evening parties with Mother and Father when she was little. How radiant a child she'd always been—and still is—with pink cheeks and hair that matches mine, dark like the velvet brown of autumn midnights.

Brushing another kiss to Lucy's temple, I ease out from under her and tuck the blanket around her shoulders.

Fatigue devours me from the inside out as my eyes trail along the grimy surfaces of our apartment. The soot-stained hearth, the mildewed sink stinking of turpentine and streaked with a rainbow of pigments. Broken dishes on the shelves, a dilapidated dining table. My tiny cot in the corner. Stacks of drawings and paintings piled in every spare space.

A shining black beetle scuttles across the floor toward me, leaving tracks in the dust. I bring my foot down hard and shudder when the tiny body crunches under my boot.

Finding an old napkin, I bend to scoop up the carcass. One of its legs twitches. Its innards ooze around the shards of its iridescent wings.

Wilburt Harris Jr.'s half smile flashes across my memory, and I pause, glancing over to the holy shrine in the far corner of the room. A faded painting of the Artist stares back, His benevolent eyes watchful and fathomless.

If He created life with His paintbrush, and it is His power that lives in my sevren, is it really so far out of the realm of possibility that I might be able to bring someone back from the dead?

I cross to the table, placing the napkin there so the beetle is visible, and arrange my paints and a canvas.

It's time to find out what my magic is truly capable of.

My body tenses as I set up my easel. I pause only for a moment to dab in some ladyrose gel with my paints before I get to work—I have less than three hours now, so I'll need to be quick about this.

The insect's crushed body takes form on the canvas in quick, trembling brushstrokes. That place at the base of my skull sparks cold with life when I've gotten the first illustration right.

Then, with my heart throbbing in my throat, I load more paint onto my filbert brush—a long-bristled one with a rounded tip—and start on the new image. The one where the beetle is alive.

I don't dare blink. My breaths gasp in and out, staccato and uneven, as the illustration unfurls under my hands.

An hour later, it is done. Rendered in deep, cool blacks mixed with ultramarine blue and viridian, the tiny beetle I've illustrated looks so alive, so real, I swear one of its antennae twitches.

"Please," I whisper to the Artist watching me from the wall. "Please let this work."

I settle my palm onto the painting and allow the electricity to wind from my hand through my heart to that place at my brain stem that crackles with anticipation.

The buzz fills my body, and I brace myself, trying to detach my thoughts from the sensation as the painting of the beetle rearranges itself into a diagram of threads in my mind's eye. Once again, my magic lunges for the pulsing knot at the beetle's heart, and I tamp it back firmly.

I'm not sure what would happen if I gave my magic free rein to attack the subject's heart the way it always tries to, but

I don't trust it. I've had nightmares of it devouring people's whole souls, and I'm not too keen on the idea of finding out if that's what it would do.

Every muscle in my body tenses as I focus it into my painting and the beetle spun in threads of oil under my fingertips. I channel small bursts of power into the insect's sevren, detangling each knot related to its death one by one.

The magic's electric buzz swells into a roar. My whole body shudders.

And then all at once, pain crunches through me. I collapse, screaming. It's like every bone in my body has splintered, every organ burst. My lungs convulse for air, my eyes ooze, thick juices crawl all over my skin.

Gasping with my cheek pressed to the floorboard, I squint through the agony. Between starbursts of white pain, I catch sight of movement.

A shimmer of lustrous black scuttles down the table leg and into the shadows.

7

"Myra!" Lucy's cry is far away.

I weep, shuddering in a tight ball on the floor.

The pain, once so acute I thought I was dying, has begun to dull. The beetle's sevren are slowly being absorbed by my body—and thank Artist for that.

As the sensation of being crushed fades, Lucy's frantic sobs break through the haze in my brain.

"Luce," I wheeze, forcing my eyes open. "It's all right. I'm all right."

"What the hell, Myra?" She grasps my shoulders as tears track down her cheeks. "Please don't tell me that was a joke. Because it wasn't even remotely funny."

"Not a joke," I manage, reaching for her.

She wraps her arms around my shuddering frame and smooths the hair out of my face. "Are you sure you're all right? What hurts?"

"I'll be fine. Just give me a minute." As my vision clears, I look at the empty napkin where the beetle's corpse once lay and tighten my grip around my sister, elation sparking to life inside of me.

It worked.

I painted that insect back to life.

I close my eyes. Leaving Lucy here, going to Rose Manor, attempting to perform the same magic on a dead young man is terrifying. But I just proved success is *possible*.

Half a million gold pieces.

For a breath, I allow myself to imagine a purse full of so many coins I can scarcely lift it. I see Lucy and me in a clean, well-kept apartment with pitchers full of gourmet orange juice for every birthday, every holiday, every Tuesday if we want. I watch Lucy inspecting river water under a brand-new, functional microscope with a bookcase full of biology textbooks behind her, just waiting to be perused.

And my bedroom. It would be filled with the scent of linseed oil, pigments, and turpentine. I'd have all the supplies I could ever want: stacks of canvases and sketch pads, piles of fresh brushes, and all the time in the world to paint for *me* as I learned to control my magic and finally put together my portfolio for the conservatory, which I would actually be able to afford.

Maybe that life isn't as impossible as we thought.

"What happened?" Lucy hiccups. "I thought you were dying."

I sit back, wiping sweat from my brow, and tell her about Mrs. Harris's proposition. Her eyes widen.

When I finish my account of what I achieved with the beetle, she raises a brow. "So what you're saying is that you're leaving me alone to fend for myself with boring old Ava?"

I elbow her. "Come on. Ava's not that bad."

"She thinks George is gross. Amphibian haters are the absolute worst." She gives me a pointed look.

I hold up my hands. "I'm sorry. He's slimy!"

"Your prejudice against the Artist's most beautiful creatures is disgusting." She crosses her arms.

"George is a lot of things, but beautiful certainly isn't one of them."

"He can *hear* you, Myra!" she gasps. "Don't listen to her, Georgie-Poo," she calls to the tank across the room. "She doesn't know what she's saying!"

I snort. "Sorry, George."

With a teasing huff, Lucy crosses her arms. "Once we're rich, you have to promise me we'll feed him live crickets. Only the best for my growing boy. It's the very least you can do after an obscene remark like *that*."

As my chuckles fade, I whisper, "Do you think I can really do it? This is the governor we're talking about—you know what he thinks of people like me."

"If anyone can, it's you." She grasps my hand and squeezes it. "Show ol' Wilburt who's boss."

Snorting, I pull her against me. "You are so odd, Lucy."

"Oh, one of us is odd, and it's definitely not *me*."

I stick my tongue out at her, and she scoffs.

"Manners, Myra. What would Pop say?"

"He would say it's time for you to get in bed."

She rolls her eyes. "He would not. He was way more fun than you." But she climbs obediently into the nest of sheets anyway.

I glance at Father's old clock on the mantel.

11:45.

Fifteen minutes until Mrs. Harris's coach will be here.

I tuck the sheets around Lucy. Her bones jut through the fabric. I take her hand in mine, feel every tendon straining beneath the skin and her pulse trembling in her wrist.

I haven't been separated from her since the night Mother

disappeared. We've clung to each other, our bond the only solid, tangible thing we've had to ground us amid a sea of turmoil. The thought of leaving her for longer than a work-day makes me nervous. What if something happens while I'm away? What if her condition worsens even more? What if she needs me?

And how do I face something this big without her? My rock, my partner, my heart?

Tears burn at my eyes, and the glint of mischief in Lucy's expression fades. "Don't worry, Myra. It'll be okay. George will take good care of me. It's only four days."

I grit my teeth. How many times has Lucy had to comfort me like this? I'm the eldest child of the family and less than a year away from adulthood, so I should be the one taking care of her, and yet somehow she finds ways to take care of me just as much.

"But what if I can't do it?" I whisper.

She squeezes my hand. "You can. And you will. You have to."

I wrap my arms around her. She nestles her head into the hollow of my throat, and I press my cheek to her hair. "I'd better go. Ava will be here any minute." I tear myself from her side, forcing down the lump in my throat. "I'll be back before you know it."

I tug a half-broken carpetbag from the broom closet and dump the few articles of clothing I own into it. Crossing to the kitchen table, I pause, staring at the medical textbook I bought from Ernest what feels like days ago.

"I got this for you." I hold it up for her to see. "But would it be all right if I borrow it to use for the portrait? I'm worried it might take a bit of research for me to know exactly how to heal whatever trauma killed him."

"You? Medical research?" Lucy feigns horror. "But your brain will explode."

"You pipe down, or I might decide to accidentally misplace this before I get back."

She chuckles. "Of course you can take it. But under absolutely no conditions are you allowed to dog-ear any of those pages. If you do, I swear on the blood of my firstborn child I will scribble on every sheet in your sketch pad."

I gasp. "You wouldn't."

She crosses her arms, sliding deeper into the sheets. "Consider yourself warned."

Shaking my head, I situate the medical textbook inside my bag before snapping the faulty latch closed. It pops open again, and I force it shut once more with a sigh before turning to unlock the door. Just as I'm about to step into the hallway, Lucy's voice stops me.

"I love you, Myra," she says softly. "Even if you're an amphibian hater."

I pause, my whole chest aching. "I love you, too."

She watches me with those shining brown eyes as I back into the hallway.

I pull the door shut and lean my forehead against it. "I'm going to build a better life for us," I whisper. "I promise."

Then I steel my nerves, descend the stairs, and venture out into the icy night.

8

As soon as I step out of the building, the wind lashes me back against the wall. Snow tears across my skin, and I wince, pulling my scarf up over my nose so I can breathe.

I catch sight of Ava trudging across the street toward me, her arms braced in front of her face to block the gusts. She gives me one last meaningful look before vanishing into the building.

Mrs. Harris's coach should be here any minute. I trek toward the curb, but just as I reach it, the latch on my bag drops open again, and the contents spill into the snow. Cursing, I bend to retrieve my things, but a violent gale whips me backward into the slush, snatching stockings, chemises, and knickers into the air.

"No!" I cry, scrambling after my clothes and stuffing them one by one back into my bag, glancing over my shoulder to make sure no one has caught a glimpse of my underthings dancing across the street.

A man snores on a stoop nearby, but no one else is out. Relieved, I scuttle through the snow, jamming skirts and books and socks into the bag and gritting my teeth as the wind burns my ears.

A clatter of hooves breaks through the howling tempest, and I catch sight of a cab headed my way. My stomach clenches as I snap my bag closed once more.

That must be Mrs. Harris's coach.

I'm really going to do this.

But as I make my way toward it, a white ghost of fabric darts in front of me.

My eyes widen.

I missed a pair of knickers.

Panic jolting through every limb, I sprint after it, but the wind is too quick. My underclothes gust right into the carriage door, twisting against its handle as the cab eases to a stop.

I'm almost to it, fingers reaching, when the door snaps open and a boy about my age steps out. "Miss Whitlock?" he asks, his voice so quiet I almost don't hear it over the wind.

Trying not to draw attention to the undergarments knotted on the door just inches from his hand, I give him a stiff nod. "Yes, sir, that's me."

"Let me get your things," he says, stepping into the snow and reaching for my handbag.

"Uh—it's broken, so I'd—I'd better keep it," I mumble, praying he can't feel the heat of my blush from where he is.

"Very well, then." He turns back toward the coach and stops.

Artist, no.

My heart drops to my shoes.

"Oh…" He reaches toward the fabric knotted tightly in the latch. "Is this…yours?"

Death would be a mercy right about now.

I swallow hard. "Um, yes." He glances at me, and blood

floods up my neck. "I mean no! I've never seen those before in my life!"

He stares at me for a long moment.

"I…" I lurch past him and yank at the knickers. The fabric tears, and the sound of it is so loud I'm certain everyone in the world must have heard it.

"Here, why don't I—" He reaches out to help detangle the fabric from the door.

"No, no, no, I've got it just fine," I say, leaping in front of him and tugging on the knot with shaking hands.

Why. Why, why, why, why, *why*?

Finally succeeding at freeing the knickers, I make to shove them back into my bag, but another gust of wind rips them from my grasp.

The boy and I both stare after them as they dart into the sky, spreading out like a kite so that every damn stitch is visible.

He clears his throat. "Should we—ah—go after them?"

"No," I say faintly. "I—I think I'll manage without…"

"Very well." He extends a hand to help me into the carriage, staring intently at our feet. A scarf is wrapped around the lower half of his face, obscuring his expression, but his cheeks are such a bright shade of scarlet I'm sure it rivals the color of my own.

"Thank you." I accept his offered hand and clamber into the carriage, clutching my bag to my chest like a shield.

The boy follows me inside and shuts the door, rapping on the window above his head for the driver to go ahead. There's a snap of a whip, and the coach jostles forward.

Still keeping my eyes trained on the floor, I mumble, "Would it be all right if we stop by my employer's art studio downtown on our way? I'd like to leave a message."

"Of course," he says, and I relay the address to the driver.

As the coach reaches the corner of my street, I press my

face to the window and watch the night swallow my apartment building whole.

"Bye, Lucy," I whisper, pressing my palm to the glass.

Now that midnight has claimed the city, the streets have quieted and the crowds have thinned. Only shadows huddled in rags curl in the alleyways, wrapped in newspaper. A few men stagger home from the taverns, but even their laughter has sobered.

The boy across from me does not glance my way or utter a word. His silence makes the embarrassment burning through my veins that much hotter. He must think me a fool, whoever he is.

I set my jaw and try to ignore his presence. Maybe if we never speak of it again, he'll forget what just happened. It's too bad our god was an artist and not some sort of memory-wiping magician. The things I could do with *that* kind of power would come in really handy right about now.

As we approach downtown, the gaslights brighten and the scrubbed streets reflect that glimmer like a mirror.

We reach Elsie's studio soon after that, and I tug a piece of parchment and a pen from my bag to compose a quick note.

Something important has come up. I will explain as soon as I return to work four days hence.
—Myra

I slide it under the studio door, trace my fingers along the gilded lettering on the window, and clamber back into the cab.

The rest of the city passes in a blur of barbershops and boutiques, bookstores and bakeries as the coach makes its way north. We drive past Old Sawthorne at the precise moment it clangs out the quarter hour, and the ringing of the bells vibrates my bones. The clock's yellow face peers down on us, its turret slicing through the clouds. When we reach the north-ernmost quarter of Lalverton, the residences grow even larger and finer. Soon, I catch glimpses of sweeping yards covered in the silver-white blanket of untouched snow and peaked roofs with chimneys spitting fat gobs of smoke into the sky.

I twist Father's ring, eyes wide. Do people really live like this? With homes the size of an entire city block, adorned with trellises and glimmering wrought iron gates? Though Father's job as a chef was steady enough to keep us comfortable in a flat downtown, I'm sure one of these houses costs more than he could have earned in a lifetime.

But the cab never pauses, never stops. Even when the gas-lights disappear, the mansions give way to slumbering fields, and the sky opens up into a wide expanse of stars.

After a time, the boy across from me tugs off his cap and loosens his scarf. A flaming shock of orange hair sticks in every direction above a pair of protruding round ears. Splotchy freckles stand out against his fair skin. He looks almost fa-miliar, but I can't put my finger on where I might have seen him before.

He avoids my gaze, his cheeks pink, and grimaces down at his hands knotted tightly in his lap.

Somehow, seeing the face of the person who just bore wit-ness to my knickers on display in the sky like some indecent constellation makes everything so much worse. I press my hands to my stomach and squeeze my eyes shut.

"You don't look well," he says after a moment.

"I'm fine," I manage, burrowing deeper into my coat. "A little motion sick is all."

He nods once.

"So," I say, trying to fill the thick silence, "do you work for the Harrises?"

A grimace tweaks his lips. "Something like that."

But he doesn't elaborate. And though he picks at the stitching in his gloves, obviously as uncomfortable as I am, he makes no effort to speak.

Perhaps I am too beneath him, a poor girl who loses her knickers in the street. My neck and ears heat, and I turn my attention back to the window and the world passing outside.

If he thinks me below him, then I don't owe this servant boy anything, least of all my attention or my embarrassment.

Finally, after we are miles out of Lalverton, the carriage turns onto a winding driveway. Massive bone-white trees lean over us like a tunnel, reaching for each other's throats. A few moments later, we stop at a massive gate whose iron finials skewer the stars. It rolls open slowly, and a pair of guards watches us with beady, pinprick eyes as we pass.

The cab trundles through more forestry over snow carved with the tracks of carriage wheels. After several heartbeats of shadows, the trees open up, and I gasp.

Snow sparkles across an expansive front lawn as though someone has scraped the stars from the sky, ground them to a powder, and scattered it thick over the ground. The jagged branches of symmetrically placed trees twist gnarled, dagger-tipped fingers into the air. Rosebushes line the drive, the bloodred of the flowers dark against the moon-spun snow, and I shiver. How did the Harrises get them to bloom like that in the dead of winter?

Up ahead, a house like a castle hulks against the sky.

"Is that it?" I breathe.

The boy looks out the window, and his eyes grow somber. "Welcome to Rose Manor, Miss Whitlock."

The mansion scowls down on us, calculating and cold, stony and silent, and in spite of the light spilling from its entryway, I feel anything but welcome.

9

Several stories of glittering glass, pointed arches, and curving buttresses tower over us as the carriage trundles into the mansion's shadow. And from the roof, a dozen gargoyles with demon eyes watch, their wings spread to the night, their claws reaching.

"Artist's teeth," I breathe. "It's beautiful."

"Yes, that is a word that many have used to describe it," the servant boy allows, and I glance back at him. The glow of the lights from the mansion's windows paint his face golden, emphasizing the resigned frown on his face.

"You don't think it is?"

He purses his lips. "I never said that."

"But you—"

"Ah, she's waiting for you," he interrupts, nodding toward the house.

Mrs. Harris stands outside the front doors wrapped in cloaks and furs. Air snakes out of her mouth and writhes in the frigid air.

The coach eases to a stop, and the servant boy pulls the door open for me. I feel Mrs. Harris's gaze as I clamber down into the snow. Forcing myself not to gape, I stride up the intricate stone steps to meet my new benefactress.

"I am pleased to see you, Miss Whitlock," she says, nodding to a butler standing behind her. He jerks into action, taking my bag and tugging open the front door to admit us. The servant boy strides past me without a second glance and disappears down a hallway.

As I trail Mrs. Harris inside, my gaze snags on the intricate knocker mounted on the door. It's some kind of devil with bulging eyes and pointed teeth. Its tongue curls from its lips in an inhuman loop to form the knocking mechanism. Horns protrude from its head, sharp enough to draw blood. Shuddering, I jog to catch up to Mrs. Harris. A maid closes the door behind us and removes my coat and hat.

Mirrors hang from black textured walls in the foyer, and smooth, polished tables bear gleaming silver vases. A fire roars in a hearth next to where a massive staircase spills out toward me. I pause, gaze trailing upward along a set of stone columns crowned by chandeliers dribbling crystals.

The air is thick with the aroma of the alizarin crimson flowers that give the mansion its name. Underneath the floral runs a distinct musty scent, one that makes me think of ancient libraries and long-forgotten cellars, and I find myself breathing deeply, as though the aroma of wealth could fill me all the way to my toes.

"You like it?"

I flinch. Mrs. Harris is watching me from the bottom step of the grand staircase with an amused expression. My cheeks heat, and I force my jaw shut. "Your home is lovely, Mrs. Harris. I have never seen its equal."

"Thank you." She smiles. "It's been in the family for over

two centuries, actually. Five generations of Harrises have lived here." She's reapplied the rosy lip stain she usually wears, and the curls that were loose from her bun earlier have been smoothed into place. But even though her expression is pleasant enough, there's something broken in the tired way she gazes past me out the window as though waiting to see a face she knows will never appear there again.

"This way." Mrs. Harris ascends the stairs. I hurry after her, trailing my hand along the glass-smooth bannister.

She reaches the second-floor landing, glides down a hall carpeted in deep plum, and pushes open a door detailed with gold.

"This will be your room while you're here. Martel has already brought your bag up." She crosses to a lantern and lights it, bathing the room in a pale yellow glow. "I hope the bed is satisfactory. The sheets have been freshly laundered, and the duvet is new."

I follow her gaze to the bed. It is so massive it could fit all four members of my family comfortably. Blankets detailed with pink stitching have been tucked neatly over the mattress, and a mountain of pillows of varying shades of mauve sits at the head. A lace canopy spills from above, casting gossamer shadows across the carpet.

"This is…" Every word in my vocabulary fails me. "Everything is perfect, ma'am. Thank you."

She nods once. "I've also taken the liberty of stocking the wardrobe with a few things I thought might fit you. Things that would be a bit more, ah…suitable."

I drop my gaze to the frayed stitching of my gown, feeling suddenly hot. The dress was Mother's, and it was lovely once. But the wear of the last year shows in the mud stains at its hem and the unraveling threads in its bodice.

Mrs. Harris is right. This garment doesn't belong in this house of ancient wealth and finery any more than I do.

She gestures to a nearby chair, over which is draped a lovely charcoal dress. "I thought you'd like to put this on."

"Oh, of course," I mumble, lifting the fabric carefully.

Mrs. Harris nods at a small changing area, and I duck behind the folding screen, fumbling at the buttons with shaking hands.

I step out a moment later, feeling exposed and out of place in such a fine gown. She regards me with a critical eye, and her lips tick upward, pleased. "Much better." Then she rubs her hands together. "Now, I would like to discuss a few things regarding the circumstances of you being here before I take you downstairs to your work space." Her voice goes a bit feeble on the final words, so she clears her throat and charges on. "First, and most important, my husband and the staff know nothing of the purpose for your stay. To them, you are Maeve, the daughter of the Duke of Avertine."

I twist my fingers together and wait for her to go on.

"What I've told him, as well as the rest of the staff, is that you've come to familiarize yourself with Lalverton in preparation for attending the conservatory to practice music next year. While everyone in this household knows of Wilburt Jr.'s death, they are all under the impression that you believe him ill."

"I'm afraid I know very little about Avertine," I admit.

"Not to worry, dear. My husband is a very busy man. In fact, he's currently out on business and won't be back until late tomorrow night. Once he returns, you'll likely only ever see him at meals. I doubt he'll say more than two words to you the entire time you're here. And, as for the servants, they don't speak unless spoken to, so as long as you ignore them, they shall give you the same courtesy."

"Begging your pardon, ma'am, but if I am successful and

restore Wilburt Jr. to life, won't everyone find out we've been lying?"

She grimaces. "My hope is that my husband will be so overcome with gratitude that he will forgive me for the indiscretion."

"But what of me?" I ask, trying to shove away memories of the governor's angry speeches on abomination during his campaign to shut down every portrait studio in Lalverton last year.

"You will be under my protection." Mrs. Harris's eyes are sharp. "As long as you are successful, I will not allow any harm to come to you."

The underlying threat in those words raises the hairs on my arms, but I force my expression smooth. "Very well."

"In order to keep up the pretense, you are required to attend our family meals. The dining room is on the first floor at the end of the hallway to the left of the staircase. We eat breakfast at eight, lunch is served at eleven thirty, and supper is at seven in the evening. Do take care to be prompt. The daughter of a duke would never be late."

"Yes, ma'am."

"And, finally, I want to make it absolutely clear that snooping about the house will not be permitted. If I discover you outside your work space, this bedroom, or the dining area, I will have you discharged immediately. Do I make myself understood?"

I nod vigorously. "Of course, ma'am. I wouldn't dream of it."

"Very well, I'll go ahead and show you to the…" She clears her throat. "Yes. Follow me." She turns and exits the room in a swish of satin.

I pause to fish the textbook I purchased from Ernest's bookshop out of my carpetbag before following her.

The house groans like an old ship at sea as we descend to

the first floor, sending goose bumps crawling over my skin. When we reach the base of the stairs, a soft murmur of voices to my left draws my attention, and I catch sight of the servant boy from earlier, all elbows and sharp angles, talking to the butler, whom Mrs. Harris called Martel. The boy's hair mirrors the fire to his right, a brilliant red with threads of amber, and his pale lashes catch the light. He glances my direction, then looks quickly away as though I'm of little interest to him.

But now, in full light, I can see why I thought he seemed familiar before. The hair color, the freckles, the jawline—he must be related to the Harrises in some way. Perhaps a cousin? His resemblance to Wilburt Jr. is uncanny. It's like he's the too-tall, too-skinny version of the boy I've seen from afar since I was a child. When I asked if he worked for the Harrises, he said, "Something like that." What could he have meant, if he was not a servant?

Mrs. Harris lifts a candle from one of the tables in the foyer and leads me along a hallway to another door that, when opened, reveals a sharply descending set of stairs. Shadows sulk in the corners, and the air is still, as though the eaves and corridors of the house are holding their breath so that I might not notice them watching me.

My nape prickles, and I tighten my arms around the textbook to force away the tingling sensation of being observed.

Deeper and deeper we descend. The air chills, and the light fades into a thick darkness lit only by the small flame Mrs. Harris carries. Finally, when it feels as though we must have plunged into the center of the very earth, Mrs. Harris comes to a halt before a thick, unornamented doorway. My breath mists in front of my nose.

Mrs. Harris fishes a large metal key from her pocket and slides it into a keyhole. The whine of metal on metal sets my teeth on edge as she pushes the door wide. Retrieving the key, she holds it out for me.

"Keep this door locked at all times," she says, her eyes sharp in the jittering candlelight.

I nod and pocket the key. It weighs heavy against my leg. As Mrs. Harris turns to step through the door and light a lantern within, a sudden panic jolts through me.

This must be where they are keeping the corpse.

My vision swims. I press a hand to the door frame to steady myself.

Since Mrs. Harris first explained the situation, I never paused to actually consider that I would be working in close proximity with a dead person. A rank sweetness fills my nose, and I swallow down a sudden rise of bile.

I don't have the luxury of fear, of disgust, of panic. I need to face this head-on, do what needs to be done, and get out of this house.

Bracing myself, I follow Mrs. Harris inside.

The room is largely bare. A desk sits to one side, stacked high with parchment and stocked with glasses of brushes and pencils. Two easels stand in one corner, and several dozen canvases lean against the wall next to them. On the opposite wall towers a bookshelf filled with everything I could possibly ever need: palettes and knives, oils, pigments, tubes of ladyrose gel, turpentine, jugs of water, and cleaning cloths. Two chairs sit in the center of the room. A smock is spread out over one, pressed and ready to use. Mrs. Harris truly thought of everything.

Finally, I allow myself to look at the table to the right of the chairs. On it lies the form of a body draped in a white sheet. Mrs. Harris stares hard at the wall behind me, her jaw rigid.

"I hope you'll find everything you need," she says, her voice uneven. "The potion that has been injected into…the body…should keep it preserved in its current state for the next four days. I hope it'll be enough time." She swallows hard and presses her fingertips to her temples. "I—I need to g-go."

"Actually, I do have a few ques—"

"I'm sorry. I m-must…" She dashes out of the room. Just before the door slams behind her, I catch sight of tears streaking through the powder on her cheeks.

10

I stare at the door for several long moments after Mrs. Harris's footsteps fade.

The cellar is an unearthly quiet in her absence, like the body under the sheet is listening. Waiting.

Gripping Father's ring through my glove, I close my eyes and hear Lucy's words from earlier. *It'll be okay.*

First things first: I need to assess Wilburt's body and its damages. With something this complex, I'm sure his sevren will be thick and difficult for my magic to unravel, so I need to get as much information as possible, including how and why he fell and which injuries were ultimately responsible for his demise. I'll only be able to infer so much by observing the state of the corpse.

I had hoped to ask Mrs. Harris a few questions before she left—about whether he tripped or if something else made him lose his balance, where exactly he landed, and how long it took for him to pass away—but I see now how troubling those questions will be for her. I suppose I can give her a bit of time. Besides, doing the baseline painting of Wilburt as he is now should take me a while to get right. I won't need to do any detangling of sevren until later. Maybe I can speak to Mrs. Harris after breakfast.

I set the medical textbook on the desk and approach the corpse. Bracing myself, I lift the sheet in one swift motion and fold it down over the bottom half of the body so that the head, torso, and arms are exposed.

Though most of the blood has been cleared away, there are still congealed globs of it caked to his shirt, and the sight of it makes my stomach turn.

"It's just a body. Just a body. Just a body," I repeat to myself in a hoarse whisper, trying to channel my inner Lucy and approach this like a scientist. What would she do now?

Notes. She always takes careful, detailed notes. Jots everything down, even things that don't seem important at first.

I breathe slowly, steadying my trembling hands as I pull out a clean notebook and a pen from the desk.

I try to focus on Wilburt Jr.'s face, but all I can see is the caved-in, crushed right side of his skull and the way internal juices have crusted on the pallid skin.

Vomit lurches into my throat. Dropping the notebook and pen, I dash across the room, yank open the door, and sprint up the stairs, palm clapped tightly across my mouth. My stomach heaves. Twists. Another bubble of acid shoots onto the back of my tongue. I force it down, searching desperately for a bathroom, a sink, anything.

I reach the first floor and whirl about. Where do I go?

Another wrench of my gut sends me hightailing it for the front door. Just as I'm tearing across the entryway, my stomach hurls its contents upward in a final, angry thrust. I dive for the decorative vase serving as an umbrella stand and retch into it everything I've eaten the past week.

Squeezing my eyes shut, I force away the image of Wilburt's mangled head and grip the sides of the vase. Tears stream down my cheeks, and bile burns my lips as I cough and heave and cough some more.

When it's finally done, I ease back onto my haunches, trembling. Saliva drips in strings from my mouth, but I don't want to ruin my gloves by wiping it away.

"Are you all right?" a male voice asks from behind me.

Heat floods my neck and cheeks.

Oh, please, no.

"I'm fine," I rasp, tightening my grip on the vase.

Someone kill me now.

"Here." A handkerchief is thrust into my line of vision.

"Thank you." I take it and dab the muck from the corners of my mouth.

Balling the handkerchief in my fist, I force a pleasant expression onto my face and look up. The fire-headed boy from earlier towers over me, kneading his knuckles against each other and staring very intently at the wall behind me.

"It's, uh, it's quite all-all right, Miss Whitlock." He gives a small nod, still avoiding my gaze. His voice is curt, his face stone.

An image of my knickers dancing in the sky flashes across my mind, and my stomach lurches all over again. How is it possible for me to have humiliated myself in front of him twice in one night?

"I suppose you've seen the body, then," he says, nodding toward the vase full of my vomit.

I gulp. "I—" Hadn't Mrs. Harris said the entire staff was told I didn't know Wilburt was dead? Then again, she also said no one would know who I really was, and this boy knows my name as well as where I live.

His jaw flexes. "It's all right. I'm aware of your purpose here."

"You are?"

"That's why Mother sent me to pick you up—so no one would witness where you'd come from or ask questions about what you're doing here."

I get to my feet and have to tip my head back pretty far to keep my eyes on his face. Then his words register, and I take a step back. "Wait—'Mother'? You mean Mrs. Harris?"

"Yes."

"You're her son?"

He dips his head in a polite bow, still avoiding my eye, his mouth a thin line. "I'm August Harris."

So not a cousin, then. "I didn't know the Harrises had two sons."

"You're not the first to be mistaken in that regard." He pauses. "You sure you're all right?"

"Once I recover from the utter humiliation of having done something so ghastly in front of a member of the governor's family, I think I will be," I say with a nervous chuckle.

He does not smile.

I clear my throat, letting the hopeful grin slip from my face. "I'm terribly sorry for ruining your vase."

"I'll call Martel to come clean it up." He turns to head down the hall.

Panic floods my body. "No!" If Martel learns of my disgrace, it's only a matter of time before word gets back to Mrs. Harris. I'd rather die than have her find out. "Please. Don't tell anyone. I'll take care of it myself." I attempt to pick up the vase, but it's heavier than I expect, and it takes me a few good tries to get it off the ground. "If you'll open the door for me, I'll go dispose of the mess outsi—"

The vase slips from my hands and clangs on the ground. The distinct slop of wetness echoes loudly from within.

I stare at it in horror.

Flee. I must flee this place and never show my face in society again.

"Why don't I—" August reaches for the vase.

"No, no, no, I can manage!" I leap in front of him, hoisting the weight in my arms and waddling for the door.

He rushes to hold it open for me. "Really, Miss Whitlock—"

"I've got it!" I say as the cold air rushes across my flaming cheeks. "If you'd just direct me to a suitable place where I could...uh...empty this?"

He inhales sharply, his jaw clenching as though he'd like nothing better than to be rid of me. Shame makes me tighten my grip on the vase.

"There's a stream on the other side of the fence. This way." He sets off for the east end of the drive. Our shoes crunch over the ice-encrusted lawn as we tread down an aisle of carefully spaced rosebushes. The deep crimson blooms watch us pass, silent, suspicious sentries the color of blood against the snow. Gooseflesh erupts on my skin as we weave among them and come to a stop at the exterior wall.

"Must we climb it?" I ask.

"No. We go through there." He moves along the fence a few more paces and comes to a stop at what looks to be a locked gate.

"Do you have the key?"

"Don't need one. Lock's broken." He yanks on the padlock, and it snaps apart.

On the other side of the fence, trees and shrubbery twist wild and free, unlike the neat rows and carefully matching sizes of the plants on the estate. We make our way over pebbles and around fallen logs to a small half-frozen stream.

"Excellent, thank you," I say, setting the vase on the icy bank. My jaw rattles, and every breath of the winter air feels like it's freezing my lungs.

"I don't suppose you'll allow me to take over yet?"

"I've got it!" I say a bit too brightly, pausing to remove my gloves before dunking the vase into the stream.

The water splashes onto my hands, a thousand pinpricks of ice, and I purse my lips to keep my teeth from chattering.

An air of awkwardness hangs between us. I feel his eyes on the back of my neck, unblinking and unimpressed.

"I would have loved to live near a place like this growing up," I say, desperate to fill the silence. "Lots of rocks and trees to climb. Did you and Wilburt ever play out here?"

"Will," August says, watching me dump water out of the vase. It cascades like a shower of diamonds back into the stream.

"I beg your pardon?"

He still won't look at me. "My brother hated being called Wilburt. It was always just Will." His words are curt, almost like a dismissal.

"Oh. Sorry." I know I'm nowhere near regal enough to run in the circles of a Harris, but would it kill him to at least pretend he thinks I'm worthy of his time?

He reaches for the vase. "Let me take that. You should put your gloves back on before you get frostbite."

"All right." I hand it over reluctantly.

He hoists it into his arms and waits as I dry my palms on my skirt and pull on my gloves.

"So did you?" I ask, watching the way the nighttime shadows play across those blotchy freckles on his cheeks.

"Did I what?"

His words are a cold slap. I jut out my chin, my embarrassment bubbling into annoyance.

"Play out here with Will." I plant my hands on my hips and nod around at the trees.

"Sometimes." He turns and stalks back up to the house, clearly unperturbed by my irritation.

If coming out here and helping me is such a burdensome chore, why did he accompany me? I made it more than clear I didn't need his help. What gives him the right to treat me like a fool? I stomp after him.

We speak not another word as we slip back through the gate and reenter the home. I sigh once we close the door behind us. Though the house seemed cold before, in contrast with the frigid wind outside, the air in here feels downright toasty.

"Thank you for your help," I force out.

August sets the vase back in its place. A few drops of water drip like tears down its side and pool on the gleaming floor. "You're welcome," he says before turning on his heel and continuing down the hallway to wherever he must have been on his way to when he found me in my disgrace.

Grinding my teeth, I follow him into the same corridor, but pause when I catch sight of the stairs that lead to the cellar. To the body.

Though the windows fill the hallway with the silver glimmer of moonlight, darkness laps at its edges, lakes of ivory obsidian paint. I twist the ring on my thumb until it knots in my glove, remembering the blood, the brain matter, the exposed skull fragments that sent me running up here in the first place.

"Are you sure you're all right?"

I jump for the second time tonight at the sound of August's voice and look up. He's watching me from the end of the hallway, as though he paused on his way through the final archway to glance back at me.

"I—" I grimace. "I'm tired, I suppose." It's not a lie. Exhaustion eats at my insides and wearies my bones. I try to ignore it. I'm well acquainted with fatigue.

August purses his lips and walks toward me. "I'll escort you down," he says, extending an arm.

"Oh, that's not necessary." I swallow my nerves and force my jaw hard. "I'm quite all right."

His eyes flick to my face. "Please. You look a little green. Trust me, it'll help to not be alone."

Trust. A word people throw around but never mean. Lucy and I trusted my parents, and now they're gone. We wanted to trust Elsie, but she's more loyal to her bank account than she could ever be to us. Ava promises we can trust her, too, but she'll vanish as soon as we can't afford to pay her anymore.

Trust is a luxury for the wealthy, the secure, the loved.

Not for us.

August clears his throat, his arm still extended.

I don't need him—other than Lucy, I don't need anyone—but I've already been such a disgraceful guest. So, taking a deep breath, I loop my hand through the inside of his elbow, taking care to touch him as little as possible. He holds very still. I'm not entirely certain he's even breathing.

With one last glance behind me at the ice-framed windows and the star-strewn sky beyond, I allow the forgotten Harris boy to lead me into the dark.

||

Wilburt Jr. is right where I left him. The sheet flutters as we move into the room.

August inhales sharply and comes up short just inside the doorway.

I release his elbow and step away. "You probably don't want to see him like this. You can go."

August shakes his head, his teeth clenched tight together. "No wonder you were sick."

I crouch to retrieve the notebook I dropped earlier and search the floor for the pen.

When I finally stand, I make eye contact with August. He flinches and turns away immediately, but something catches in my chest. His eyes are palest aquamarine, translucent and bright. Watery and open and not at all condescending or disgusted. They look almost…afraid?

"Were you very close with him?" I keep my voice hushed as though the sound of it might disturb Will's dreams.

August shakes his head once. "We didn't get along."

The words are as clipped and short as the rest of the words he's said tonight, but now that I've seen the vulnerability in his eyes, I notice the cracks around the edges of his tone. The gentler points in the syllables and the soft, crumbling undertones.

Not sure why I'm doing it or what I think might come of it, I lay a careful hand on his shoulder. He blinks once but doesn't otherwise react.

"Thank you," he says after what feels like an eternity. "For coming. For trying to bring him back." His Adam's apple bobs as he forces a swallow. "Will always seemed so large before. He had a presence that filled a room, you know? He looks so much smaller now."

I nod, and we lapse into silence for several moments.

"Did it hurt terribly?" I whisper. "When he passed?"

"Hurt," he echoes the word slowly, "is not deep enough. Not raw or serrated enough to capture how it felt." He reaches out a hand and brushes his brother's thumb, still and lifeless on the table, and presses his other fist to his lips, squeezing his eyes shut and breathing slowly. "I never thought... Well, I can't say I imagined losing him, but if I had, I wouldn't have pictured it would feel like this."

I ball my hands into fists. "I will try my best to bring him back. I promise," I say. "I don't claim to be a great Prodigy— or even a good one. But I've never let my own mediocrity stop me from trying."

The faintest hint of a smile ticks the corner of his mouth upward. I smile back.

A footstep creaks somewhere above us.

We break eye contact at once, both of us looking down at our shoes, at the floor, at the shadows lurking in the corners.

August starts to turn for the door but pauses at the threshold. "I don't know much about what you do or how it works, but if I can be of any help to you, please don't hesitate to ask."

"Actually…" I hold up my notebook. "In order for me to undo the effects of Will's fall, I need to know as much as possible about the circumstances surrounding his death. I meant to ask your mother, but I didn't get the chance."

His jaw tightens, but he nods and crosses to one of the chairs, giving the table and the cold, quiet body atop it a wide berth. "I'm not sure how much help I'll be, but I can certainly tell you what I know."

"Thank you." I move the apron to the desk and take the chair opposite him. Then a sudden realization drops a stone in my gut. I wasn't raised in proper society, but it's always been drilled into me how important propriety is.

"I'm so sorry," I say as blood rushes up my neck. "I just realized how dreadfully inappropriate it is for us to be here together alone at this hour."

"Yes, my mother would probably have some kind of heart episode if she found us." August snorts, then covers his mouth with his hand and composes himself. "I'm sorry. This is really not the time to make a joke, but she can be a bit intense."

"Really? I hadn't noticed." I quirk a sarcastic eyebrow, and he almost smiles.

"It's all right," he says. "A few questions won't hurt anybody."

I glance down at the blank notebook page on my knee. "All right." I shake the pen to get the ink running and ask, "What can you tell me about how he died?"

"I was upstairs in my room around nine o'clock this morning. Someone started screaming, so I went to the window." He gulps. "All I could see was blood. I ran down and found our cook, Nigel, shouting for help. He was the one who found him. He'd been taking out the remnants of our breakfast when Will fell."

"Did Nigel say if he saw what happened?" I scribble notes as August speaks.

"He told us Will had been up on the balcony outside his room. Sitting on the railing. I guess he lost his balance."

"No one was up there with him?"

August shakes his head. "Not that I'm aware of."

"All right." I pause, tapping the pen against my chin. "Any guesses why he was on that balcony? Did he go out there a lot?"

"That's the odd bit about it." August frowns. "He was afraid of heights. Kept the balcony doors locked at all times. That he would be out there sitting on the railing of all things doesn't make any sense."

"What had his emotional state been like as of late?"

August almost scoffs. "He wouldn't have fallen on purpose, if that's where you're going with that question." He considers me for a long moment, as though trying to decide how much to tell me.

"August," I say quietly, gently. "The more I know about him and what he was like before he died, the better. My magic deals with how a soul is spun together. If I'm going to have any chance of healing him, I need to understand what that soul was like."

August's jaw tenses, and then, finally, he sighs and rubs his eyes. "He was a pompous dolt, if you want the truth. Had the whole city in the palm of his hand, girls throwing themselves at him wherever he went. And he loved it. Bragged about it like he'd done a damn thing to deserve it." August shakes his head. "I honestly think sometimes he forgot that the only reason he was anything at all was because of who his father was."

The bitterness in August's tone is taut, almost angry. He grimaces down at his fists. "I shouldn't be talking about him like this. He was far from my favorite person, but he was my brother."

"His death doesn't erase how he behaved toward you during his life," I say. "It's okay to dislike him and mourn him at the same time."

August twists his fingers together and stares at my notebook. "So how does it work exactly? Your magic?" His voice drops to a whisper, as though he's uttered a bad word.

"When I paint, I can alter reality," I say. "Erase a blemish or a mole, mend a wound."

He watches my pen skate across the page warily but doesn't speak.

"I—" I lick my lips, trying to decide how to phrase my question. "I know how your father feels about what I do."

His Adam's apple bobs. "Yes."

"Are you... Do you think it's an abomination like he does?"

He glances to his brother, and his face pales. "I'm not sure," he says after a moment. "But if your magic is the thing that could bring my brother back...that can't be evil, can it?"

I shrug. "I think the Artist has His ways of making miracles. Why can't magic be one of those methods?"

August ponders that for a moment, then asks, "Have you ever done anything like this before? Raising the dead?"

I shake my head. "Not a human. I'm not even sure it's possible. But I'm trying anyway."

"What comes next?"

I sigh and get to my feet, gathering my wits. "The first step is to paint him as he appears now. Then I layer over that a healed, living version of him. Once that's finished, I use my magic to make that new image reality. It might take me a few portraits...or many."

"You can't use the same one over and over?"

I shake my head. "For a minor cut or blemish, sure. But

for something like this, I have to infuse the painting with the emotions he was likely feeling in the moments leading up to his death. Focus on the specific ways in which the most lethal injuries were sustained. Each painting may look largely the same, but the manner in which I paint it—the things I'm feeling and thinking as I do it—has an immense effect on whether I'm successful or not."

I cross to the table and try not to breathe through my nose.

It's just a still life, I try to tell myself. *Not a person. Not blood and tissue.*

Steeling my nerves, I set everything up. A small canvas on the easel. Paints laid out on the palette: alizarin crimson, phthalocyanine blue, cadmium yellow, raw umber, burnt sienna, and titanium white. Always in the same order so I never have to go looking for the color I need.

The room fills with the gentle scraping sound of my palette knife as I mix the colors. Then I squirt a dollop of ladyrose gel onto the palette so it'll be ready to mix with each color once I'm ready to use them. If I have only four days to pull this off, I'll need to work fast, which means I don't have time to sit around waiting for my paints to dry.

Once everything is set, I pull out some turpentine and mix it with my burnt sienna to make the paint as lean as possible. Taking my long-bristled flat brush, I scrub it onto the canvas, falling into my rhythm. Then I block out the underpainting with more turpentine-loosened paint, studying the body carefully as I diagram its shape. I note the crushed and mangled ear, the blood congealing on the hair, the fragments of skull and brain tissue. I take in the scraped skin and the way the blood has pooled on the bottom of the body. August stands to my side, observing silently.

"You're free to leave," I say. "I think that's all of my questions for now."

He studies me for a long moment, those furtive eyes searching every inch of my face. I force myself to focus on the corpse in front of me, but as I take in the blood and the mangled flesh, my head spins. I press my hand against the table until the sensation clears.

August frowns, running his fingers along the glass bottles of pigment and linseed oil on the shelf next to him. He doesn't speak for several moments, but when he finally does, his voice is quiet and soft. "I'm happy to leave if that's what you wish. However, I'd like to keep you company, if that's all right."

I force a small nod. "Suit yourself."

Why is he so eager to stay? There's no way this is solely about him wanting to keep me company so I don't have to be alone with a corpse. He doesn't know me and surely has no reason to care. I steal a glance his way as I load more paint onto my brush. He's ruffling through his pockets with tense hands. It's clear he doesn't like being near his dead brother any more than I do. Has Mrs. Harris sent him to supervise my work? To spy on me and make sure I'm doing what she wants?

Something is off about this family, about this house. Gritting my teeth, I focus on my painting. The faster I do this portrait, the sooner I can get out of here and back to Lucy.

12

As the painting slowly begins to take shape under my hands, my magic's faint prickle crescendos into a distracting buzz. I stifle a sigh, shaking out a cramp in my wrist, and glance at August, who has returned to his chair. He pulls a notebook and pen from his jacket. My eyes catch on a glint of gold, and I pause in my painting to study the pen. It's gilded at the ends and has a wooden body threaded through with intricate engravings.

"That's a remarkable pen," I say.

"Oh, this used to belong to Thomas Kenwick," he responds, holding it up to the light. "You've heard of Kenwick, right?"

"The…" I scrunch my forehead, trying to place the name. "The poet?"

"Yes, that's the one!" His face brightens, and it's like sunshine breaking through clouds, his whole demeanor growing suddenly brighter and, at the same time, more vulnerable. I can't help but grin with him in spite of my suspicions as his tone takes on an excited lilt. "He's my favorite author. I met him once, and he gave me this as a gift." He runs a thumb along its length, admiring it as though it were a puppy or a long-lost friend.

"It's beautiful."

He nods. "I never write without it." Then, as if to prove it, he leans in over his notebook and starts inking in another line.

Smiling faintly, I turn back to my work. Soon, the gentle scratching sound of his writing fills the silence. It's soothing, making the gore in front of me seem less horrific and the impossibility of my task less daunting. And, somehow, the icy itch of my power doesn't seem quite so unbearable, too. It's not quite the comfort of having Lucy nearby, flipping through her medical notes, jotting down hypotheses, and making sarcastic quips about the odd expressions I make when I'm concentrating, but there's something about the quiet camaraderie of sharing space with another human that makes life seem less bleak. I mix colors and dab them carefully onto the canvas. The preliminary illustration of Will's body soon materializes under my brush.

"I'm curious," August says after about half an hour of silence.

"About?"

"Can Prodigies alter their own bodies?"

I give a sort of half laugh. "It's not very pleasant, but yes, it's possible."

"Have you changed yourself before?"

"I broke my ankle when I was fourteen and used my magic to fix that. And I've changed my hair color at least a billion times. You wouldn't believe how stunning I look with fuchsia curls." I snort, remembering how Lucy laughed so hard she choked on her own tongue when I did that.

"Why is making changes to your own body unpleasant?"

"Well." I step back to survey my painting, then load my

brush with a bit more phthalo blue. "When I paint away a feature from someone else, I experience the sensation of that feature for a time. Like if I heal a wound, I feel the pain of it. But when I make the change on myself, it's like the sensation of the feature I painted away compounds upon itself."

"So fixing your broken ankle made it hurt worse?"

I nod. "Only for a couple of hours, though. Then it was gone. And it was worth it to me."

"But what about with the hair color? That isn't painful, so how would you experience the sensation of that?"

"Oh, it's hard to explain. It's like every emotion I'd ever felt about my hair—the good and the bad—all hit me at the same time and then was doubled because I was altering it. Insecurities and frustrations about how it looked combined with pride in how much it made me resemble my mother. It felt as though I was drowning in it all at once."

"Interesting." August glances at his brother on the table. "So if you're able to heal him, you'll feel what he felt when he died?"

"That's how it works."

He goes silent for several moments. "You're willing to put yourself through that?"

I force a shrug even though the thought of taking on the agony of Will's injuries makes my hands shake. "Your mother offered me a lot of money. Besides, the pain will only be temporary."

We lapse into silence as I finish up Will's face. Time to do his shoulders, chest, and arms. I lean around the canvas to look at his body again.

His shirt is still buttoned, though it's stiff and blotted with crimson, and there are a few black streaks near the hem that look almost like charcoal or ink. I set down my paintbrushes and cross to the table. Gingerly, I unfasten the buttons and expose the chest so I can get a look at the damage there. When I ease the shirt open, something topples out of the breast pocket and hits the floor. I bend to retrieve it and hold it to the light. It appears to be a piece of wax the color of midnight with the corner of an intricate-looking letter on it. Maybe an *A*? Or a *V*? I drop it into my pocket and continue my inspection of Will's torso.

I pause to study an odd-looking wound right over his heart. A sort of puckered split in the skin. There's no blood around it, but whatever pierced him there went deep, going in right between the ribs. It might have even gone through his heart.

"Do you see that?" I point.

August leans closer. "It looks almost like…"

"A knife wound, right?"

He frowns. "But there's no blood. And the other injuries are all mostly on the opposite side of his body."

"It's extremely odd." I return to my painting and start illustrating Will's torso, making sure to add in the detail with a deep mixture of alizarin crimson and burnt umber. "You didn't notice anything protruding from his chest after he fell?"

"There was nothing like that." August pinches the left side of Will's shirt and examines it. "Look. There's no tear in the fabric or blood here, either."

"Hmm." I frown, leaning back to survey my illustration from a different angle. "Would you actually cut the shirt away from his arms? I need to paint them, too."

He retrieves a pair of scissors from the desk and approaches the corpse. As he makes to lift Will's arm, however, his hands begin to shake, and his face goes green.

"Are you all right?" I ask.

He squeezes his eyes shut. "I'm fine. I just need a moment."

"I'm so sorry." I leap from my seat and take the scissors from him. "This is your brother. I can't imagine how difficult—"

"No, I want to help," he says, but he doesn't object when I slice through the stiff, blood-soaked fabric of the sleeve.

"You have already helped so much," I say, giving him a reassuring smile as I return to my canvas. Retrieving my brushes, I take special care to get the details of the shattered right arm as accurate as possible.

August returns to his chair, his coloring returning to normal as time passes. Soon, he tugs what looks to be a cinnamon candy stick from his pocket and gnaws on it as he writes. The sharp scent of it fills the room. I focus on each detail of my portrait, losing myself in the colors. Time spins away from me. An hour passes. Then two.

It must be close to five in the morning when I step back, adding in one final flourish. The place at the base of my skull flares so cold a shiver runs through my whole body.

"Finished," I say. "Do you think I missed anything?"

August comes around to get a look at the final product. His jaw drops. "It...it looks exactly like him. How did you *do* that?"

"Oh, this is nothing compared to what an actual professional could do."

"This is not nothing. This is..." He gulps, going a bit greenish again. "Well, it's disgusting, to be honest, but it looks so *real*." He takes a step back, as though in awe. "It's just like a photograph...like I could reach out and—" His eyes meet mine, and he freezes. Color floods his cheeks. He turns back to the painting, clenching his jaw. "I mean. I'm sorry. I— This looks good."

"August—"

"Forget I said anything. Please." Gone is the warmth that was starting to thaw his stoic expression. His jaw is as tense as it was in the hallway upstairs, his lips pursed as tight.

"You don't need to be sorry," I say quietly. My pieces have

always seemed so juvenile in comparison to Mother's, and every one I've done has always been thoroughly critiqued by both her and Elsie so I could improve. I've never been able to look at a painting I've done and see anything but its flaws.

But the way August's eyes just lit up and the way his brows rose like I was some kind of artistic genius... Pride floods through me, and a smile trembles on my lips.

"What's next?" he says abruptly. "You paint him healthy, right?"

"Right." I try to catch August's eye again, but he avoids my gaze. His hands clench into fists, and the veins in his temple twitch.

Sighing, I cross to the desk and leaf through the medical textbook I brought.

"This part's more complicated," I say, pausing to study Will, tapping the handles of the brushes against my chin, then turning a few more pages, looking at diagrams of fatal injuries in the book and comparing them to Will's. "I need to be able to understand precisely what caused his death. Which specific injury." I glance at August. "Do you know if the death was immediate?"

He shakes his head. "I'm not sure. He had already died by the time I got there, but that was several minutes after it happened."

"See, and that's the other part." I sigh. "If he hit the ground and was still alive for a moment or two, that'll make it harder for my magic to unravel." The sevren will be much thicker and more tangled if he experienced pain for several minutes.

"So what are you going to do?" August asks.

"Guess, I suppose." I flip through the medical text, but diagrams and tiny scrawl blur together as though written in some foreign tongue. Human anatomy and science have always been Lucy's passion, not mine. If only she were here to help me sort through this… I purse my lips and turn to August. "Is there a telephone I might use?" The house obviously hasn't been wired for electricity yet, but maybe…

August nods. "In the parlor. Father had a special line set up to take calls there. Who are you trying to contact?"

"My sister," I say as he leads the way up the stairs, along the corridor, and through the foyer. The fire in the hearth has burned down to glowing embers, orange coals flaring in the cold. "The apartment building where we live has a communal telephone. Perhaps I might be able to reach her."

August lights a candle on a table next to a gleaming black telephone. I take a seat in the chair and lift the earpiece from its perch, dialing in the numbers carefully. The wheel clicks sudden and loud in the quiet.

The superintendent of my apartment building growls into the phone first, upset at the early hour, but soon he agrees to find Lucy. A moment later, Lucy's voice, thick with slumber, crackles across the line. "Myra?"

"Lucy!" Just hearing her voice sends a wave of comfort through me, settling my frazzled nerves. "I need your help. I've been looking at the body, and I can't for the life of me figure out what injuries might have been responsible for the death."

"I told you your head would explode," she teases. "Why don't you describe the state of the corpse? I'll see if I can come up with anything."

I scan through my list of notes, describing to her the fractured skull, broken bones, shattered arm, caved chest, and the blood pooling at the bottom of the body.

"The most likely thing would have been the head trauma," she says without pause. "The fall most certainly caused intraparenchymal hemorrhages and contusions."

"What?"

"It means the impact damaged brain tissue and caused irreparable damage, bleeding, and swelling. Not being able to look at it myself, I can't say for sure, but if those were severe enough, he likely died either instantly or within minutes. You can't mess around with brain trauma."

I jot that down in my notebook. "All right. I'll try that. If the intrapare-whatever doesn't work, what else could I try?"

"Hmm..." I can practically see her chewing on her thumb knuckle the way she always does when considering a tricky scientific problem. "My next guess might be internal hemorrhage—bleeding inside the body cavity—though, again, without looking at it, it's hard to say which organ would have caused that. You could take your pick of any organ on the left side, though. Pancreas, spleen, kidney... The lung could have been punctured by a rib."

She goes on, listing possibilities, and I scribble each one into my notebook.

"All right," I say once I've got a list of close to a dozen. "I'll try these."

"Don't mess it up."

I snort and roll my eyes. "Thanks, Luce. I owe you."

"Big fat crickets for Georgie, that's all I need," she says with a yawn. "I love you."

"I love you, too."

The line goes dead, but I don't replace the earpiece right away. I listen to the crackle, imagining her trudging up the stairs in her slippers, mumbling responses to Ava about what I wanted, and giving George an extra kiss before sinking back into her pillows.

"You all right?" August asks quietly.

I jump. Blushing, I set the earpiece into its cradle and gather up my notebook. "I'm perfectly well. Back to the cellar?"

He extinguishes the candle, and we steal soundlessly the way we came.

Once back in my work space, I flip through the textbook until I locate a section specifically on head trauma and scan the images, frowning. The fact that I might have to experience the sensations of any one of these injuries makes my stomach twist.

"So a brain injury first?" August asks, glancing over my shoulder at a carefully labeled drawing of the interior of a human head.

I nod. "I'll try several paintings, going through each possibility one by one until something sticks. Lucy thinks it was most likely head trauma that did it, so we'll start with that."

August frowns. "I could also ask Nigel for more specifics in the morning, if that would be helpful. Like whether Will died on impact or if it took him a few minutes to pass away."

"No, that's all right." I shake my head. "I'll talk to him myself. *I* know what I need to know."

"But you can't," August says, crossing his arms.

"I beg your pardon?" I raise a brow. "I'm perfectly capable—"

"You're not supposed to know Will is dead."

I deflate. He's right. I grind the toe of my boot into the stone floor.

"Despite what my mother thinks, I'm not totally inept," August says quietly. "Let me help you."

I sigh. "Fine. But I want you to take notes."

"Of course."

"And be thorough."

He nods.

"Ask follow-up questions," I say. "I need to know absolutely everything that man saw."

"Don't worry, Miss Whitlock. I'll interrogate him within an inch of his life." His tone softens into a sort of teasing, but I glare down at Will's corpse.

He's right. I can't talk to the cook. But his eagerness makes me wary. As much as I'd love to let him share the burden of this task, every single nerve in my body is tensed for attack. I can't trust him. He's the governor's son.

"Why are you so set on helping me?" I mutter. "You said yourself you didn't like him."

He frowns. "Just because I didn't like him doesn't mean I didn't love him. He was my brother. Surely I shouldn't have to explain that."

I sigh. "I'm sorry."

My life and Lucy's depend on my being able to paint Will back to life. The fact that I have to rely on this boy I know nothing about makes me feel like jumping out of my own skin, but he just lost his brother. And while my presence here has given him and his mother reason to hope the death isn't permanent and made it possible for them to put off grieving for now, I've seen enough cracks in August's exterior already to know his brother's passing has affected him deeper than he lets show.

"It's okay, Myra," he says. "You can trust me."

There's that word again.

Wiping my sweating palms on my skirt, I force a smile. "Thank you."

He nods and returns to his seat.

I sort through my pile of brushes and begin working in a new layer of Will over the damaged one. Since Will held such a prominent role in Lalverton society, his photographs featured frequently in the papers, and I saw him often at city events. All of that is playing to my advantage now, as I've got a pretty clear memory of what he looked like.

As I work, that buzz in my fingers fills my whole body with the chill of magic. As long as I focus on the art, I don't have to think of Mother and Father's disappearance. I don't have to wonder whether we'll still have a home next month or why my sister's illness has gotten worse. I don't have to stop myself from imagining all the could-have-beens. All I have to do is get the lay of Will's hair right, dot in the glisten of light on his skin, dab on the freckles, and, all throughout, keep my thoughts focused on the brain injury that must have caused his death.

The small, precise movements of my brush keep me grounded, keep me focused. The snick of the bristles over the canvas. The tap of my knife on the palette.

It's close to seven by the time I finish. I sit back and let out a slow breath. *Please, let this work*, I pray as I press my fingertips to the canvas.

My eyes fall shut. I block out the thud of my heartbeat in my ears and the quiet scribble of August's fancy pen across the room. I focus only on the thrum of cold electricity in my hand as it builds its way along my arm, snapping and crackling all the way up until it meets the base of my skull. Colors and light flow through me, fill me until my whole body vibrates with magic.

When the painting morphs into the diagram of Will's sevren, I gasp.

It's far more tangled than anything I've ever seen.

My magic lunges forth, and I dig my hand deeper against the canvas, grounding myself in the sensation of the cold paint against my skin as I force it back, direct it toward the parts of the painting I want it to focus on. The injuries. The motionless chest, the closed eyelids. Allowing the tiniest stream of power out through my fingertips, I trace over the knotted sevren of Will's head trauma slowly, praying my magic can detangle it in spite of how thick and impossible the snarls seem.

I brace myself for the crush of pain Will must have felt when he died as I imagine the circumstances that led to his passing.

Him sitting on the railing of the balcony, losing balance, and plunging through the frostbitten wind to the patio. I experience the emotions of panic, of terror in the seconds before his skull smashed into the ground.

My magic builds, and the current jolting through me reaches its peak.

I clench my jaw as it consumes me.

And then, all at once, it releases.

I wait for the crunch of bone and the squelch of blood like I experienced with the beetle back in my apartment, but it never comes.

August clears his throat. "Did you do anything yet?"

Disappointment wells in my chest as I drop my hand from the painting. "It must not have been the head trauma that caused it." I sink back into my seat. Tears sting at the corners of my eyes, and I knuckle them away. Of course I knew it was unlikely that I would get it right on the first try, but I had allowed myself to hope.

"It's all right. Your sister gave you a whole list of possibilities to try next." He tugs out a pocket watch and studies it. "Besides, it's seven thirty already. Almost time for breakfast."

"You'd better go on up first. Don't want anyone to know we spent the night together."

August stiffens, and my words echo back to me. Heat floods my cheeks.

"I—I'm sorry. I didn't mean—"

"No, you're right," he says crisply, getting to his feet. "It would look bad."

He ducks out the door without another word.

I let out a slow sigh as I gather up the dirty paintbrushes, wondering just how many more times I can make a fool of myself in front of August before I combust.

13

With the governor not returning home until later this evening, it's just Mrs. Harris, August, and me at breakfast. The servants bring out plates of flaky biscuits topped with oozing jams, meats soaked in heavy cream sauces, and fresh cranberry juice. My mouth waters as the food is placed in front of me, and the temptation to take the plate and dump its contents straight down my throat is so strong I can't see straight.

But I've already embarrassed myself enough since my arrival last night, so I watch Mrs. Harris, take my cues from her, and eat only as much as she does—which is barely more than a few bites.

Once we've tucked in, Mrs. Harris launches into what must be the most recent gossip circling among the prominent members of Lalverton's governing elite. August laughs along and responds in kind, never once glancing toward me.

I stare at him as he speaks. This cannot possibly be the same August who acted so indifferent, so cold to me last night. Neither can it be the same August who later on warmed into the kind, charming boy who was such a comfort to me in that frigid cellar afterward.

No, this August is completely different. He reminds me of… well, his brother. Will. He holds his chin high, defiant. One eyebrow cocked as though he finds her amusing. His smile suave and diplomatic.

But whenever I saw Will at public events, he seemed to genuinely *be* that person. August, however…there's something off here. When his mother makes a joke at someone's expense, he laughs a little too loudly. When he answers her questions, his words are too sweet, too practiced—like he rehearsed them all night long to say them in precisely that order with precisely that intonation. He barely eats a bite of his breakfast and instead spends the whole meal with his hands under the table.

Who is August Harris, really? The stoic, unperturbed stranger who witnessed me vomit into an umbrella stand? The slightly sheepish, quiet boy who sat all night with me scrawling in his notebook while I painted? Or this not-as-smooth-as-he-means-to-be politician?

As the meal draws to an end, August tosses his napkin onto the table next to his untouched plate.

"Auggie!" Mrs. Harris's tone is shrill as she snatches his hand and inspects his fingers. Scabs circle his fingernails, some of them open and weeping little trickles of blood. "Your cuticles look terrible. You said you'd do better."

August's eyes flick to me as his ears redden. He yanks out of her grasp and shoves his hands into his pockets as he gets to his feet. "Doing my best, Mother."

"Well," she huffs. "You'd better keep your gloves on when the Ambroses come tomorrow. What an embarrassment. It's a filthy habit, you know that."

"Yes, Mother, I do." He gives a slight bow of the head.

"Excuse me. I'm late for the, uh—" He mumbles something unintelligible and departs in a rush.

Mrs. Harris harrumphs, folding her napkin and exiting the room after him without a backward glance at me.

Taking full advantage of being left alone with the food, I wolf down the rest of what's on my plate and drink three more glasses of cranberry juice.

Artist, it feels good to have a full stomach.

When the stitching in my bodice feels ready to burst, I excuse myself from the empty table and return to the cellar, pockets stuffed with extra biscuits.

My second portrait of Will is one where I focus on if he might have died of a broken neck, which seems to me to be the next most likely cause from Lucy's list. I choose a smaller canvas this time, so I'm able to complete the portrait by eleven.

Once again, my magic has no effect on the body.

August won't meet my eye at lunch, and we never get a chance to speak. Praying he'll find a way to tell me soon if he got anything out of the cook, I return to my task once the meal is over.

It takes me until late afternoon to finish my third painting—this time imagining Will died from having one of his broken ribs puncture a lung—and by that point, my head is throbbing and I can scarcely keep my eyes open.

When my magic fails once more, I lean my forehead against the portrait and weep.

I'm exhausted. Everything in me wants to curl into a ball on the floor and never get up again, but I try to shake away the fatigue. I don't have time for a break. There are only three days left before I'm out of time and they have to bring an embalmer for Will's body. Three days before Mrs. Harris makes good on her threat to expose me.

But as I try to sort through a jar of paintbrushes, my vision blurs. Blood thumps in my ears, and my mind swims. How long has it been since I slept? Close to forty hours?

Smudging away the paint and the tears from my face, I stagger out of the cellar, lock the door, and climb leadenly up to my bedroom.

I can afford a small nap. Two hours won't put me that far behind.

I collapse on the bed without even bothering to remove my shoes.

Supper is a quiet affair, and though the soup is better than anything I've eaten in months, it pales in comparison to what my father used to bring home from his restaurants. August stares at his wineglass all through the meal, responding to his mother's inquiries and gossip just as he did this morning—in a voice that doesn't quite sound like it belongs to him and with an expression that appears painted on. He's wearing black leather gloves now and rigidly keeps his hands on either side of his plate all the way through dessert as though they've been glued there. He doesn't eat a single bite and looks a bit peaked by the time Mrs. Harris dismisses him for the evening. Shoving his fists into his pockets, he all but dashes out the door.

Once supper is over, I allow myself the luxury of a quick bath in my chambers to calm my nerves. It's been ages since I last soaked in hot water, and though I would give anything to lie here in the steam for hours, I force myself to scrub quickly and towel off. The longer it takes me to heal Will, the longer it'll be before I can go home to Lucy. And I already wasted enough time with my nap earlier. I need to get back to work.

Wrapped in a fluffy towel, I cross to the wardrobe and push its doors open wide. A dozen dresses finer than anything I've ever owned hang daintily within, their silks and satins shimmering in the candlelight. I run my hands over them, reveling in the colors and the intricate stitching. If only Lucy could get a look at these. She would be absolutely beside herself. Smiling, I sort through them, my fingers stilling on a pastel pink one adorned with pearl buttons.

Pink has always been my favorite color. Like sunrises and springtime, new beginnings and hope.

Holding my breath, I pull the dress out and tug it over my head, then step in front of the floor-length mirror, pinching color into my cheeks and pinning up my hair.

Once finished, I twirl, admiring the way the skirts flare around my legs. With a flourish, I bow to the mirror, extending a hand for an imaginary suitor to kiss. "The pleasure's all mine, kind sir," I murmur with a giggle.

But when I meet my own brown eyes in the mirror, my smile fades.

I wish Mother could see me in this dress. Father would tell me I look just like her, take me in his arms, and dance me across the kitchen. I would trip, and he would laugh, and Mother would fuss that we were going to soil the gown with our nonsense while Lucy would ask if we could buy her frog a bow tie so he could match.

I press my fingertips to the glass. If only I could pass through it back to that world where things were so simple. Where Mother and Father were near and my worries were fewer.

As much as I want to believe my parents are somewhere out there, that they're trying to find their way back to me and my sister, deep down I know that the days when our family was complete, days of laughter and security, are nothing more than distant memories.

It will never be like that again.

Tugging on a pair of lace gloves, I turn away and shuffle downstairs on leaden feet.

With the fourth portrait, I focus on the possibility of broken bones crushing through one of Will's arteries and filling his internal cavity with blood.

If this one doesn't work, I have only a handful of options to try next. Beyond Lucy's remaining suggestions, I can't think of anything else that would kill him within minutes of striking the ground, especially since the left side of his body is undamaged. Well, undamaged except for that odd wound in his chest that looks like it came from a knife, but I still haven't figured out what could have caused that.

August returns shortly after ten o'clock, just as I'm finishing up the version of Will as he is. I look up expectantly.

"I'm sorry it's taken me so long," he says stiffly, taking his seat once more. "Mother kept me quite occupied all day."

"It's all right." I wave away his apology. "Did you talk to Nigel?"

"I did. He wasn't sure if Will died immediately or not. He didn't want to talk about it."

I clamp down on a frustrated sigh. I knew I wouldn't be able to trust August to get the information I needed. "Did he give you any insight that might be useful? I told you to take notes."

August shakes his head once. "He didn't tell me anything I didn't already know, so I didn't have anything to write down."

I grit my teeth and turn back to my portrait. "Well, then, this had better work."

August is silent as I paint, and though awkwardness hangs in the air between us at first, as the hours pass and the sound of my brushes against the canvas mingles with the scratch of his pen on the pages of his notebook, the tension softens into something almost friendly, the way it did last night.

I finish the portrait around midnight. When my magic once again fails to make any change to the corpse on the table, I toss my brushes into the corner. They clatter loudly against the stone floor, and the sound reverberates in the silence.

What else could have caused Will's death?

Lucy would be able to figure this out, I'm sure of it. She'd have graphs measured out for probabilities, and she'd have diagrams of each injury and how long each one could have taken to kill him on its own. She'd know how much blood he'd lost and where to find the missing pieces.

My notes are messy and full of questions. I push the notebook aside and pull out the textbook to scour it, but the more pages I turn, the more tears blur over my eyes.

I could call her again, but what would she be able to do from across town? Without looking at the body herself, she can only give me the same hypotheses she already shared.

I wish my sister were *here*. Not only because she'd know what to do, but also because things are just *better* when Lucy's close.

Closing the textbook, I lean forward in my chair, studying my portrait. The careful orange-and-red brushstrokes swooping across Will's brow, the dab of his brown freckles. I frown.

What if it wasn't that I got the injuries wrong? Maybe it's just that my magic is being persnickety, as usual, and it wants me to get the healthy version of him as accurate as possible. Get the placement of his freckles correct and the quirk of his brow angled precisely.

Sighing, I turn to August. "Are there any recently done paintings of Will I can look at?" I ask. "Maybe my illustration isn't exactly right."

"Do you have to get it exactly right in order for it to work?"

"For the general Prodigy, no. My mother has altered people's appearances drawing stick figures in a pile of flour before. Prodigy magic is more about understanding the feature you're trying to change than being able to render it perfectly. But my magic seems to be quite a lot more temperamental than hers, and in this case where what I'm altering is so complex, getting the details right can't hurt. A portrait of Will would be very helpful."

"I'm afraid my father has forbidden paintings of any kind in the house," he says. "We've never even had family portraits done. He says that doing so would be making light of artistry's holy significance."

I try not to roll my eyes. "What about photographs from one of the newspaper articles, then? You've got to have some of those lying around, right?"

"Probably. Will kept a collection of them. Would you like me to run up to his room and find one?"

"Actually." I pull off my apron and gather the notebook and pencil. "Could you tell me where his room is? It would be really helpful for me to have a look around it and the balcony where he fell."

August ponders a moment and then nods. "All right. But we need to be quiet. If anyone catches us in there…especially alone…" He swallows and offers me his arm again.

I eye his extended elbow. As nice as it would be to have him along, part of me still rankles at the idea of depending on him. On anyone. "You don't have to come with me if you don't want to," I say quietly. "I'm sure I'll be all right on my own."

"It'll be easier if I show you. And besides, if we're both looking, we'll be able to find the photos faster." He lifts the lantern down from the wall.

"All right." I glance at the corpse slumbering still and silent on the table. Trying to shake the feeling that Will's unseeing, glassy eyes will flick my direction as soon as I turn away, I take August's arm and allow him to lead me out of the room. But when the prickle of being watched dances down my spine, I yank the door closed behind us and lock it tight.

14

As we climb the stairs, we take care to tread softly. The rest of the lighting in the house has been extinguished, and the night claws around our small halo of yellow light, dragging its slippery fingers along my nape and whispering my name on an exhale. Fear crawls through my veins, but I keep my head high, my eyes wide-open, and my steps steady.

We reach the main floor and steal soundlessly down the hall. The hearth in the entryway glows red with cooling embers, and the scent of smoke lingers in the air. Each decorative vase and potted plant looms against the wall, and every time we pass a mirror and I catch sight of our reflections hulking in the night, I nearly jump out of my skin.

Instead of ascending the main staircase, August leads me down another hallway to the back of the house, where a smaller set of stairs climbs to the upper floors. I glance out a window and pause.

Blanketed in white, a garden intricate enough that the Artist Himself could have painted it slumbers under a cloudless violet sky. Pristine and perfect and untouched. Like something from a dream. The snow on the ground glows as though lit from within.

Peering through the frosted glass, I catch sight of a large patch of the outdoor patio area where the snow has been cleared away.

"Is that where he fell?" I whisper, pointing.

"It is. The servants scrubbed it immediately after his body was removed." August leans away from the window as though he doesn't want to look. "Shall we continue upstairs?"

"Actually, I'd like to poke around while we're here, if that's all right." I need to be able to picture the moment when he died like I was there. Like I lived it.

We tiptoe through the door onto the beautifully crafted back veranda. A fountain composed of an intricate sculpture of the Artist and His Dear Lady with their backs pressed together and their hands reaching to heaven stands at its heart, frozen water blossoming from their mouths.

We pick our way through trampled snow over to the cleared area. The tiles there shine with ice, and I take care not to step on it in case it's as slippery as it looks. August holds the lantern as I crouch to inspect the floor.

It's been scoured absolutely clean. If I didn't know someone died here, I wouldn't think it possible.

"Here," August says, draping something over my shoulders. I've been so intent on studying the tile that I didn't realize how violently I was shivering. His jacket tucks in around me, smelling distinctly of cinnamon.

"No, you'll freeze." I start to take it off and give it back, but he holds up a hand.

"Please." His gaze is intense, his jaw set. He's entirely serious. "It's the least I can do."

"Thank you," I say, and he drops my gaze quickly. The lantern illuminates his features in a soft yellow light, and I can't help but study his face for a moment. How similar to Will he looks—and yet so different. Will always seemed chiseled in stone, a masterpiece to behold. My first impression of August was that he was the complete opposite. But now, I can't help but notice the sharp, masculine jaw and the handsome cleft in his chin. And his ears...well, they certainly weren't Will's style of rugged handsomeness, but they've got their own endearing charm.

August shifts uncomfortably. Dear Lady, how long have I been staring? I clear my throat, turning back to the scene. "Can you tell me what position the body was in?"

"Uh... Artist... I think his feet were over that way." He points, wincing as though seeing the scene all over again. "Kind of crossed diagonally over each other. He was on his right side. And then his head was over closer to the house. His right arm was pinned under him, and the left one was kind of drooping in front."

I scrawl a few notes into my notebook. "What happened after you found him?"

"Father came out." August's tone darkens. "He instructed the servants to bring the body inside and set them to work cleaning up the mess. And then he swore everyone to secrecy."

"Why?" If the governor didn't intend to have Mrs. Harris hire me, then why would he want to keep his son's death such a secret? "Did no one call the police? Why are the papers reporting that he is ill?"

"Politics." August says the word like it's the vilest thing he's ever tasted. "Can't allow Father's precious reputation to be tarnished, especially not now with the election looming. The papers have been publishing questionable pieces about his moral compass for weeks, claiming that he makes all of his decisions only with his head and never with his heart." He scoffs. "Funny how accurate the assessment is, actually."

"So he thinks that Will's death will reflect poorly on him somehow?" I mull it over slowly. "But it's not like he can put them off the truth for long...if my magic doesn't work, that is. Eventually, the story is going to have to come out."

"But he wants to control that story."

"How?"

August shakes his head. "There have been several articles recently disparaging him for the amount of pressure he's put on Will the past few years. People have accused him of forcing his son to grow up too quickly. I think Father's afraid that even if the papers reported that Will's fall was entirely accidental, people would spin the story into a suicide, and the gossip columns would have a field day blaming him for it."

"That makes sense," I muse, and then my gaze catches on something in the snow outside the line of August's lantern light. "What's that?" I cross to it.

A few sets of footprints trail this way through the snow. They lead around the east corner of the house.

"That's where they took the body inside," August says.

Tiny flecks of red glimmer in the slush like melted ladyrose petals, and the hairs rise on my arms. I follow the trail along Rose Manor's wall to an unadorned back entrance. "What's in there?"

"The kitchen," August says. "There's a sink they use for rinsing the meats from the butcher, and Father...well, he wanted as much of the gore cleaned off the body as possible before it was brought any farther inside." His face has taken on a grayish sheen, and he presses a hand to the wall to steady himself.

"Are you all right?"

He nods, but his sour expression tightens. "It's just...not pleasant to relive it. I'll be okay."

"I'm sorry. I shouldn't—"

"If it'll help you bring him back, then I can handle it."

I purse my lips. "Thank you."

He pushes himself upright and forces his expression into something less pained. "What else do you need to see?"

"Uh..." I look around, studying the area. Something doesn't quite seem to be clicking together.

A big rectangle of dead grass is visible through the snow to the left of the door, as though a bin used to stand there. I glance to the right where a dumpster now stands, exactly the size and shape of the section of missing snow.

"Did someone move that?"

He frowns. "Looks like it."

"Why?"

"No idea."

I catch a glimpse of something dark lining the bottom of the bin. "Can you shine the lantern over there?"

August holds it closer to the ground. The light glints on a line of blackened red. "Is that what I think it is?" I approach the trash bin and cinch my hands into the handles to move it aside, revealing what looks like a dried puddle of blood. My gaze trails up to more flecks of red on the walls.

"This is the dumpster used by the kitchen staff," August says as the blood in my own body curdles. "It's actually not uncommon for there to be blood out here from the meats brought in from the butcher." He wrinkles his nose. "Though they are usually better about cleaning up after themselves. I'll have to let Mother know."

"Oh, I see." A wave of emotion floods my system. Most of it is relief, but unease prickles under my skin as I let the dumpster thunk back into place and tug August's jacket tighter around me. "All right, why don't we go ahead and take a look at Will's room, then? I think I've seen everything I need to out here."

August leads the way past the fountain and through the back door. Once inside, I shrug out of his jacket and hand it to him. His face flushes as he takes it from me, and, when I offer my thanks, he turns away with a mumbled, "You're welcome."

We tread carefully up several flights of stairs to the fourth floor. A grandfather clock lurks on the landing, tall and scowling, its pendulum swinging back and forth with a soul-rattling *tick-tock, tick-tock*. I squint to make out the time.

A sudden single deep *gong* slams through my eardrums. I leap back, knocking a pot of flowers off a table. August catches it before it crashes to the floor, and I double over, pressing my hands to my knees, gasping. Adrenaline zings through my system.

August makes some sort of muffled sound. I glance up at him. He covers a laugh and composes himself. "Sorry," he whispers, a grin tickling at the corners of his mouth. "Are you all right?"

I scowl at him. "Perfectly fine, sir."

He forces a serious expression. "Oh, good."

Once I've gathered my nerves and willed my heart rate to return to its normal pace, I nod at August to continue. He slinks farther along the corridor, coming to a stop before a set of double doors trimmed in gold. Twisting the handles, he leads the way inside.

I shut the doors behind us, and he turns up his lantern, filling the space with a dull orange glow. I look around. A bed commands the center of the room. Its sheets and duvets are tangled in elaborate knots, and pillows lie scattered everywhere—there's even one atop the writing desk in the corner. Papers and books make piles on the floor, and the air is thick with the unmistakable scent of young man. Sweat with a hint of expensive cologne.

The memory of the cinnamon aroma of August's jacket fills my mind, and my cheeks warm.

Shaking that thought aside, I pick my way across the floor, moving to the balcony doors. I try to open them.

"These are locked," I say, frowning and jiggling the knobs. "That's odd."

"Do you think Will might have locked himself out there on accident? Maybe he fell when he was trying to find another way into the house."

"Maybe." August frowns. "Or I guess one of the maids could have locked it later on? Though—" he glances around the room "—it doesn't look like this room has seen a maid in weeks."

"Could it have been your mother or father?"

"I suppose." He doesn't seem entirely convinced. "But why would they come in to lock the doors and leave everything else untouched?"

"August," I say, running my thumb over the keyholes. A cold, terrible thought leeches through me, filling my blood with ice. "You don't think it's possible that… I mean…maybe he didn't…" I swallow, giving up on the knob and pulling the journal out of my pocket to scribble down a few notes. "Was there anyone who might have disliked Will?"

He snorts. "The list of people who didn't like my brother is miles long," he says, his voice threaded with an emotion I can't quite name. "What are you implying?"

I finish scrawling in the notes about the footprints in the snow and the puddle of blood under the dumpster, struggling to keep my hand steady in spite of the fear making it shake as I write. "What if he didn't fall, and he also didn't jump?"

August wraps his own hands around the knobs and gives

both doors a tug. They rattle but hold firm. He steps back several paces, mopping a hand over his face. "You think he could have been pushed?"

"It's a possibility, isn't it?"

"But Nigel said he was alone." August's mouth is a grim line.

"Maybe whoever it was ducked out of sight before Nigel noticed them up there. Or maybe Nigel was so fixated on Will that he didn't see that there was someone on the balcony."

August sits heavily on the end of Will's bed, and the mattress doesn't even creak. I stare at it a long moment. Have I ever slept on a mattress that didn't creak?

"If someone pushed Will, they could have locked the door when they came back in," August says softly, almost like he's talking to himself. Thinking aloud. "But who would do something so terrible?"

"Who might have wanted to hurt him?"

August shakes his head. "I don't know. Though he was a dolt, I can't imagine him doing anything meaningful enough to tempt someone to kill him."

I chew on the end of the pen. "What about your father?"

"What about my father? You think *he* did this?"

"Oh, no, I'm not saying that! I mean... People dislike him. Maybe somebody did it as a warning or threat to the governor?" I begin to pace, taking care not to tread on any of the books and trinkets on the floor. "What if someone is really upset with your father, or maybe wants to boot him out of the running for next year's election?"

August sighs, knotting his fingers, and I notice that the tips of them are stained black with the ink from his pen. "That actually could be a possibility. People have tried drastic things over the years in an attempt to get my father's attention. Climbing our fences, accosting him in our driveway.

It's why we have so many servants now and why the entrance to the estate is gated and guarded."

"I suppose a hazard of being in charge is that no matter what you do someone is going to be unhappy about it."

August nods, then drops his face into his hands and massages his eyes. "I thought Will dying was terrible enough on its own. But murder?"

"I'm sorry," I say, closing my notebook. "I'm sure you're exhausted. You lost your brother this week, and here I am forcing you to parade me around the house like a tour guide. You're more than welcome to go get some rest. I'll finish up here and make sure to close the door when I'm done."

He raises his head, his expression something between anguish and shock. "No."

I blink. "No?"

"If someone murdered my brother, I want to find out who."

I consider him for a moment. As much as I don't trust him—or anyone else in this house, for that matter—I wouldn't have been able to learn as much as I have about what happened to Will without his help. Maybe it wouldn't be such a terrible thing to have him on my side.

"Then why don't we look around in here?" I say. "See if we can find any clues?"

"All right." August crosses to the wardrobe and begins rooting through it.

I turn to the desk. One by one, I pick through the trinkets of the boy who died.

The boy who might have been murdered.

15

We spend the better part of an hour combing through Will's things. As I examine odds and ends on a pair of bookshelves against the wall, my thoughts stray across town to a dilapidated apartment building and the spitfire girl within. I imagine Lucy arguing with Ava about bedtime, promising she'll go to sleep as soon as she finishes the pie chart on bacterial microbes she's working on. Ava will relent, of course, because there's no arguing with Lucy when she's made up her mind about something. And then, twenty minutes later when Lucy has fallen asleep with her cheek stuck to the notebook page, Ava will have to tuck a blanket around her and ease the pen from her grasp. Then, finally, Ava will fall asleep on my bed, only to wake in the night to the sounds of Lucy moaning and weeping, clutching her abdomen.

I'm all too familiar with the jerk of panic those sounds would wrench through me. Sometimes I would slip into the sheets next to her, holding her squirming body in my arms. After having stayed up so late, the fact that the few hours of sleep she got were full of pains, dozens of trips to the chamber pot, and insomnia was so frustrating it would bring her to tears.

No, nights offer no respite, even for the most weary and determined of us all.

My heart aches as I shove a book back into its place.

Is Lucy crying now? Will Ava even wake to hear it? Will she lie next to her and hold her until she falls back asleep?

I force myself to focus. The only thing I can do for Lucy now is unravel the mystery of Will's death as quickly as possible so that I can return to her.

Rubbing my eyes, I consider the facts.

If Will was pushed, and we're looking at a murder instead of an accident, that complicates things significantly. Accidents don't give as much time for the soul-threads to tangle, and they aren't as complex. If he merely fell, all I need to know is which injury lead to his passing and imagine how he felt in that moment.

But if someone killed him, that would explain why Will's sevren are so much more knotted. In that case, more emotions were likely mixed up in the events prior to his death, leading to tightly snarled sevren—which means that instead of just needing to know which injury caused the death, I'd need to understand what Will was feeling in those moments before it occurred, as well.

It becomes not just a matter of *how* he died, but also of who did it and why, as well as what Will's relationship was to the killer and how he felt about that person.

And I still have so little to go on.

I glance over my shoulder at August, who is rifling under the bed. "Anything?"

"A lot of dust." He coughs as though for emphasis.

I sigh as I give up on the bookshelves. So far everything

I've found has been entirely ordinary. Messy, but nothing un-usual. Planting my hands on my hips, I glare around the room, seething as though it's keeping its secrets from me on purpose.

"I think we've been through everything," I say. "Is there another place where we could find a photo? Or any other clues about what might have happened?"

August frowns, getting to his feet. "I don't think so."

A faint noise in the hallway makes us both freeze. We stare at each other, wide-eyed. August presses a finger to his lips and creeps to the door, inching it open a crack.

The sound grows louder, and I recognize it for what it is: the soft padding of feet on carpet.

August watches for several long moments until the noise fades.

"Who was it?" I whisper.

"Mother."

Mrs. Harris's earlier warning rings sharp in my ears. *If I discover you outside your work space, this bedroom, or the dining area, I will have you discharged immediately. Do I make myself understood?*

A flicker of panic flares in my chest, but I tamp it back down. If Mrs. Harris were to find me here, I have a perfectly good reason for straying from my work space. But even as I reassure myself of this, sweat gathers on the back of my neck.

The truth is, I don't know what Mrs. Harris would do if she caught me. From what I can tell, she wouldn't take kindly to being disobeyed, no matter the reasoning. It would be best to keep this midnight exploration a secret at all costs.

After another few minutes, August deems it safe enough for us to go. He grabs the lantern, opens the door, and gestures for me to come with him. We slink onto the landing, and he leads me in the opposite direction of where Mrs. Harris's footsteps went.

August ushers me through a small door. It leads into a plain-looking, quaint hallway that must be some kind of servants' passage. A set of stairs leads steeply upward to my right.

The ceiling creaks directly over our heads so loudly we both jump.

"What was that?" I whisper.

"I don't know."

A burst of cold air whispers across our faces from the stairway.

"What's up there?"

"The fifth floor." A timbre of fear quivers in his voice.

"Well, yes. I figured as much, considering this is the fourth floor. But what is *on* the fifth floor?"

He shakes his head. "Nothing."

"Then what's it used for?" I raise a brow.

"It isn't. No one goes up there."

"Ever?"

He swallows. "It's strictly off-limits. For everyone. Not even Father dares."

I squint at the shadows curling beyond our lantern's glow. The air shifts again, and there's another creak.

"Was that a footstep?" I ask, scarcely daring to breathe.

August doesn't reply. The lantern sputters in his hand.

"Maybe it's your mother?"

He shakes his head. "Not a chance."

"Why not?"

"The fifth floor is haunted."

I smirk, but when he doesn't laugh, when his grip tightens on the lantern, I let the smile fade. "You're serious?"

"My great-grandfather Bertram Harris owned this house when he was alive," August says so quietly I have to lean in closer to hear. "His quarters were on the fifth floor. Legend says he was a Prodigy."

"There are Prodigies in your bloodline?"

He shakes his head. "No one knows for sure, but the stories say that he became drunk on his power, that he thought himself some kind of twisted god and used his magic to torture people. Paint them with massive wounds, eyeballs hanging out, things like that. He killed men, women…even children. His daughter was found by her brothers with her body wrapped in her own entrails with a portrait next to her to match."

Horror wraps a fist around my throat. "What? Why?"

"It's hard to say. Bertram was locked up after that and died in prison. But all the roses on the estate? He planted them. And there has to be some truth to the stories, because how else do the flowers bloom in the winter? I have a theory that he used his magic on the seeds to make them resistant to the cold."

I think of the bloodred flowers encrusted in snow outside, and a shiver rolls up my spine. "But our magic only works on people and animals, not plants."

He pauses, considering. "Oh, I didn't know that. Are you sure there isn't some strain of Prodigy magic that can do more?"

"I…" Frowning, I stare at the flickering flame in his lantern. "I suppose there could be a lot to my magic I haven't learned yet."

"Well, regardless, I don't know how much of it all is true," August goes on in a whisper, "but it's because of the stories that my father is so against Prodigy magic. He believes Great-Grandfather Bertram's violence was a result of the corruption of his soul."

Goose bumps rise on my arms that have nothing to do with the cold. "But why do you think the fifth floor is haunted?"

"I've heard things in the night. Weeping. Screams. Father says it's the souls of the people who died there, bound by their agony to the place where Bertram killed them."

Another creak above makes me jump so badly I almost

knock the lantern out of August's hands. Shadows spider across the ceiling, crawling along the place where it slopes upward above the stairs toward the gaping maw of the fifth floor. Beckoning us to follow.

"There's someone there," I say.

August shakes his head. "No one goes up to the fifth floor."

"But what if they do?" I turn to face him. "What if they only perpetuate the stories so that no one will investigate the screams you've been hearing?" I pause, wringing my hands. "If Will really was killed, maybe the person who did it is on the fifth floor right now."

August looks like he's about to be ill.

My mind whirs, but I set my jaw. "I'm going to have a look."

August shakes his head. "It's too dangerous."

"There are a lot of things I'm afraid of, but ghosts are not one of them." Clenching my fists, I head up the staircase.

August's hand wraps around my arm. "It's not just the ghosts," he says. "No one's been up there in decades. There's no telling what state it's in. Even when the rest of the house was remodeled to preserve and update it, they skipped over the fifth floor. It could be unstable."

I level his gaze with a fierce one of my own. "I have to do this," I say, and though my voice is a whisper, it cuts through the air like a blade. "In order to bring Will back, I need to find out what happened to him. I don't have the privilege of playing it safe."

August swallows hard, his eyes tracking over every inch of my face. Finally, he releases me. "All right. But I'm coming with you."

16

The darkness of the fifth floor sucks hungrily at our light, smacking its lips as we tread along hallways slumbering under blankets of dust.

Unlike throughout the rest of the Harris house, where the only ornamentation is mirrors and vases, faces stare down at us from the walls here. Cobwebs cling to dozens of paintings, trailing gossamer threads across high foreheads and somber eyes immortalized in faded oils.

Neither August nor I utter a word as we make our way along the corridor, but when a rush of icy air whips the hair back from my face and a squeak of terror chokes out from my lips, he tucks my arm in his. No longer the polite, gentlemanly gesture it was an hour ago, it's like a life raft. An offer of comfort. Of solidarity in the face of whatever—or *whoever*—might be waiting for us in the shadows.

We peer into room after room, shining the lantern inside long enough to see that there are no footprints in the dust. Furniture covered in faded white sheets hulk quiet and sul-

len as we check behind them for any hint of something having been disturbed.

But we find nothing.

The fear eating at me soon gives way to frustration. What
made that noise? Where did the cold air come from?

As we retrace our steps onto the landing after scouring another empty, untouched room, the glow of August's lantern
illuminates a section of hallway leading from another set of
stairs where the dust only clings in clumps to the edges of the
carpet, leaving the center of it clear.

I tug on August's elbow, which is still looped around mine,
and point wordlessly.

He frowns, and we follow the trail to a plain, nondescript
door. I press my ear to the wood paneling and listen for several long moments.

Not a single sound emerges from within. Not a breath, not
a step, not a rustle of fabric.

I ease the door inward. The hinges whine, raising the hairs
on my nape.

As our light fills the space, I stifle a gasp. The room looks
like it could be the storage area for a museum, not a suite on
the top floor of the governor's mansion. Paintings and drawings in various mediums stand in massive stacks and cover
nearly every inch of the walls. A built-in bookshelf bowing
under the weight of a hundred texts reaches straight to the
ceiling in one corner.

August stands stock straight, staring at a portrait over the
mantelpiece directly in front of us. My lungs squeeze in on
themselves at the sight of Governor Harris glaring down from
within the frame. It is a fearsome image, and not a kind ren-
dering. Governor Harris's eyes protrude, the whites like pus-
tules ready to pop and snaked with thick, bulbous veins. His
fanged teeth drip blood down his chin.

"Someone *has* been up here," I breathe. "That couldn't have been painted by Bertram Harris over a century ago."

August's face shines with sweat in the glimmer of amber light, and his eyes are far away, like he's seeing but not understanding.

I glance back at the portrait, shuddering at the gruesome image and its intricate details and practiced brushstrokes. It's flawless. Horrible. I look around at the other paintings. Illustrations of bloodred skies with jagged, reaching tree branches and others of demons spreading muscular wings and people distorted into gruesome positions close in around us. I flinch as I take in each one, my empty stomach twisting against my ribs.

The curtains hanging on a window in the corner stir, and my gaze snaps to the portrait hanging directly next to them. I approach cautiously.

It's of Will. Dark auburn hair and thick eyebrows. Cut, striking jawline and freckled high cheekbones. A cravat knotted carefully in a starched white collar.

His eyes are piercing and blue like August's, but the color is deeper. Oceanic. Myriad emotions tangle in that gaze. Threads of longing, hints of frustration and anger. Determination. Fear.

Even when it isn't done by a Prodigy, art holds magic. It captures how it feels to be alive, with all its aches and sorrows and joys.

The curtain twitches again, and the cold puffs across my face, fanning the downy hairs on my cheeks. I tug it back, and a whoosh of chilled air rushes into the room from the window, which is wide-open. I duck my head through it. Vines tangle along the stone wall outside, gnarled and naked and thick enough to hold a grown man.

I scan the gardens sprawling beyond the back veranda of the house. Twisting hedges curl in a massive onyx maze dusted with snow. Icy rosebushes dripping red snake their thorny branches to the sky.

Nothing stirs on the grounds. Nobody moves in the shadows.

But that doesn't mean no one is there.

I yank the window shut and latch it tight, then step back from it, teeth chattering as I tug the curtains closed. Whoever was here is long gone now.

As I turn away, I loosen my grip on the fabric. Just before I let go of it completely, however, moonlight shafts across three paintings next to the one of Will.

Mrs. Harris's calculating eyes glint like tiny gems from another expertly done portrait. Alongside her is one of Governor Harris, but in this piece the monstrosity of the other image exists only in the slightly wolfish curl of his lip.

On the far end is a painting of August. Whoever the artist is must know the warm version of him. Instead of the oiled hair of Politician August, floppy, unruly locks the color of fire frizz around his forehead, and his eyes crinkle in a soft, kind smile. The artist even captured the shy charm of his aquamarine eyes.

"Did you see this?" I ask, turning to face the real August.

He's still staring at that portrait of his father as a monster, and his hand is shaking so hard the lantern light gutters.

"August?" I approach him. "Are you all right?"

He jerks as though I've awaken him from a nightmare. His breathing is uneven, like it's catching on his teeth on its way in and out. He sets the lantern down on the floor and sits next to it, draping his arms across his knees. His eyes are wide, and he twists his fingers together, his thumbnail instinctively digging at the cuticles of his right hand.

"I'm sorry," he says in a breath. "I knew Father had all of Great-Grandfather Bertram's paintings stored away up here, so I expected to find *those*. But this? These are obviously new. It's...a lot."

I settle down next to him and sift through a pile of canvases on the floor. "On the bright side, whoever painted this was probably not a Prodigy like Bertram. Otherwise your father's real face might look like *that*."

"Do you think one of the servants could be behind this?" August continues tearing at his nails. "Maybe they knew my father wouldn't come looking up here, so they thought it would be a good place to hide things?"

"But why, though?"

"I don't know." He shakes his head. "What if Will might have come across all of this? Maybe whoever painted these was afraid he'd tell someone, so they got rid of him."

"It's a possibility," I say, flipping through the pictures in my hands.

Each one is of a maimed, injured person. Ankles snapped in half, arms twisted at horrible angles, massive wounds rotting in puckered, oozing flesh. When my stomach twists with nausea, I let them fall back into a heap. The resulting poof of air rattles papers on a nearby shelf. A notebook slips off and lands on the floor next to me.

I pick it up and fan through it. More of the same ghastly images flash past. Diagrams of the human body and notes written in messy, haphazard clumps litter every page. One image catches my eye, and I stop to study it.

It's a pencil sketch of a woman facing away from the viewer, the back of her head splayed wide, exposing the glistening brain matter within. At the place where the spinal column connects to the sliced-open skull, an intricate mass of a thousand tiny threads knots in a tight bundle like a ball of yarn.

It's in the exact place where I feel my own magic come to life, at the base of my skull.

The tiny threads, labeled "sevren," extend out from the little bundle, which has been labeled "fervora" by the artist. Some of those threads weave into the brain, while others trail down the spinal column and spread into the neck, disappearing beneath the woman's skin.

Is that what the hub of my magic is called? Fervora?

I trace the illustrated sevren trailing out of the fervora. No one but Prodigies knows about the network of sevren, as far as I'm aware. Since they're threads of soul, they aren't visible to the human eye, not even if a surgeon were to open a person up.

My chest constricts.

Whoever all of these paintings belong to seems to have a bit of an obsession with Prodigies. A gruesome obsession.

If they find out I am one...

Stars dance in my vision, and I force myself to breathe.

Maybe Mrs. Harris's threat isn't the only one I should be worried about in this house.

"I can't stop thinking about how much more we'd be able to figure out if I'd only paid more attention to Will," August says darkly. "If I'd been a better brother, I would have more answers right now."

"You can't blame yourself." I close the notebook and tuck it into my pocket to study later. "Friendship goes both ways. He didn't make efforts, either. There are likely just as many things about you that he didn't know."

August gives a gentle "ha" and shakes his head. "There were things, but..." He gestures at the painting of Governor Harris. "The idea of him coming into contact with the type of person who painted that..."

"You know what's sad about all of these portraits?" I muse. "Whoever did them is extraordinarily skilled. My mother's been teaching me my whole life, and I couldn't do anything like this. The talent...it's remarkable."

"Where is your mother now?"

My smile slips. "I don't know. She and my father disappeared about a year ago."

"No one knows where they went?"

I shake my head.

"I'm sorry," he says softly.

I hate speaking about my parents, but something about the late hour, the fragility of August still picking at his nails, and the fatigue turning my thoughts fuzzy has me wanting to fill the silence with all the worries I've locked away in my heart these last several months. "The day before she...well. I overheard her and Father talking. She sounded so worried. Frantic, almost. She was saying that someone had come into her studio that day asking her odd questions. It wasn't normal, wasn't right, she said. They were too eager."

August seems to have stopped breathing, and so have I.

"She told Father that she was almost certain the person had discovered she was a Prodigy," I continue. "'You have to stay home,' Father told her. 'It's not worth the risk.' Mother only shook her head. 'I'll be careful,' she promised him. But the next day she went to the studio and never came home.

"We searched for days. Father called the police, and they scoured the neighborhood—the whole city—looking for her. Father was beside himself. So were my sister and I. Then one night, Father decided to go looking, too. He never returned."

"They both just vanished?"

I nod numbly.

"That's awful." August stares at me. "Myra... Hell. Did the police ever find out anything?"

I shake my head. "And I didn't know the first thing about hiring a detective or investigator to pursue it further. It's probably a good thing I didn't try, though, because we ran out of funds soon enough after that."

Pausing, I curl my knees against my chest and rest my chin on them. "I miss them terribly."

"I bet they'd be proud of you."

I shake my head. "They most certainly would not."

"What do you mean?"

"I've sort of made a mess of things."

He gives a bleak chuckle. "Then we make a fine pair. I've been ruining my parents' plans and embarrassing the family name basically since birth."

"Oh?"

"I've never been great with people. An unfortunate character trait in the firstborn son of the governor, let me tell you." He pauses, snorting. "At a big important dinner about two or three years ago, I tripped and knocked the prime minister's wine all over the bodice of his wife's dress. I was so mortified I instantly grabbed a napkin and tried to mop it off of her. It wasn't till she slapped me that I realized what part of her body I was trying to clean. So, naturally, I attempted to apologize, and in bowing, I lost my balance and knocked into her chair, which promptly toppled, and she went crashing into a waiter, who lost control of the platter of food he was holding. Four dishes of pudding slopped onto the queen of Haltenland's head."

"No!" I gasp, trying to stifle a laugh.

"Not my best moment, I'll admit." He chuckles. "Mother and Father were furious, and they forbade me from going to events with them after that. Which, honestly, was a mercy. I hated those things." He smiles ruefully. "Luckily, it seems that life manages to go on no matter how catastrophic my blunders."

"It does," I say. Then I turn to him. "So do I get to know the secret?"

"Secret?"

"You said there were things about you that Will didn't know."

"I've just met you, Miss Whitlock," he says with a coy grin. "What makes you think I want to share my secrets with you?"

"I've just met you, too, Mr. Harris, and yet you already know the most dangerous secret I have." I keep my tone light and airy, though the stark truth of what I'm saying weighs heavy on my tongue. "I think it's only fair you tell me something about you."

"It's not my fault I know what you are. Mother told me."

"Still."

He sighs. "Fine. I write."

"Write?"

"You know, like poetry. Stories. It's silly." A blush creeps up his neck and turns his ears faintly purple.

Poetry. That must be what he's been working on in his notebook and the reason for the ink stains on his fingers.

"It's no sillier than painting," I offer.

"Yes, it is."

"Why?"

"Because I'm the governor's son. My whole life is mapped out, and that map doesn't include any detours for things like poetry readings, literary accolades, or publications."

"Can't you do both?"

He snorts. "You obviously haven't met my father."

"No, I'm afraid I haven't yet had the pleasure."

"He's a strict man with very rigid ideas about what sorts of things are worthy uses of time."

"What's his plan for you, then?"

"To be one of my brother's advisers. I'm set to begin studying law and politics at Lalverton University this fall. The idea was that Father would win reelection next year and train Will at his side for the term. By the time the following election came around, the public would be so enamored with Will it'd be an automatic win. So then, once Will took over the governorship from Father, I would be one of his most trusted lackeys." He pauses, smoothing his palms over the knees of his trousers. "Though I suppose that plan might be changing now that Will is gone. Unless you revive him, of course."

I ponder that for a moment and then say, "If I'm unable to bring him back to life, will you have to take his place as heir to the position? Train under your father if he is reelected?"

August grimaces. "I thought I'd hate nothing more than to be my brother's adviser, but it seems I was mistaken. Being the governor would kill me. And I'd be horrible at it."

"You wouldn't be horrible."

He laughs this time, really laughs, and it's a humorless sound. "You're terribly kind but sorely misguided. I could barely manage to talk to *you* when I first met you. Imagine me in front of a crowd of strangers."

Was that what his cold indifference had been? Fear?

"I guess people aren't really your thing?" I ask.

"That's an understatement." He gets to his feet. "And if I weren't so Artist-damned awkward, I would tell my father to find someone else to be his bleeding heir."

"What would you do instead if you could?"

"There's this symposium coming up." He flicks through a stack of yellowed canvases in the corner. "A literary symposium. In my dreamworld, I would present at it."

I stand. "You should do it."

"It doesn't work like that."

"What doesn't?"

"Me."

"Why not? You could do it."

"No, I couldn't."

I smile and shake my head gently. "Come on, August. You could."

"No!" He whirls to face me, his eyes suddenly fierce. "Believe me, I want to go. I have a manuscript I've been working on for months, and I think it stands a real shot at publication, but I *don't* do crowds."

"Why?" I search his face, desperate to understand, desperate to see.

"Because that's how it is."

"But—"

"No. Don't do that." His voice hardens.

I take a step back. "Do what?"

"Stand there and tell me that if I just tried, if I just 'put myself out there,' I could get over it." Though he's still speaking barely above a whisper, it feels as though he's shouting, and I take a step back. "Have you ever felt like your heart was about to beat itself to death? Like your lungs were seizing up? It's not a pleasant experience. Your vision goes splotchy, and your body feels like it's shredding itself inside. Hot sweats. Dry mouth. It feels like dying, and I'm sorry, but I don't have to force myself to go through that because you think I should." He pauses to take a slow breath and turns away. "The more I try to force myself to be something I'm not, the worse the attacks get. So, no. I'm not going."

"I didn't mean—"

"I know." He pinches the bridge of his nose between his fingers. "I know."

I set the pile of sketches I was leafing through on a nearby desk and turn to the bookcase, my stomach jittery with shame. Heat licks up my neck, and I'm sure my skin is as flushed as his.

"I'm really sorry," I say. "This is just like me. Thinking I know exactly what someone needs and missing it entirely.

You're right. I don't know what that feels like. I shouldn't have said anything."

"Thank you."

Neither of us speaks for several minutes after that. I scan the titles of the books on the shelves but don't really see them.

At last, August breaks the silence. "I'm sorry, too. It's not you I'm upset with. Not really. My parents used to bring me to events back when they still had dreams of me, their glorious firstborn, carrying on the family legacy. They thought that if they forced me to 'push through' the discomfort, it would eventually go away and I would grow out of it. But unfortunately, their attempts seemed to have had the opposite effect.

"It took me going into a full-on panic at one of his speeches when I was eight for them to stop. It was so bad I ended up in the hospital, and Father's publicity team had to work overtime to keep the press quiet about it. From then on, Will took my place. We were so close in age—only ten months apart—and we looked so much alike that people kind of just accepted him and forgot about me. Ever since then, it's been like there's this cloud hovering over me, choking the life out of this family. For a while they would still bring me along to some of their dinners, but when I accidentally accosted the prime minister's wife *and* ruined the queen of Haltenland's hair in one night, they put an end to that, too." He pauses, and when he speaks again, his voice is barely a breath. "They wanted me to be so much more."

"I'm sorry, August. You deserve better than that."

He grimaces and rifles through another stack of canvases. "I'm not so sure."

I think of last night, of him offering to help me clean the vase. Him escorting me to the cellar and insisting on staying with me so I didn't have to be alone. Him offering to talk to the cook on my behalf.

If I'd known how uncomfortable doing those things had made him, how much he was pushing beyond his fears in order to help someone he'd just met...

Maybe I've had the wrong idea about him—and maybe his family has, too.

I turn my attention to the bookcase next to me and begin leafing through the books. After several minutes, I feel August's gaze on my face. I glance at him, and he offers me a tentative smile. "Thank you, Myra."

"For what?"

"For seeing me. You're the first person who's done that in a long time."

As I return the smile, something settles in my chest. Something warm and bright. I'm not quite sure what to call it—hope, maybe? It's small and tentative, but after a year of hardship, I cling to it.

Maybe I'm not as alone in this as I thought I was.

17

"There are a lot of paintings of this baby," August says, holding up a small portrait of a newborn. As I glance over my shoulder at it, a chill snakes under my skin.

Though the subject is a sweet, black-haired baby fresh from the womb—the painter even included traces of white-and-red birth fluids clinging to the child's face—something about it makes my skin prickle.

At least the infant appears normal, with its wrinkled skin and its mouth wide-open in what looks like its first wail of life. "None of them are—you know…?" I nod toward some of the other paintings with the subjects in various states of torture.

August goes green and shakes his head. "No, thank Artist for that." He looks down at the illustration in his hands, frowning.

I return the stack of sketches I was perusing to the small table where I found it. As I proceed to the other side of the room, the movement of my skirts knocks a few pieces of parchment onto the floor. Stooping to retrieve them, I pause, staring at the hardwood.

"August, bring that lantern over here," I say, my throat going tight.

The glow creeps across the floor in front of me as he approaches, illuminating crimson-brown smears on the old wood leading to the wall where the four portraits of the Harris family hang.

I take a step back. "Is that—?"

But a sharp creak in the hallway outside cuts me off. August and I stare at each other when the sound repeats.

"Footsteps," August breathes.

I whirl and catch sight of a wardrobe in the corner. "Come on!" I yank on his arm, dragging him across the room. He extinguishes the lantern as we stuff ourselves inside the cramped space. Old linens reeking of mold crowd in from all sides, and we crush ourselves against each other in order to get the doors shut.

The footsteps grow louder, and I twist into a position where I can peek through the crack between the wardrobe doors.

Hinges whine.

Air stirs the papers on the table.

Shadows flicker along the walls.

I hold my breath and crane my neck to get a better angle, to see if I can catch a glimpse of whoever—or whatever—has entered the room.

August's heart thuds wildly against my chest, echoing my own. Blood thunders in my ears. Sweat trickles down my spine.

A shape crosses between the table and the wardrobe.

It moves closer.

One step. Two. Three.

I cover my mouth and nose with my hand and turn, pressing closer to August to stop my trembling. We lean on each other for support. One of his hands grips my elbow, and I focus on the touch, use it to ground myself as the shuffle of feet grows nearer.

Just when the scream building in me is so strong it's ready to burst forth, the door to the room whines again on those rusty hinges.

The footsteps outside the wardrobe pause.

Hushed voices swirl upon the air, making my hair stand on end. I strain my ears, but I can't make out anything distinct.

We wait, our bodies flush against each other, pulses skittering.

After what feels like an eternity, the footsteps move away. The voices fade. The door outside clicks shut.

The relief is acute and overwhelming. I sag against August, my legs wobbling.

We stay like that for several long moments, making sure whoever was out there isn't going to return.

Finally, August lets out an unsteady breath. "I think they're gone."

My whole body is twitchy with adrenaline, yet my limbs are so weak I'm certain if August weren't holding me up, I'd collapse to the floor of the wardrobe among the mothballs and dust.

My hand is still pressed over my mouth. I let it fall onto August's chest.

His breath catches, and I freeze.

Now that the danger of being discovered by a possible murderer has passed, I'm acutely aware of how inappropriately close I am to him.

I look up.

Though it's too dark to see his face, I feel his eyes on mine. Our breath tangles.

The faint scent of cinnamon makes my mouth water. His hand is steady on my elbow, and his chest rises and falls under my palm.

Every nerve in my body pulls taut. Blood pounds in my ears, but it's different now. Where the terror of before was cold, something warm curls its way through the ice, sliding its tantalizing thaw through every vein.

Something forbidden. Something desired.

August shifts, and one of the buttons on his suit jacket catches the shaft of starlight coming from the crack between the doors, glimmering white like a pearl.

Heat floods my cheeks.

He's the governor's firstborn son. Heir to a massive family name and all of the wealth that comes with it.

I wear drab, threadbare clothing and sleep on creaky mattresses.

We do not belong in the same world.

"I—I'm sorry," I mumble, pushing the wardrobe doors wide and stumbling out. The frigid air leeches across my skin, sudden and biting after the warmth of August's breath on my cheeks.

"It's quite, uh…" He clears his throat, stepping down behind me and pressing the wardrobe closed again. "Quite all right."

I cannot even look at him. Humiliation warms my neck, flames across my cheeks.

I straighten my dress and make my way for the exit. "Shall we?"

He reignites the lantern and follows me into the hall.

We double back the way we came. I'm not entirely certain where we're going next, but my mind is too muffled with embarrassment to make sense of it.

As we descend the stairs in the servants' passage, movement twitches in the hallway below. I stop, my heart jump-ing straight into my throat. August comes to a halt in time to avoid knocking into me. His lantern illuminates someone hurrying along the passageway at the foot of the stairs.

The heel of my boot scrapes noisily against the edge of the steps, and I hold my breath.

The figure stops.

What if this is the painter from upstairs? Or the murderer? What if it's Mrs. Harris?

I cling to the bannister as the figure turns and looks over its shoulder. The lantern light illuminates a girl around my age with a pale face. Her silky black hair is pulled back in a tight bun, and her eyes glitter obsidian in the night.

"Mr. Harris?" she says, as though meeting us in this stair-well at past two in the morning is absolutely normal. "Is there something you need, sir?"

"Oh, Ameline," he says, lowering the lantern. "Uh, no. Thank you."

"Very well, sir." She disappears into the shadows.

I exhale. "Is Ameline a servant?"

August nods as we descend the rest of the way. "Kitchen staff. No idea what she's doing here at this time of night, though."

"Do you think it could have been her? On the fifth floor?"

He frowns, gesturing for me to follow him out of the ser-vants' corridor. We pad softly into the fourth-floor hall. "I don't know. But even if it was her, there's no way she was re-sponsible for Will's death."

"Why not?"

"They were…involved."

"Involved with what?"

"They were in a sort of relationship. Until a few months back. I don't know a lot about it," he says. "I walked in on them…uh…you know." He coughs, and even in the dark, I can tell his ears are coloring. "They were in a closet. I've never fled a scene faster in my life." A ghost of a smile flits across his lips. "He asked me not to say anything to Mother."

"I see."

"He was betrothed. I don't know if you'd heard about that? Felicity Ambrose, the Duke of Miltonshire's niece?"

I raise an eyebrow. "I didn't. Why haven't the papers mentioned it?"

"Mother and Father were waiting until the reelection campaign was in full swing to announce. Probably thought it would endear the public to us or something." He harrumphed. "Everything is a calculated move in this house. Nothing is as it seems. Ever."

I ponder what he's told me, gazing through the frosted windowpanes as we pass. Ladyrose vines curl up over the sills outside, and moonlight reflects off the diamond ice crystals clinging to the blood-crimson petals.

Such beauty, those roses, blooming in the cold.

My eyes catch on a faint glint in the shadow cast by one of the flowers, and I squint to see what it is.

A thorn. Sharp as a needle, as long as my forefinger.

Nothing is as it seems. Ever.

I shudder away, refocusing my attention on August as we tread deeper into the house.

Could Ameline be the artist behind all of those horrid paintings upstairs? Somehow, with her petite frame and fine-boned face, I can't imagine that kind of brutality in her.

Maybe she isn't the painter, but she could still be responsible for Will's death. What if she's one of the jealous types? Perhaps they were on his balcony when he told her about the betrothal, and, in a fit of anger and pain, she shoved him.

I almost laugh at myself. It sounds like the dramatics of one of the novels on the racks at Ernest's bookshop.

Still, I can't assume it wasn't her. Something about all of this seems personal to the Harris family. I think of those meticulously detailed paintings of each of them, framed and carefully hung on the wall upstairs.

It would have been extremely difficult for a murderer to have escaped the scene of Will's death without detection in broad daylight. But if it had been one of the staff, someone whose presence wouldn't have been questioned...

Fear slicks an oily fist around my heart.

"What if the killer works here?" I ask, breaking the silence so suddenly that August jumps. "How many servants do your parents employ?"

He frowns. "There's the cook and about five kitchen staff, including Ameline. Then we have three butlers. Seven maids. Several groundskeepers. Three guards who rotate out at the front gate. So maybe two dozen in total?"

Two dozen possible suspects, if my theory about it being a member of the staff holds true, plus the three members of the Harris family.

"How well do you know them?"

"Most have worked here for years."

"Would any of them have had a reason to want Will dead?"

August shifts the lantern from hand to hand as he walks, obviously uncomfortable with the conversation. "I honestly can't imagine it. They're like family, most of them."

"Did Will treat them well?"

"Well enough, I suppose. He was a bit ignorant and self-centered, but he certainly wasn't unkind."

Maybe something was going on that August doesn't know about. It wouldn't hurt to do some looking around, at least. "Where are the servant quarters?" I ask as we trail into another hallway. Starlight glimmers on golden-framed mirrors hung from velvet-black walls.

"East of the kitchens. Why?"

"Is it ever empty? I'm curious if I could find any clues there."

August shakes his head. "They work in shifts, so there's always going to be at least a handful of them there." He pauses. "I could go, though."

"What?"

He blows out a breath through his teeth. "I have something I have to do in the morning, but I could come up with an excuse to poke around later on in the day."

I sigh. Though I'd much rather do things myself, I can't be caught sneaking around. So, even though my stomach twists at the thought of relinquishing control over something so important yet again, I nod. "That would be most helpful. Thank you."

"My pleasure." His smile is soft, so soft I almost miss it.

Trying to ignore the way that smile makes it hard to breathe, I tug out my notebook and scan back through each detail I've written down. The paintings upstairs. The locked balcony doors. The odd injury in Will's chest. Brushing a thumb along that last one, I frown.

"What about that bloodless wound?" I ask. "Does anybody in the house have experience with knives?"

"Well, the kitchen staff, of course," August muses. "Nigel. Ameline. And—" He cuts off, eyes widening. Turning abruptly, he grabs my arm and tugs me after him down the nearest set of stairs.

"And what? Where are we going?"

"My father has a collection." He's nearly jogging now, his fingers tight on my elbow. When we reach the main landing, he leads me through a parlor. Exquisite chandeliers dangle from the ceiling and catch the moonlight, reflecting it in silvery-rainbow streaks on the walls.

We pass a gleaming, polished door. "What's in there?" I whisper.

"His office." But he steers me to the next room, pulling one of the cuff links off his sleeve and jamming it into the lock. It pops open almost immediately.

"That looked incredibly practiced."

August chuckles. "Will and I used to break into this room all the time." He pushes the door wide, and I gasp.

A hundred blades shine from the walls inside. Swords and daggers of varying lengths and styles adorn nearly every surface, displayed proudly like art.

I reach for the nearest one—a long, medium-width blade—and lift it. It's a lot heavier than I expected. "What are all of these for?"

"Father collects them." August tugs a dagger from its mounting, holding it up to the light. "This was hand engraved by a famous artisan in Elddat. Do you think it looks like the right size?"

I cross to him, examining the width of the blade. "Maybe too thick. The wound was longer but more narrow."

He nods, returning it to the wall and selecting another. "What about this?"

We spend the better part of the next quarter hour inspecting a dozen daggers and comparing them to our memory of Will's wound. Despite the late hour and the harrowing discoveries we've made tonight, the small weapons room soon feels oddly cozy, like August and I have found some pocket of time where the horrors of what we're investigating don't feel quite so terrible. As long as I don't let my mind actually picture one of these blades cutting through flesh and bone, I can fool myself that the murder wasn't real, that no one's dead.

I'm just sorting through daggers with a boy who smells like cinnamon, trying to find a match. Simple.

I slide a particularly stunning weapon from its mounting and inspect the gems glittering on its hilt. "What kind is this one?"

"That," August says with a slight grin, "is a broadsword. And I highly doubt that is what killed my brother."

"Why not? It's the right width!"

He holds up his hands. "I'm just saying that it doesn't seem likely. Swords are much more conspicuous than daggers. If someone was carrying that around, I think people would have noticed."

"En guard!" I say, swinging it.

He snorts. "Very terrifying."

"This is heavy. How do people actually fight with these things? I feel like I'm going to lose my balance."

"That's because you're standing all wrong. You need to spread your feet more and sink into your knees." He demonstrates for me, bouncing a bit to show me his knees aren't locked.

I try to mimic the stance.

"Good," he says. "Now grip the sword. One hand under the cross guard and the other down close to the pommel."

I move my hands into the places he indicates and thrust the sword as though stabbing an imaginary foe.

He snorts again. "No, no, no."

"Stop laughing. I'm fearsome."

"I guess that's one word you could use."

"It's the *only* word." I stick my tongue out at him. "Then tell me, oh wise one, what am I doing wrong now?"

"Your elbows. They look like chicken wings."

"Well, I'm sorry, but they're the ones I was born with."

He chuckles again. "Here. You need to lower them a bit."

He sets the lantern on the floor at our feet, steps around behind me, and presses his hands against my arms.

My breath catches in my throat, and I turn my head. His nose is inches from mine, but he doesn't back away. Instead, his eyes dip to my lips.

My whole body goes weak.

The door slams open, smacking the wall with a sound like a gunshot, and we leap apart.

Mrs. Harris steps into the room, eyes hard, arms crossed. "What in Artist's name is going on here?"

18

Mrs. Harris's small frame seems to fill the entire doorway. She's wearing a white dressing gown, which is knotted tightly around her waist. A braid drapes over her shoulder and hangs past her hip, tendrils of red fraying its entire length. She surveys both August and me in turn over the dancing flame of the small candle in her hand and raises a brow.

August straightens, and his jaw lifts. It's like he's awkwardly tugging on the Politician August costume before my eyes. Hastily yanking his gloves back on, he opens his mouth to speak, but I jump in before he can.

"I'm sorry, Mrs. Harris. It's just that I was working on my paintings downstairs, and in surveying Will's injuries, I noticed... Well, I'm not entirely convinced the fall was an accident. There was a wound in his chest that looked like it might have come from a knife. I was trying to see if any of these blades matched..."

Her other eyebrow raises. "You think someone stabbed him?" Of all the things she was expecting me to say, apparently this was not one of them. "And in looking for the perpetrator of something so preposterous, your first thought was not of the servants, who have access to the kitchen knives, but *my husband*?"

"I—" The blood drains from my face. "No, of course not, I—"

The color in Mrs. Harris's cheeks is bright, and her eyes are like coals. "I bring you into my home at great peril to my name. I provide you with food and clothing and the prospect of compensation far beyond what you deserve, and you presume to make an accusation like that?"

"I didn't mean—"

Her glare bores through me. "My only rule was that you not leave your work space."

"In order for my magic to work," I say, trying not to stumble over my words, "I need to know as much as possible about how his death occurred. I wasn't saying it was your husband necessarily. There is the possibility that one of the staff—"

Mrs. Harris shakes her head. "No. Wilburt fell. It was an accident."

"If his death was an accident as you say, then my magic should have worked by now, and it hasn't," I explain quietly. "Something else had to have been the cause."

Mrs. Harris presses a hand to the door frame as though suddenly weak. I rush on in an attempt to comfort her. "Don't worry. There's still a possibility it wasn't a murder. Like I said, all we really know at this point is that his death wasn't caused by a simple fall. But as far as what actually happened…it could have been anything."

She squeezes her eyes shut for a long moment, breathing slowly as though considering my words one by one before straightening and giving a firm shake of her head. "I'm sorry, but I cannot permit you to be snooping about the house. My husband just returned home from his trip, and if he were to hear from one of the servants that you were digging about the estate… Or if, Artist forbid, he were to discover you himself, especially alone, unchaperoned with his son…" She glances over her shoulder before raising a brow in my direction. "Why can't your magic work unless you know exactly what happened? You certainly didn't know what caused Peony's cut on her leg, and you were able to get rid of that."

"Painting away a small cut like that on an animal is fairly simple magic. Bringing a boy back to life after being murdered?" I shake my head. "I need to know exactly how his soul bonded to his injuries, and those bonds are forged by the emotions he was feeling immediately prior to the incident."

"He was likely scared. Why can't you go with that?"

"Humans experience a dozen emotions at a time, particularly in traumatic circumstances."

Mrs. Harris sighs. "Well, I'm afraid you're going to have to do your best with what you have. I cannot allow you to nose around the house."

"But—"

She holds up a hand. "We won't discuss it further."

"Mrs. Harris!"

Her eyes flash. "I am sorry. I am doing what I can, but this is where I draw the line. I have a place in this household, and I have already put that place in great jeopardy by bringing you here. Allowing you free rein of Rose Manor would be pushing it too far. My husband would not be pleased."

"I—"

"And you." She turns to her son and glares daggers at him. "Do you know how it would look if it got out that you were found unchaperoned in the middle of the night with a young woman? You're going to ruin all of our chances of a marriage arrangement with Miss Ambrose before we've even begun pursuing it."

Marriage arrangement? Like a betrothal?

"Yes, of course, Mother. It won't happen again," he says, his voice as smooth and practiced as it was at breakfast. The Politician August mask is securely in place again. I dart a glance up at his rigid jaw and his forced smile. I hardly recognize him.

"It is two thirty in the morning," she goes on shrilly. "Felicity will be here after breakfast. Do you intend to sleep at all before that?"

"I do," he says.

"If I could—" I cut in, but Mrs. Harris's lips thin, and I snap my jaw shut.

"You are here as an employee, not as some nighttime companion for my son. Do I make myself absolutely clear?"

I gulp down every protest rising in my throat and nod. "Yes, ma'am."

"Very well, then. Off you go to the cellar."

With the anxious churning in my stomach making me jittery, I retrieve the lantern, replace the sword on the wall, and slip past Mrs. Harris into the hallway, taking care to give her a wide berth. Once I've passed her, I look over my shoulder at August. He's watching me go, an expression almost like a wince on his face. We make eye contact, and he holds it. I see a thousand words in his eyes, like he's trying to say something to me, but I have no idea what it is. I nod goodbye and hurry away.

As I weave through the hallways toward the cellar door, a scratching sound echoes somewhere in the house, raising the hairs on my arms. I slow my pace, straining to hear.

Scratching...and breathing. Quick and heavy.

My heart stops.

I glance back the way I've just come, but August and his mother haven't left the weapons room yet. Odds are she's still lecturing him about impropriety.

The scratching continues, echoing against the floors and walls. My mind conjures up images of what August's great-grandfather Bertram might have looked like—the prominent cleft chin the Harris boys both got from their father, maybe the telltale red hair and broad shoulders, too.

August's words about the fifth floor being haunted swirl around in my head, and for a moment, I swear I see the power-hungry old man lurking toward me in the shadows, knobby fingers stretched out toward me.

I shake the image away.

Bertram Harris is not here, and this house is not haunted. The two people we heard whispering upstairs prove that. The stories are nothing but tales to frighten and entertain. Tales that have been recently commandeered to keep people from stumbling upon that stash of portraits upstairs. Nothing more.

I should leave whatever is making this noise alone, turn back toward the cellar, and forget I ever heard it.

But I don't move.

Someone painted all those ghastly images upstairs. Opened that window. Held that whispered meeting in the middle of the night. And if whoever is responsible for the horrors we discovered there is the same person responsible for Will's death, I cannot simply turn away.

What if the person who nearly found August and me in the wardrobe is the one sneaking through these hallways now making that noise?

So, with my heart gargling in my throat and every muscle in my body tensed to flee, I extinguish the lantern, leaving it at the mouth of the corridor leading to the cellar, and take a hushed step toward the sound. And another.

The house groans around me, wooden beams settling in the cold, and a gust of wind whispers from somewhere far away. In spite of myself, I listen for the screams August talked about—the cries of Bertram's victims.

Maybe ghosts would be better than whatever awaits me in

the dark. Ghosts are dead. Intangible. They can't harm anyone. Can't kill.

But whoever attacked Will did…and still can.

And I am all alone.

As I trail my fingertips along a windowsill, snow swirls in
my peripheral vision, casting unearthly reflections through
the glass. My own breath twitches like a spirit from the un-
derworld in front of my face.

The heavy breathing noise is near now. Around the corner.
Short, staccato, shallow snorts stifled as though they are being
muffled against something else—a hand maybe?

I steel my nerves and peek around the corner.

Instead of a hulking shadow, I catch sight of a small furry
form with its snout pressed to the bottom of a door.

Peony, Mrs. Harris's poodle.

Letting out a huge breath of relief, I hurry to the tiny animal and crouch. "What are you doing out here?" I whisper.
"You gave me such a fright." The dog must have gotten out
of Mrs. Harris's bedroom when she came downstairs.

Peony digs her paws against the floor near the crack at the
base of the door, her claws scrabbling loudly over the hardwood.

"What's in there?" I stand and tug on the knob. As I pull
the door wide, Peony scrambles over my ankles and leaps inside. Moonlight shafts through the nearby window, illuminating an array of coats hanging in a tidy row.

I shiver, suddenly acutely aware of how cold I am. Is this
where the maid took my hat and coat? I search among the
linens. It takes only a moment before I locate the old, worn
wool of my jacket—so very out of place next to the expensive fabrics and gleaming buttons of the Harris family's things.

As I pull it on, my eye catches on a glimmer of gold in the
closet. I recognize it immediately—it's Mrs. Harris's brooch,

the one she fiddled with during our conversation in the taxi-cab. I reach out to rub a thumb over its smooth surface.

What if Mrs. Harris's reasoning for keeping me from searching for clues isn't simply a matter of upsetting her husband? What if it's more? Is she trying to hide something from me?

I frown. That wouldn't make sense, though. If she were the one behind Will's death, why would she hire me to bring him back to life?

I run my fingertips along the sleek material of her coat. My fingernail scrapes along a sliver of white poking out of the pocket, and I reach in and tug out a small folded piece of parchment.

Peony snorts at my feet, and I jump so high I nearly drop the note. Stuffing it into my pocket, I crouch to see what the dog has gotten into.

"Peony, come on!" I whisper.

She's sniffing obsessively behind a pile of boots.

I wrap my hands around her middle, hoisting her out of the closet. Grasped in her mouth is some kind of garment.

"What have you got there?" I ask, easing it gently out of her teeth so as not to tear a sleeve. Once I've freed it, I set her down and hold it up to the light while she jumps around my calves, snapping excitedly at it.

The material is stiff and obviously soiled, but it's still too dark to see clearly. I carry it closer to the window. As the starlight illuminates it, my heart plummets to my shoes.

Blood.

My whole body starts shaking so hard I can barely keep my grip on the fabric.

What on earth is this doing stuffed in the back of the coat closet? Whose blood is this?

I untangle the material. It's a cook's uniform. Torn across the left breast, missing a sleeve, and bloodied almost beyond recognition, it bears a design that's almost identical to the white uniform Father used to wear to his restaurant.

Mrs. Harris's voice echoes from around the corner, and Peony goes streaking toward it, her little claws rattling across the floorboards.

If I try to show this to Mrs. Harris, will she balk at me again?

I could leave out the part where I was looking through her closet and say Peony brought it to me. But if Mrs. Harris is somehow involved...

I shove the bloodied uniform back where Peony found it and slide the door shut. Then I take off at a quiet run up the hallway. As I swing around the corner, I catch sight of someone ahead.

Pressing myself against the wall, I squint to see if I recognize who it is.

Tall, though slightly stooped, the figure moves purposefully away from me. As he passes a window, moonlight illuminates a halo of silver hair and a starched white uniform exactly like the one I found in the closet, except the one he's wearing is clean.

This man must be the Harrises' cook, Nigel. But what is he doing up and about in the middle of the night?

I wait until he's turned down another hallway before peeling myself away from the wall and dashing to the nearest washroom. Trying to stop my trembling, I turn on the sink. The frigid water makes my fingers ache as I scrub and I scrub and I scrub.

But no matter how the rose-scented soap burns into my skin, I cannot seem to get the feeling of dried blood off of my hands.

19

Once I've retrieved my lantern from where I left it and returned to the eerie, stale quiet of the cellar, I tug the notebook I found on the fifth floor from my pocket and pull one of the chairs next to the desk. Removing my gloves, I flip carefully through the pages, taking care not to smudge the ink. The handwriting is small, cramped, and written in clumps that trail diagonally across the pages or outline the edges of the parchment instead of running in straight lines.

Most of the text corresponds to diagrams of human anatomy. I pause on the sketch of the woman with the back of her head splayed open. Once again, I study that knot of sevren tangled like a ball of yarn at the base of her skull. A line has been inked from it to a few scrawled thoughts on the opposite page. I squint to read the tiny writing.

Prodigy magic is based in the fervora, which is attached to the brain stem. Powerful sevren extend from it into the brain and out to the body. Fervorae are present only in Prodigy specimens.

My hand trails instinctively to the back of my neck, and chills snake through my body. "Specimens"? Who wrote this?

That's all it says in this section. I flip to the other side, but there's nothing else about the fervora or the sevren, just a small note in the corner of a diagram of a human heart.

When a Prodigy alters another Prodigy, the sevren the painter acquires from the subject is permanent. Example: painting away an injury from a Prodigy results in the permanent sensation of that injury to the painter.

Wait, what? Mother never told me that.

I always imagined she knew everything there was to know about our magic, but now that I think about it, how could she? It's not like Prodigies are common. Mother said she'd only ever met one other in her life besides Frederick Bennett, who she was never able to confirm was one. There might have been a lot she hadn't yet learned about how our magic worked.

She kept a journal, though. I found it when Lucy and I moved out of the downtown apartment. It's full of all her thoughts and ideas about magic. I'll have to check it again when I get home to see if she might have mentioned anything like this.

I flip through the rest of the pages in the notebook from the fifth floor but don't come across anything else intriguing. Sighing, I toss it onto the desk, rubbing my eyes. So much for that.

I spend the next couple of hours scouring the medical textbook I bought from Ernest's bookshop, using it to craft another painting of Will. This time I focus on the traumatic brain injury in the context of if someone had pushed him. As I layer on the healed version of him over the dead one, I imagine a possible scenario that could have played out. Perhaps someone accosted him on the balcony. Maybe they had a fight. I think of the emotions he might have felt—anger, frustration. Then when the person pushed him, there might have been a moment of shock, followed by a tangle of terror and betrayal as he plummeted to the earth and hit his head on the ground.

But when I press my hand to the portrait and try to channel my magic through my fingertips into Will's sevren, nothing happens.

I collapse into my chair and toss my palette and dirty brushes onto the desk.

Mrs. Harris is being ridiculous. If she's that desperate to get her son back, why should it matter if her husband finds out she hired me? Guessing how Will might have felt as he died when I'm not even sure how it occurred isn't going to get me anywhere. His sevren knots are far too complex.

I'm not going to be able to pull this off.

How long will I last before Mrs. Harris leaks my secret? How long will I walk free before someone else decides to kidnap or blackmail me? Or before the governor comes up with a reason to have me put in prison to keep me from defiling his city?

I rub my fists across my face. Fatigue gnaws at every part of me, making my movements twitchy. My stomach grinds irately against my ribs, and I sit up straight. It's got to be approaching breakfast time. Did I miss it?

I stand, hurriedly yanking on my dress to straighten it. I really can't afford to make Mrs. Harris upset again, and she was pretty adamant about my attending family meals. I pat at my bun. My straight, wiry hair seems to still be largely in place. I comb at a few stray hairs with my fingers and adjust the pins in a few of the sections by feel before rushing out of the room, pausing only to put out the lantern and lock the door. I take the stairs two at a time and dash into the hallway on the first floor, breathless.

Pink light spills from the windows and laps at the floor around my feet. Where the corridors seemed ominous and haunted in the night, Rose Manor creaks as she stretches, blushing in the morning sun. The hearth in the main entryway crackles with a roaring fire, and the warmth fills me up and makes my skin tingle. I catch sight of a clock resting on the mantel, and I let out a sigh of relief that there are still twenty minutes until eight o'clock.

I rush through shafts of dust motes sparkling like rose gold on the air as I hightail it up to my bedroom, pull the door shut, and cross to the wardrobe to find something clean to wear. As I look through the dresses, I pause on one that's palest turquoise, like August's eyes. I rub my thumb over the lace on the sleeve, and a memory of the way those eyes locked on mine as I left his father's room of blades fills my mind. So many emotions, so many words swam in his expression.

As I think of the moments that preceded that look, my stomach sinks.

Are his parents truly hoping to arrange a betrothal for him?

"It doesn't matter," I mutter to myself.

But why didn't he say anything about it?

"Because you're nobody," I answer my own question aloud, trailing my hands over a fine network of beads stitched into the dress's bodice, stroking the shining pearl buttons down its back.

And yet I still slip the August-blue gown from its hanger and pull it over my head, shivering as the delicate fabric slides down my body. Buttoning it up and taking one last look in the mirror to pinch some color into my cheeks, I head downstairs to the dining room, pulling a pair of lace gloves into place as I go.

The grandfather clock upstairs strikes eight o'clock as I enter the room. The Harrises are already seated—Governor Harris at the head of the table reading a newspaper, his wife at the opposite end with her hands neatly folded in her lap, and August to his father's right staring so hard at his plate I'm afraid it might crack.

"Good morning," Mrs. Harris says, her voice tight.

"Morning," I repeat, taking the empty place across from August.

As soon as I'm seated, a swinging door in the corner opens, and a pair of servants dressed in black-and-white carry in our breakfast. Scoops of chopped fruits slathered in cream are dropped onto my plate, and thick slabs of toast dripping yellow butter are placed on bread platters. Slices of ham soaked in some kind of fragrant glaze are brought in next, and I'm positively drooling.

Back when Father used to bring home leftover food from his restaurant, Lucy and I were pleasantly plump and content. We were picky, even. We could afford to be, because there was always another meal cooked in fine sauces and tossed with exotic spices.

As I take a bite of the toast, I stifle a moan. Sweet Artist, how I've missed butter. Father always used to say a meal wasn't a meal without butter. A lump rises in my throat, making it difficult to swallow. I grip my fork tightly, blinking away the film of wetness fogging across my vision.

The Harrises eat in silence. Mrs. Harris doesn't look up from her meal, but somehow it feels as though her eyes are on both August and me, boring into the sides of our faces with a simmering heat.

I glance up at August, but he doesn't meet my gaze as he spears a slice of ham.

His hair, cadmium orange, has been freshly styled with

some kind of gel. I follow the lines of his sideburns to the splotchy dusting of freckles across his cheeks. How striking they are, offset by a faint hint of auburn stubble on his chin. I can't help but trace the line of that angled jaw down to the lavender cravat at his throat. His gray suit was obviously tailored to fit him perfectly, accentuating the broad lines of his shoulders.

He looks…nice.

With a jolt, I remember Mrs. Harris's words about his outing this morning with Felicity, and I drop my gaze back to my plate.

How well do they know each other? Does Felicity know he likes to write? Has she noticed the faint ink stains on those long, slender fingers? Does she find his protruding ears endearing?

"The ham is tough," the governor says, setting down his newspaper for the first time.

His appearance is even more impressive in person than it is in the photographs. A prominent chin and the high cheekbones Will inherited make him look regal and handsome. His dark auburn hair is streaked through with lines of distinguished silver. But unlike Will or August, his eyes are a deep brown, and his mouth is set in a stark line that gives the impression of perpetual dissatisfaction.

"And the cream is too runny," he goes on, tossing his spoon onto his plate with disgust. "Where is Nigel? This meal is simply unpalatable."

I swallow the bite of ham I'm chewing, which doesn't seem tough at all to me.

"Wilburt, darling, don't be too hard on him," Mrs. Harris says soothingly. "He's had a rough week, what with witnessing—" She glances at me and coughs. "Well. He's been through a lot."

I do my best to make my expression as blank as possible.

"I'm paying him," Governor Harris retorts. "I refuse to waste good money on substandard work."

"You didn't see what he was like right after, though, sweetheart," Mrs. Harris goes on, her voice weak as butterfly wings, as though the words pain her to say them. "He was... Well, I've never seen him like that." She pauses, dabbing her mouth, and lowers her voice. "You remember how close they were. Will so loved to tag along behind him in the kitchen learning about the spices and things. I do think Nigel felt...ah, *feels*, I mean..." She clears her throat. "I think he *feels* a kinship with Will. Like a grandson. So he's taken the news of the illness quite hard."

"He's a good man and a loyal friend," Governor Harris allows. "But if I have to work in spite of—" his eyes flick to me "—recent events, then I expect no less from him." He turns and snaps his fingers. A servant girl I hadn't even noticed moves from her place in the corner and approaches the governor.

I try not to jump when I recognize her as the girl we saw in the servants' hallway last night. Ameline. With rosy cheeks, full eyelashes, and shining black hair, she looks exactly like the type of girl a boy like Will could have been interested in.

"Bring Nigel in here. I would like a word with him," the governor says to Ameline, who nods, curtsies, and swishes through the swinging door.

"Really, Wilburt, he's—"

"That's enough, Adelia." Governor Harris's eyes flash. "You've said your piece. Do not forget that *I* am the head of this household as well as this city, not you."

Mrs. Harris clamps her mouth shut, but her eyes blaze and her cheeks redden. Her gaze snaps to mine, and I focus my attention on my food.

A moment later, Ameline reappears, followed closely by the older man I saw in the corridor last night. He's slender and tall, and his moustache and hair are a silver so pale they almost seem translucent in the sunlight streaming through the windows. The freshly starched uniform that hugs his frame triggers flashes of the starlit, blood-crusted version I held in my hands a few hours ago, and I stiffen as icy fingers trail down my spine.

As Nigel bends to speak to Governor Harris, a glimmer at his throat catches my eye. A silver chain with what looks like a few large trinkets strung along it slips from his collar. He reaches a gnarled hand up to tuck it back in, nodding solemnly as the governor lectures him about the quality of the meal.

"Yes, sir. I'm sorry, sir," he says, his nose twitching to the left as he clasps his hands in front of him. "You are absolutely right."

"You know I hold you in the highest regard," Governor Harris goes on, retrieving his newspaper. "I look forward to eating a better lunch in a few hours' time."

"Of course, sir." Nigel stands upright and turns to leave, but just before he does, something flashes in his eyes. Something hard and cold, something lethal. But his expression melts to warm kindness again so quickly I wonder if I imagined it.

As he and Ameline retreat to the kitchen, I set my fork on the table, my appetite suddenly gone.

The cook was the only one who saw Will fall. He was the only one present for Will's death. His uniform was covered in blood.

What if he's been lying?

If Nigel's story cannot be trusted, we don't even know for sure that Will fell from the balcony at all.

I swallow hard and knot my fingers under the table.

Nigel. Ameline. Mrs. Harris. The governor. Any one of

them could have been the one to hurt Will. Or maybe I'm looking in the wrong places, and it's one of the other members of the staff. Or someone outside the house entirely.

Martel, the butler, enters the room, interrupting my thoughts.

"Felicity Ambrose and company are in the foyer," he says, his tone smooth and professional.

August keeps his head bowed as he stands and sets his napkin carefully on the table next to his plate.

"They're a bit early." Mrs. Harris takes one last sip of tea before dabbing her mouth and getting to her feet. "Come, August. Keep those gloves on, and stop fidgeting with them. Fix your posture. I've taught you better than that."

August adjusts his stance, forcing his head upright. His eyes dart in my direction, and his cheeks turn splotchy.

Servants' quarters, I mouth at him while Mrs. Harris's attention is focused on straightening his tie.

He gives the barest of nods before his mother ushers him toward the door, reminding him not to yawn, as though anyone has any control over that.

20

Just like that, I am alone with Governor Harris. Ameline has returned to her spot in the corner, but she is so quiet and still it's like she's simply a fixture on the wall.

My appetite has returned in full force, and the servants have left behind the platters and bowls full of food. Good manners likely dictate that a lady is not to take second helpings, but the governor's nose is buried once more in his newspaper, and no one else besides Ameline is here.

Propriety be damned.

I scoop fruit and cream onto my plate and pluck another slab of toast from the platter, taking a moment to dollop a healthy gob of marmalade on top of it. I devour the meal in seconds and serve myself three more slices of ham. Only when the ribbons of my dress begin to dig into my waist do I finally set down my fork and fold up my napkin.

"Excuse me," I murmur in Governor Harris's direction, getting to my feet and crossing to the door.

"I never knew a duke's daughter to have such a hearty appetite."

I pause in the doorway, nerves bubbling in my chest. "I'm sorry. I quite enjoyed the meal, sir," I mumble.

"How are you finding Lalverton so far?" His voice is smooth as silk, measured as he peers at me over the top of his paper. Like he's trying to create some sort of recipe reaction in me.

"Lalverton is…" I search my mind for anything I know about Avertine and what someone from there would think about Lalverton. It's in the south, an arid, desert-type terrain. I remember that from a commissioned landscape painting Mother did for a client down there. "Cold," I say. "Lots of snow?"

He grunts a single laugh and folds his newspaper. "I'd like to have a word with you. Come. My office is just down the hall."

"But—" I search my mind for a suitable excuse.

"It will only take a moment." When he speaks, the words drop like heavy stones. Loud, resounding, and final.

"Yes, sir." I follow him out of the dining room.

I trail in his massive shadow through the hall. The whole house seems to tremble as he moves along her arteries, shrinking back to allow him the space his very aura requires.

As we pass through the main entryway, I catch a glimpse of August in the parlor. He's perched at the end of a plush, flowery sofa across from a small young woman with raven hair twisted into an intricate knot on the top of her head. Diamonds sparkle from her ears with every movement, lovely against stunning skin the color of gold ochre paint.

Something clenches in my gut, and I tear my gaze away, hurrying to keep pace with Governor Harris's long-legged stride.

I recognize the door to his blade collection as we pass. He pauses to unlock his office and ushers me inside. He lights a lantern on the wall as I take a seat in one of the wooden chairs opposite a shining mahogany desk.

Every inch of the walls is crammed with bookshelves groaning under the weight of massive tomes. Encyclopedias and dictionaries, history books and atlases wink their titles golden in the flickering lamplight.

Governor Harris settles heavily in a broad-backed leather chair and steeples his hands in front of his face, resting his elbows on the desktop. He regards me for several long, measured moments, and I am suddenly acutely aware of every errant hair quivering in my peripheral vision and the tired set of my face.

"I don't know if my wife explained to you our...situation," he finally says.

"Situation, sir?" I feign ignorance with a smooth expression and a raised brow.

"My son Wilburt Jr. has fallen very ill."

"Oh, yes, Mrs. Harris did mention that." I nod vigorously, trying to channel the air of a young duchess-to-be—polite, poised, and eager to please.

"Good. Good." He taps his fingertips against each other slowly, one after the other, like he's playing some kind of musical instrument. His eyes are sinkholes, reeling me into a suffocating, uninhabitable place. "As such, I wanted to make sure that you are aware that it is of the utmost importance that you keep to designated areas of the house. For your own health and safety. We wouldn't want you coming into contact with him or any of the servants attending him. That said, I want to impress upon you how...displeased... I would be if I were to learn of you straying into areas where you have not been invited."

The words are said in a kind, airy tone, but they drop like a threat. Did Mrs. Harris tell him she found me in his blade room last night?

"The fifth floor is strictly off-limits," he goes on. "As are the third and fourth floors where our family residences are."

"Yes, of course, sir."

"I would hate if you made a misstep here, as your actions could tarnish your father's reputation." His mouth curves up in a smile.

"I will keep to myself," I say, my voice warbling on the final word, betraying the knot of butterflies in my chest.

"Yes, you will." He opens his mouth to continue, but a sharp rap on the door interrupts him. "One moment." He crosses the room and pushes the door wide.

"A quick word, sir?" Martel asks.

"Yes." Mr. Harris slips into the hallway, and the door clicks shut behind them.

Heart skittering in my chest, I look around his office. It's in pristine, orderly condition. Every book is in place, arranged from tallest to shortest on the shelves.

Could there be clues about Will's death in here? I won't likely get another chance to search this room. Dodging a glance at the door, I sprint around the desk and tug open drawers, rustling as quietly as I can through their contents. Ink bottles, parchment, stacks of letters...nothing out of the ordinary. I frown, turning on my heel to survey the books on the shelves.

I pull a few files down, but nothing seems relevant, so I return them carefully to their places.

Planting my hands on my hips, I stare at the desk. What if there's some kind of hidden compartment somewhere? I yank open the top drawer and feel along the underside of the desktop.

My thumb catches on a lip.

"Aha," I breathe, nudging it downward. Out slides an envelope. I hold it to the light.

A black seal clings to the parchment, but it seems to be missing a chunk. It looks so familiar... Where have I seen a seal like this one before?

A memory unfurls in my mind. Didn't a chunk of wax fall out of Will's pocket the other night when August and I were inspecting his wounds?

With my heart rate buzzing in my ears like an electrical current, I dig my fingers into the envelope and extract the note within. It has only one line written in looping cursive.

The papers, as promised.
-V

The doorknob rattles behind me, and I ram the compartment and then the drawer closed. I stuff the envelope and note into my bodice and leap for my seat, trying desperately not to pant as adrenaline sparks through my body.

"Sorry about that," Governor Harris says as he opens the door and returns to his chair.

"It's no problem," I manage in a voice that comes out a bit too tense.

"Anyway, as I was saying, you are certainly welcome in our home, but due to the debilitating nature of my son's illness, I must insist that you exercise the utmost caution."

I nod, hoping he can't hear the slamming of my heart.

"Very well, then." He stands and opens the door for me. "Best run along."

"Good day, sir."

It takes all of my self-control not to sprint away from his office. I force my steps steady and keep my chin high, trying to get the oily feeling of Governor Harris's gaze off my face. I am Maeve of Avertine, not a girl terrified for her life.

As I come around the corner to the front entryway, I nearly

run into August. He's standing with one hand braced against the wall, the other clutching his chest.

"August, are you all right?"

He nods but doesn't meet my gaze, his breathing short and staccato. His flushed skin glimmers with a faint sheen of sweat.

"Hey, what's going on?" I reach out and brush his shoulder. "Aren't you supposed to be in the parlor?"

He flinches and nods, gasping. "Felicity's father. He wasn't supposed to… He wasn't…supposed to be…here…today. He wants…wants…"

"August?" Mrs. Harris's voice is muffled through the closed parlor door. "When are you coming back?"

"One moment!" he shouts, his voice ringing too high, too loud.

"What's wrong with her father?" I ask quietly. "Is he unkind?"

August squeezes his eyes shut and shakes his head, gasping, yanking at his cravat. "I need air. There's no air."

I fumble for something to say.

"I just wasn't…wasn't ex-expecting…" He coughs and knots his fingers in his hair. "I'm… I'm fine. Don't w… Don't worry. You can go."

I bite my lip. I can't leave him here. Not like this.

"Hey." I place my hands on either side of his face.

He wheezes.

"Breathe with me," I whisper. "Inhale, exhale. Inhale, exhale. Through your nose. That's it."

His hands wrap around my elbows, cling tightly as he forces the air in and out.

We breathe together for several long moments, grasping onto each other the way I've done with Lucy a hundred times. Riding out the pain, breathing through the storm. The clock

ticks on the mantel. The fire crackles in the hearth. The footsteps of servants upstairs creak softly in the ceiling.

Slowly, his breathing evens out. His grip loosens, and he
opens his eyes.

"Thank you," he whispers.

I meet his gaze. "You've got this, August. Just keep breathing."

His Adam's apple bobs. Hair sticks to his brow. I tug a handkerchief from my dress and dab the sweat away, arranging the
strands back into place.

"There. Good as new."

Once again, we are closer than we should be. My left palm
on his face, his lips so close I can taste the cinnamon on his
breath.

"August!" Mrs. Harris's voice is shrill in the parlor. "Really, where has that boy gotten off to? I'm terribly sorry, Miss
Ambrose…"

"I'd better go," he says, tugging his suit coat into place.

My cheeks warm as I let my hands fall. "Yes, you'd better."

He turns to the parlor door but pauses with his fingers on
the knob. "Miss Whitlock—"

"Myra," I correct.

He smiles. "Myra. I—"

"August!" Mrs. Harris calls again.

"Go ahead. We'll talk later," I say.

He nods, bracing his shoulders and rearranging his face
into the poised, undaunted Politician August as he reenters
the parlor.

I take the stairs two at a time, not pausing for anything
until I've dashed into my room and locked the door behind
me. I stand there for a moment breathing, my elbows still
warm where he touched me, the taste of cinnamon faint on
my tongue.

Leaning back against the door, a grin steals across my lips. But I force it down.

August is the firstborn son of the governor of Lalverton. His parents are in the process of arranging a marriage for him to a girl who wears diamonds, sits with perfect posture, and knows exactly how to behave among members of high society. I may be wearing a fine silk dress today, but I'm not part of August's fine silk world.

The thought grounds me, pulls my head out of that starry place.

I extract the envelope from my bodice and examine the broken seal. Where did I put the piece of wax that fell out of Will's shirt? In my pocket?

Praying that the maids haven't taken my clothes to be laundered yet, I cross to the hamper. In a heap on the bottom is the dress I wore the first night. I rifle through it until I find the wax piece from Will's shirt.

Sure enough, it fits perfectly into the missing space of the seal. When pressed together, the *V* is obvious. An intricate emblem that sends a shiver down my spine.

Who is this "V"? What papers is the note talking about? Could this have something to do with Will's murder?

Just as I'm about to close the hamper lid, I catch sight of a little piece of parchment sticking out of the fabric of the dress I wore yesterday.

Frowning, I pull it out and instantly recognize it. It's the note I found in Mrs. Harris's coat. I carry it, the envelope, and the letter I found in the governor's office to my bed. Climbing in among the pillows, I spread the items out on the bedspread in front of me.

I unfold Mrs. Harris's note. On it is scrawled a list of a dozen names, and it's titled *Prodigies?* Some of the names seem familiar. *Roseann Dumont. Robert Swarthon. Louisa Mark. Martha Lantt.*

Most of them are crossed out. I frown as I read through the names. Where have I heard them before?

When my eyes catch on the final name in the list—the only one without a line through it—my heart stops. *Elsie Moore.*

I gasp. That's it. That's where I know these names.

These are all of the painters who own studios like Elsie's in Lalverton. Well, at least all of the ones who *have* owned studios. Every single one of the painters who has gone missing, other than my mother, is on this list, crossed off one by one.

Is Mrs. Harris involved in the disappearances? And is this related somehow to Will?

The handwriting looks strangely familiar…cramped and scrawling off the lines like they don't exist. Haven't I seen handwriting like this before?

An illustration of a woman's skull splayed open flashes across my mind.

Fervorae are present only in Prodigy specimens.

The handwriting of this list is nearly identical to the writing in the notebook I found on the fifth floor.

I lean back, clutching the list to my chest, staring at the lace canopy overhead.

If the same person wrote both the list in my hand and the notebook I found upstairs, then whoever is responsible for the disappearances of the artists in town could be here in this house with me now. The person oddly obsessed with Prodigies. Who paints people with their eyes hanging from their sockets and limbs twisted at grotesque angles.

And this list was in Mrs. Harris's pocket. Could she have written it? Blackmailed me for something beyond the revival of her son?

My brain whirls, and my hands shake.

I press my palms to my stomach, crinkling the parchment between my fingers as I try to ground myself.

Have I made a dangerous mistake in coming to Rose Manor?

I pull a pillow over my face, blocking out the light. Fear pulses cold through my system, draining the last of my body's energy. My eyes ache.

I'm so, *so* tired. If only our money problems and this new apparent danger could be blocked out so easily with a fluffy throw pillow.

For the thousandth time, I wish Lucy were here. She'd know where to look next. And even if she didn't, at least we'd be together. The miles separating us feel like entire countries, and my bones yearn for her like I'm missing half of myself. That, combined with lack of sleep, makes a lump rise in my throat.

I force the tears back and inhale the rose scent of the pillow to ground myself.

What I wouldn't give for a nap.

I cannot afford to let my exhaustion get in my way. I have only a few days left.

But what can I do? It's not like I'm going to be able to find any clues during the day—I'm not supposed to be snooping around. And painting more portraits of Will is useless since I still don't know how he died. The only thing I can do is wait for August to tell me what he sees in the servants' quarters.

My breakfast sits heavy in my belly. Every muscle aches, and this bed is so comfortable… I settle into the pillows. I can rest for just a moment.

I'm thinking of August's strawberry blond lashes feathering across his blotchy freckles when I finally drift off to sleep.

21

A sharp rap on the door sends a jolt through me, awakening me like a slap to the face. I sit bolt upright and blink around at my surroundings, trying to piece together where on earth I am and why.

And then it all comes slamming back. The Harrises. The body. The murder. The money.

How long was I asleep?

Another knock sounds, and I scramble off the bed to answer it. August stands in the doorway holding a basket. "Hi," he says to the wall behind me.

"Hi." I fiddle with Father's ring. "How did it go with Felicity's father?"

He clears his throat. "Um. Fine. They left about two hours ago."

"I see." The awkwardness between us is thick. I shuffle my feet.

"Thank you. For earlier," he mumbles. "You were… I… It was…good."

"Oh, uh." My cheeks are so hot they might melt my eyes. "Don't worry about it."

He digs the toe of his shoe into the floor.

"Did you go to the servants' quarters?" I ask.

He nods and holds up the basket. "Would you like something to eat?"

I gasp. "Wait, did I miss lunch?"

"You did."

I feel sick. "Was Mrs. Harris angry?"

He shakes his head. "She was too busy lecturing me for being such garbage at wooing women."

A giggle pops out of my mouth before I can stop it. I compose myself. "I'm sorry."

He grins, darting a quick glance at my face before resuming his staring contest with the wall. "I suppose it is a bit humorous."

"What's for lunch?" I point to the basket.

"Sandwiches and fruit." He clears his throat. "I…uh…don't think we should stay here to eat it, though. In case Mother sees. Can we go outside? In the garden maze?"

"It's frigid." I stare at him in horror. "We'll get frostbite."

"Not if we bundle up. Please." Desperation breaks through his stoic facade. "I need to get out of this house."

I give him a fake long-suffering sigh. "All right. But if I catch my death, that's on you."

He snorts. "Fair enough. Give me a five-minute head start, then come down. Enter the maze through the opening past the fountain. Take three lefts. There'll be a bench."

I nod, and he sets off down the hall, his head bowed so the flushed pink skin on the back of his neck is visible above his collar.

I shut the door, then return to the wardrobe and pull out a winter coat much thicker and warmer than the drab one I wore here. A scarf and hat hang from pegs on the wall, and I put those on as well and swap out the lace gloves on my hands for thick wool ones. As I pass the bed, I collect the papers and wax and shove them into my jacket pocket to show August.

When I slip outside five minutes later, the sun is a white fire, reflecting off the snow so that the whole world is shining. The air is cold and still, and as I breathe it in, the icy freshness of it seems to loosen something in my soul. I feel lighter. Almost hopeful. Days like these always remind me of my sister. Lucy Days, we called them when we were little. When the world glows. Perfect for gathering samples for scientific research and catching tadpoles in streams.

My boots crunch in the snow as I weave around the fountain and past the patch of scrubbed space on the ground that August and I inspected last night. In the sunlight, the tiny flecks of blood shine like garnets, and I force myself to walk past without pause.

The maze looms ahead, its leafless branches dripping icicles like jagged claws.

After taking my first three lefts, I come upon a tiny circular area with a frozen pond at its heart. On one side sits a bench in the sun. August, who was perched there, stands as soon as he sees me. "You found it."

"Yes. It was very difficult to follow those extremely complicated directions."

He frowns. "Wait, are you joking?"

"No, no...there were two whole steps. Way too many to follow unless one happens to be a genius like I am."

A grin quirks the corner of his mouth. "You *are* joking."

"You *are* observant."

He points a menacing finger at me. "I'm the one who brought lunch. You be nice or I won't share."

"Are you threatening me, young Master Harris?"

"What if I am?"

"Then I'll have you know that I learned how to use a longsword last night, so you should be very terrified."

"It was a broadsword, actually. For a genius, your memory needs work."

I throw him a mock glare. "For a gentleman, your *manners* need work."

He hisses as though burnt and laughs. "Do you want a sandwich or not?"

Grinning, I cross to him as he opens the picnic basket. Pulling out a pair of sandwiches wrapped in waxy parchment paper, he hands me one.

"So," I say, taking a bite. "Did you find anything in the servants' quarters?"

"I wasn't able to do a lot of looking," he admits. "I told the off-duty servants who were in there that I was checking up on the state of things for my mother, and they all got really squirrely."

"Sounds suspicious to me."

"Maybe..." He pauses, dabbing his mouth with a napkin. "But then again, my father can be intense. They might have been genuinely afraid they were in trouble for something."

"Oh." I ponder, watching the little bits of lettuce flutter from the ends of my sandwich as my breath plumes against them. "Was Ameline there?"

"No."

"Did you check her room?"

He nods. "This was under her pillow." He extracts a piece of paper from inside his jacket and hands it to me.

I unfold the parchment and read.

Tomorrow night. Midnight. Make sure you aren't followed.
–V

My eyes widen. I fish in my coat and extract the envelope. "Look. I found this in your father's office."

"You snuck into my father's office?" His eyebrows shoot to his hairline. "Do you have a death wish?"

I shake my head. "I didn't sneak. He asked me in."

"What for?"

"He said he was only concerned about my health, but he sort of threatened my alleged parents with ruin if he finds me stepping any toes out of line."

August blows a breath out through his teeth, and the white cloud it makes in the air obscures the look of disgust on his face for a moment. "I'm sorry. I told you Will was a pompous dolt... I guess you've now seen where he got it from. With Father, everything is about appearances. He probably wanted to make sure you weren't going to report anything about him to the newspapers. He's paranoid about things like that."

"But look. This letter's signed the same as Ameline's." I hold it out for him to see.

August frowns. "I've seen a letter like these before. Signed with just a V."

"Where?"

"One of my buddies, Thompson, was applying for an apprenticeship this past summer, but he was afraid they'd reject him for it because he has a bad heart." He ducks a glance past me, leans in, and lowers his voice. "He and I spent several weeks trying to find someone who could falsify some medical records."

"Like a forger?"

He nods.

I raise a brow. "You?"

"What?"

"I don't know, Mr. Harris. You just don't strike me as the criminal type."

"Oh, there are *so* many things you have yet to discover about me, Miss Whitlock." He winks.

Taking a small bite of my sandwich to hide my blush, I ask,

"So I assume you discovered one, then? Someone to do the medical papers?"

He nods. "Thompson found him. I don't know a lot about who it finally was, but he did show me the papers before he turned them in for the apprenticeship. The forger signed his notes like that. A solitary *V.*"

My mind whirs, and I chew my bite of sandwich slowly, mulling everything over. "What on earth would Ameline be doing with a forger? And your father, too?" I wonder aloud, extracting the chunk of wax from my pocket. "Did I ever show you this?" I fit it into place with the rest of the seal on the envelope like a puzzle. "I found it in Will's pocket."

August frowns. "So Will was involved with him, too?"

My thoughts stray to the room full of daggers next to the governor's office. That bloodless wound in Will's chest suddenly seems even more ominous, and I shudder.

"What if it was Father who killed him?" August asks quietly.

"I have thought of that, but for the life of me I can't come up with a motive. Your father had that whole plan for Will to take over after him and continue his legacy. Seems like an awful lot of work to go through if you plan on killing someone."

"Maybe killing Will was an accident?" August grips the letter so hard it crinkles. "What if he's hired this forger to put together some kind of alibi? False medical records for Will so no one will suspect murder. Or maybe he wants a psychologist note dictating that Will was mentally unstable or dangerous in some way? Something that would keep people from pointing fingers in his direction?"

"I don't know." There are too many threads involved. "What if your father was involved with the forger before all of this, and Will discovered the connection? Maybe Will intercepted the paper meant for your father. That would explain why the piece of wax was in his pocket. And then he could have confronted your father about it, and your father pushed him. Or stabbed him."

August clenches his jaw. "Maybe."

"I found something else." I reach into my coat again. "This was in your mother's jacket."

August takes the list of painters from my hand, brows rising. "What were you doing with her jacket?"

I fill him in on how I followed Peony to the closet, fished the list out of Mrs. Harris's coat, and discovered the cook's bloody uniform. The crease in his forehead deepens the more I speak.

"But how does it all fit together?" he asks when I finish. "Nigel has been with us for decades. His father worked for my grandfather. He's practically like family. And he and Will were particularly close. Will had a fondness for cooking, and Nigel loved teaching him how to make things. I can't imagine any world where Nigel could be involved in this. It had to have simply been the uniform he was wearing when he found Will's body."

I think of the flash of cold hatred I saw in the cook's eyes this morning. "At breakfast earlier, didn't you think Nigel was acting a bit…angry?"

August frowns. "Father was chewing him out. If he seemed angry, he had good reason."

"True." I sigh and take another bite, glancing down at Ameline's note. "I wonder when she got this."

"No idea." August picks a shiny crimson apple from the basket and takes a hearty bite. Juices trickle down his chin, and he wipes them with his napkin.

"Do you think Thompson would be able to tell us where to find this forger?" I ask.

"I imagine so."

"Then let's go see him." I get to my feet.

August pulls a pocket watch from his jacket and studies it a moment. "All right. Mother's taking me into town for some fittings at four, but we've got two hours until then. Should be plenty of time."

Dumping the remnants of our lunch into the basket, August tucks it all under the bench and offers me his arm. He only stiffens a bit when my hand settles against the inside of his elbow and seems to relax after a moment as we crunch through the snowy grass.

Instead of leading me toward Rose Manor, he pulls me deeper into the maze. "Let's head for the back exit. Don't want Mother to see us leaving together."

"All right."

August seems to know every twist of the maze by heart. I imagine him as a child dashing among these hedges in the amber light of summer, playing chase with his younger brother. His skin freckling golden in the sun, his hair shining like fire. Back before politics and family expectations squashed him.

As we come around a bend, my feet fly out from beneath me. August cinches my arm against his chest to keep me from hitting the ground, but when he tries to step forward to help me regain my balance, his own feet go skidding. We crash against each other and land in a heap on a thick, glossy sheet of ice covering the entire expanse of the path we're on.

"Ow," I moan, trying to extricate myself from August's tangled limbs.

"I'm sorry. I didn't see—"

"Me neither." I scrabble across the ice on all fours to the nearest hedge to pull myself upright.

August follows suit, and we manage to get back on our feet.

"That way?" I ask, indicating the path ahead, which glimmers in the afternoon sun.

He nods, panting a bit.

"We'll have to take it very…very…slowly…" I say each word as I slide my boots one after the other. I manage to make it halfway toward the end of the icy patch before my ankles twist out from underneath me once more.

Luckily, August is behind me, and he grasps my waist as I go down, managing to keep me upright by sheer force of will. I turn to face him and try to use his biceps for leverage. His heels start to slip, and we cling to each other, our arms wrapped tight.

I look up at him. The silver air of our uneven breathing clouds in the space between us. His hair hangs down across his forehead, orange red like a sunrise, and his blue eyes shine watery in the afternoon light.

"Are you all right?" I manage, though my heart has lodged itself in my throat.

"I—I…" he stammers, his ears as purple as ever. "I'm sorry. I didn't mean…"

"To save me from splitting my head open?" I say as my boots scrape against the ground for purchase. "Why are you apologizing?"

I try to ignore the way my legs go weak when he looks at me like this, all tentative and shy and honest. Like he's sharing a secret with me just by meeting my eye. It's as though every moment I spend with him, I ache for the moment when he'll catch my gaze. And then when he does… I can't breathe. Can't think. I'm as frozen as the air sparkling like diamonds around us.

"Maybe if we balance against each other we can make it across without falling again," I say.

He nods, his lips slightly parted like he wants to say something. But he doesn't speak, only braces his arms around my back until I regain my balance. Once I'm situated, we turn to face our feat. Something in me wilts when his eyes leave mine.

We clutch each other and maneuver forward slowly, one step at a time. Though the afternoon is cold, his grip on me is warm. I find myself wanting to lean into him.

Though he comes from a completely different world—one where people have garden mazes in their yards and glazed hams served for breakfast on fine china—he seems to know the ache I feel. The ache of trying so hard to be something that seems impossible. Of wanting desperately to do more, be more.

When our feet finally scrape solid ground, I don't want to let go. His hand strays for a heartbeat on my lower back.

"Thank you," I murmur.

"You're welcome." We break apart, and cold seeps in through my coat in all the places where he was touching me. He shuffles forward. "We're almost to the exit."

Trying to catch my breath in a world that feels suddenly devoid of air, I stumble after him.

22

The cabby barely looks at us when he picks us up from the road a mile away from the Harris home. I suppose it is some small consolation that August's face isn't as recognizable as Will's was. However, I'm not too keen on ruining August's reputation, so I take care to keep away from the windows as we enter the city.

"So what's she like?" I immediately want to kick myself as soon as the words pop out of my mouth.

"She?"

No going back now, I guess. "Felicity. I got only a glimpse of her." I try to keep my tone light even though my stomach is tying itself in knots.

"Oh, her. She's nice."

"You're going to be betrothed to her, right?"

"If you don't bring Will back." He twists at the fingers of his gloves, avoiding my gaze. "She's technically still betrothed to *him*. But if you are unsuccessful, my mother is hoping that the Ambroses will be amenable to a new arrangement with me. Her uncle is the Duke of Miltonshire, and a show of co-operation with that sector of the country would look good for my father. Politically."

"Do you want to marry her?"

"It doesn't matter what I want." A muscle twitches in his tightly clenched jaw.

"I'm sorry," I whisper.

He makes a noncommittal noise in the back of his throat, and we don't speak again until the carriage comes to a halt in front of an expensive-looking flat downtown. I offer to wait in the carriage while August runs up to talk to Thompson.

"We're in luck," August says when he climbs back inside twenty minutes later, his cheeks pink with cold. "Thompson says the forger's name is Vincent, and his place is not too far from here. We can't let on how we found out that information, though. If this Vincent guy discovers who told us how to find him, Thompson's as good as dead."

"All right," I say, fiddling with the buttons on my coat.

August directs the cabby where to take us next, and the carriage lurches into motion. I watch the scenery as we pass. People throng the streets, wrapped in fur coats and scarves, bustling quickly through the snow, their heads bowed against the cold. Buildings tower around us, imposing and adorned with wrought iron balconies, painted shutters, and trellises.

Soon the streets begin to look familiar, and the embarrassment I was feeling before turns sour. Suffocating. Painful. This is the eastern part of downtown—where I used to live before Mother and Father disappeared. I tighten my grip on Father's ring as we pass the corner where his restaurant once was. It's decorated differently now. Where a bright red awning and green shutters adorned the front windows before, white lace curtains now hang inside behind swirling black lettering on the glass.

"That used to be my father's restaurant." I point numbly.
August follows my gaze.

"He was the best chef in the city," I go on, not even sure
why I'm talking. "Did an apprenticeship with Varlo Larkin."

"*The* Varlo Larkin?"

"The very one." My chest swells with pride. "He used to
make the most delicious cream sauces. I begged him to bring
some home with him every night."

Memories of evenings curled in Father's lap with plates of
roasted duck and bowls of vegetable stews balanced on my
knees fill my mind. I close my eyes. "He always smelled like
basil and butter, no matter how hard he scrubbed. Mother used
to tease that it was a good thing he kept her well fed, otherwise she'd be tempted to take a bite out of him."

August chuckles.

I smile, letting the vision fade as I open my eyes. "My sister, Lucy, is the spitting image of him."

"Are you close with her?"

"Pretty sure we're made of the same soul." I snort. "Though
she would object to that assessment. Say her soul is much more
fun than mine and a lot smarter." I chuckle, shaking my head.
"And she would be correct in that. She's absolutely brilliant.
Going to be a biologist one day. She prefers studying amphibians and water–dwelling animals, but she's also really good
with medical stuff and human anatomy, as you saw the other
night when I called her."

"How old is she?"

"Thirteen."

He gives an appreciative whistle. "It's remarkable she's so accomplished. When I was thirteen, all I cared about was how to
sneak more bacon from the kitchens without Nigel noticing."

"She really is a wonder. I want to be just like her when I
grow up." I grin, leaning back in my chair. "Funny. Cheer-

ful. And passionate. I've never seen someone so fierce about pursuing their dreams." My chest tightens as I think of Lucy the way she looked when I last saw her. Funny and cheerful and passionate, yes, but worn down. Exhausted. In pain.

"What's wrong?" August prompts.

I look at him, and he cocks his head, waiting.

Part of me doesn't want to tell him. It seems that as soon as people hear about Lucy's illness, they stop thinking of her as Lucy and define her only as "the sick girl," when her illness is just one small fraction of the many pieces that make up who she is.

And telling him about her condition means showing him the most vulnerable part of me. The part that's terrified things might continue to get worse. The part that's desperate to find a way to ease some of her pain. The part that doesn't know who I am without Lucy and will fight heaven and hell to stop the world from forcing me to find out.

I'm still not sure if I want to trust him.

But my eyes stray to his hands, where he's twisting at the tips of his gloves like he's trying to dig through them, and my fear softens a bit.

August has done nothing but help me. He told me I could trust him that first night. And every time I've needed someone since I came to Rose Manor, he's been there for me.

So I take a deep breath. "Lucy's sick," I say quietly. "It's something she's lived with since childhood, but about three months ago it took a turn for the worse. She hasn't been doing very well. We keep hoping the flare will pass like the others did, but if I'm being totally honest with you, I can't shake the fear that—" I choke on the words as they come out "—that she might not make it through this one. And I don't know what to do."

He peers at me, Adam's apple bobbing. "What do the doctors say?"

"We haven't been able to afford one." And then all at once, I'm telling him about the endless nights Lucy has spent writhing in pain. I tell him about the bloody chamber pot, the sunken cheeks, the way no matter what foods she eats or doesn't eat, what tonics she takes, or how much rest she gets, her symptoms only seem to get worse. As I speak, tears tumble quietly down my face. August watches them fall, the lines around his eyes deepening the longer I go on.

Maybe I'm making a fool of myself. Maybe trusting him with all of this is a huge mistake. After all, life has proved to me time and again that I can't lean on anyone but Lucy. It's just the two of us against the world.

But he's here, and he's listening.

The words spill out in a rush, and I let them, praying to the Artist that for once choosing to lean on someone else won't result in more hurt.

"That's why I agreed to paint your brother," I finally say when the carriage pulls to a stop. "The money your mother offered me could change everything."

"We're here!" the driver shouts.

August doesn't move. "I don't have any money that is strictly mine yet," he says, his voice quiet and yet full of emotion at once. "Everything to my name is actually my father's. But maybe if you aren't able to do the painting and bring my brother back, I'll..." He takes a deep breath. "I'll talk to my father. See if he'll pay for a doctor."

I don't respond for a long time. Beyond his regular shyness, I've seen the way he tenses whenever he speaks of his father. I'm sure asking the governor for money is one of the most terrifying things he can imagine doing. And he just offered to do it for me. For Lucy.

Tears film over my vision again. I reach a hand out to brush his knuckles, and he inhales sharply but does not pull away. "Thank you," I whisper.

His eyes dart to my lips for a fraction of a second before he clears his throat. "Well, should we…should we go in and see this forger?" He hops out of the carriage and holds the door open for me.

I smooth the tears from my cheeks, tighten my coat, and follow him.

The beautiful sunlight from earlier has been swallowed by thick, bulging clouds. Wind rushes against us, whipping my skirts around my legs. With my teeth chattering, I trail August into a slumping building with broken-windowed eyes.

When we close the door behind us, the screaming of the wind cuts to silence, but the cold is just as fierce. I inhale the dank scent of mold.

We are in what appears to be an old office building, but each office we pass is boarded up. Rats scuttle past, their tiny claws scrabbling across the floor, and I lift my skirts, prickles crawling under my skin at the sight of their beady eyes and wormlike tails.

"Thompson said there'll be an elevator shaft, but the lock on it is false," August whispers. The walls seem to lean in, listening. "We'll find an old man in there who we're supposed to give a code to."

"What's the code?"

"Old Sawthorne."

I blink. "Like the clock?"

August nods.

We continue along the hallway. Though the building appears to be uninhabited, there is no dust in our path. Whoever this Vincent is must have enough clients filing through here that grime hasn't been able to settle on the floor.

We turn a corner and catch sight of the elevator, coated in rust and chained across with a padlock.

"What do we do after that?" I ask, my voice barely a breath, my heart skipping in my throat.

"He fires up the elevator, I suppose."

"You suppose?"

"All Thompson said was that the man in the elevator would know what to do."

"Well, that's very reassuring." I wrap my arms around myself to try to keep in some warmth. And to keep my heart from leaping clean out of my chest.

When we reach the elevator door, August tugs on the lock. It twists open, just like Thompson said it would, and the chain falls at our feet with a clang that rattles through my bones. Taking a deep breath, August pulls open the door to reveal the wrought iron cage dangling in its shaft. The accordion grate creaks aside to reveal a bent old man with hair so thin the moles on his scalp are visible.

He turns milky eyes on us and grins. His mouth is gaping and toothless, and I force a smile in return, not entirely sure if he can see it.

"Where do lovers clasp their hands?" the man wheezes in a breathy, singsong voice.

"At Old Sawthorne," August replies.

The man steps aside to allow us into the cage, wrenches the door shut, and cranks a lever.

We plummet.

My stomach lurches into my throat. I instinctively grasp August's arm to keep from toppling.

All is dark as night. I cannot even see the old man less than a foot away from me.

Maybe this wasn't such a good idea. I may be poor and desperate, but I've never broken the law. Never associated with people who participated in illicit activities. What if August and I don't make it out of here? What will happen to Lucy if I never return?

The elevator slams into the ground, and the bars around us ring like the tines of a tuning fork. My teeth smack together, punching holes in my tongue, and I swallow a cry as my mouth fills with blood.

"You shall find what you seek in the third door on your left," the old man says as we stumble out of the elevator.

Unlike the dilapidated corridor upstairs, this one is carpeted in a deep color like the burgundy born of a mix of alizarin crimson, raw umber, and black. Like the oozing blood of burning ladyroses. The wood-paneled walls gleam the color of chocolate in the flickering light of ornate torches in ebony sconces. Scenes of shadowed figures dancing beneath crescent moons and depictions of bony winter trees stretching into lightning-heavy clouds hang in elaborate frames on every side.

The elevator door creaks closed behind us, and the old man disappears as the lift rises.

I pause in front of a painting of a still pond under a starless night sky, finally steady enough to release my grip on August's arm. Two glimmering orbs watch me from within the glassy water. I pull off a glove and run my fingertips along the oils, feeling the ridges and sweeps of the brushstrokes.

"These are remarkable," I breathe.

"'Disturbing' is the word I would have chosen," August says.

"You ready?" I nod toward the third door.

"Not at all. Let's go."

We pad across the carpet. An opulent onyx knocker with a ghoulish face adorns the wood. The knock mechanism hangs from the ghoul's neck like a loosened noose. Its bulging eyes remind me of the painting of Governor Harris on the fifth floor, and I shiver.

August raps the door three times.

"Come in," a deep voice says from within.

August sucks in a gulp of air and opens the door.

The room is the color of blood. Textured crimson paper lines the walls and ceiling. A lavish black chandelier lurks overhead like a spider with curling, flaming legs. It is a quaint space, made even smaller by the massive hulk of a polished obsidian desk.

A young man sits behind it in an expensive-looking high-backed chair. Something about him seems wizened and ageless, though he can't be more than a year or two older than me. His features are striking—a pointed nose, delicately arched eyebrows, eyes like charcoal. His hair sweeps away from a regal, high forehead. An ebony beard trimmed close to his skin is shaped with precise, curling edges, like an artist painted the facial hair on as an intricate tattoo.

"Ah, Mr. Harris." The deep timbre of his voice unsettles something in my soul.

"Are you Vincent?" August asks, rattling his thumb against his thigh.

"At your service." The forger stands and gestures toward a pair of plush scarlet seats in front of his desk. "Please, sit."

We obey.

"I admit you are one of the last people I expected to see in my office," Vincent says, sitting back in his chair and crossing one ankle over the other knee.

"We need information." I force my voice to stay even and measured though every nerve in my body is screaming at me to flee.

"What kind of information?" Vincent's smile does not slip, but as his gaze slides to me, I begin to tremble.

"The governor. What sort of papers did he have you do for him?"

Vincent's eyes glitter. "You want me to incriminate one of my clients? A businessman willing to be so indiscreet would not last long in my line of work."

August unbuttons his coat and reaches into his jacket. Pulling out his pocket watch, he thunks it onto the desk. The chain pools around it. "That is worth five thousand golds. It's yours if you talk."

The forger reaches out long, slender fingers to inspect the watch. His expression is smooth, impassive. After a moment, he raises his gaze to me, taking in my face, my cap, my dress. I feel like he's assessing my worth just as thoroughly as he did the watch, and it makes my skin crawl.

"Who is your young escort here, Mr. Harris?"

"Maeve," I say carefully. "Of Avertine."

He purses his lips. "Maeve, hmm? Daughter of the duke and duchess?"

My stomach clenches, but I force my expression to remain smooth. "Yes."

The forger regards me silently for several long moments, as though waiting for me to tell him more. I force my hands to remain still, my face impassive, as August's pocket watch ticks away the seconds one by one.

Finally, he smiles. "You know, I've met your father. You don't look a thing like him."

"Everyone always says that." My voice quavers, and I pray he doesn't notice.

He runs his thumb absently over the face of the watch. "I have fond memories of my visit to the duke's household. That painting in the parlor? Exquisite."

I nod along mechanically. "One of my favorites."

"I always loved myself a Whitlock."

Every nerve in my body goes numb. "Whi-Whitlock?"

His lip curls into a satisfied smile. "Lavinia Whitlock. The painter." He nods toward the door. "I commissioned that pond piece from her just over a year ago."

My blood turns to ice at the sound of my mother's name on his lips. "Oh...yes, she's quite...quite good."

"Do you paint, Lady Maeve?" His eyes bore into me like he's asking me so much more than that simple question. Like he's pulling out my sevren one by one to see how they hold me together.

"Why does that matter?" August asks. "We came here to talk about my father."

"See that wall there?" Vincent continues as though August hasn't spoken, nodding toward the wall to our right. It's completely bare—no paintings, no shelves. Not even a decorative table. "I had wanted to commission a portrait from Lavinia for it. A larger-than-life one of me. Wouldn't that be impressive?"

I force a swallow, though my mouth is so dry it grinds like sandpaper. "Yes. It would."

"It's a shame so many portrait artists have gone missing." He sighs. "I suppose I'll have to contact someone overseas to do it for me."

August clears his throat. "Are you going to tell us about my father or not?"

But Vincent is still looking at me, and the smile on his lips twitches the tips of his mustache upward. "For a watch like this, I will answer one question and one question only," he finally says, dropping the timepiece into his pocket. "Choose wisely."

August leans forward. "What sort of papers did you forge for my father?"

"Medical documents for one Wilburt Harris Jr."

"What kind of medical documents?" I ask.

Vincent shakes his head, holding up a single finger. "I told you I would answer one question, and I have done so. Now, unless you have more to offer me for my time, I'll need you to leave. I have important things to do."

"But—" August says.

"Do you have something else to offer?"

August shakes his head. "No, but—"

"Then you are dismissed. If you do not walk out on your own, then I will call in my men to take you. Believe me, they aren't gentle."

"Come on, August," I say. "He's not going to tell us anything else."

As we retreat through the door and into the hallway, Vincent's voice trails after us.

"Meeting you was very enlightening, Lady Maeve."

I dash past August in my hurry to escape.

23

Neither of us says a word until we are back in the cab.

"It was my father." August buries his face in his hands. "That bastard."

"We don't know that for sure," I say.

"What other possible explanation is there?" He lets his hands drop, and I catch a glimpse of pain—real, stark, aching pain—in his eyes. "He hired Vincent to create false medical reports to make everyone believe Will is sick! That way, when he comes back in a few days to say Will died, the whole world will believe it happened because of the illness. No one will even think to ask questions."

"How could he have had it done so quickly, though?" I ask.

"He's the governor. He hasn't had to wait for a thing in his life." August slouches back against the seat and glares out the window.

"But the papers were running stories about Will's illness the same day he died. Either your father managed to find this forger right after the incident happened, hire him on the spot, and have the medical documents done in time for the newspapers to run the story—all of that within a matter of hours—or it was a premeditated thing."

"What do you mean?"

"The timing only makes sense if he had the medical papers drawn up before Will's fall in order for the story to be in the papers the same day."

"That bastard," he repeats.

"What are we going to do?"

"I don't know." He mops a hand over his face. "The worst part of it all is I *still* don't want to upset him. We're sitting here, talking about how he's an *actual* murderer, and all I can think about is how I hope he doesn't notice my watch is missing."

I can tell he has more to say, so I only nod.

"Ever since I was a child, I've been trying to live up to this life he's made for me. And I've come up short at every turn. But Will? He was the perfect replacement, their golden boy. From day one, he did everything right. He was handsome. A genius. Did you know that by the time he was ten, he was sitting in on meetings with the prime minister?"

"I didn't."

"And then there was me. So humiliatingly awkward. More elbows and knees than man. Terrible at mathematics, an embarrassment at public events, and to top it off, I inherited my grandmother's damn ears."

"I think your ears are nice," I offer.

He glances down at his hands. "I wish my mother shared your opinion. They're like the icing on the cake for her. Every day since Will was born, it's always been 'Why can't you be more like your brother?' and 'That's not how Wilburt does it.'"

"That must be awful."

"Don't get me wrong," he says, balling his hands into fists. "I was happy to let him do the political stuff, but could it have been so hard for my parents to acknowledge me? To love me the way they loved him? I'm their son, yet everyone in this whole blasted country has forgotten I exist."

"As far as I'm concerned," I say quietly, "you're by far the most memorable person in your family, and for reasons that count."

He gives me a soft smile. "That's kind of you to say, but I've given up hoping my parents will ever see me as more than a disappointment. I'll never forget the day Father found one of my notebooks. He went into a rage, cursing me for squandering the family name in pursuit of frivolities." August glares out the window. "What I wouldn't give to have him look at me the way he looked at Will. Like I'm worth something. Like I'm an Artist-damned human being."

He tugs his gloves off one finger at a time. Pursing his lips, he holds his hands up so I can see the cracked cuticles.

"They hate that I'm like this," he says, his voice so quiet I have to lean in to hear him. "I try so hard to be the man who has it all together, who doesn't worry, who's as solid as stone. And yet it's never enough for them. Mother's always looking for new treatments, a cure-all that would make me calm and collected like my brother, as though she cannot be happy with me as I am."

I grasp his hands and pull them down to his knees so I can meet his eyes. "You are not weak because you are not stone. In fact, I would say you're stronger *because* you feel things so acutely. The internal battles you fight every day—you've conquered far more than you give yourself credit for. Despite what they've made you believe, you do not need to apologize for the things that make you different. And you shouldn't have to pretend to be someone you're not."

He stares at me, and his hands tighten on my fingers. "You really believe that?"

I nod. "Take Lucy as an example. Yes, she has an illness, and fools may claim that makes her weak, yet she is the furthest thing from weak I've ever known. She deals with everything I do—the grief of losing our parents, the fear of the unknown, even the days of hunger when we can't afford meals—and then a whole array of things I don't. Physical pain, eating restrictions, fatigue, not to mention the emotional weight of living in a world that refuses to accommodate her. As far as I'm concerned, I may be the one with magic, but *she's* the truly powerful one. Because she's fought where I have never had to." I lean forward. "And if anyone ever even insinuated that her illness needed to be cured in order for her to amount to anything, well…" My jaw tightens. "Let's say I would have some *very* choice words for those people. Just like I have a whole pile of words I'd love to spit at your mother right now, too."

"Thank you, Myra," he says softly. "Lucy sounds remarkable."

"Oh, she is. And so are you." I look down at his fingers in mine, at the chewed nails and torn skin. "Being kind is much more important than being able to give impressive speeches, and creativity is a sign of a brilliant mind. You are worth more than a pocket watch, more than whatever genetic traits you did or didn't inherit from your grandmother." The words stumble over themselves on their way out of my mouth, but I press on. Because he deserves to hear this. Because he *needs* to. "I've known you for only a couple of days, but even in that short amount of time, I haven't seen a failure. I've seen a strong, determined man. One who cares deeply and loves fiercely even when those he cares for and loves treat him poorly. I've seen sharp intellect and keen understanding." My voice warbles. "And I've seen tenderness and mercy when none was required."

"Myra, I—" he begins, but I'm not finished.

"Don't let them cage you, August. You may not be impassive as stone, but you are a force to be reckoned with."

My cheeks heat, and I turn away.

He doesn't speak for a long time, but I feel his gaze on me, tender and tentative. Warm. Tingles fill my whole body.

He pulls the notebook from his jacket and flips through the pages until he finds the one he's looking for. "I wrote a poem," he says softly. "I'd like you to read it." He holds it out, his hand quaking in the air. His breath comes in shallow spurts. "I'm not good at saying what I think, but I'm good at writing it."

"You sure you're okay with me reading this?" I ask, taking the journal from him.

He nods.

The poem is written in an elegant cursive so precise it could have been printed on a press. My name adorns the top of the page.

Myra
Who are you?
Child of brilliance and light,
Daughter of quiet and night.
With paint like raindrops down satin cheeks—
Who are you?
Fists clutched tight on yesteryear,
A white-knuckled grip
On tendrils of smoke.
Ghosts in her smile
And walls oiled thick round her heart.
Who are you?
Warden and executioner
Or
Liberator?

Chills dance along my arms. He's been paying closer attention than I realized. Noticing things about me I never knew people could see from the outside.

I scan through the poem again, and my chest aches at the details he's included. My white-knuckled grip on yesteryear, the way I hold everyone at arm's length... But it's those last few lines that hit me the hardest. Because I don't know the answer.

Who am I? Have I built my own prison, reinforced it with beams of guilt and bricks of loneliness over the months since Mother and Father vanished? Pushed away anyone who wanted to care, bowed my head and resolved to not lean on anyone, not trust anyone besides Lucy since we lost them?

Could things be different?

"You get to choose, Myra," August says quietly, as though reading my mind. He takes the notebook back and tucks it into his pocket.

"Choose what?" I ask on a breath.

"Which you want to be."

His words are soft, but they strike me to my core. I can choose to imprison my heart, be the warden and executioner of my own dreams...

Or I could liberate myself from the weight of all the guilt I carry for the many ways my life has become so far out of control.

"August," I say with sudden fervor. "*This* is how you tell them."

He stares blankly at me. "Tell them what?"

"Everything!" I jab a finger at the place where the corner of his notebook sticks out of his jacket. "*That* is how you use your voice."

"Poetry?" He frowns.

"You just communicated a whole speech to me in a single

poem. You could write them a letter about how you really feel. Be honest about the life you desire."

He shakes his head. "It's not that simple."

"But—"

"My father wouldn't even look at it. Did you forget the part where last time he found one of my notebooks he flew into a rage?"

"August, you may be a Harris, but you should get a say in your life. They can't treat you like this."

He sighs. "Can we not talk about that anymore?"

I slide back into my chair, thoroughly deflated. "Sorry."

We watch the rest of the city pass in silence. It isn't until the carriage turns onto the road that leads to Rose Manor that August speaks again. "We can't tell anyone."

"Can't tell anyone what?"

He watches the snow-frosted fields and ice-spangled trees pass with a face carved from stone. "About what my father has done. We leave it alone."

"But—"

"My mother has been through enough. Will's death has affected her far deeper than she lets on, and I can't put her through a public scandal when she's this vulnerable. We have to give her time." He turns to me. "Will you promise me you won't tell anyone? I'll keep an eye on Father, make sure he's not dangerous for the time being. In a few months, when things have settled down and Mother is in a more stable place emotionally, I'll go to the police." His Adam's apple bobs as he grasps my hands in his and squeezes. "Do this for me. Please? You know who committed the murder now. That should be enough for you to be able to do the painting, right?"

"I still don't know *how* he did it, though, if it truly was him."

"Then I'll make you a deal. If you aren't able to paint my

brother with the information you have now, I'll hire you to paint me."

My eyebrows rise. "You? Why?"

"Fix the ears. The freckles. The hair. Make me at least *look* like the man my parents need me to be now that my brother is gone."

I gape at him. "But August, haven't you been listening to a word I've said? Your parents are *wrong*. You are perfect *as you are*. I can't take that away from you." I tug my hands out of his grasp. "And I don't want to!"

"Please, Myra," he says, his voice steady. "I'm sure about this. If you cannot bring Will back, then my family will need someone to take his place. August Harris is not enough for that."

"Yes, he is!"

"No, he isn't. I will get my mother on board to pay you for the painting. It should cover the cost of the best doctors in Lalverton."

"But—"

"Please, Myra." There's a finality in his tone, in his eyes. "I have to do this." He holds out his hand for me to shake.

I glare at it. "Your parents are fools."

"Do we have a deal?"

"Don't do this, August."

"Artist's teeth, Myra, it's just a painting. You need the money."

"Fine," I say, gripping his hand so tight he winces. "It's a horrible idea, but it sounds like my opinion doesn't matter."

We don't speak again.

24

The cab drops me off near the back exit to Rose Manor's grounds. As it clatters away to take August to the front drive, I skirt around the outside of the garden maze, tugging my coat in tight and stuffing my nose under my scarf as the ravaging wind drags frigid claws across my face. The sky is so thick with clouds it feels like twilight, though it's only four o'clock in the afternoon—we got back just in time for August's appointment with his mother.

I come around the corner of the maze, and Rose Manor glares down at me with ill-concealed fury in her gaze.

I trudge up the steps to the veranda and in through the back door. As I pass the foyer on my way to the cellar, I catch sight through a window of August and his mother tucking into the cab on the front drive. The butler shuts the door for them, and they trundle off, disappearing among the trees.

I can't do the portrait of August. I won't.

Which means it's even more imperative that I get this painting of Will right. And I have only two days left.

Stomping down the stairs, I yank off my gloves and slam a canvas onto the easel, then turn to fill my palette with paints. I'll do this one and try to imagine how it might have played out if Governor Harris pushed Will and he died of a brain injury once more. The complexity of emotion in a son being threatened by his own father—a man he may have loved and hated in equal measure—could account for the thick sevren snarls.

Artist, please let this work.

As I turn to the shelf, I reach for the tube of ladyrose gel and curse.

It's nearly empty. I paw through the rest of the supplies, but there is no more. I inspect the other mediums, but none of them could speed up the oil's drying time enough for me to finish this painting today.

Maybe I could call a cab and go back to town to pick up more. It's not like I can ask a servant to fetch me some. If the governor were to find out I requested it…

Locking the door, I hightail it to the main floor. I cannot afford a cab, but perhaps I could offer a cabby one of the pearls on this dress.

As I near the entryway, heavy footfalls creak on the stairs. Governor Harris.

Fear shoots through me, turning my blood even colder than the air outside, and I press myself into an alcove behind a potted tree.

The governor doesn't seem to notice me as he dons a scarf, a sleek top hat, and a pair of white gloves. Taking a decorated silver walking stick from the vase I vomited into the other night, he allows Martel to open the door for him.

"Tell Adelia that I should be home in time for supper," he says as he strides onto the porch. "I'm stopping in at Jeb's to meet with Colonel Gloucester."

Jeb's is a pub right around the corner from Elsie's studio. If I could find a way to tag along unnoticed on the governor's cab, I could stop in and ask her for a few tubes of ladyrose gel and hope Mrs. Harris will be willing to pay her back later.

My heart stutters. Governor Harris might be a murderer; do I really want to risk getting caught stowing away on his carriage?

Short of risking Mrs. Harris's wrath for pawning the pearls off this dress, I don't have much choice.

Steeling my nerves, I slip onto the front porch and hide behind a pillar until Martel has returned into the house. Then I dash after Governor Harris's carriage, leaping onto the back of it with my heart pounding like a drum in my ears.

The cab jolts a bit when I latch on, and I hold my breath, grasping tightly to the ribbing. But when it doesn't slow, I slither my way into the luggage rack hanging from the bottom, tucking my dress in and thanking the stars that the thick cloud cover will likely obscure me from notice.

As the carriage turns onto cobbled streets and makes its way downtown, my bones jostle and my teeth rattle against each other. Shadowed businesses and tall apartment buildings lurch past. Old Sawthorne clangs half past four, its music vibrating through my whole body as we get closer.

The cab makes its way south, and soon I begin to recognize the shops we pass. I crane my neck as Elsie's studio comes into view. Light glimmers from the massive front window.

Scrambling from the luggage rack, I push myself out and land in the mud. The cab continues on its way, leaving me rubbing my hip where it struck the cobblestones.

I cross the street quickly and press open the door. The familiar tinkle of the bell greets me, along with the scent of paint and new canvases that fills my whole soul up.

"Ms. Moore?" I call, scanning the front room. Portraits

stare down from the walls, and a blanket on the back of a set-tee flutters, but there is no other movement and no response from Elsie.

The wind rattles the window behind me, but inside all is silent. Unearthly. A place that has always felt so warm and alive to me in the past seems suddenly so empty. Like it ex-haled, and there's no oxygen left.

"Ms. Moore?" I say a bit louder, stepping deeper into the room, glancing past easels, searching for a glimpse of Elsie's gray curls or her oil-stained smock.

Shivers snake through my body. Did she step outside for something? Run to the market for extra supplies? She never leaves the studio unlocked when she goes out—not even if I'm here.

"Elsie!" I cry. "Where are you?"

My boots smack through something wet, and I glance down.

I'm standing in a puddle of blood.

I shriek and leap back, knocking into an easel. As the paint-ing that was on it crashes down, I catch sight of her on the floor.

"Myra—" she gasps, reaching a shaking hand for me. Her dress is stained dark alizarin.

I gasp, rushing to her side, my dress trailing in the blood as I press my hands against what looks to be a knife wound in her chest. "No. No, no, no!" Tears sting my eyes as panic sends a jolt through my limbs.

Her skin is still warm, but her pulse is aflutter.

"Go…" she rasps, her hands wrapping around my wrists, her glassy eyes widening. "Looking for you…"

"Who did this to you?" I sob as hot wetness seeps around my fingers and stains my skin.

She coughs, clutching my arms, and mumbles something unintelligible.

"What?" There is too much blood. It crawls over my wrists, slicks across the floor, laps against the wall.

"Asking...questions..." she wheezes as her eyes shutter. "Said..." she chokes, "killed... Harris..."

"What?" I shout into her face, shaking her as tears stain my lips salty. "Who was it?"

She coughs once more and goes still.

I shake her harder. "Elsie!"

Her head lolls forward and back, and I press shaking fingers against her neck.

"Come on. Stay with me, stay with me, stay with me."

But there is no pulse.

"No!" I scream into Elsie's face, lifting her head between both of my hands, forcing her to look at me. "Stay awake! We'll get you to a doctor. I'll call the police!"

Her eyes are empty.

I set her down, stumbling across the studio to the door and wrenching it open. "Help!" I shout, but the wind swallows my cries as snow blasts into my face. I choke on it, doubling over on the threshold. "Someone, please," I whimper.

But no one hears me. No one comes.

Sniffing hard and mopping at my eyes, I totter back to Elsie's side, gathering her in my arms and holding her to my chest.

She never hugged me. She was not a touching, loving kind of woman. She was crabby and stingy with her money and critical of me at every turn. But in spite of her refusal to give me money, she was the only one there for Lucy and me when Mother and Father vanished. She stepped up, offered me more hours, recognized a need. Though she didn't fill it the way I wished she would, she did more for us than anyone else was willing to.

I press my cheek to her neck, willing the pulse in her carotid to jerk beneath my touch. For her to gasp, for her arms to move.

"Please," I whimper as my lungs seize in on themselves. "Don't leave me here."

Lucy's voice echoes everywhere. *Don't worry, Myra. It'll be okay.*

But Elsie is gone.

Nothing is going to be okay.

I lay her back down as more sobs heave through me and lean my head against a desk.

I cry, and I cry, and I cry.

I'm not sure how much time has passed by the time my sobs finally slow, but when they do, Elsie's blood on my skin has gone sticky and cold. My stomach twists, and I rush to the sink, turning on the faucet with shaking hands.

The basin stains red.

I scrub until my fingers are raw and soap foams up to my elbows.

Once my fingernails are finally clear and the only remaining blood is the spatter on my dress, I shut off the faucet and lean against the counter, toweling my hands, hiccupping.

Elsie's words claw through the silence.

Go... Looking for you...

Said...killed... Harris...

If Will's killer and Elsie's are one and the same, it cannot be the governor. I was with him until I got here. Unless he hired someone to do it for him, I suppose.

Either way, the killer is still out there.

And I'm apparently next on their list.

I drop the towel into the sink and yank my sleeves down,

gripping a nearby table to keep steady as I stumble to the door, all the while avoiding Elsie's unseeing gaze.

I should go to the police to report her murder, but if I do, I'll likely be held there for questioning, and if someone's hunting me, I need to act fast. Lucy could be in danger. I need to find August and see if he can get me that money he promised now so I can take her and get out of Lalverton as quickly as possible.

I grab an apron and tie it around my waist so that it covers the blood on my skirt. Then I cinch my coat closed over the top of it. "I'm so sorry," I whisper to Elsie, pausing to press a kiss to her cooling forehead. "So sorry."

Go… Looking for you… Elsie's wheeze is so loud in my head I pull back to stare at her motionless body for several seconds. Goose bumps ripple across my skin.

Suddenly, the smiles of the faces in the portraits on the walls seem more like hungry grins and bared, angry teeth.

Tearing away, I dash out into the frostbitten wind.

And I don't stop running.

25

My vision goes splotchy, my legs go numb, and still I push onward.

As I run, my mind whirs.

Elsie's attacker was looking for me, asking after me. Why? Is it because I've been meddling in things? Is it because of my power? Is someone trying to stop me from bringing Will back to incriminate them?

My feet pound the slushy pavement, jarring through my limbs. People blur past, their faces obscured by the twilit swirl of ice on the wind. Mud slaps my legs from carriages clattering through sludge in the street, and I dodge out of the way of gas lamplighters as they make their slow trek across the city, igniting Lalverton in a dull gray glow.

Could it have been Nigel? Ameline? What would either of them want with Elsie?

I just need to get to August.

But there are miles between here and Rose Manor, so I bow my head, ignoring the stitch in my side, and increase my pace.

Thud. Thud. Thud.

The beat of my boots on the frozen pavement drills through my bones as minutes and then hours pass. Frigid air burns in my lungs. The muscles in my legs cramp.

But still I push on.

My thoughts swirl in circles, replaying the scene at Elsie's studio, echoing her gasping last words.

Go... Looking for you... Said...killed... Harris...

It wasn't the governor, but that doesn't mean he couldn't still be responsible, does it? Maybe he hired someone to question Elsie. He would certainly be the one with the most reason to hate me, especially if he suspects I'm a Prodigy.

But then I think of Mrs. Harris's list. Elsie was the only one left on it. And Mrs. Harris had acted so strange that day when she came to the studio—she was oddly fixated on Elsie.

Yet, if it was her, why would she kill her own son and then hire me to try to bring him back to life? And if she wanted me dead, why hasn't she done it already? I've been in her house for two days.

Snow is soon pelting down from the sky so thick I can scarcely see. A choking dusk smothers the gaslights. Pinpricks sting in my toes, and I think I hear Old Sawthorne's bells, but the wind is so loud I'm not quite sure. The streets empty as people take cover in their homes. Cafes and bookshops and markets shut their doors and pull in their awnings.

By the time I stumble up to Rose Manor's front gate several hours later, my whole body is quaking, and I can no longer feel my own fingers. I collapse against the iron bars, banging on them weakly.

Please, Artist, help me keep Lucy safe.

A guard approaches me. "Can I help you, miss?"

"I'm a g-guest of th-the Harrises," I stutter through chattering teeth. "M-M-Maeve..."

"Ah, yes, they've been looking for you." He allows me through.

"Th-thank you," I manage as I trip past.

There's nothing more I want in the world than to turn away from this place. I'm so unbearably tired, and the person hunting me could be waiting just ahead.

But August is my only hope now. He said he could ask his father for money. I can only pray he'll make good on that promise so that I can take Lucy and get far away from Lalverton and whoever is hunting me here.

So though each step sends a jolt of pain up my frozen legs, I force myself on. One foot after the other, past curling rosebushes whose alizarin crimson blooms cock their heads at me in the moonlight, until I reach the front steps of Rose Manor. Digging deep for whatever strength I have left, I pull myself by the railing to the front door. Grasping the handle, I twist it, and the door swings inward. I slump onto the entryway floor.

"Myra!" August leaps for me, pulling me upright. "Where have you been?"

"I need your help," I say through lips that are so frozen I can scarcely feel them. "You told me I can trust you. Is that true?"

"Of course it is," he says. "But you need to keep your voice down."

"Why?" I ask as he all but carries me to the fire. The warmth of the flame feels so good I yank off my gloves and thrust my hands closer.

"It's my parents. They're not happy with you." He dodges a look over his shoulder.

"What happened?"

"It seems Father noticed the forger's letter was missing from his office. He got pretty upset, and when he interrogated the staff about it, Nigel mentioned he'd noticed you snooping about."

"What? I've barely seen Nigel!"

"Then Father came upon the supplies downstairs."

"Oh, no."

He nods grimly. "It was not good. And Mother acted like she had no idea what you were doing—said you must have been sneaking around painting without her knowledge."

My knees wobble. "What did you tell them?"

"I—" He swallows. "I didn't tell them anything."

I stare at him. *What?*

"I'm sorry, Myra. What was I supposed to say? That Mother was lying?"

"Yes, that is precisely what you were supposed to say!"

He shakes his head. "She would have me eviscerated!"

"She—" Fury burns through the chill in my bones, stinging through my veins like smoke. "You want to know what I think, August? You say *they're* the ones obsessed with appearances, but you're no better."

His jaw tenses. "That's not true."

"Isn't it?"

"Keep it down," he says.

"You find out your father could be a murderer, and you want to *cover it up*. Your potential-murderer father thinks I'm here scheming against your family, and you *let him*. Your family sets up a marriage with some diamond-dusted dainty, and you say 'Sure, where do I sign?' You're a sell-out, August. You are just as concerned with your image as they are."

"August?" Governor Harris's voice booms from the other room.

But before August can respond, the governor appears in the doorway. His eyes meet mine, and his mouth curls into a snarl. "You."

"Please, sir, I—"

"August, call the police."

"But—" I say.

"The police!" he shouts at August, pointing a finger at the parlor, where the telephone I used the other night sits waiting on a small table. "I want her arrested immediately."

"Please, Father," August says, digging at his fingernails, hands shaking. His eyes are on the floor, and his jaw is tensed so hard it might crack. "Don't do this."

"Excuse me?" The governor turns his gaze from me to August. He takes four slow, heavy steps toward his son.

August, though taller than his father, ducks away from the blaze of his scowl. "Don't arrest her." His voice is a whisper. A plea.

"Look at me when you're speaking to me, son!" The governor bellows, making August jump. Governor Harris thrusts a hand out, grasps August's chin, and forces his head up, but August still can't meet his eye. He wheezes in his father's grasp, still tearing at his fingernails. The governor leans his face in close and growls, "You're a disgrace."

The governor shoves him aside, and August crashes to the floor.

"Sir—" I begin.

"Get out," Governor Harris snaps.

His wife appears behind him, her expression as fierce and hateful as her husband's. I focus on her eyes. They're cold and hard, but there's something in them I can't quite decipher. Sadness? Despair?

I was her one shot at getting her son back, and I've failed her.

Like I've failed Lucy, failed Elsie. Mother and Father.

Myself.

"Please don't send me back out there," I whisper. "Give me at least until the storm passes."

The governor glowers. "Leave the premises, or I will have you taken by force."

"But you don't understand—*she* hired me to paint him. I—"

He gestures for Martel, who's been standing on the stairs grasping my carpetbag in his hands. "Get her out of here."

"Wait, no! Please! You could be in danger. Will didn't fall!" I shriek as Martel and another servant yank me toward the door. My body is still convulsing with shivers, but a blaze of desperation has ignited in my soul. "He was murdered!"

It's like they don't hear a word I'm saying. They watch me, their fury and disgust apparent in their glares.

"August!" I screech as the door is pulled open behind me and the icy air wraps its fist in my hair. He stands at his father's left shoulder, his face stricken, his knuckles bleeding. "Tell them!" I cry.

He licks his lips as though about to speak, but when his father shoots a withering glare his way, he shrinks back like a turtle into a shell, his ears reddening. *I'm sorry*, he mouths before dropping his gaze to the floor.

"August, please!" I scream as the servants drag me onto the porch.

He flinches as though I've struck him.

Tears stream down my face as I topple down the stairs and land in the snow. The butler tosses my bag out next to me and slams the door shut.

Not even bothering to quiet my sobs, I gather my things. My fingers are stiff and frozen already, and my teeth chatter so hard my jaw aches.

I mop up my tears and hoist my carpetbag with both hands. As I start the long trek back up the driveway, I cast one last, angry glance at Rose Manor.

A figure watches from a window on the second floor—the window of the room where I was staying. He wears a white uniform, and the lamplight behind him highlights the glow of silver-white hair.

Slick fear douses the fire of my fury, and I hobble into the night as quickly as I can, the sensation of the cook's eyes like spiders' legs on the back of my neck.

26

As the cold leeches the life from my bones, I stumble through the gate and onto the street.

I don't think about Will. I don't think of his killer or the list or Elsie's dead eyes. I don't think of Ameline, the governor, or Mrs. Harris.

I don't even think of August.

I think of Lucy. I focus on her face. Her laugh. Her summer smell. Her bright eyes and even brighter smile.

I think of the day she found George, rescued him by detangling the twine from his legs. "Myra!" she cried. "Look at him! He's so *cuuuute!*" And of all the times she chased me, threatening she was going to let him kiss me as I ran away screeching. How she'd shout between giggles, "But he likes you!"

Then there was the night Mother and Father took us onto the roof to point out constellations and tell us their tales. Lucy kept interrupting them, telling them what scientists had discovered about the universe and how the stars in each constellation were actually billions of light-years away from one another, so even though they looked close enough to make pictures, they most certainly were not. "And," she'd said, "to top it off, whoever made up those constellations obviously was prejudiced against amphibians. There's not even *one* up there!" So she decided to tell her own story about George the Great, who saved Lalverton from an infestation of giant man-eating snails.

That was the life we were meant to have. The four of us, laughing so hard we were crying. Warm and fed and loved and *together.*

My tears begin afresh, sliding down my frozen cheeks and slipping into the scarf at my neck.

I have no money. No job. No hope.

I feel the pain of each one of those half million gold coins as they're wrenched away from me. How will I pay Ava? How will Lucy ever be able to find treatments to ease this flare of her illness?

How can I protect us from whoever the killer is if I can't afford to get us out of here? And even if the killer by some miracle doesn't come after me, how long before Mrs. Harris lets slip I'm a Prodigy to her husband or someone else?

If I were you, I would try very hard to be successful.

Her threat repeats over and over in my ears.

I wasn't successful, and I am certain Mrs. Harris will make sure I pay the price for that.

The snow is so thick I barely notice when I reach the outskirts of the city, barely see the flickers of yellow candlelight through the windows of the houses I pass.

The streets are empty and congested with snow.

Hours pass. My feet are massive blocks of ice. Heavy. Too heavy.

What if I die out here?

Part of me wishes I could. That I could lie down, let the pressure of the many ways I've failed finally release.

Old Sawthorne is only a block away now, and the blaze of its glowing golden face pierces the gloom.

I glance up at the black iron hands slicing through the light. There are fewer than ten minutes left until midnight.

Thunder cracks overhead, and the snow turns to rain. Slick like ice, it cuts through the night in sheets. I stumble into Sawthorne Square. The clock is so far above my head that I can no longer see its face. The grinding of gears fills the air with rattles and pops, vibrating my frigid bones.

I stagger toward the small overhang at the base of the tower. I'll ride out the storm there.

An icy bench crouches in the shadows, sheltered from the rain, and I slump onto it, setting the carpetbag next to me and leaning against it like a pillow, shivering.

I let my eyes fall shut, let my mind wander as I curl in against myself for warmth.

A scrape of a boot over cobblestones jolts me upright. A small figure stands in the corner, and the light of Old Sawthorne flickers across a face I recognize.

"Ameline?" I ask, peering into the dark. "What are you doing out here?"

"Waiting for the rain to pass, same as you." Her mouth barely moves as she speaks, and her voice is low and quiet and monotonous.

Mopping fat, wormlike clumps of dripping hair away from my forehead, I offer, "I'm sorry about what happened to Will."

"Yes. I hope he recovers soon."

I sigh. I'm so tired of lies. "I know he's not ill, Ameline."

Her eyes snap to mine, inky and hollow. Empty. The way Elsie's eyes looked after she died.

"August told me you were close to Will," I go on, unease curdling in my gut. "I'm sure this hasn't been easy for you."

"Oh? And what else did August tell you?" Her voice is sudden and sharp, and it slaps me across the face.

"I— He—"

"August sees only what he wants to see." She turns her dead gaze back to the rain as it slashes puddles across the square. "Want my advice? Stay away from him."

The clock tolls, and the sound is everywhere. It rocks through my bones, throbs in my skull. I grit my teeth as the reverberations fill the air. Twelve gongs, slow and methodical.

And then the world goes silent once more.

Ameline doesn't speak again, and neither do I.

We watch the night through sheets of ice, two silent sentries. My heart beats quadruple-time in my chest, and a thousand questions pummel one another in my head, but I don't utter a single one aloud.

When the storm finally subsides to a light drizzle an hour later, I get to my feet. Nothing sounds better than putting as much distance between myself and Ameline as possible. "Good night," I say.

She does not look at me, does not utter a word. She is stone.

I gather my bag and trek into the gloom, my boots and stockings soaked through with ice. As I tread along the deserted streets of midnight Lalverton, something twitches in the corner of my eye. Footsteps echo behind me.

I whirl and scan the streets for any sign of movement.

There is no one there.

I turn back, quickening my pace.

"It's all in your head," I say aloud. "Sleep deprivation. That's all it is."

Another scuff on the cobblestones. I look over my shoulder. A cloak whips into the shadows.

Lifting my skirts, I sprint.

My bag knocks against my legs, heavier with each footfall.

Boots pound behind me. Closer and closer.

I wheel around one corner, then the next, no longer aiming for home, only looking for a place to hide.

Buildings with gaping eyes glare down at me from every side. Frigid water splashes up my legs. I gasp for air as my muscles burn.

My pace slows. My limbs twitch. My knees wobble.

And still, the footsteps grow nearer.

I won't be able to outrun them. I can scarcely keep myself upright.

As I career around a corner, I catch sight of a man crossing the street ahead. I dive for him.

"Help me!" I screech, grasping the back of his jacket. "There's someone—"

But he turns and meets my eye, and the words die in my throat.

"Oh, hello. Maeve, was it?" Vincent the forger surveys me with a smile.

Trepidation coils in my gut, but footfalls echo from the next street over.

"Are you all right?" His voice is smooth as silken chocolate. "I—"

There's a clatter on the sidewalk behind me, and his gaze snaps up. I throw a glance over my shoulder but only catch sight of a shadow ducking behind a building.

"Why don't you let me escort you home?" Vincent asks slowly, still watching the street with a wary eye. "It's not wise for a young lady to be alone at night in this part of Lalverton."

A covered carriage, wet and gleaming, waits at the curb. Its windows reflect the hulking shape of the deserted office building to my left, the same one where August and I found

Vincent earlier today. As much as I'd love to get away from whoever is trailing me, the thought of climbing into a cab with the forger doesn't seem like a good idea. "Uh, no, thank you."

"Are you sure? You look rather pale."

I tighten my grip on my bag. "I'm fine, though I appreciate the concern."

He purses his lips. "Very well."

Sucking in a frigid breath, I step past him.

My knee buckles, and Vincent's hand wraps around my elbow in time to keep me from landing face-first in the mud.

I sag in his grip. My whole body aches like I've been trampled by one of the horses harnessed to the cab. When was the last time I actually got a full night's sleep? Has it been more than a week? Two?

"Are you sure you wouldn't like a ride?" Vincent asks, his voice gentle, like he's speaking to a stray kitten.

I shouldn't accept his offer. But I'm *so* tired. And home is still miles away. It's either get into the carriage with him, or find somewhere to sleep in the slush and hope I wake up in the morning.

So, though a thick fist has clenched around my heart, I force out, "Very well. Thank you."

Vincent helps me into the cab and then takes the seat opposite, pulling the door shut. I shiver with relief and sink into the cushions, grateful for the reprieve from the night's frigid wind.

The cab jerks into motion, and Vincent regards me with his mouth tied in a tight knot. "I'm glad you accepted the ride, Miss Whitlock."

The sound of my name sends a jolt through me. "It's Maeve," I manage. "Of Avertine."

He chuckles. "I didn't get where I am by being gullible. You're the spitting image of your mother."

My tongue sticks to the roof of my mouth.

He sits back, his lips curling into a pleased smile. "You needn't look so surprised. I make it my business to know everybody in town."

I swallow and turn my gaze out the window, trying to focus on the streets we pass. Instead, I'm intensely aware of him and his calculating eyes on the side of my face.

The cab jostles in silence.

What am I going to do when I get home? What do I tell Ava when I have no money to give her? How do I protect Lucy from the mess I've made, Mrs. Harris's threats, and the murderer on our trail? Where will I get the funds to buy our next meal or pay rent?

The panic of each question crashing through my mind makes my head spin.

"So," Vincent says quietly, "I asked you earlier, but you seemed pretty determined to carry on the lie about being the duke's daughter. Do you paint like your mother did, Miss Whitlock?"

His words light a spark in my chest, and an idea takes shape in my head. A risky, terrible idea.

But I might be desperate enough to try it.

I turn to face Vincent, forcing my chin up and my expression as poised and smooth as possible. "Yes, actually. I trained with her and her colleague, Elsie Moore, my entire life and was planning to attend the conservatory next year."

His lips curl into a smile. "Impressive."

I take a deep breath and steel my nerves. "You said you were looking for someone to do that portrait for you for your office earlier? For the right price, I would be willing."

Vincent raises a brow, and I force my shaking hands still. I can't let him see how terrified I am of him, of what I'm offering.

"And what exactly is the right price, Miss Whitlock?" he asks.

I run a quick calculation in my head. Enough to compensate Ava, buy some supplies, purchase train tickets for Lucy and me, and pay for food and lodging for at least a month until we find somewhere safe. At this point, I don't think I could also ask for funds to pay to get Lucy to a doctor—no simple portrait, even a larger-than-life one, would be worth enough money for all that. No, I need to focus on getting Lucy to safety first, then I can worry about finding a job to pay for medical help later. And pray she can hang on until then.

"Twenty thousand golds," I say with finality.

Vincent's other eyebrow rises. "That's a fair sum for a portrait."

I meet his gaze with fire. "You said you wanted a Whitlock. I am one, and my style and methods are closer to my mother's than you'll be able to find anywhere else. It'll be worth every copper."

His eyes glimmer as he sits back in his seat, crossing his arms over his chest and regarding me as though I'm an interesting equation he's trying to work out.

I don't allow my gaze to drop from his. Though I feel as if I might pass out any second, I force my jaw to stay hard and determined.

Doing this painting might be dangerous. All I know about this young man is that he's a forger, and therefore likely associates with some of Lalverton's most despicable criminals. He's obviously cunning and smart, and he has a complex network of people who owe him favors. Entering into a deal with him could be a very stupid move.

But with that complex network likely comes an understanding of the inner workings of Lalverton. If anyone is going to know secrets, it's him. Plus, he worked for the governor to draw up Will's false medical records, so it's possible he's aware of how the death actually occurred. He could know who the killer is.

Now that that killer is hunting me, it's more vital than ever I discover their identity. Lucy's life as well as my own may depend upon it. We need to know who to hide from and how to protect ourselves.

If I can endear myself to this forger, make him like and trust me over the course of our painting sessions, perhaps I could get him to reveal what he knows. A deal like this might get me both the money *and* the information I need to keep me and my sister alive.

So I wait with bated breath as he considers me, praying to the Artist I haven't made a serious mistake.

Finally, he grins and extends a hand. "You have yourself a deal, Miss Whitlock. You can start first thing in the morning." His voice is slick as ladyrose blood, and my stomach curls in on itself like the withering petals do before they bleed.

With my pulse rushing like rapids through my temples, I take his hand and shake it once. "I look forward to it."

As he releases me, he glances out the window, and his mouth pops open. "Oh, blast. We forgot to tell the cabby where to take you. It looks like we're halfway to my home by now." He raps on the smaller window behind him to alert the driver. "Why don't you give the cabby the address where you'd like to be dropped off, and we'll get that sorted out?"

Surveying the unfamiliar streets outside with a sudden burst of alarm, I nod and move next to him to relay my address to the driver.

The carriage slows and turns around, heading in the direction of the way we just came as I settle back into my seat.

Vincent makes small talk as the carriage winds its way to my building. I respond politely, but throughout our whole conversation, my mind keeps whirling back to the fact that I've struck a deal with this young man I barely know. This dangerous forger who not only knew my mother but was well enough acquainted with her work that he recognized the painting at the Duke of Avertine's home as one of hers.

But I remind myself it's unlikely he was directly involved with Will's murder, since his presence in Rose Manor wouldn't have gone unnoticed that day. Still, he is part of the puzzle. A puzzle I don't yet have all the pieces to. A puzzle that holds my life and my sister's in its balance.

By the time the carriage slows to a stop on my street, my stomach is tied in so many knots it's starting to cramp.

"I'll send a cab to retrieve you in the morning." Vincent's white, perfectly straight teeth glitter in the lamplight as a smile cuts across his face. "I look forward to seeing you again, Miss Whitlock."

Dear Lady, what have I done?

27

It feels like it's been an eternity since I last was inside my apartment building, since I last inhaled the must and the mold, since I last felt the soft give of the stairs under my feet. After the splendor and enormity of Rose Manor, my home feels even smaller and grimier than before.

I knock softly on the apartment door with one knuckle, and shuffling footsteps approach from inside.

"Who is it?" Ava's voice asks.

"It's me."

The bolt scrapes, and the door opens. I step inside, my eyes going instantly to the table. Lucy looks up from her microscope—a broken, taped-together piece of equipment she salvaged from a dumpster—and blinks at me with the knuckle of her thumb frozen between her teeth, as though she'd just been chewing on it, working through some hypothesis.

"You're back!" She leaps from her chair, knocking it over, and crosses to me, wrapping her arms tight around my neck as Ava closes and locks the door.

"How are you?" I ask, returning the embrace, inhaling her scent, settling in the comfort of finally holding her close once more.

She releases me and returns to her chair, wincing. "It was a hard day. But I'm hanging in there."

My stomach sinks. I should have been here.

Her eyes flick to my skirt. "Are you bleeding?"

I follow her gaze to where the stains of Elsie's death glisten wet from the snow. "Ms. Moore was killed today."

"Killed?" Ava gasps as Lucy's brows rise.

"Yes. Stabbed. I don't know who did it, but it sounds like they were trying to get information from her about me. I found her body."

Lucy's face has gone ashen. "But why?"

"I wish I knew. You and I are going to have to lie low for the next little bit until we can afford to move out of the city."

"What about your job with the governor's wife?" Ava asks, wringing her hands.

"That was... Well, it didn't work out."

Ava's eyes follow the jerky movements of my hands as I tug off my gloves. She purses her lips but says nothing.

"I'm sorry," I say to Ava as heat prickles up my neck. "I don't have the money to pay you now, but it's coming. Someone else has hired me to do a portrait. A big one. I promise I'll get you what I owe by the end of next week."

She grimaces. "I cannot feed my family on promises, Myra."

"I know. By the end of next week, I swear."

Sighing, she pulls her coat from the peg on the wall. "If you don't, I'm afraid I'll have to look elsewhere for employment." She places a cool, callused hand against my cheek. "I care for you both dearly, but I have my own children to think of."

"I know. I'll get you the money. Every last copper."

Her palm slips from my cheek as she retrieves her cap, scarf, and gloves. "I suppose you'll need me here in the morning, same as usual?"

"Yes, please."

"All right. I'll be here. But only until you finish this job. Helping Lucy is one thing, but hiding from killers?" She glances at Lucy and shakes her head. "I can't, Myra. My girls need to come first."

"I understand. We appreciate you even staying through next week."

She gives me a soft, worn smile that makes her look twice her age. Worry lines frame her mouth, and purple circles ring her eyes. She's seen her own fair share of hard times. Everyone in this part of Lalverton has.

As she makes her way for the door, she pauses and points to the line of glass bottles on the table, all of Lucy's medicines lined up like little soldiers. "The willow bark tonic is running low. You'll need to pick up more."

"Thank you."

Once she's gone, I pull off my coat. The apron I took from Elsie's studio sticks to the blood on my skirt. Trying not to dwell on the stiffness of the fabric or the faint scent of iron, I strip off the dress and set it aside. As much as I'd rather never look at the thing again, it is a very fine gown, and if I can get the bloodstains out, it would be a nice replacement for the old one I've been wearing for months.

"Who is the new job for?" Lucy asks, watching me solemnly from the table, her dilapidated microscope forgotten next to her.

I look at her, all of the stresses and the uncertainties and the fear piling up, building like a torrent until I can't breathe.

As if sensing my emotions, Lucy's on her feet in seconds, leading me to her bed, encircling my shoulders with one arm. I curl against her and tell her everything. The body, August, his parents. The balcony's locked doors, the fifth-floor room of horrors, the governor's blade collection. Visiting Vincent, finding Elsie dying, being kicked out into the snow like a criminal and chased through the streets downtown. And, finally, I explain the proposition I made to Vincent.

She listens quietly, never interrupting once. When I am finished, she grasps my hand in hers, interlacing our fingers, ducking so she can look me in the eye.

"We are going to be all right," she says, and in this moment, she looks like Mother did, with her deep brown eyes and hair, her chin jutting, determined and resolute. "No matter what happens. No matter if we lose everything. We will always have each other, and that is worth more than all the money in the world."

I nod. "You're right."

And, for this moment, it's that simple. Whether we get kicked out of our apartment at the end of the month, whether we can afford our next meal, whether the whole city finds out about my magic...none of that needs to matter tonight. In this tiny cocoon spun from threadbare sheets and the scent of Lucy's soap, with my head pressed against hers, I let that we are together be enough.

The ghoul in the ebony knocker mounted on Vincent's door grins down at me the next morning, its bulbous eyes wide with hunger. I meet its stare even as every instinct tells me to flee.

"Good morning," Vincent says when he opens the door, stepping aside to let me pass. He leads me through a side hall into what looks like a dining area. The table has been moved aside to make room for a massive canvas that has been set up against one wall. Though morning light blazes in through a window, the bloodred walls hoard shadows in their corners that twitch like phantoms in my peripheral vision.

"I made sure to purchase only the finest materials." He indicates the pile of supplies on the table. Palettes, knives, brushes, tubes of paint, bottles of mediums, and jars of turpentine. "I asked the shop owner what you would need, so I hope I haven't forgotten anything."

"No, this looks good," I say, scanning the items.

"Perfect. Now. Where shall I sit?" He grips the back of a chair, and when I point toward the corner by the window, he moves it into place.

I settle into the familiarity of pigments and oil, of turpentine and brushes. Though I'm aware of the faint flicker of my sevren in my fingertips as I gather the colors I want to use, I brace myself against the sensation. Under no circumstances will I allow it to distract me from what I need to do. Not today, not ever again.

Vincent asks me questions about my training, my experience, and my time working with Elsie as he sits languidly in the chair, his perfectly symmetrical chin propped on his hand. Though he's as intimidating as he was the moment August and I first saw him, there's an ease about him now I didn't notice before. A gentleness, almost. His smile is not cold or cunning or calculated. It's kind.

Isn't he supposed to be a criminal? Aren't criminals dangerous? Somehow, with sunlight streaming in and illuminating the laugh lines around his eyes, he doesn't seem quite so terrifying.

"You said your mother taught you to paint," he muses. "I always imagined she'd be a marvelous teacher."

My hackles rise at the mention of my mother. I shrug, sorting through the brushes on the table.

"I'm sorry. It's probably difficult to speak of her," he says, his tone gentle.

"Yes." Taking a large long-bristled brush, I begin coating

the canvas with burnt sienna thinned with some turpentine. Though all Vincent has had to say about my mother has been praise for her work, the idea of discussing her as though she's something from the past, like she's not coming back, makes my chest ache.

"That's all right," he says. "We can talk about something else."

I need him to trust me. The first step to getting him to do so is to share things with him.

So I take a deep breath. "No, it's all right. I just miss her." I squirt out more burnt sienna onto my palette and mix in the turp. It'll take most of the tube to cover the whole canvas. My arm is already getting tired. "She was an amazing teacher, possibly even better than she was a painter."

"Which is certainly saying something!" He smiles. "I am so interested to see how this portrait turns out. If your work is anything like hers, it's going to be a masterpiece."

I smile. "Don't set your expectations too high, sir. I don't want to disappoint."

He laughs and then launches into a tale about the first time he ever came across one of my mother's paintings. It was at an alumni display at the Lalverton Conservatory, and it was the most gorgeous, haunting thing he'd ever seen.

"I had nightmares about it for weeks," he concludes, shaking his head.

I snort. "Oh, me too."

"You did?"

"The shadowy, possessed ballerinas in the branches? I couldn't walk anywhere near a tree for at least a month."

He looks at me, his eyebrows raised almost like he's surprised, and then he lets out a laugh, deep and low. "Let's get one thing straight about this portrait you're doing for me," he says, holding up a warning finger. "No ballerinas."

"Oh, come on. Not even a little one?" I jut out my lower lip in a mock plea. He chuckles again as I step back from the canvas. "All right, I'm going to need to you to sit forward a bit. And put your hands on your knee."

He tries to obey, but he looks anything but comfortable.

I snort. "Why are you wincing like that?"

"I'm not wincing. This is just my face."

"Here," I say, stifling a laugh. "Let me help." I set down my brushes and cross to him, grasping his hands to arrange them into a position that looks more natural. Then I reach up and tip his chin sideways. "Hold it there," I say softly as the coarse texture of his finely trimmed beard scrapes against my thumb.

"Better?" he asks, meeting my gaze with those intense eyes—eyes the color of charcoal and shuttered by thick lashes just as dark.

"Much."

"Thank you."

"Of course." I return to my canvas and use my palette knife to mix in a bit of extra linseed oil as a medium to the paint colors. The oil will lengthen the drying time, which is the way I prefer my paint—especially on a piece as large as this one. The longer it takes for the paint to set, the more workable it is. It really allows for me to get the details absolutely right. But I take care not to add too much to this first layer—the base paints need to stay leaner than the fattier layers that will come later on. "But...no more wincing."

"Yes, Miss Whitlock."

"Myra," I correct him before I can stop myself.

"Myra." He smiles.

As I block out the underpainting, Vincent launches into a bit of gossip about a duchess I've never heard of who said this or that at a party last week. His mildly amusing story does little to distract me from the magic sparking to life in my veins, begging me to use it. Trying to force away the sensation, I distract myself with thoughts of Elsie and Will's killer—the killer who might be after me. The panic that courses through me is enough to dull the chill in my palms for now.

If I could get Vincent talking about the Harrises, maybe he'd let something slip. It takes all of my self-control not to spew forth a thousand questions. How did he meet them? What exactly were the medical papers he forged for the governor? Why did he have a meeting with Ameline?

But I cannot ask any of these questions directly. I need to ease him into sharing, make it seem like I don't care. So when there's a lull in the conversation, I say, "August Harris was surprised you recognized him yesterday."

Vincent's smile fades slightly. "I'm afraid knowing everything about everybody is part of my job."

I manage a disinterested chuckle. "So you know the Harris family well?"

"To some extent."

"And the staff?"

He narrows his eyes. "Don't think I don't see through these inquiries, Miss Whitlock."

"Excuse me?" I feign confusion even as my heart threatens to bludgeon itself through my rib cage.

"For the record, I think he returns your sentiments, though he'd never admit it."

"He...?" I stop painting and stare at him a long moment until his words piece themselves together. "Oh, you're speaking of August!" The room grows suddenly hot. "No! He... I... That's not..."

"It's fine." He holds up a hand, a satisfied quirk to his brow. "We won't speak of it. And to answer your question, yes, I know the majority of the Harrises' staff quite well. Even the most innocent people have lies percolating beneath their skin, things they would pay to keep others quiet about."

My cheeks burn. I turn back to the painting, angling my head so he won't see.

"Speaking of the Harrises..." He crosses to a bookshelf in the corner, retrieving a rolled-up newspaper. "Have you seen this?"

"Now I'm going to have to arrange you again," I complain. "Sit back down."

"Time for a break." He thrusts the newspaper into my line of vision. "Have a look."

Setting aside my brush and wiping my hands on a clean rag, I take it from him and unfurl it.

Staring back at me from the front page is a black-and-white photograph of Will. He's laughing at something past the camera. No blood. No bits of brain matter or shards of bone.

Wilburt Harris Jr., Son of Governor Wilburt Harris, Dies of Influenza at Eighteen.

The headline is bold and stark, and I have to read it three times before the words register.

"I always love to see headlines like that," Vincent says.

I look up at him in horror.

When he catches sight of my face, his eyebrows shoot upward. "No, I don't mean that I love to see when people die of influenza. Heavens no." He shakes his head brusquely. "I only meant that the headline is proof my autopsy reports were well done. People believed them. That's all." He rubs the back of his neck, clearly ruffled. "Would you like a drink? I'll get us a bottle of wine." He rushes away.

Autopsy reports.

Last time he only said "medical documents." August and I thought maybe he had been providing medical proof that

Will had been ill to send out to the papers to make the story seem valid. But autopsy reports?

I read through the article, but it doesn't offer any important information. Sighing, I close the paper and toss it onto the table behind me.

A face on the back page makes my heart shoot into my throat.

August, in his perfect, pressed, tailored suit, smiles shyly out at me from the top of the stairs of some important-looking building downtown. I recognize the girl hanging on to his arm immediately as Felicity, though I saw her only the once from afar in the Harris home. Her dark hair is coiled into an intricate bun at the crown of her head. Her neck is long, her shoulders slight, her eyes bright.

And her smile looks real.

I pick up the paper and sink into a chair, gripping the photo so tight it crinkles.

Felicity Ambrose. Even her name sounds like it fits in a world of people like the Harrises. With the elegant lace on her dress, the elbow-length gloves, the sparkling pins in her hair… I scan the article for the word "engagement" or "betrothal," but it only mentions that they attended a dinner event together yesterday evening.

I sniff hard and chuck the paper back onto the table.

So what if he ends up engaged to her? It's not like there could ever have been a possibility of something happening with me. I'm a nobody from nowhere who wears the same old stained dress day after day and who vomits into umbrella stands. He obviously didn't care enough for me to save me from being thrown into the snow.

Maybe he thought me a fool.

Maybe I am one.

Vincent returns a moment later with a bottle and two glasses. He fills mine, and I take a slow sip.

Red wine was always Father's favorite.

"Something wrong with the drink?" Vincent asks, filling his own glass and pulling a chair out to sit next to me.

"Oh, no, it's good." I run my thumb along the rim of my glass. "My father used to collect wines. He had a whole wall of bottles, some almost a century old. I was just thinking of him."

"Do you miss him?"

"Terribly."

He swishes his drink, staring into its depths. "You're very lucky you had such a good relationship with him. My father loathes me."

"Why?"

"You know, to be honest, I'm not sure. Maybe I'm too much like him." His expression sours. "He probably doesn't like being reminded of his own worst traits. Can't blame him for that, I suppose."

I'm not sure how to respond, so I give a sort of half chuckle and take another sip of wine.

He looks at me a moment, a soft smile twitching his lips. "Have you ever been to one of the conservatory's charity dinners?"

I shake my head. "I'm afraid I'm not fancy enough for anything like that."

"They're holding one in a few days to raise funds for the new orphanage downtown, and as one of the main contributors to the cause, I've been named their guest of honor. Would you like to accompany me?"

"Me?" I purse my lips. It would be the perfect opportunity to continue to build his trust, break down his walls. "I suppose, though I don't know what I would wear to an event like that." My cheeks burn as I smooth my hand over the thread-bare fabric of my worn dress.

"Don't you worry about it. I'll take care of finding something suitable."

"Oh, no, that's really—"

He holds up a hand. "It's not a problem."

"All right, then," I say. "I'll go with you."

His smile is bright as he stands, setting his glass down on the table and returning to his chair.

I leave my own glass next to his. My eyes stray to the newspaper, to August's shy smile, and I turn away, retrieving my palette and brushes to continue my work.

But as the hours pass, every inch of me is painfully aware of that face in black-and-white behind me, his freckles and cleft chin and untidy hair. And his arm looped with that of another girl.

28

Vincent sends me home with several bags full of food—fresh breads, bunches of grapes, four different types of cheese, a basket of eggs, and about a dozen other things. It takes everything in me not to burst into tears when he loads them into the cab.

"You didn't have to do that," I say, my voice warbling. I swallow hard.

"Think of it as a small bonus." He flashes me a smile before glancing over his shoulder at the shadows cast by the night. "Please be careful. I'll have the cabby keep an eye on you once he's dropped you off to make sure you get inside safely. I think someone might have followed us to your building last night."

I peer past him, heart skipping into my throat. "What? Why?"

"I saw someone lurking in the alley across the street. Could have been nothing, but..." He frowns. "Best not to take chances. Keep your apartment locked tonight just in case. The cabby will pick you up again in the morning."

"Thank you," I say as he shuts the door.

The next several days pass quickly. Every morning the cabby arrives at sunrise to whisk me across Lalverton to Vincent's. Every night I stay up into the early hours of the morning with Lucy, discussing any clues I might have been able to pick up during my painting sessions, dissecting his words for any hidden meanings. But so far, even with her sharp mind to the task, we haven't been able to come up with anything. He's an extraordinarily careful man.

Vincent's portrait slowly takes shape under my hands. I've never done a piece this large before, and I find it invigorating to have the space to capture the glisten of sunlight on skin, the texture of the hair in his finely trimmed beard, and the web of gold threads woven through his charcoal irises.

The more time I spend with him, the less I fear him. I ask him about his background, and he tells me how he's always had a knack for business and stocks, so he started pursuing that when he was only fourteen. Then, when trying to take on some clients of his own and forging his age and identity on certain official documents, he discovered he had a knack for falsifying records and copying signatures. He's been doing forgeries for only four years now, and he takes great pride in his meticulous attention to detail, which is what has allowed him to become so successful so quickly. "It truly is an art," he tells me. "Like painting, I suppose. Maybe I would be good at what you do. I should try it someday."

Only a very few select clients use him for this illicit work, however. The community at large knows him solely for his work as a businessman, a successful investor who works with the most prominent companies in the country, even at only eighteen years old. He doesn't say as much, but I can tell from the way he speaks and the things he says that he's absolutely brilliant. The more he talks, the more I can see how he became so successful at such a young age. Passion, precision, and pure genius. He's remarkable. In many ways, he reminds me of Lucy.

He sends home a small paper sack full of sweets the day I tell him about her—though I talk as though she's a neighbor's child, not my sister, out of caution for her safety. Just because I'm getting mixed up with a man who deals in illegal documents doesn't mean she needs to. He says he'll say special prayers to the Artist on her behalf. Lucy's eyes narrow when she sees the bag, however. "I don't trust him one bit," she says, though she still pops a candy into her mouth. "What's he bribing us for?"

But though my conversations with Vincent are many, he does not divulge any further information to me about the Harrises or their staff, and he never leaves me alone long enough to search his office.

Soon, it is the night of the charity dinner. I'm in Vincent's kitchen scrubbing paint from my hands when he enters with a big white box in his arms.

"What's that?" I shut off the faucet and dry my hands on a towel.

"A dress." He holds out the box. "You still wish to attend the dinner with me tonight, don't you?"

I nod, my stomach tying itself in knots. The idea of leaving the protection of his hidden lair and waltzing out to a public event when there's a murderer hunting me doesn't feel like the wisest decision, but I force myself to breathe. No one would try to hurt me at a party with so many witnesses. And Vincent wouldn't let them. As long as I stay among the crowds, I'll be fine.

"Of course," I say.

"Why don't you come in here to change?" He leads the

way down a back hallway to an unornamented door. Pushing it open, he ushers me inside.

It's a small bedroom. Quaint, inelegant. A simple bed with a faded quilt, a mirror hanging from one wall next to a sturdy wooden armoire. He sets the box onto the bed with a flourish and retreats out of the room. "I do hope it fits. I gave them the measurements you wrote down exactly, but I know sometimes these things don't always—"

"I'm sure it'll be fine," I say.

He smiles and ducks out, closing the door behind him.

With careful fingers, I lift the lid and unfold the tissue paper within. An elegant dress the color of smoking ladyroses slides smooth as silk over my hands.

Once I've stepped out of my own gown and into this one, I move in front of the mirror and tug on a pair of matching lace gloves. Intricate black-and-red beadwork covers the bodice, and an onyx sash ties high on my waist. The sleeves flutter like gauzy crimson shadows from my shoulders.

My gaze trails upward to my face and hair, and I stifle a snort.

The dress is gorgeous, but my hair is stick straight, as usual, my cheeks and lips unstained, my eyes unpainted. Beauty products haven't been high on the list of things I've wanted to use my money for lately, and it shows.

A soft knock sounds at the door.

"Ready," I say.

Vincent steps inside and stops, his brows lifting, his mouth dropping open. "It—it suits you well, Miss Whitlock."

"I feel rather silly," I admit, testing out a few steps in the heeled shoes that came with the gown.

"Well, you don't look it."

"Thank you."

He extends an arm. "Shall we?"

With nerves jittering in my stomach, I loop my hand through his elbow, and he leads me out into the night.

As we ride through the city in the cab, Vincent chats animatedly about a client he's supposed to meet at the party tonight—a stockholder who sorely needs his help. I can't help but remember riding in a similar cab last week with August.

How different they are. Vincent is confident and charming, and he knows it. August, on the other hand, was always quieter, gentler, unaware of his own endearing allure. But imagining him here with me instead of the forger makes my emotions swirl into tight knots. Fondness and longing tangle with humiliation and betrayal until I feel queasy.

I should not be angry at August for what his parents did to me, for the fact that his family cast me into the snow. He did try to stand up for me. And yet...why did he wait so long? Why didn't he tell the truth the moment his mother incriminated me to save her own skin in front of her husband?

How much did I truly matter to him?

"Here we are," Vincent says cheerily, yanking me from my thoughts as the cab pulls up to a massive building lit like a gilded beacon in the night. Music drifts out from the open balcony doors of the upper floors, which billow with red velvet curtains.

I force a smile as Vincent helps me out of the cab and leads me up the polished stone steps to the double-door entrance.

The scent of butter and roasting meats makes my mouth water, though, thanks to Vincent's care over the past few days, my stomach doesn't growl like it would have last week.

"What did you say the charity was for?" I ask as we enter the building. The swell of voices surrounds us, and we follow it along a hall.

"Governor Harris and the conservatory are raising funds

to build a new orphanage downtown," Vincent says, nodding politely to a man as we pass.

My blood goes cold. "The Harrises will be here?"

"Of course. The governor invited me himself," Vincent says breezily as he opens the door to the main dining room. The noise of conversation, the tinkle of glasses, and the strum of violin strings swallow the choking sound I make in response.

A server dressed in crisp black-and-white leads the way to our table. I cling to Vincent's elbow, heart hammering, eyes flitting from face to face as we pass among glowing candelabras and lace tablecloths toward the front of the room.

Suddenly, the most terrifying person I could run into at this party is no longer the killer. In this moment, seeing Governor Harris scares me far more.

The server comes to a stop at the head table. Governor Harris, Mrs. Harris, August, and Felicity all look up simultaneously. August's eyes widen when he catches sight of me. The governor's mouth twists into a thin-lipped grimace, and Mrs. Harris raises a brow. Only Felicity seems blissfully unaware of the impact my presence is having on her companions.

My whole body tenses to flee, but I force myself to stay still and paste on a smile.

"Good evening," Felicity says to us as Vincent reaches out to shake the governor's hand and kiss Mrs. Harris's knuckles.

August opens his mouth to speak, but his father clears his throat and places a hand on his forearm. August snaps his jaw shut.

"Young Maeve. I should have thought you would have returned to Avertine by now," the governor says, his voice clipped.

"I—" I begin.

"I've been showing her around Lalverton until her father can get a cab through the mountain pass for her," Vincent breaks in. "The storms have made travel to Avertine quite troublesome, as I'm sure you're aware."

"I see," Governor Harris says as Mrs. Harris's gaze intensifies.

"Yes, Vincent's been very kind," I mumble, giving a quick, polite bob of the head in each of our tablemates' directions before sliding into my seat and staring very intently at my plate.

"You're just in time, Vince," Governor Harris says after a moment, shifting his attention to the forger. "They're about to bring out the first course."

"Perfect. I'm famished. Do you know what they're serving?"

"Lamb. Shipped from Tenault."

Vincent smacks his lips appreciatively as he arranges his napkin in his lap. "Excellent choice."

The two men immediately launch into an intense discussion about the state of several of the governor's investments, with Mrs. Harris occasionally interjecting. August and Felicity speak in hushed tones to each other across the table from me. I keep my eyes trained on my plate and twist Father's ring around and around my thumb.

I'm thankful for the distraction once the hors d'oeuvre is served, but I can't seem to get more than one bite down. My nerves have me far too jumpy, so I turn my attention to my drink. The champagne is cool and bubbly, and I swallow down one glass, then two.

As the evening progresses, I sneak glances at August. Every now and then he looks my way, and our eyes lock for a moment before I drop my gaze to my food and take another sip of my champagne. Whenever he laughs at something Felicity says, she positively glows.

She seems nice. Sweet even. Funny.

I wish she were awful.

As our plates are whisked away and we wait for dessert, Governor Harris pats his stomach and says, "It's always good to get a fine meal. Our cook has been missing for several days now, and I daresay our replacement is not as competent as he was."

Vincent pauses with his glass of champagne halfway to his mouth. "Nigel is missing?"

"Yes." Governor Harris's tone is grim. "No one knows where he's gone. I do hope the old chap's all right. He's been with our family for decades."

"Have you called the police?" Vincent asks.

"I have a private investigator on the case, and we're keeping it quiet for now. Wouldn't want word to get out, not with the election coming up so soon."

Vincent nods. "Of course, of course. Utmost discretion, as always, Governor. I'll keep my ears open and do some digging, see if I can't find out anything for you."

"Thank you. Most appreciated."

Their conversation moves on, but my mind is whirring. Their cook is missing? Where is he? Could his disappearance be related to the murder somehow?

I remember the way Nigel watched me from the window as I left Rose Manor last week. Chills crawl all over my body.

The servers come out, arms laden with trays of some chocolatey-looking mousse, but the champagne doesn't seem to be agreeing with me.

I need air.

"Excuse me," I say, pushing my chair back and getting to my feet.

"Oh, are you going to freshen up?" Felicity asks, placing her napkin onto the table next to her own bowl of mousse. "I'll join you!"

"Uh…" I'm about to say no, but thoughts of the killer swirl

in my foggy brain. Going anywhere alone would probably be unwise, so I sigh and nod. "All right," I say as she gets to her feet.

Linking arms with me, she leads the way to the exit as I try not to trip over my own feet. The dining hall seems suddenly louder, longer, and the floor heaves angrily beneath me as though we're on a boat at sea.

"So what's Avertine like?" she asks as we enter the hallway. The door swings shut behind us, cutting off the din, and I press my free hand to my temple to ward off a shooting pain.

"Hot," I manage.

"Are you all right? You're looking a little green."

"I'm fine. Just a little too much champagne, I think."

We find the lavatory, and Felicity waits outside while I have my turn. I rush to the sink and splash cold water over my face. Gripping the rim of the basin, I lean over it and let the water drip from my chin.

I cannot bear the thought of going back out there. Why couldn't Vincent have arranged for us to sit at someone else's— *anyone* else's—table?

A soft knock sounds on the door. "Maeve?" Felicity's voice comes muffled through the wood. "I think August is about to give his speech."

Speech? Since when does August give speeches?

"One moment," I call back, wiping my face with one of the clean cloth napkins provided and gulping down a few deep breaths before exiting the lavatory and allowing Felicity her turn.

I lean against the wall as I wait for her, my eyes darting up and down the empty corridor, watching for any sign of attack. As the seconds tick by, the crowd in the dining hall begins to hush. My mind fills with an image of August, his freckles and endearing ears and shy smile, and a fresh wave of anger and embarrassment takes over me. My stomach heaves, and the world tilts so violently I have to grip the wall to keep on my feet.

"All right," Felicity says as she emerges. "Ready?"

I stare at her for a long moment. She smiles at me, and it is an elegant smile. One of curving, perfectly stained lips and powdered cheeks.

August probably likes that smile.

I press a hand to my stomach. "I'm going to need a few more minutes. You go on without me."

Her brow knits. "Should I fetch a doctor?"

I shake my head. "I'll be fine. You don't want to miss August's speech."

"All right, then. If you're sure…" She frowns doubtfully. "I'll come check on you once he's done."

And then she's gone in a rustle of pink satin.

I tip my head back and try to breathe.

More chandeliers hang here in the hallway, and their tiny, flickering flames dance, casting sparkling rainbow starbursts along the carpet.

The dining hall is completely quiet now. If I strain really hard, I can almost make out the gentle timbre of August's voice.

A footstep creaks somewhere overhead, and I jump so high I nearly trip. Flashes of that night on the fifth floor with August burst across my thoughts. Whispering shadows, sinister footfalls, gruesome paintings.

I should not be out here alone.

Glancing over my shoulder, I stumble to the dining room door and nudge it open a crack. Golden light spills out, and I squint until I find August.

He's standing on a stage behind a podium gripping a small stack of papers. Sweat glistens on his brow.

"As you all are, uh, well aware—" he clears his throat twice "—my father has, um, he's always had a, hmm, a special...a special...special bond with..." He shuffles his feet and tugs a handkerchief from his jacket to mop across his forehead. "With children," he finally forces out.

I step into the room, easing the door quietly shut behind me.

"Breathe, August," I whisper, wishing he could hear me.

"He has been a longtime donat—donator to the, uh, the Lalverton—" His voice cracks on that last word, and even with the lights washing out the color of his face, I can see the blood pumping into his cheeks. He glances up at the crowd, and his eyes widen.

I move along the back wall until I'm directly across from him. He darts a glance toward Felicity, and his grip on the papers tightens so much they crinkle audibly.

"I, uh—" He's gasping now, yanking on his collar like it's trying to choke him.

Then his eyes lock on mine.

Someone in the room coughs. People shift uncomfortably.

"Look at me," I mouth to him, pointing to my eyes.

He licks his lips and glances down at his paper. When he looks back up, he doesn't allow his gaze to stray from mine.

"My father has, uh, made it very clear that our...our children are our future. When we invest in them, we are investing in progress."

I nod for him to go on.

He continues, his voice gaining strength, his breathing evening out. "With the construction of the new Lalverton City Orphanage, the governor is showing us how imperative it is that we...that we invest not only in the ch-children of the wealthy and the influential but in the homeless and the penniless as...as well."

The speech is not a beautiful one. It will not be written about. People won't quote it or speak of it in hushed tones. Tomorrow it will be forgotten.

But I will remember it. I will remember every crack in his voice, every shaking breath. I will remember every pause. And I will remember how his eyes held on to mine from across the room, clung to them like a lifeline.

29

It isn't until August finishes his speech and gives a small bow that he finally relinquishes the eye contact.

I fumble to keep my balance by clinging to the back of a nearby chair. The applause that follows is polite. There is no enthusiasm, no whistles or whoops.

But my chest is so full of pride I want to weep.

August steps off the stage and slouches back to his seat. Felicity leans against his arm and whispers something into his ear, and his cheeks redden.

The warmth in me sours.

The orchestra begins to play, and servers usher people out of their seats so they can clear the tables away to make room for dancing.

I retreat to the exit and duck into the hallway, where small groups of people are gathering to mingle. Their chatter blares in my ears, making my head pound. Turning, I catch sight of a pair of red velvet curtains. I slip between them onto a marble balcony overlooking the city, drinking in gulps of fresh, cold air as the curtains flutter closed, softening the noise of the conversations inside to a dull murmur.

Tugging my gloves off and dropping them to the floor, I let my bare palms settle against the ice-frosted railing.

I'll go back inside in a moment. I'll find Vincent, I'll smile, and I'll be the perfect guest. I'll charm him until he tells me what I need to know.

But first, I need to breathe.

The curtains rustle behind me. "May I join you?" a quiet voice asks.

"Hello, August." I do not turn.

"Myra." He says my name on a slow inhale, like he's drinking it in.

I don't look at him, but I feel his gaze on me, tracing my face, studying my bare hands. After a moment, he removes his own gloves and settles his palms on the railing inches from mine.

We stand side by side, gazing out on the buildings spread like a garden maze below us. Starlight dances on frostbitten shingles. A thousand ribbons of smoke intertwine on the air. Gaslights flare. Shining carriages navigate the streets like tiny beetles.

"She's really sweet," I whisper, trying to infuse my voice with more warmth than I feel. "Felicity."

His grip on the railing tightens. "She is."

"Is the betrothal official yet? Are you engaged?"

"Not yet."

"You don't have to do it, you know," I say.

"Excuse me?"

I sniff. "Forget it. It doesn't matter."

"No, what did you mean? I don't have to do what?"

The gentleness in his voice pulls me in, makes me want to sink into him. I shake my head as a knot swells in my throat.

"Myra. Tell me, please," he says softly.

"You don't have to play their game." I lift a hand to cup his cheek. "You don't have to do what they want you to. Not if it would make you unhappy."

He raises his own hand and settles it atop mine. "Yes, I do."

"But why?"

"This is the life I was born into. The dance we do. I didn't choose it, but they're my family. I can't turn my back on that."

"Can't?" I say, trying not to let the tears in my eyes spill over. "Or won't?"

He looks at me for several moments, his Adam's apple bobbing as he considers me. "What are you asking me, Myra?"

"I—" I shake my head and tear my gaze from his face, slipping my hand out from beneath his and glaring hard at the place near the horizon where the craggy cityscape gives way to rolling, snow-blanketed hills.

The silence between us stretches, spins, whirls to the thud of my heart. I swallow several times, trying to breathe, trying not to let myself look at him because if I look at him I might say what I really mean, and I'm not sure I'm ready to see how he would react if I laid everything bare, not ready to see just how much it would hurt if he broke me.

Finally, after what feels like eternity, he takes a deep breath.

"If you're asking whether I wish I could choose you instead," he says, his palm settling over my fingers on the railing, "then the answer is yes."

I glance up at him, but when my gaze locks on those summer-blue eyes, my tears spill over. "Then why don't you?"

"It's not that simple."

"Why? Because I'm poor? Because I don't have the right parents?" The sting of his rejection burns in my chest, undamming every insecurity I've felt since the moment I met him. "It's all about appearances, isn't it? Playing the role. Looking the part." The words tumble from my lips too fast for me to grasp onto them, made slippery by the liquor and my tears. A sob chokes out, and I swallow it back. "Making promises to impoverished nobodies that you forget the next moment." *I'll talk to my father*, he said in the carriage last week. *See if he'll pay for the doctor.*

"Myra…" he says, his voice quiet, almost pained.

I stare out at the city, trying to get a handle on my thoughts, on my voice, on what I'm saying. "You're fabricating a persona that doesn't exist, August, and it's not fair to you or Felicity."

He hisses as though burned and turns away from me. "You don't know what you're talking about."

"Don't I?"

"This is *my life*, Myra. If I turn my back on my family, I have nothing. *Nothing.* It doesn't make me a bad person to pretend I belong in this world. It's survival. I thought you of all people would understand that."

I mop the wetness from my cheeks with a fist. "*I* would not have allowed *you* to be humiliated and kicked out into the snow, no matter what I had at stake or how scared I was. I would not have made a promise I never intended to keep. And I would not stand there now and defend those choices."

"Of course you wouldn't," he snaps. "Because you're not me! You get to live your life free of this!" He thrusts his hands up between us, baring cuticles trickling with fresh blood. "Just because my battles aren't visible doesn't mean they aren't as real or as difficult as yours." His eyes blaze. "Every single day is a fight. Every moment. I can't shut it off. So I'm sorry. I'll apologize until the end of time if that's what you need in order to believe how awful I feel for what happened with my parents, but I won't apologize for doing my damn best." His voice drops to a whisper. "This part of me? It's *not* a weakness. It's not a fault or a flaw. It is a fact of my life, and I'm a better, stronger person for it." He steps closer, his chest heaving. "My being afraid does not lessen my passion for the things I care about."

The eye contact between us is a tether of electricity, snapping and buzzing bright. I take another step, and we are so close that the silver plumes of his breath curl around my cheeks and tangle through my eyelashes.

And I see his power, right there in the clench of his jaw and the fervor in his eyes.

Didn't I tell him a week ago that he should never let anyone try to make him feel small because of this very aspect of him? Yet here I stand, doing the same thing his parents have done, judging him because of a part of his life I have never experienced, never fought through, never known.

Anger blazes through me, but this time it is not at him. It's at myself.

"You're right," I whisper around the lump of shame in my throat. "I'm sorry. I only thought about what it would have been like if I had been in your place. I didn't stop to consider that it was unfair of me to assume we face the same battles in any given situation."

He swallows. Nods.

"But you still don't have to bow to their prejudice," I say, grasping his fingers and squeezing them between mine. "Make them see your strength like you just made me see."

"I... I can't," he says.

"Your whole life, they've forced you aside, trampled over you because they've made you believe you have to earn their love by hiding the truth. Don't give them that power. They don't deserve it." I step closer. "You are one of the fiercest people I know, and I hate watching them treat you like you need to be ashamed of the things that have made you that way."

His Adam's apple bobs.

"Your battles *are* as valid as theirs, as mine, as anyone's. I'm sorry that I let myself forget that."

His thumbs stroke over mine, quiet and slow, and he tips his forehead closer. "I didn't break my promise to you. I asked my father for the money like I said I would. I told him I wanted to set up a small medical fund to help a child in need pay for care."

My brows rise. "What did he say?"

"He wouldn't hear of it. For all his talk of providing for the future and helping the impoverished, he's not about to actually do so unless it makes him look good in a significant, public way. He told me that if he gave money to every sick child in the city, he'd go bankrupt."

My chest constricts. I sniff, letting go of August's hands to wrap my arms around myself.

"So," he says softly, "I sold my pen. Just now, before you got here tonight."

"The one you got from Kenwick? But you never write without that."

"I think I'll manage." He smiles as he extracts a pouch from his jacket. My ears catch on the distinct clink of coins within. He holds it out. "This is for you. It isn't much…maybe only fifty golds, but I hope it will help."

I stare at the pouch.

"Come on, Myra." He shakes it in my face. "Take it." He grabs my hand and pushes the bag inside of it. "You and your sister don't have to bear everything alone."

I swallow hard as tears film over my vision. "But we do. We're the only people we can count on."

He wraps his hands around mine, squeezing my fingers against the pouch of coins. "You can count on me."

His breath traces designs across my cheeks. Warm and soft. I shiver.

Snow flurries around our heads, sparkling like diamonds. His face is cloaked in shadow but for a thin sliver of light shafting across his nose from a gap in the curtain.

His gaze dips to my lips, and my whole body ignites.

I'm suddenly vividly aware of how close we are. Barely an inch of space separates us. He exhales slowly, and I taste cinnamon. He tugs on my hands, pulling me closer so that my knuckles brush against his chest.

He's the governor's firstborn son. We shouldn't be standing out here like this, alone. Especially with him telling me he would choose me over Felicity if he could. Not where people might see us. Not while my veins are still buzzing with champagne.

But I cannot make myself move away. If anything, my body drifts nearer, drawn by the tether between our eyes.

"Myra…" he says, and his voice is barely a breath. Heat floods through me, and I'm trembling. Hungry.

He raises a hand, and his thumb catches on my lower lip, dragging it downward.

His eyes are a storm. Heavy and fierce.

And slowly, ever so slowly, he leans in.

I cannot breathe, cannot see.

My eyes shutter, and my whole body tenses.

His mouth hovers over mine, not quite touching. The air between us thins. Tremulous. Hot. Intoxicating.

"Myra…" he says again, and as his lips move, they graze mine.

A tiny moan escapes me.

I feel his smile. His hand moves to my cheek, and his fingers feather against my skin as his thumb comes to rest like a fluttering moth wing at the corner of my mouth.

And just when I can bear it no longer, when I think I might

die if he doesn't close that space between us, a shout erupts from behind the curtains.

"Maeve!" Vincent's voice punctures the air.

I jolt back, whipping around.

The curtains billow, and Vincent ducks through. He surveys August and me for a moment, and my cheeks flush. Even though August is no longer touching me, though my lips are cold and unkissed, I'm almost certain Vincent can see the tremors shaking through me and hear the roar of my heartbeat.

"There you are," he says, his voice suddenly quiet. "Miss Ambrose told me you weren't feeling well. I was worried." His eyes flick toward August. "Though it looks like my worry was misplaced. You were in good hands."

My blush intensifies at the thought of where August's hands just were—and where else I'd have liked them to go—and the earlier twisting of my stomach returns full force. I shove the coin pouch into my sash and snatch up my gloves from where I dropped them earlier. "Yes, I'm sorry. I wanted some fresh air. What do you need?"

"I thought if you weren't feeling well maybe I should take you home." He pauses and raises a hopeful brow. "Though if you'd rather stay—"

I tug on my gloves. "Of course. I'm sorry. I'm feeling much better." I glance at August, whose face has gone quite violet. He's staring so intently at his shoes I wouldn't be surprised if he bored a hole through them. "Thank you for the, uh, conversation, Mr. Harris."

He manages a tiny nod. "Good evening."

With my heart in my throat, I take Vincent's arm and allow him to lead me back inside, my mouth still watering with the taste of cinnamon and snow.

30

Focus. I need to focus.

I didn't come here to get distracted by young men with storm-cloud blue eyes. I didn't come here to get drunk on champagne. I came here because a killer is hunting me, and the one person willing to pay me enough money to get me and my sister out of Lalverton asked me to. I came here because I need Vincent to trust me, to want to tell me what he knows so I can protect myself and Lucy.

Yet I've spent hardly a moment with Vincent all night.

So I push down my thundering heart and hold my head high as I walk with him back into the dining hall. People dressed in every color sparkle beneath the chandeliers as they dance. The air is hazy with cigar smoke and the dull murmur of voices. Diamonds sparkle, tuxedo shoes shine, satin rustles. It's like I've stepped entirely out of the past year of my life and into the world Lucy and I occupied when our parents were here. The sights and the smells and the sounds swirl around me as though they're bits of a dream, like I might wake up if I focus too hard on any of the details.

Vincent tips his head toward me. "Would you like to dance?"

I laugh. "The extent of my dance experience comes from my father waltzing me around the kitchen floor on stockinged feet."

"Perfect." Vincent's smile is bright as he takes me by the hand and leads me out among the couples twirling in smoky light.

Champagne still has my head spinning, but if I'm going to get anything out of Vincent, tonight is my best bet. I settle my left hand on his shoulder as he pulls me in close.

The orchestra strikes up a new, slower song, a minor, melancholic melody that fills the air with low tones. Vincent leads me across the floor, his movements effortless and graceful, his hand steady on my lower back.

"You're a very good dancer," I say.

"Thank you. It's one of the few skills my father forced on me as a youth that I'm actually grateful to know how to do."

"Oh? What other skills did you learn?"

"The usual. Horseback riding, fencing, archery... Like I said, useless."

"Those sound like very useful skills to me."

He raises a brow. "When is a forger ever going to need to know how to nock an arrow?"

"When he needs to shoot someone with said arrow, of course."

"Who am I going to shoot?" His eyes glint.

"An evil warlord. Or maybe a bandit?"

He lets out a full belly laugh. "Of course, how could I forget about all the bandits after me?"

"Careless of you, really."

He grins down at me, his laughter slowly fading. Glitter and silk swish past, but he keeps his eyes locked on mine. He cocks his head, bites his lower lip. The way he's looking at me—it's like he's seeing someone else in my face. Someone he knows. And while the intimacy of that gaze makes me feel like I'm pretending to be someone I'm not, it doesn't unsettle me as it should.

"You're nothing like I expected," he says.

"What did you expect?"

His eyes dart back and forth between mine, endlessly enigmatic. "I don't know," he says after a moment. "Not this."

I smile and open my mouth to ask him if he has any ideas about where the Harrises' cook might have disappeared to when he cuts in.

"Would you care for a stroll outside?" he asks, slowing our dance to a stop. "A bit of fresh air? There's a magnificent garden off the back porch."

"Uh…" I blink, glancing in the direction he's indicating. Maybe outside it'll be quieter, and I'll be able to find a better opening to ask him what I need to know. I give him a smile. "Why not? I'd love to."

He fetches our coats and, after helping me put mine on, leads us out onto a lovely veranda lit with a thousand tiny candles. As we step into the night, the flickering lights surround us like a sea of stars.

"Is it always like this?" I ask.

"They do it up special for events," he says as we make our way down a set of marble steps onto a path winding among flower bushes and trees. Ice sparkles from every leaf, reflecting the glow of the candles behind us.

"So the Harrises' cook…do you have any idea where he might be?"

Vincent frowns. "Very odd, his disappearance. I'm afraid I don't have a clue."

"There have been a lot of disappearances in Lalverton lately..." I try to keep my voice light, like I'm making casual conversation.

But he doesn't give me much to go on. "True" is all he says.

I switch tactics. "It must be interesting to be friends with so many important people. The director of the conservatory, the governor..."

Vincent purses his lips. "Interesting indeed."

"Would you say you're friends with Governor Harris?"

"Friends?"

"Or is your relationship all business?"

Vincent thinks for a moment. "Maybe somewhere in between, I suppose. But I'd rather not talk about the governor right now, if it's all the same to you."

"Oh, I'm sorry," I say in a rush. "I hope I haven't been rude."

"No, of course not." He fidgets with my hand on his elbow and licks his lips. "Never mind."

We walk for several moments in silence broken only by the crunch of our feet in icy gravel. My mind whirs. How am I supposed to get answers out of him when he so clearly doesn't want to speak of the governor or his family?

Vincent finally clears his throat. "So, Miss Whitlock...are you involved with August Harris?"

The question is like a shock of cold water to my system. Every thought flees my brain.

"I— No. Of course not. He's— I'm— No." I bite down on my tongue to keep from stammering any further as heat floods my cheeks.

He sighs, tightening his arm around mine.

I peer up at him. The moon shimmers on the planes of his

face, curving white along the furrow in his brow. "Why do you ask?"

He glances at me and shakes his head. "I wasn't going to say anything, but after seeing you two together like that, I—"

"What?"

"Well, I've heard things about him."

I focus on my feet as we mount the crest of a small bridge overlooking a pond. Long-dead lily pads glitter just under the surface of the water, crystallized in its frozen depths. We pause, leaning against the railing.

"What sort of things?" I ask.

"It could be nothing." He trails a gloved thumb along the carving in the wood of the rail. "But I know some of their staff very well. They've told me stories about the two Harris boys. They fought all of the time, and those disagreements at times became violent. I've been told that August seems nice enough to those who don't know him well, but he's got a temper."

I shake my head. "Not August. He wouldn't hurt a fly."

"I'm only passing on what I've heard." He sniffs and ducks his nose into his scarf. "I don't want to see you harmed."

I tighten my grip on Vincent's elbow. "I don't want to talk about August."

"Neither do I." He nods toward the pond. "Do you recognize this place?"

I follow his gaze to the frozen water and the stars reflected like diamonds on its rippled surface. "No. Should I?"

"The landscape I commissioned from your mother. It was of this pond."

"The one hanging next to the door to your office?" I think of the day August and I first met him, standing outside his door staring at a painting of an eerie lake with a pair of yellow eyes hovering in its depths. "But this is so beautiful. Why did she paint it like that?"

"Because I told her to." He stares across the water, his eyes distant, like he's looking past it to another place, another time. "I met a girl here, once. Fell in love with her. Kissed her for the first time on this very bridge. And now she's gone. For a long time now, this place has reminded me only of pain." He turns his gaze on me. "But it doesn't seem so terrible tonight."

The questions I want to ask, about the Harrises, about the murderer, lie waiting on my lips, but as Vincent's confession trembles in the air between us, those questions crumble to ash.

"I'm sorry," I say.

"I am, too." He lifts a hand and tucks a stray lock of hair behind my ear. I shiver as his gloved fingers brush my skin.

His eyes dip toward my lips. "I should get you home," he whispers, his breath dragging slow, silver fingers across my cheeks. "It's late."

I swallow. "Yes, it is."

We don't speak again the whole way back to the ballroom.

A half hour later, Vincent grasps my hand to help me into his carriage on the curb.

"One moment," he says, patting his pockets. "I think I left my cigar lighter inside. I'll be right back."

I wave him away with a polite nod and settle into my seat to wait.

I'm going to do it this time. I got distracted in the garden, but I'm going to ask him about Will Harris directly on the ride home. I've played my role, I've done my work. If he doesn't trust me now, he never will.

A shout punches the air outside, and the carriage jostles.

I frown. That sounded like Vincent's driver. I peek out the window just as a figure in a cloak wrenches the driver off his perch, shoving him into the street and taking the reins.

My blood runs cold.

I dive for the door as a whip cracks the air and the carriage jerks forward. The sudden movement tosses me onto the floor, and I wince when my teeth slam against each other.

The carriage jolts as the horses break into a full canter.

Clinging to the seat to keep from falling, I reach for the doorknob and jam the door open.

Buildings rush by, and frigid water splashes up from the wheels as the cab speeds across the cobblestones.

I gape at the snow and the ice, at the jagged edge of curb as wind whips my hair back from my face.

If I jump, I could break a limb. Or get trampled by another carriage.

But all I can see is Will's smashed-in skull. Elsie's bloodstained lips telling me to *go*.

Staying in the carriage is not an option.

Gathering my skirts, I throw myself out the door. I slam into the cobblestones, and a scream breaks through my lips. Pain spasms through me, and I roll several yards until I come to a stop.

The carriage slows. The whip cracks again. Horses whinny.

Ignoring the way my whole body feels as though it's been shattered, I shove myself upright and take off running.

Frigid puddles slick ice into my stockings. Gusts of frozen air slice my cheeks. Panic lights my muscles on fire.

I don't know where I am or where I'm headed. I don't recognize the buildings, shops, or homes I pass. The pain in my legs is sharp. A stitch stabs through my ribs.

And still I run.

Horse hooves clatter behind me, louder and louder.

I dive into the nearest alleyway and shimmy through. If I can at least get my pursuer off their horse, I might stand a chance at escape.

Nickers echo in the distance, but the sound is drowned out by the roar of blood in my ears and my own gasping breaths.

Shadows claw at me from every side. I don't dare look back even when the sounds of pursuit fade to nothing. My legs scream, my feet ache, and I can scarcely breathe.

But all I see is Lucy.

Her bright eyes, a pencil perched on her ear, her hands full of river muck.

I must escape. I have to get back to her.

Icy wind closes in around me, thick and quiet and sharp as a knife. Buildings hulk overhead, sullen in the night.

I see no one. I hear nothing.

My legs wobble, and I dodge a glance over my shoulder.

There's no one there.

I allow myself to slow. Panting, I cling to an unlit gas lamp-post with both hands to keep from collapsing.

Something scrapes behind me, and I look up in time to see a shape barrel in at me from the dark. A scream tears through me as my pursuer slams into my back, and I hit the ground hard. Sludge spatters my face with cold.

I squirm beneath the weight of the person on my shoulders, wrenching my head this way and that trying to get a look at who it is, but their cloak shrouds their face. They knot their fist in my hair and yank my head back. Hot breath gropes at my cheek.

"Who are you?" I whimper. "What do you want?"

The frigid steel of a blade bites into my neck.

Adrenaline zaps through me, and I can practically feel the fear and panic weaving a thick snarl of sevren under the skin on my throat.

Tears warp across my vision. "Please—" I rasp. "I have a little sister. She needs me. I—"

But the knife digs deeper into my skin. Blood slicks into the collar of my jacket.

"No!" I scream, bucking backward and flinging an arm out. My attacker's blade slices across my forearm, and whoever it is topples into the snow.

As my blood paints the snow the color of death, I flee.

Something moves from the shadows of the street in front of me. I catch a glimpse of Vincent sprinting for me, his eyes wild with worry, just as my pursuer knocks me to the ground once more.

My head slams into the curb, and everything vanishes.

31

Pain fractures through my skull, and I wake screaming.

"Shhh," a man soothes nearby, and something cold is pressed to my forehead. "You're going to be all right. You're safe."

Vincent. My mind registers his voice, and I collapse against him, weeping. I try to open my eyes, but the pain is so acute stars eat away at my vision.

All I can see are cloaked, hooded figures lurching at me from the snow.

"You hit your head pretty hard," Vincent says, "but I think it's only a bad lump. If you keep ice on it, it should go down."

I brush my fingers over my temple. A hard knot protrudes above my ear, and my hand comes away slick with blood.

I squint until my sight clears. We are still out in the snow under a midnight sky. Vincent has pulled me under the shelter of a nearby stoop and wrapped me in his cloak. He cradles my head against his chest, dabbing at my wound with what looks to be a handkerchief.

"I'm sorry," he says, holding up the wet mound of cloth. "Soaking this in the snow was the best I could come up with on the spot."

I let my eyes drift shut as pain pulses through my head and into my neck. The wound on my arm stings. "Who was that? Did they get away?"

Vincent sighs. "They took off the second they saw me coming, so I didn't get a good look."

My chest squeezes. So my pursuer, Elsie and Will's murderer, is still out there.

Pain throbs in the skin on my neck where my attacker sliced me with his blade. I press my fingers to the cut. It's mercifully shallow and already beginning to crust over.

Vincent purses his lips. "Maybe you should stay at my office tonight. I could set up a bed for you in—"

I shake my head. "Take me home."

"I'm not sure if that's—"

"I want to go home." I scramble to my feet. As soon as I'm upright, the world pitches violently, and I topple against him.

"Easy, easy," he murmurs, hitching one hand under my knees and one beneath my shoulders and hoisting me into his arms. "What's so important about getting home?"

"My sister..." I let my head fall against his chest, squeeze my eyes shut until the ringing in my ears subsides. "I don't like being away from Lucy for too long."

"I thought Lucy was your neighbor." His voice rumbles against my cheek as he carries me down the street.

"I lied."

But he doesn't seem upset. His thumb brushes circles on my arm, and I let the gentle back-and-forth of his steps soothe the pounding of my heart. But as I focus, I notice that the pace of his steps is a bit uneven, more like a *shuffle-thump* than a steady *thud-thud*. I raise my head.

"Are you hurt?"

He frowns. "What do you mean?"

"You're limping."

"Ah." He nods. "That. 'Fraid I have a bit of a bad foot. Don't you worry about it."

"You shouldn't be carrying me if—"

"It's really quite all right, Miss Whitlock. I know my own limits. I promise if I reach them, I'll take a rest."

Sighing, I let my head droop once more. "Fine."

"So, how old did you say your sister was?" he asks.

"Thirteen."

"That's young to lose your parents," he says softly.

"I know," I say, and, as tears burble to the surface once more, the whole story comes loose. How heartbroken we were when Mother and Father never returned. How terrifying it was for us, suddenly alone in a world that seemed so bent on making us suffer. How things only got worse when we ran out of money and were forced out of Mother and Father's apartment downtown.

I tell him about the way Lucy's illness took such a horrible turn, how she's only gotten sicker and sicker no matter how many things we've tried, how she reminds me of a corpse walking, with her limbs jutting out like daggers through her skin.

I tell him about how desperate I've been to keep her with me, how she's less like a sister to me and more like a piece of my heart living in another body. The story of how Mrs. Harris came to find me comes out. I leave out the part about my magic, talking instead about her wanting me to do a special memorial painting for Will.

Vincent listens intently, his somber expression illuminated periodically by the grayish glow of the gaslights as we pass beneath them.

If I'm going to get answers, now's my best shot.

"Something was off about that family," I say carefully. "They have so many secrets."

"What do you mean?"

"Well, Governor Harris hiring you to forge false autopsy reports is one of them. If Will died of an innocent fall, why would it be so imperative that he lie to the public?" I meet his gaze straight on. "Do you know how he really died?"

Vincent frowns, adjusting my weight in his grip. "I never saw the body. All the governor said was that he needed autopsy reports declaring that the cause of death was influenza."

"When did he contact you?"

"Right after the fall. Within the hour. I've done papers for the governor on many occasions in the past, so he's able to get hold of me pretty quick when he needs something done."

I sigh and slump into his shoulder. That nullifies the assumption August and I made that the autopsy reports were drawn up in advance of the death. At least if the governor was responsible, it wasn't as premeditated as we presumed.

The gentle thrum of Vincent's heartbeat thuds against my cheek.

"Why do you care so much what happened to him? Why not do the painting and leave?"

I try to come up with a feasible excuse. "If someone killed him, I think the world ought to know, especially if the governor or anyone he associates with had something to do with it." I glance up to see if he buys my lie.

"Ah." Vincent's lips draw into a thin line. "You feel it is your moral, civic duty."

I frown. "What do you know?"

Vincent shakes his head. "I don't know anything about a murder, but I do agree with you that there is something very strange about the Harrises."

"Like what?"

"Well, I do business with the owner of an art supply shop downtown. I've seen the receipts of all his recent sales, and quite a lot has been purchased by someone in the Harris household. I wasn't able to decipher the first name, but it was very clearly a Harris signature." He pauses. "I suppose that wouldn't be that odd on its own, but the governor has made it quite clear how he feels about painting in secular pursuits."

I frown. "That might have been Mrs. Harris purchasing supplies for me. She had a whole bookshelf stocked with things when I went there."

"Perhaps." He glances sideways at me. "Does August have an artistic streak?"

"Of course not."

"You're sure about that?"

I chew on my lip.

Am I sure about that? I suppose I'm not, but if August were the one behind all of this, why would he accost me in the street instead of hurting me any number of times when we've been alone together?

As Vincent and I turn onto the road where I live, I search the shadows for any sign of the cloaked figure who attacked me.

But there is no one.

We reach the door to my building, and Vincent eases me down. "Here, I'll get the door."

"No, that's—that's all right." I move in front of him, barring his path. "I can make it up the stairs by myself." Letting him see the drab outside of the building again is humiliating enough. He doesn't need to glimpse the inside.

"It's really not a problem," he says, reaching past me.

"Please don't." I meet his gaze.

With his hand gripping the doorknob behind me, the inside of his arm presses against my waist.

He looks down at me, his midnight lashes casting spiderweb shadows across his cheeks. A smile plays at the corners of his mouth. "You've become quite the nuisance, you know. Ruining all of my plans."

I cross my arms. "Excuse me? What does that—"

He presses a gloved finger to my lips, and the words die in my throat. "I wasn't finished," he says. Snowflakes catch in his eyelashes as he cocks his head. "I had everything figured out. I knew where I was going, what I wanted. And then you came along with your propositions and your determination, and you threw a wrench in every plan."

My heart hammers in my throat. I can scarcely breathe.

"I've been walking around like a dead man for what feels like centuries, and now here you are, this explosion of life. Suddenly I remember what it feels like to breathe again. To laugh. To wake up with hope."

"I really haven't done anything," I croak.

He smiles, eyes crinkling up, and his hand slips to my cheek, tilting my face up toward his. His breath caresses my skin as he whispers, "And that's where you're wrong."

Our lips are inches apart now, and his other hand has moved from the doorknob at my back to rest against my waist.

Hours ago I stood this close to August and wanted with every part of my body for him to kiss me. But he didn't. August and I will never be anything. He's a Harris—heir to the family legacy and the governorship. Set to be engaged any day now to a future duchess. He can't choose me over that— he cares about what his family thinks far too much. He made that abundantly clear tonight.

Even still, as Vincent stares down at me, a thousand questions chasing each other across his face, all I can think of is how much I wish it were August instead. That the scent stroking my lips was that of cinnamon instead of some expensive musk from one of the stores downtown. That the eyes searching mine were storm-cloud blue and framed by strawberry-light lashes.

Why does it have to be Vincent who's so willing to choose me?

Vincent leans in slowly, his hand trailing to cup under my left ear.

I could let this happen. I could close my eyes, kiss him, allow him to make me feel beautiful and cared for and worth something. It would be easy. He's handsome and charming, warm and gentle.

But I press my palm to his chest and turn my mouth away from his. "Vincent, I..."

He lets out a slow breath as though deflating. "I'm sorry. I shouldn't have... Of course." He steps back, dropping his hand from my jaw and running it through his hair. "That was entirely inappropriate. Please forgive me."

"It's not..." I mumble, but I cannot finish the sentence. What am I wanting to say? It's not a problem? It's not that I don't like you, it's just that I like the governor's unattainable son more, even though the odds of anything ever actually happening with him are basically zero, and I'm a hopeless case, so don't waste your time?

But Vincent smiles, grasping my hand and bringing my knuckles to his lips. "It's quite all right, of course. I'll see you tomorrow, Miss Whitlock."

I slide his jacket from my shoulders and hand it to him. "See you," I say faintly.

He tugs the coat on and flips the collar up to shield his ears from the wind. Then he gives me one last smile and steps off into the street, disappearing into the swirling snow.

32

"What on earth happened to you?" Ava rushes at me the instant she opens the door, pulling my face down to her level. "Why are you bleeding?"

I scrub at the blood on my cheek. "I was…" But the words dissolve as I look over at Lucy. She's curled up in a ball, asleep, but her face is strained, her jaw is clenched, and her arms are wrapped around her middle. Sweat glistens on her brow, and her whole body quakes violently.

"Lucy!" I rush to the bed. "What's going on?" I press my hand against her forehead. It burns through my palm.

"She seemed to be doing all right this morning," Ava says, wringing her hands. "But this afternoon she started screaming like she was in excruciating pain. She collapsed into slumber a few hours ago, and I haven't been able to rouse her since."

"What?" I push the soaking clumps of hair away from Lucy's face. Her skin scalds my fingertips. How can she be worse? "Lucy!" I shout, shaking her shoulder.

She does not wake.

"Lucy!" I scream, panic turning my vision splotchy all over again.

"That won't do anything," Ava says quietly, placing a gentle hand on my arm. "She's in some sort of unconscious state."

I stare down at my sister, tears running down my cheeks in earnest. "I should have been here."

"You're doing what you can," Ava says.

"It's not enough, though, is it," I spit through my teeth. Lucy gasps for air like she just sprinted a hundred miles. The veins in her neck pulse wildly.

"Has the man you're painting for paid you yet? Even a partial sum you could use for a doctor?" Ava asks.

I shake my head. "I'll probably finish the portrait tomorrow, so I expect that's when—" The memory of August handing me the pouch of coins strikes like lightning across my thoughts. "Wait. I do have some money. We could—" I dig at my waist for the purse.

But my sash is empty. I paw through the fabric, hands frantic.

"No," I whisper, suddenly dizzy. "No, no, no…"

"What?"

"It was—it was right here—"

The coins he gave me are gone.

I let my skirts slip from my hands and stare blankly ahead, thinking back through all of the times when the pouch might have fallen out of my sash. In the garden. When I jumped out of the cab. During the scuffle. Maybe the attacker even stole it.

There are a thousand places it could be.

I bury my face in my hands as my sobs begin anew. "I'm such a fool."

Ava murmurs comforting, meaningless words, but I don't hear them. All I can see is that little pouch clinking with the sound of coins. Coins that August got for me by selling his most prized possession.

And I lost it.

"Lucy needs a doctor tonight," Ava says.

I whirl, my blood boiling hot. "I *know*!"

Ava's forehead creases.

"No matter what we do. No matter how we try. She just keeps getting worse, and the money keeps disappearing." I hiccup.

Ava has every right to leave. To pack her things and go home to her own children. She's not family. Not even a friend. She owes us nothing.

But I'm weak, and when she holds her arms out for me, I sink into her embrace, close my eyes, and pretend she's Mother. That I'm not alone.

"Maybe we can go out after Vincent," I weep. "Ask him to give me the money now." I turn to head for the door, but the room swims before my eyes, and my legs give out. Ava catches me before I hit the floor and hoists me over to my cot.

"You're not going anywhere right now." She takes a whiff of my breath and frowns. "Have you been drinking?"

"Only champagne," I weep.

She tsks, smoothing my hair out of my face and tugging off the elegant shoes Vincent got me for the party. Then she helps me sit down on my cot, tucking a ratty blanket over my legs. When my sobs finally begin to quiet, she asks, "Why the sudden interest from all of these important people, Myra? First the governor's wife and now this businessman... And then there's also a killer on your trail? I know it's not my place to pry, but I can't help but wonder... Why wouldn't either of them have commissioned a portrait from someone with more of a reputation? Or more experience? And why would anybody want to hurt you?"

I search her eyes. I've never admitted to her what I am—never admitted it to a soul. But I'm so *tired*. And Lucy is so ill. If she's got a fever, something must be infected, and if that's the case, her odds of surviving are low without medical help.

Maybe August is right. Maybe it's time I finally trusted someone to help us.

We can't bear this alone anymore.

"Do you believe in Prodigies?" I ask, mopping tears away from my eyes.

"I don't know. I suppose I haven't really thought about it." Ava pauses. "Why?"

Folding my arms across my chest, I rub warmth through my sleeves. "My mother was one. And so am I."

Ava laughs, but when I don't join in, don't even smile, she stops. "You're serious?"

"Never been more serious in my life."

"Do the Harrises know? And this businessman?"

Letting my hands fall back to my sides, I launch into a watered-down explanation of what Mrs. Harris really asked me to do and why I failed. "And as for Vincent… I don't think he's aware. As far as I can tell, he just wants a regular portrait. But sometimes I wonder how much he suspects."

Ava gapes at me. "If you're a Prodigy capable of raising a boy from the dead, couldn't you have done something about Lucy's illness before now?"

I glance back at my sister, whose cheeks shine pink in the gloom. "No. It doesn't work like that. My magic is only capable of healing wounds or changing appearances," I say quietly. "Lucy's illness is such a part of her life—it has defined so much about how she experiences the world and helped influence the young woman she has become to such an extent that my magic never could unravel it, even if I wanted to do so."

"Well, I'd say that what's going on in her body now is no

longer about her illness. Something has ruptured or perforated internally. There's an injury now that's entirely separate
from her illness."

I consider that for a long moment. "So you're saying that
if we are able to figure out what has been injured, maybe I
could use my magic to heal just that and get her stable again?"
My thoughts blur as Ava nods. "*Maybe* I could pull it off...
though I've never been great at understanding biology. That's
always been Lucy."

"What if I help?"

"You?" I blink at her.

She juts her chin out. "I'm no doctor, and I certainly don't
know anything about painting, but I *am* a nurse."

"I—"

"Do you have any medical records for her I could look
through? And Lucy's biology books would be very helpful."

I shove the covers off and hobble across to Lucy's bedside
table, where an orderly stack of her research stands, along with
her symptom journal and food diary. As I hand those to Ava, I
say, "I've also got a book about medical anatomy and injuries.
Should be over here." I stumble on leaden, bruised legs to hoist
my bag up from its place on the floor by the door. Dumping
out its contents, I slam the textbook from Ernest's bookshop
onto the kitchen table. Breathless, I turn to her. "Bought it
with the last gold pieces we had to our name."

She joins me, setting Lucy's notes next to the book and
heaving open the cover. "Go get your paints. I'll start searching."

"But your family—"

She shakes her head. "If anything ever happened to me and
my husband, I would hope someone would look after my little
girls. They will understand."

Wetness stings my eyes all over again, but she points at the pile of paints and brushes on the floor. "Get to work, Myra. There will be time for tears when Lucy's awake again."

Setting up my mother's old easel, I slap on a burnt sienna turpentine mix with my biggest brush. My head throbs, and my hands are still smudged with dried blood, but there's no time.

Once the canvas is coated in brownish orange, I swap out for a smaller brush—a filbert—to block out the underpainting, my mind humming through how best to approach this.

Until Ava comes up with a theory on what might be injured internally, I need to focus on keeping Lucy alive. Maybe the key to helping her will be to make small alterations focusing on the symptoms. Instead of trying to restore her in one go, perhaps I should do it in smaller steps. It'll take me hours and hours to do that many paintings, but I'm out of options.

So I mix in some ladyrose gel and begin by illustrating Lucy the way she looks now. My magic lurches to life, cold and snapping, at the base of my skull. My thoughts flick back to the drawing I saw in that notebook August and I found on the fifth floor—what had the nest of sevren in the woman's brain been called? Fervora?

Two hours later, and the first painting is dry enough for me to layer on the new version of Lucy. I detail in her sunken cheeks, the clumpy, dull hair, the bony wrists just as they are now. I imagine her the way she was when I left for Vincent's— still in pain, but at least conscious. I dot in beads of sweat and outline her chest in arcs that show the way she's breathing so rapidly. The only thing I focus on changing is that she's awake.

My body aches. Fogginess eats away at the edges of my mind, and the wound in my arm burns with each brushstroke. But I grit my teeth and continue, reminding myself that no matter how terrible I feel, Lucy feels worse.

In a sharp contrast to the gentle whisper of my brush over

the canvas, the pages of the medical textbook ruffle behind me as Ava flips through, jotting down notes alongside Lucy's, muttering under her breath.

The night wears on, and as the clock on the mantel ticks away the hours, I settle into a haze of work. The scent of linseed oil and pigment fills my nose and settles my nerves. I imagine Mother standing behind me, murmuring small encouragements as I work. *That's it. Make sure to blend the white in a bit more to give the essence of light. Use some cerulean blue—it will brighten your titanium. That cadmium red is a bit too harsh—tone it down with some viridian. Don't worry about the mistakes—you can always paint over them.*

When Old Sawthorne's bells strike two o'clock, I sit back, surveying my work. "First one done," I say, setting my brushes aside and getting to my feet for a quick stretch. My fingers pop as I work out the stiffness in my knuckles.

"It's very good," Ava says, pausing on a page midway through the book. "Looks just like her."

My eyes dart to the shrine on the wall. "Artist, let this work." Focusing on the buzz that has slowly been building in my fingers since I started painting, I press my palm against the wet paint and close my eyes. *Please, please, please…* I repeat over and over in my mind as the magic spreads icy tendrils along my arm, into my chest, and up to meet the nest of electricity in my brain, a braid of power linking me to the portrait.

And, slowly, the image of the painting in my mind's eye ripples. The brushstrokes rearrange themselves into a colorful web, the silhouette of Lucy's body coalesces into an intricate diagram of her sevren.

My magic tries to drag my fingertips downward, away from her head. Gritting my teeth, I keep my hand where it is. I can't afford to let it have its way, not when I don't know how it could hurt her.

"Stop fighting me," I hiss.

With all of my might, I imagine the Lucy lying comatose in the bed across the room as the Lucy I've illustrated—ill, but at least awake, and I press my fingertips to the knots of sevren in her temples, sifting through them until one looks right. The cold brew of my power builds until my whole body is alight and shivering with it.

Then all at once, it releases.

"Myra!" Ava's shout breaks through a thick fog, and I force my eyes open.

I'm on my back on the ground staring up at the water-stained ceiling.

"Are you all right?" she asks.

I blink around, getting my bearings. And then it hits me. I leap to my feet.

"I passed out?"

"For only an instant. You fell not two seconds ago."

With my hands shaking and hope making my knees weak, I trip across the room to Lucy's bed.

"What happened?" Ava whispers.

"When my magic works, I take on the feature I changed for a brief time. If I passed out, then maybe…" I kneel at the bed, dazed and desperate. "Lucy?" I take her hand in mine and squeeze her fingers. "Lucy, are you all right?"

All is silent as I wait for her to respond. Her eyes rove beneath her lids, twitching. Her gasping breaths seem to slow a bit.

Then her eyelashes flutter. Her dark eyes focus in on mine, and she grimaces.

Relief floods through me. "Lucy!" I gasp, wrapping my arms around her, laughing and crying and shaking. "Lucy, you're awake!"

But then she shrieks, doubling over. She retches, and I pull her hair away from her face and shove the bowl on the floor she keeps for exactly this purpose under her mouth. Nothing but bile drips from her lips, but her body keeps heaving. Despair claws through every inch of me.

"You're going to be all right, Luce," I whisper as her body convulses. I squeeze my eyes shut. "It worked. I just have to keep going."

Lucy collapses in my arms, her body twitching a few times before going eerily still. The sudden quiet after her vomiting is loud in my ears.

"Hey, Luce, are you all right?" I ask, nudging her gently.

She does not respond.

"Lucy!" I grip her shoulders and shake her. Her head lolls back. "Wake up!"

But she does not wake.

"No…" I press my fingers to her neck. Her pulse is faint but very fast, and her breathing is back up to its earlier, impossibly rapid pace.

"Is she—?" Ava doesn't finish her question.

I shake my head. "She's back to the way she was before." I lay my sister against the pillow and settle the blankets around her. "But it worked. My magic did something. It *finally* did something!"

Ava's smile is a sad one, full of grief and worry, but in it flickers a trace of triumph. I cling to that as I get to my feet.

"I've got to try again," I say, but as I take a step forward, my legs buckle, and I topple against Ava.

"Easy," Ava says, shouldering me back to my seat and easing me down. "You're shaking. When was the last time you ate?"

"Lunch, I think? I'm fine."

She crosses to the kitchen and rifles through the cupboards. "Unfortunately, I just fed Lucy the last of what Vincent sent home." She frowns, turning to the sink and filling a cup. "This is what's going to happen. You are going to drink this while I run across the street to my house for some food."

I accept the water when she hands it to me and guzzle it down. "Be careful," I say. "Watch out for strangers."

She pauses, glancing back at me. Nodding toward the book and papers on the table, she says, "I haven't been able to find anything promising yet, but I'll keep looking when I return."

I scoot to the edge of my chair and load my biggest flat brush with more burnt sienna. Ava slips out of the door, and then I am alone with the rapid gasps of my sister's labored breaths.

33

It seems as though only moments have passed by the time Ava returns. She enters and locks the door immediately, a quiver in her movement.

"What is it?" I ask.

She deposits a small sack of food on the table. A pomegranate rolls out, and I catch it before it hits the ground. "It's probably nothing," she says, but her hands are shaking. "There's someone watching the building."

Unease prickles through me as Ava crosses to the window and tugs aside the curtain an inch.

"There. In the alley across the street."

I peer through the grimy glass. At first I don't see anything, but after a moment, one of the shadows twitches, and moonlight slices across a familiar black cloak. The figure leans against the wall of the building, the shadowed recesses of its hood turned in our direction.

Though I cannot see the person's eyes, I feel them on me,

and it's like I'm back in the snow with a blade at my throat. Shivering, I let the curtain fall.

For the thousandth time, I run through my list of who it could be. Mr. or Mrs. Harris? The cook? Ameline? Or someone else entirely?

"Do you know what they want?" Ava asks quietly.

I shake my head. Sparks dance in my vision as I back up to my chair and sit down.

"What do we do?" She hands me a knife and a bowl.

"We take care of Lucy," I say, digging the blade into the pomegranate. Juice dribbles onto my fingers. "That's the only thing we can focus on right now. Once she's stable, I'm going to take her and get out of Lalverton as quickly as possible. Somehow. We aren't safe here anymore."

Ava returns to her place at the table. I feel her eyes on me as I scoop pomegranate seeds onto my tongue. The juices are extra tart, but I wolf them down ravenously and say nothing more to her.

There isn't anything else to say. Only my magic can save us now.

If it would behave.

Once I finish the pomegranate, I retrieve my paintbrush. I'm still hungry, but I should be all right for now.

For this portrait, I focus on an even more incremental change. Instead of intending for Lucy to immediately regain consciousness, I take it from unconsciousness to slumber. Maybe going all the way to entirely awake was too much for her.

Once the painting is complete, I press my hand to the image, letting the shiver of magic braid its way through me. The chill blasts along every strand of sevren, reaching its peak, and it takes every ounce of strength in me to keep it contained as it splits shards of pain through my skull trying to take control.

And then it releases.

This time, when I regain consciousness, I cross immediately to Lucy's side and study her face. I can't quite tell if she's still comatose or if it worked and she's merely asleep. Stroking my fingers along her face, I hiss at the temperature of her skin.

"Her fever is getting worse," I say.

"Look at her eyelids," Ava whispers from my side. "Her eyes are moving. They weren't doing that before."

Relief floods through me, making my toes and fingertips tingle.

But a moment later, her eyes go still again.

Grinding my teeth, I set up a fresh canvas.

As the night wears on, my vision grows hazy and my hands begin to cramp as I paint image after image. Thankfully, the ladyrose gel makes each layer dry quickly, and I keep the portraits small and undetailed, so I'm able to churn out half a dozen paintings in a few hours. I succeed in small ways with each one—lowering her temperature, getting her breathing to slow—but only for a moment or two. Each time I paint one of her symptoms away, the alteration takes hold just long enough for my hopes to soar. But then she slips right back to where she was, and as the hours tick by, her condition only seems to worsen.

By the time Old Sawthorne's bells chime four o'clock, I'm barely holding on.

"Haven't you found anything yet?" I ask, kicking over my easel when my newest illustration fails to make any lasting effect.

Ava flinches at the earsplitting clatter of the canvas on the floor. "I've found some notes in Lucy's research about allergies."

I shake my head. "No, she and I already discussed the possibility of allergies weeks ago. Her symptoms don't fit. There's no itchiness, no swelling of the nose and throat, no rash or hives…"

"Well, true, but the book here says that there are some food allergies that cause gastrointestinal upset. Were there any foods that she seemed particularly sensitive to?"

"Only during her flare-ups," I say, frowning. "When she was having symptoms, then eating greasy foods or lots of fiber would make it worse. But when the illness was dormant, eating those foods didn't have much of an effect on her that we could tell."

"Maybe the foods were still affecting her, but not in ways she noticed?" Ava asks.

"It's possible." I read the entry in the book about food allergies over her shoulder. But my elation quickly dissipates when I see how little information there actually is. Only about a paragraph before it moves on to discuss a body's reaction to poisons. "What sort of organ damage might that do?"

Ava squints back and forth between Lucy's symptom journal and the textbook. "It looks like certain food sensitivities and allergies can cause significant damage to the kidneys, which can lead to infection. Any kind of infection could result in blood poisoning if it gets bad enough, and her symptoms match that now."

"So I could paint away the blood poisoning. And maybe repair the kidney? That wouldn't be taking away her illness or anything like that, only healing the wound that's currently killing her, right?"

Ava ponders. "I think so?"

"It's worth a try, I suppose," I say, leaning over to peer at the paragraph Ava indicates before stooping to hoist the easel from the ground and set it upright.

But the hope, the thrill of possibly being close, isn't there. I only feel hollow.

What am I even doing?

I sigh, leaning my head against the easel as I look at my sister. She's always been so brilliant. So spirited. She deserves someone better to fight for her. Someone smart, like she is. Someone capable. "What would you do if you were me, Luce?"

I press my palms to my thighs, imagining her lifting her head to roll her eyes at me. *Well, first off*, she would say, *I'd sit up straighter. You're going to wreck your back with posture like that.*

I almost laugh.

And second off, I'd say you need to try something new, imaginary Lucy goes on. *Think outside of your normal parameters.*

My eyes fly open.

Maybe that's it.

For hours I've been painting Lucy and focusing on her overall health and symptoms, but now that we've got this kidney hypothesis, maybe it would be more effective to paint that directly.

I whirl to face Ava. "Can you find me an illustration or photograph of a pair of kidneys in that book? And does it have any visual depiction of what an infected one might look like?"

Ava fans through the pages and spins it around to face me. "Here's one."

I study the colors in a drawing of a dissected cadaver.

"Lucy, you're brilliant," I breathe.

Periodically throughout the night, Ava has been checking out the window to see whether the figure is still watching our building. She gets up from her seat now as I set a new canvas in place and peeks through the curtain.

"Whoever it is…they've gone," she whispers.

"Gone?" I cross to look over her shoulder. Sure enough, the alley across the street is empty.

Unease rakes at my insides as I return to my paints.

"Do you think they've given up?" she asks, letting the curtain fall back into place.

I sigh as I mix cadmium red with yellow ochre and titanium white in an attempt to get the pinkish-orange color of the kidney right. "I would love it if they had, but I don't want to assume so."

She nods. "Better to be careful."

Once I've got a damaged set of kidneys illustrated—swollen and angry red—on the canvas, I allow a moment for the oils to dry before starting on the new layer. The healthy one.

The flare of cold in my fervora is duller than usual this time.

But it wouldn't be there at all if I hadn't gotten it right, would it? It's probably just my magic being unruly again.

Ignoring the uneasy fist gripping the pit of my stomach, I press on.

When the new layer is finished, I step back from my painting and toss my brush and palette onto the table. "Please work," I whisper.

Ava sits up straighter, and I give her a hopeful grimace before settling my palm over the shining colors. This time, I let my eyes fall shut and focus entirely on the possibility of the food sensitivity. I imagine Lucy's kidneys mending, healing, the blood poisoning dissipating. Then I seize up the energy flowing through my fingertips, my hand, my wrist, wrenching it as hard as I can through my system until it fills me entirely. It flares, icy and white, and then releases.

I wait.

No pain overtakes my midsection. I remain completely conscious.

Dread lacing acid through my veins, I peek through my

lashes at Lucy. She hasn't moved. Her breathing continues its frantic pace, and sweat snakes tiny, shimmering lines down her face.

It didn't work.

Sinking to the floor, I bend my knees against my chest and press my face into them.

The air is too thick to breathe. The weight of it too much.

"What am I missing, Luce?" I squeeze my eyes shut so the tears cannot collect, cannot drip onto my paint-stained dress, cannot admit defeat for me.

"You're so close," Ava says.

"Am I?" I don't even bother to raise my head.

"We need to keep trying. Keep looking. Maybe it isn't a food sensitivity. I've been reading about appendicitis—"

"It's not appendicitis. I had a friend who had that once, and it came on quite suddenly. This has been building for months." I knead my aching fingers against each other so hard my knuckles pop. "Maybe what she has is something that hasn't been studied yet. Maybe even a real doctor couldn't diagnose it. If that's the case, then it won't matter how many pages you read in that stupid book."

"So, what, you want to give up?"

I press my face harder into my knees. Images of Will's body, rigid and silent, fill my mind.

Will Lucy be as cold as he was?

I shake my head. No. I refuse to go there. Refuse to imagine that.

Wobbling, I force myself to stand. "Never."

One more painting. I just need to try once more.

With shaking hands, I mop the moisture from my cheeks and comb through my supplies. I'm running low on burnt sienna. Frowning, I shuffle across the room to where I left the carpetbag I took to the Harrises' house and paw through it to see if there might be some extra paint in there. A few bottles and brushes roll between my fingers, but no burnt sienna. As I dig into one of the outer pockets, my hand grazes across the cover of a book.

The only book I took with me was the textbook Ava's reading now, so what's this? Squinting to see in the meager light of the almost-spent lantern, I tug it out.

I recognize the deep brown leather cover instantly. It's the journal I found on the Harrises' fifth floor. I'd taken it and left it in the cellar where I was working. The Harrises' servants must have thought it belonged to me when they were packing up my things.

Flipping through, my fingers stop on a page where an excerpt from what looks to be a textbook has been pasted to the paper.

In some of the most popular versions of the Prodigy myth, the strength of the Prodigy's magic depends entirely on how stubborn the artist is. Many people hypothesize that it might not even be a gift from the Artist that makes the Prodigy powerful—it's their own sheer force of will to bend reality to fit the version of it they wish to be real.

I pause, tapping my chin. That reminds me of something I once read in my mother's journal. What had it said? Something about Prodigies needing to have faith?

I push back from the table and cross to my cot in the corner, pulling out a small box of assorted items I kept from my parents. My father's measuring spoons. My mother's favorite paintbrush. I sift through it until I locate the small tattered notebook underneath everything else.

Pulling it out, I wipe away the dust and search through the pages. My heart gnaws in my chest at the sight of her familiar cursive handwriting—so lovely. Like it was an art all its own.

It takes only a moment to locate the entry.

I'm beginning to realize my magic isn't dependent upon how well I render an image or how thorough I am at getting all the details right. It seems like it could be more based on trusting my magic to know what it needs to do. Allowing my magic to be the one to control an outcome. Accepting it as part of me, an extension of my instincts. When I do so, I've discovered that the stronger my faith in my chosen reality, the deeper the changes my power is able to accomplish.

I've read through my mother's journal a thousand times, and this passage never struck me before as anything special. I'd assumed it was a simple platitude that didn't change much about the actual function of our power. But now... Maybe I just need to have a stronger faith in my own ability to create that chosen reality, like she said. Rely on my sheer force of will.

Every time I've painted my sister tonight, I've clenched my teeth and prayed *please work this time. Please, please, please.*

Maybe that's my problem. Maybe I've been too convinced that it wouldn't work. Is it possible that I've been foiling my own attempts with my lack of confidence?

I set the book down and return to my newest painting, studying the careful, swooping lines and the gentle swell of the kidneys.

"I'm going to try this one again," I say quietly, standing before the illustration. Taking a slow, deep breath, I lay my hand at the center of the canvas. This time, instead of closing my eyes, I focus on the hues of the oils between my fingers. The alizarins and cadmiums and titaniums. The darks and the lights, the cold and warm colors blending together.

As the prickle in my hand grows, my skin numbs, almost like my fingertips have gone frostbitten. The feeling leeches up my arm toward my heart.

Gasping as though I've been doused in ice water, I grit my teeth. *You are strong enough,* I say to myself, to my magic. *I know you can do this.*

As the cold pressure in my chest builds to fill my entire

body, I imagine Lucy's fever breaking, her eyes opening. And once again, my magic rears its head, lurching against my will.

I can control this. My magic is my tool.

As I clench my jaw and tamp it down, directing it to the knots of sevren under my fingertips and forcing it through me into the painting, the familiar zaps of pain inside my skull increase until my ears are ringing.

When the magic releases, a rush of warmth floods me.

The air crackles, and my hair stands on end like lightning has struck.

I blink as the room comes back into focus, and then I totter on unsteady feet across the room to Lucy's bed.

"Luce?" I ask.

She's unresponsive, but as I comb hair out of her eyes, I realize that the fever has gone. She shivers uncontrollably. No longer scalding, her skin has turned clammy.

"Ava," I say. "Come here."

Panic singes through me, making my whole body jittery.

Ava kneels next to me, checking Lucy's temperature and then pressing her fingers to her neck to count her pulse. Her eyes widen as she moves her hands to press on Lucy's abdomen.

"It's distended," she says.

"What does that mean?"

"The dropping of her temperature, the faintness of her pulse, and the swollen belly are all indicators that she might be in some form of sepsis."

"What is that?"

Ava swallows and places a hand on my arm. "She has hours left. A day at most, if we're lucky. If her blood has started forming clots, or if she is going into multiple organ failure, there might not be anything anyone can do in time." She squeezes my arm gently. "I'm afraid I don't have the training to know without the testing they'd do in a hospital. Her low blood pressure is not promising, though."

I rock back, shaking my head. "No. No. You're wrong. It's not..."

But she's biting her lip, and her eyes are shining with tears. "She's young, Myra. Children are very resilient in times like this. They often hang on longer than we expect. There is still hope."

I stumble to my painting, staring at it but seeing nothing. My vision warps and swirls. The room bleeds. The light fractures.

"I was supposed to take care of her," I whisper, smudging my fingers through the oils on the canvas, dragging my fingernails through the colors. "I was supposed to be able to help her. I've only made it worse."

"It's not too late," Ava says quietly. "You could try again."

"Are you kidding?" My lip curls, and I wrench the painting off the easel. With a growl, I slam my foot through it and hurl it across the room. It hits the wall, smearing paint on the peeling wallpaper as it slides to the ground. "Mother was the true Prodigy. I'm nothing but a shadow of what she was."

"You are only seventeen." Ava takes a step in my direction. "You cannot hold yourself to the same standard."

"I don't have a choice!" I shout, my whole body shaking. "She's gone! Our parents left us here to pick up the pieces all alone. I didn't know the first thing about raising a child, the first thing about making a living or paying rent or keeping a damn house. They abandoned us here with *nothing*!"

I turn to my easel and, in one violent sweep of my arms, smash it to the ground. Then I turn to the bottles of oils and pigments on the table, and I fling them one by one into the fire. They explode against the hearth, the mantel, and the

bricks surrounding the fireplace, leaving dribbles of color that
ooze to the ground.

With each crash, another scream bites through my lips, and
when the last one shatters and the glass tinkles to the floor,
I sink to my knees, burying my face in my hands, not even
caring that I'm smearing oil all over my cheeks.

"My magic was supposed to work," I weep. "I was supposed to be able to help her."

"It's not your fault," Ava whispers from behind me.

"Please," I say between hiccups. "Go home. I've kept you
from your real life long enough."

"But—" she begins.

"I said go!" I cry. "Leave!"

Ava pauses, and for several moments there is nothing but
the sound of my sobs. But then, finally, she gathers her things.
"I'll be back first thing in the morning," she says as she slips
out of the door, locking it behind her.

Once she's gone, I crawl over to Lucy's bed and pull myself on top of it, sliding into the space next to her. I ease her
against me, pressing her head to my chest and wrapping my
arms around her small frame.

As I run my fingers through the knots in her hair, I press
my lips to her temple.

We used to lie like this back when our parents were here.
Father would tell us bedtime stories, and we would fall asleep
all tangled up in each other. I would inevitably be awakened
an hour later once Lucy started her routine sleep-flailing.

A laugh chokes through my sobs as I remember the morning I woke with a massive purple bruise in the middle of my
back exactly the size of Lucy's kneecap.

"You remember how Mother used to say that love was
the most powerful magic of all?" I murmur as my tears spat-

ter onto her face. I wait for her to respond, to move, to wrap those arms around me and squeeze.

But of course, she doesn't.

"She must have lied," I whisper. "Because the love I have for you? It's… I'm certain it's more than anyone has ever loved another human being in the history of the world." My voice cracks, and I squeeze her tight against me. "If love were magic, it would have saved us long ago."

Her breath wheezes, and her swollen belly presses against my ribs. Her screams from earlier echo in my mind, cracking through my soul.

"You've been hurting for so long…" I take a deep, steadying breath as the words puncture parts of me on their way out of my mouth. "But if it's a choice between me suffering or you, I will gladly take the pain if that means you don't have to anymore." I wind my fingers around hers and squeeze them. "If you're ready to be done fighting, if you're tired, I—" My voice falters. "I promise I won't be mad at you."

She doesn't move, doesn't speak. My angel sister stuck somewhere between life and death, fluttering on broken wings, gasping for air in a body that can scarcely breathe anymore.

I turn my face into her pillow and cry.

And cry.

And cry.

The fabric smells of her, her sweat, her tears, and that bright fragrance that's always just been *her*. The aroma of sunshine and ponds, of laughter and summer.

I cry until my body is too weak to do it anymore. Until dawn's light feathers palest pink between the curtains and the lantern on the table sputters out. Until the coals in the fireplace are cold.

It wasn't supposed to be like this.

34

I lie awake listening to the flutter of Lucy's breaths and the ticking of the clock on the mantel, staring at the gap between the curtain and the window where the light of two tiny stars dance like pinpricks in the gray sky, slowly fading as the sun rises.

In the almost silence, I think of August's eyes. The way I craved having them meet mine, and the feeling that rippled through me when they actually did. *You get to choose which you want to be*, he'd said.

Before Mother and Father disappeared, I planned to attend the same art conservatory my mother did, to open my own studio, to have my paintings displayed in museums across the country like hers—across the globe—and purchased by wealthy, influential people to hang in their offices and sitting rooms where people could ooh and aah over them long after I die.

That life is not a choice for me anymore. I don't even know where I will be next month.

If Lucy's gone, it won't matter anyway. None of that will mean anything if she's not there.

August can write as many poems about me as he wants. It doesn't make me any less useless, and it doesn't make anything he says more true.

But even as I want to hate him for not understanding, the emotion isn't there. I don't feel anger, or even the humiliation of his rejection.

I don't feel anything but empty.

"Hurt" is not deep enough, he'd said of his brother's death. *Not raw or serrated enough.*

He was right. Now that I'm faced with the very real possibility that Lucy will not live, my insides feel as though they're being sliced with jagged, rusty claws. Oozing blood. Weeping fluids.

Does August have an artistic streak? Vincent asked me last night.

August certainly has an artistic way with words...

My eyes widen.

What if...

The ink stains on August's fingertips. Hadn't there been black streaks on Will's shirt?

My lungs constrict.

Elsie's gasping last words. *Said...killed... Harris...*

What if that wasn't one fragmented sentence—not "they said they killed the Harris boy." Could she have been trying to tell me her killer *was* a Harris?

And the stab wound without blood.

What if it was magic that created that wound in Will's chest? That could certainly explain why it didn't bleed the way a normal wound would have, couldn't it?

Could August be a painter, too?

Were all those portraits on the fifth floor his?

Maybe he offered to help me in my search for clues in an attempt to throw me off his trail? Many of the clues we worked with came from him—the note from Ameline, the information about Nigel's story. Maybe the reason he insisted so much on helping me was so that he could distract me. Build my trust. And perhaps he knew about his father's dealings with Vincent and used that to make me believe the governor was guilty.

August certainly had enough of a motive. He was the disappointing firstborn, always in his younger brother's shadow. What better way to assert himself than to get rid of his competition?

And the way Vincent spoke of him... *August seems nice enough to those who don't know him well, but he's got a temper.*

I shake my head. This is *August*. The kind, gentle-hearted boy I've come to care for. The August I know couldn't do something like that, isn't capable of even the tiniest amount of cruelty.

And yet...what if he is? How well do I know him, really? I of all people am keenly aware of how easy it is to dress up the truth in pretty lies, hiding reality with the right hues.

I think of the way I looked at August last night, the way I gazed into his eyes and trembled for the caress of his lips.

Have I been played for a fool?

Not just for thinking someone of his rank could care for me in that way, but for not seeing through to what he might have hidden beneath?

For someone who considers herself fairly observant, it's possible I saw only what he wanted me to see. Took his forgery of friendship and kindness at face value.

Was it he who attacked me last night in the snow?

Has it been him all night, watching my building from across the street?

My heart pounds loud and hard in my ears, but I shake my head and curl my hands into fists.

It can't have been.

Can it?

My eyes stray to Lucy. She is so still that a shiver of fear prickles through me. I rest my hand on her chest to reassure myself she's still breathing.

It wasn't him. There's no way it was him.

And yet, if it somehow—impossibly—is true, if he is a Prodigy and he did kill his brother with magic, that would mean he has to be a pretty powerful one. One who could be strong enough to save someone on the brink of death.

My head spins.

August has asked me several times to trust him. He's proved to me even more times that I can. Whether he's a killer or not, whether he's got magic or not, whether what happened between us was real or not, I can choose to trust him anyway.

And, even if he isn't the killer and he's no more a Prodigy than Ava, he's still a Harris. That counts for something in this city. Surely he can get us into a hospital somewhere, pull some strings to get us a doctor.

He's my only chance.

I sprint across the room, tug on my stockings and boots, wrap a scarf around my neck, and yank a hat over my half-unraveled bun. As soon as I have my gloves on, I kneel at Lucy's bedside, taking her hand in mine.

"I know I said it was okay to go if you needed to, but I'm going to need you to hold on for just a bit longer. Fight this. Stay here. I need you. I'm bringing someone to help." I press her knuckles to my lips. "I love you."

A soft knock sounds on the door.

Ava has returned.

I stand, letting Lucy's hand drop limply onto the sheet.

And then, before I can dissolve into another puddle of tears, I let Ava inside.

"I'll be back soon," I say. "Keep her alive."

"Where are you going?" Ava's fierce whisper feathers after me as I dash into the stairwell.

But I don't pause to answer.

The winter air is cold and still when I emerge from the building. The rooftops of Lalverton are limned in the white light of sunrise. I pull my scarf up to cover most of my face and steal across the road, pushing my aching body as fast as I can to the place across the street where I saw the person who might have been August lurking earlier.

But he's gone. The alleyway is empty. I walk the whole length of it. There's nothing but footprints. I sigh, and the air silvers in front of my face.

Guess I'm headed back to Rose Manor.

Wrapping my arms around myself to keep in my body heat, I begin the trek across the city, praying for a cab. I don't have money to pay for one, but I will give the driver the shoes off my feet, the dress off my back if I need to. Hell, I'm not above stealing a cab at this point if it comes to that. Lucy doesn't have long.

The air smells of ice and smoke and fish, and I drink it in gulps. I haven't slept in days, haven't eaten anything but champagne and pomegranates since lunch yesterday at Vincent's. My temple pounds like someone's slamming it with a sledgehammer. I'm covered in paint and dried blood and hardly sure whether I'll make it to the next block, let alone across the whole city.

Fishermen, dock workers, and factory men pass me in their dirty garb, headed south toward the Lawrence. They greet me in their guttural street accents, and I tip my head in their direction, not pausing to say hello in my hurry north.

As I reach the end of my street, a familiar cab clatters around the corner, and I almost weep with relief.

Vincent's driver pulls up to the curb next to me and clambers down. "I'm sorry, miss. Am I late?"

"Not at all!" I gasp as he helps me inside. "But I can't go to Vincent's today. Would you please take me to Rose Manor?"

The driver's mustache twitches. "Of course, miss."

Dawn's light has blossomed into the blaze of morning by the time we reach the street where the Harrises live.

Instead of going to the front gate—there's no way the guards would let me back in at this point—I have the cab drop me off by the east wall. Once the cab has jolted out of sight, I trek into the slushy mud of the forested area, aiming for the side gate August took me through to clean out the vase that first night.

It doesn't take me long to find it. I run my hands along the iron poles, hissing at the cold, before locating the best place to reach my hand through to the padlock. Mimicking August's motion from before, I tug it sharply open, and it drops to the floor. The gate whines open on rusty hinges, and I pause, holding my breath.

When several minutes have passed and no one has come to investigate the noise, I slip inside, easing the gate back into place slowly enough that the hinges barely whisper.

The mansion is foreboding and ominous in spite of the morning sun. The gargoyles perched on its gutters glare down on me, their spiked wings and sharp claws poised to strike.

Shivering away from their gazes, I inch closer to the house, skirting along the wall until I come to the kitchen's back exit.

The doorknob rattles, and I dive behind the dumpster as the door swings open. Ameline emerges, hoisting platters of uneaten breakfast food. As she tries to lift the lid to the dumpster, the stack of plates in her arm tilts, and the whole pile goes crashing into the snow. Cursing, she stoops to gather them up, and I take my chance, darting through the open door and into the heat of the kitchen.

A pair of servants stands with their backs to me scrubbing plates in the sink. With my heart gargling in my throat, I tiptoe across the room to peer through the door to the dining room.

A man dressed in a cook's uniform is clearing away dishes on the table. Glancing at the servants at the sink, I make my way to another door across the room and steal through it.

It spits me out into what looks like some sort of servants' hall, much like the one August and I took to reach the fifth floor. Trailing my hand along the wall, I creep forward, praying to the Artist that I won't run into anyone on my way.

It only occurs to me once I've followed the passage for several minutes that I have no idea where August's room actually is.

A few branches of the corridor break away, and I choose the first left, praying it will lead me to a part of the house I'm familiar with.

Finally, I reach a door. I press my ear to the wood for several moments. When I hear nothing, I twist the knob.

I instantly recognize Governor Harris's office door across from me, and my heart drops to my shoes. Steeling my nerves, I slink past, pausing outside the door next to it.

The room where the governor keeps his blade collection.

I'm choosing to trust August, but if he really is capable of murder, confronting him defenseless would be a stupid idea.

Glancing over my shoulder, I dig a pin out of my hair and jam it into the lock the way August used his cuff link that night. It takes me much longer to work at it, but eventually

the mechanisms inside give way with a sharp *click*, and I tiptoe into the room.

It's dark as pitch. Trying to force away the image of someone—alive or dead—lurking in here with me, I press my hands
to the wall and trail them along until they brush steel. Working entirely by feel, I locate the dagger August showed me.

My cheeks flush at the memory of his body warming the
air around me, his hands pressing gently down on my arms.
I tuck the knife into my waistband and find my way back to
the door.

As I ease it open, voices fill my ears, and I freeze. Two men,
sounds like, farther down the hall. I wait with my heart slamming in my chest.

Soon, they finish their conversation, and I catch a glimpse
of Governor Harris striding toward his office. As he reaches
for the knob, he pauses, eyes flicking in my direction. He
frowns, and I jump back, adrenaline stinging through every
inch of my sevren.

"Who left this unlocked?" Governor Harris mutters, his
footsteps approaching.

I press myself into the space behind the door and pray.

35

The door swings open, pinning me against the wall. I stuff my hand over my mouth as the hallway light glints on steel and jewels and pommels.

For a moment, he doesn't move.

Blood rushes so loudly in my ears I'm certain he can hear it. Sparks lick at my vision as I hold my breath, but I'm too terrified to inhale in case it might make too much noise.

Finally, after an eternity, the governor mumbles something about negligent servants and yanks the door shut. The lock slides home, and his footsteps retreat. I hear his office door open and close.

I sink back against the wall, gasping. My whole body trembles.

What would he have done if he had found me here?

The thought makes me physically ill.

Forcing myself upright, I unlock the door again with shaking hands.

The sooner I get this over with, the better.

As I dart into the hall and close the door behind me, I consider my options. I don't know where August's bedroom is, but I do remember where Will's is. Up on the fourth floor. I imagine their rooms aren't far from each other, so that'll be my best bet.

Keeping my palm against the hulk of the dagger at my waist, I steal along the corridor until I find the stairs.

When I reach the fourth-floor landing, I catch sight of a maid backing out of a room, and I duck behind a potted tree until she disappears into another chamber.

I start at one end of the hallway and make my way along it, listening at each door before peeking inside. I find a library, some kind of parlor, bathing rooms, and what looks like the governor and his wife's suite.

I skip over the door where the maid disappeared. There's only one left besides Will's. Uttering a prayer to the Artist on a faint breath, I wrap my hand around the handle and twist it open.

The room is bright with midmorning light. A bed stands rumpled, and a discarded pair of trousers and a jacket lay strewn on the floor. I recognize them instantly from the suit August wore last night to the charity dinner, and I gulp down the trepidation bubbling like bile in the back of my mouth.

Pushing the door open farther, I catch a glimpse of someone bowed over a writing desk in the corner under the window. The gentle scratch of a pen against paper jars against my nerves. I slip the dagger out of my belt.

August sits back, and the sunlight ignites in his hair, violently orange, cadmium bright.

I grit my teeth.

I can do this.

Forcing away my fears, my nerves, and my doubts, I dart

across the room and, in one motion, grasp a fistful of hair, yank his head back, and press the blade to his neck.

A quiet gasp escapes his lips. His pen drops to the tabletop and rolls off, hitting the floor with a loud *smack*.

"Don't move," I breathe, trying to make my voice sound much more lethal than I feel.

"Myra?" he asks, splaying his quaking hands against the desk atop his open journal. "Why are—"

"Are you a Prodigy?"

He lets out a nervous laugh. "Myra, I don't paint. My father—"

I spin his chair around and point the dagger at his chest.

He holds up his hands, eyes wide. "What's going on?"

"Did you kill him?"

"Kill who?"

"Will, damn it. Who else?" I snap.

Confusion crinkles his brow. "Of course not!"

I frown, studying his features as they go from afraid to bewildered to angry. His cheeks redden, the splotchy freckles darkening as he scowls.

"Are you seriously accusing *me* right now?"

"They say you and Will used to fight. That it would get violent sometimes," I say.

"You've seen Will." August scoffs. "He was twice my size. Do you honestly think that if things got 'violent' between me and my brother, I would have ever stood a chance of coming out on top?"

My eyes dart along the bony points of his shoulders jutting through his shirt, his knobby wrists peeking out from his sleeves, and my resolution falters.

"If you used magic, then it doesn't matter how big he was," I say, but my tone isn't quite as sure as it was before.

"I didn't kill him, Myra. I wasn't fond of him, sure, but I'm no murderer."

My dagger quivers between us. The air grows thin as I search his face for lies. I keep settling back on those stormy eyes, the electric way my body reacts when they meet mine, the way they spread everything open.

They are not cruel eyes. Nor are they merciless or angry.

And I know as he meets my stare, as I search the aquamarine depths of his soul worn like drops of water round his irises, that it can't be him.

He might lie, but his eyes never could.

The tiny bubble of hope I'd allowed to fill my chest bursts.

"But," I whisper, gripping the knife so hard that spasms jolt up my arm, "I *need* you to be."

"Why?"

His face swims. My body sways.

"It had to be you." I gulp for air, but there doesn't seem to be any. My lungs constrict on themselves, and my heart races so quickly spots eat across my vision.

"Myra." August's voice distorts.

Lucy is going to die.

I cannot breathe.

Where is Mother? Why isn't she here to fix this?

I shudder, gasping for air.

"Myra!"

Something grips my shoulders, and I flail against it.

"Breathe!" August's voice is suddenly loud in my ears, and it jolts my vision clear.

He moves his hands from my shoulders to my face, cupping either side of it, holding my gaze steady with his.

"Breathe with me," he says, more quietly this time. And then he inhales slowly.

The dagger drops from my hand, clattering away on the floor, and I wrap my hands around his, grounding myself in them.

And I breathe.

Together, we stand in the sunlight.

In and out. In and out.

And slowly, ever so slowly, the tidal wave of panic and fear ebbs. Air fills my lungs, and my body sags.

"I'm sorry," I whisper after several moments.

"Never apologize for feeling your fear," August says, letting his hands fall to his sides. "Not to me." He pulls his chair out. "Sit down."

I totter into the seat and lean against his desk.

"What's going on, Myra? What happened to you? Why are you covered in blood?"

"It's Lucy," I say. "She's in some kind of sepsis or something. I thought if you were a Prodigy, if you were more powerful than me, you could help her."

"How long does she have?"

I shrug, and a sob escapes my lips. "She might already be gone. The nurse I hired said she only had hours."

"Did you take her to the hospital? Where is she? Was the money I gave you not enough?"

"I—" I swallow. "I was attacked last night on my way home from the party. I lost the money. We couldn't afford to take her to a doctor."

His eyes widen, and his eyes track across my face, pausing on the scrapes and bruises. "Artist."

"Lucy's at home. There's not much time."

"Let's go. I'll call a cab. I don't have any more money, but I'll get her into the hospital. Tell them it's government business. We'll worry about funds later."

"Thank you." I let him hoist me to my feet.

Poking his head into the hallway, he tugs me out of the

room. "Let's take the servants' passage. We'll be less likely to run into my parents there."

He leads the way down the corridor. When he opens the door to the passage, it is dark as night.

"That's odd," August says, stepping inside. I follow. "Why are the lanterns out?"

Something scrapes behind me, and I whirl.

There's no one there. Just the open door.

"Did you hear that?" I ask.

"Hello?" August says. "Who's there?"

The hall door slams shut, plunging us into darkness.

36

I reach for my belt, but the dagger is gone. I must have forgotten to retrieve it from where I dropped it in August's bedroom. August presses me behind him against the wall. "Show yourself," he says, his voice warbling.

A shadow moves toward us.

"Young Mister Harris." The voice raises the hairs on my arms. It's gravelly and deep and vaguely familiar.

"Nigel?" August says. "Where have you been? What's going on?"

"I saw someone sneak into your quarters with a knife," the cook says quietly.

"That was me," I say, trying to mask the unease in my voice. The hairs on my neck are still standing on end, and goose bumps ripple down my back. I remember the flash of fury I saw in the old cook's eyes that morning at breakfast, and the memory sends a shudder through me.

"August, you'd better return to your room." Nigel takes a step forward. "I'll make sure Miss Whitlock gets home."

"Thanks for the offer, but that won't be necessary." August's hand finds my wrist and wraps around it like a vise. "I appreciate your concern, but I have an urgent matter to take care of with Miss Whitlock. If you'll please excuse us…" He makes to lead me past the cook, but the old man steps in our way.

"Nigel…" August's warning, which I can tell is meant to be threatening, comes out raspy.

Nigel holds his ground. "Your father spoke to me last week about Miss Whitlock. I've been studying up on her, and I have reason to believe she might be a Prodigy. According to your father, whose opinion I value very much, that means she's dangerous."

August's laugh is high-pitched. "You of all people should understand what a paranoid fool my father is when it comes to magic."

"Paranoia and prudence are two sides of a very similar coin, son," Nigel says calmly. "Your father asked me to look after you. I'm only doing my job."

August's grip has gone sweaty, and I can feel the heat rolling off him. My own body is alive with tension and adrenaline.

"Why don't you head on back now? I'll take care of the girl."

"No," August says. "You're dismissed, Nigel."

The cook's teeth gleam, and they're the only thing I can see in his shadowed face. A predatory smile of bared white in a sea of night.

Could Nigel actually be dangerous? He's definitely frail and likely wouldn't hold up against us if we were to take off at a run, but he's also quite large. If he did manage to catch up to us, he'd take me down easily.

Every second that passes tightens the wire around my heart.

I'm so close to finally getting a doctor for Lucy.

"What do we do?" I whisper to August.

"I'll tell you what you do," Nigel says. "Go, August. If you leave now, I won't tell them. They'll never know you were here, never know you saw her. I'll even consider keeping what she is a secret from them."

"But—" I begin.

"What do you want from her?" August asks quietly. "What's in this for you?"

Nigel gives a laugh. "There's nothing in this for me, August. There's never anything in any of it for me when it comes to this family. You're all the same…you and your parents. You take and you take and you never consider what you're taking or who you're taking from."

"I…" August swallows. "I had no idea you felt that way."

"It doesn't matter. Go on, son. I'll make sure Miss Whitlock gets a cab and is safely on her way."

Something about the way he says the word *safely* makes my stomach twist.

August seems to sense the same thing, because he solidifies his stance. "No. Step out of our way, or I'll be forced to speak to my father about your position."

Nigel laughs, high and hard, and the sound fractures the enclosed space. "You aren't the only one who can make threats," he says. "How about I phrase it like this—leave the girl with me, or I will kill you both."

The air goes deadly silent as his words slither along the stone floors and shudder in the cobwebs hanging in the corners.

August lets go of my wrist. His whole body is trembling with the same fear and anxiety that's throbbing through my own system, but he raises his fists.

"You will not lay a finger on her."

Nigel moves lightning fast. A blade whines as it's wrenched from a sheath. Steel arcs through the air, and I barrel into August to knock him sideways. The cook's knife barely misses us as we topple into the stairs.

"Run!" I cry, scrabbling upright.

But August doesn't run. He jumps up, pulling the belt from his waist and snapping it through the air toward Nigel, who is advancing slowly, his hair hovering like a halo around his head. He dodges August's makeshift whip, somehow as lithe and quick as though he were a youth and not a bent-over old man, and slashes his knife toward August's face.

August ducks and pummels into his stomach, wrapping his arms around his torso and pinning him to the floor.

I wrench off my boot and totter forward.

August and Nigel are a tangle of limbs in the shadows. A mess of grunts and shouts and scuffs that echo along the stone floor. With a growl, August throws all of his weight against Nigel's right forearm, slamming it hard against the wall. The impact makes the cook roar. The dagger slips from his fingers and slides away down the hall.

But his hand knots in August's hair.

Now that I've got a free shot to Nigel's face, I hurl my boot with all of my strength. It hits him in the nose, and though my throw was feeble and likely didn't hurt, it shocks him just enough that August is able to land a punch to his jaw.

Nigel goes careening back, spitting blood.

August scrambles off him, wincing and shaking out his now-bleeding knuckles. "Please. I don't want to fight you. Let us go."

But the cook dives for August's legs, wrenching them out from underneath him. I scream as August's head slams against the bottom stair. He crumples and goes still.

"August!" I leap toward him on limbs that won't move fast enough and press my fingers to his neck. His pulse is warm and steady under my touch, and I let out an exhale of pure relief. The shine of wet blood trickles down his forehead.

But he's alive.

Footsteps approach behind me, and I whirl, backing up until I'm pressed against the wall.

"That was a lot messier than I intended for it to be," Nigel says, straightening to his full height. "I did not expect him to fight for you like that—he's much more the turn-tail-and-run-screaming type."

"No, he's not," I snap.

My boot is still behind Nigel on the ground, but I doubt I'd be able to get to it from here, so I brace myself and try not to think about what might happen next.

"What do you want from me?" I ask.

He retrieves the discarded knife and pulls his uniform jacket aside to slip the blade into its sheath at his belt. The jacket falls back into place, covering him, but for an instant I catch a flash of the clothing he has on underneath. Black, expensive-looking fabric with gold embroidery. I've never seen him in anything but the chef's uniform, but I certainly never imagined him to be the type of man who would wear something like *that*. The Harrises must pay him well.

"What do you want from me?" I repeat, grinding each word out through my teeth. Every moment he wastes is another that Lucy does not have. "Whatever it is, you can have it. I just need to get my sister to the hospital. Once she's taken care of, you can do with me as you wish."

"What do I want from you?" He smiles, a beastly expression of too many teeth and glinting, hungry eyes. "Come and see, Miss Whitlock. I think you'll quite like what I have to show you."

And then he's upon me, pressing a wet cloth to my nose until the world winks out.

37

"Myra?" A familiar voice jerks me from somewhere cold and quiet. I jolt, scrambling away from the figure leaning over me.

"Let go of me!" I shriek, pressing my back to a wall.

The figure raises its hands in surrender. "I'm sorry. I didn't mean to frighten you."

I squint as his face comes into focus. Dark eyes, manicured beard, long, slender fingers.

"Vincent?" I look around. I'm against the wall next to the wardrobe in that room we found on the fifth floor of Rose Manor. Governor Harris's demon painting glares down at me quiet and watching and lethal. "Where'd Nigel go? How did you find us?" My heart pounds. "Oh, Artist. August! We have to get back to him!"

"How's your head?" Vincent asks, reaching a hand toward my temple where the hard knot from earlier still throbs. His fingers are soft. "It's swollen."

I grasp his wrist. "Vincent. August could be hurt. And Nigel—"

"I took care of the cook. You don't need to worry about him anymore."

"You…" The casual finality in his tone makes my skin prickle. I watch his face with a sudden trepidation. Vincent has only ever showed kindness to me, but I hardly know him. Given his illegal work and the types of criminals he must associate with, there's no telling what he could mean or what he might be capable of. I force my voice steady. "Vincent, what did you do to him?"

Vincent gets to his feet, crossing to a cupboard in the corner and digging through the bottles and boxes inside. He sorts through the contents with confidence, as though he knows precisely where to find what he's looking for.

I get to my feet. "I'm going back for August. He—"

"He'll be fine."

"Where is he?"

"Still at the bottom of the stairs unconscious. He'll wake soon enough."

I frown. "But—"

"I promise he's okay. I checked on him, made sure he was all right, got him all situated. I have a few things I need to tell you about first, and then we can go back for him."

Scrubbing the hair out of my eyes, I relent. "Fine. What is it?"

With a sigh, he tugs out a bit of cloth from the cupboard and dumps a clear liquid onto it from a small glass bottle. "I'm not sure where to start." He approaches me, raising the dampened cloth to my wound. It's cold, and the chemical bubbles audibly on contact.

I hiss as it stings, but I let him continue, meeting his gaze straight on. "We don't have time. Lucy's dying, and August—"

"I lied to you," he cuts in. "I'm so, terribly sorry." His other hand comes to cup my jaw. "I won't keep anything from you again, I swear it."

"What lie?"

"I told you last week that I'd like to try painting someday, but I already have. I've been painting since I was a child."

"That's hardly something you need to keep a secret from me, Vince."

He winces, and his hand stills against my face.

"I'm sorry, do you not like to be called that?" I ask.

"No, I do. It's just—" He swallows. "That wasn't my only lie."

I wait for him to go on, but he drops his gaze from mine, pulling the cloth away from my temple and twisting it between his fingers.

"Art has been my escape for as long as I can remember," he says quietly. As he speaks, his tone softens into something almost wistful. "When I'm working on a piece, everything else seems to fade away. Almost like reality is only as limited as my imagination." He glances at me. "Is it like that for you, too?"

I nod, trying to dodge a look at the clock across the room. "I don't really see what that has to do with—"

"Of course, you had your mother to teach you," Vincent continues. "You grew up in a home where art was celebrated. I wasn't. I had to hide it from everyone. But…" He smooths the cloth on his palm, staring at the designs my blood has made on its surface. "Even in spite of my restrictions, it did not take me long to realize I was different. That I could *do* things with my art. Change people."

I blink. "You're a Prodigy?"

He steals a glance at me, an almost bashful smile tugging at his lips. "When I discovered the magic, it was like this huge weight had been lifted from my back. Finally I meant something. Finally I wasn't a new version of my father, set to do only the things he did, able to only live up to his accomplishments. There was a power that I was master of, not a power I got by default simply by being born to the right parents."

"Who was your father? What did he want you to do?" I'm getting twitchy, praying he can spit out all that he wants to tell me so that I can go to August and get back to Lucy.

But it's like I haven't spoken. His eyes gleam white, reflecting the tiny sliver of light coming from under the door in a way that makes him look possessed. "This world has treated me as though I'm nothing more than a reincarnation of my father since the day of my birth. It's the name they care for, not who I am. They won't let me be anyone but who they've planned for me to be, won't allow me to make my own way, won't give me the space to build my own life. So I turned to my painting, to my magic. It was the one thing that made me different. The one thing I had total control over. With it, I had the power to build the exact success my father had. Not to inherit it, but to *win* it."

"I'm not sure I'm following you, Vincent."

"That's when I started the forgeries," he goes on. "It began as a few jobs here and there, a means to earn enough coins to pay for the paints and canvas and things without my father knowing. But I found I was good at it, found that I liked being a forger. Living two lives like that wasn't easy, but it was enough for me for a time. Until I met her."

"Her?"

"I knew from the moment I met Ameline that she would change my life." He moves to sit next to me, tipping his head back against the wall and looking up at the ceiling. "I'd never seen anyone more beautiful. She was everything to me." His expression sours. "But my father would never hear of it. She was a servant, and I was destined for bigger things."

He turns his gaze to mine.

"That's when I really threw myself into the forgeries and started to make a name for myself as a businessman. I figured if I could build a successful life that depended on no one but me, I could choose how I wanted to live it. Choose who I wanted to spend it with."

The voice of the old man in the elevator echoes in my mind. *Where do lovers clasp their hands?*

And the answer: *At the Old Sawthorne.*

I think of the note we found in Ameline's quarters. *Tomorrow night. Midnight. Make sure you aren't followed.*

Old Sawthorne must have been some kind of meeting place for them, somewhere they could escape to be together.

That rainy night, when the clock's hands had met and the bells clanged midnight, Ameline had been there waiting for Vincent, hadn't she?

"I'm sorry." I make to get up. "I really have to get back to my sister—"

His hand clamps on my arm, locking me in place. "But then, a little over a year and a half ago, I accidentally got her pregnant," he goes on, his eyes glassy. "And I've never been so simultaneously overjoyed and terrified in my life. She kept telling me it was time to leave my family for good, but I wasn't ready."

"Vincent, you're hurting me." I dig my fingers against his grip, trying to pull my arm out from his grasp.

"Then," he says, "one night when she was only in her sixth month, she and I were fighting about it again, and she started bleeding."

I stop yanking on his hand and stare up at his face, which has gone deathly pale.

"Artist, there was so much blood," he whispers. "We needed to get her to the hospital. But I was a fool. I was too concerned with the possibility of being seen by someone who would tell my family. I took too long to take her in. I needed time to put on a disguise so no one would recognize me."

My mouth is dry, my desperation to get back to August and Lucy paused for just a moment at the thought of a pregnant Ameline bleeding in the night. "What happened?"

"The baby came in the street on our way to the hospital." Tears gather in the corners of his eyes, but he paws them away with his fist. "He never cried."

"Vincent." I touch his arm. "Artist, I'm so sorry."

He sniffs, shaking his head. "It was my fault. I shouldn't have hesitated."

"No. You made a mistake. That doesn't mean it was your fault."

"If we'd gotten to a doctor in time, Silas wouldn't have died." He finally releases my arm and covers his face with his palms, shoulders shaking.

I need to get back to Lucy, but my heart aches as I watch him weep. I push up onto my knees and pull him into my arms. He wraps his own around me, burying his face into my shoulder.

Tears sting at my eyes as I imagine what that night must have been like for him. In the dark, alone with their fear as they wept over their stillborn child.

"It broke her," he says quietly against my neck. "Ameline was never the same after that. I should have done as she said, abandoned my parents and that life long before. Then she wouldn't have had to hide the pregnancy or belt down her belly so my father wouldn't see. She would have been able to get proper medical care." He sucks in a breath, pulling back. "Silas would have survived."

His cheeks shine wet, and his eyes are fierce and rimmed in red. "I've never felt so useless in my life as I have been the past year watching Ameline become a shadow of what she once was."

"I'm sorry," I say. "That must have been awful."

"There's never going to be a future for Ameline and me anymore. I destroyed my chances of that. But I still care for her, and I'm going to fix this. So she can move on with her life. Be happy, even if it's with someone else."

"How?"

He offers me a sad, tearstained smile. "I'm a Prodigy. My magic is the same magic the Artist Himself wielded when He built the world, when He painted mankind into existence. If the Artist could create life with His paintbrush, then I should be able to, too."

My eyes widen as his words register. "You want to create life?"

"Not just any life. Silas. I want to re-create my child, bring back the son that Ameline was meant to have. That's why I need you."

38

Vincent's eyes are wide and bright and determined. He puts his hands on my shoulders. "Don't you see? Ameline doesn't have to feel that loss anymore. Not if you help me. We'll combine our power. It will work. It has to!"

I stare at him. "Vincent, I don't think…"

He shakes his head. "No. It *will* work. I need it to work. I can't be the reason for her pain anymore. I can't bear it." His expression breaks. "Please help me. Please."

His words echo in my head to the beat of my heart as he looks at me, desperate with those wet cheeks and red-rimmed eyes. Lifting my hand, I press my palm to the side of his face. "I want to help, Vincent, I do. But I'm not sure… Even if this magic is possible, which I honestly doubt, I don't think this will fix it."

His mouth thins.

"It's only that…even if you were to create a baby some-how out of nothing—and I don't know how you would do that—but if you did, and even if it looked exactly like Silas, it…" I take a deep breath. "It wouldn't be the baby you lost."

He draws away from my hand. "You won't help me."

"No, I do want to help," I plead, trying to take his hands in mine, but he yanks out of my grasp. "I just don't think it would erase Ameline's pain. She still lost her son. Giving her a new child wouldn't undo what happened to her. Losing someone changes you fundamentally."

"You don't think I know that?" he snaps, glaring at the floor. "He was *my* son, too."

"Of course he was. And of course you'd want him back." Tears are running freely down my cheeks now. "What you're trying to do is good and noble, but I don't think it will fix what's been broken."

He continues to stare hard at the floor, his jaw working. A vein pulses in his temple as he kneads his knuckles against his knees. But he doesn't speak.

"Vincent?" I whisper, ducking lower in an attempt to make eye contact. "Vince?"

"I should have known you wouldn't help," he says, his voice quiet and cold as steel. "I thought you would be different. I thought you would understand."

"I do understand. Please…"

He stands and finally makes eye contact, and I shrink away. Where his eyes were kind and pleading before, they burn hot with fury now.

"Fine. If you're not going to give me what I want, I'll have to take it for myself."

"What?"

He reaches into his jacket pocket and extracts a wire. "Hold still."

Panic ignites in my chest as he approaches me. "What are you doing?"

His lip curls as he reaches for me.

"No!" I bolt past him, yank the door open, and dash into

the hallway, but I make it only halfway down the corridor before Vincent's hands wrap around my forearms and pin them behind my back.

I lift my one booted foot and jam my heel hard into his groin. He hisses, pinching my arms tighter, so I muster up my strength and land another solid hit.

This time, his grip slackens barely enough for me to get a hand free, and I fling an elbow into his nose.

He growls, and hot, wet blood spurts against the side of my face. I wrench my arms loose and sprint.

His footsteps are loud behind me, and they pound in syncopation to the rush of my heart. The walls rattle, and dust plumes around my feet as I run. Light shafts in through moth-eaten curtains, shimmering in twitching cobwebs, filtering among sparkling motes in the air.

I've nearly reached the other end of the landing when Vincent slams into me from behind, knocking me flat into the dank carpet. A silver chain with three pendants hanging from it drops out of his collar and smacks against my injured temple, and I wince.

I ram my head back into his still-bleeding nose. Pain punches through my skull, reverberating with a ringing sound loud and shrill enough to shatter glass. He howls.

Yanking out from under him, I dash forward, but he jerks me by my hair, flinging me back the way we came. I scramble to my feet and dive up the corridor into the painting room, slamming the door and sprinting for the window. Remembering the thick vines I saw outside before, I drag the curtains back. I should be able to climb down. As long as I can get this window open... Sunlight sears my eyes, making them water as I fumble with the latch.

The door bangs open behind me, and I scream. But my hands are shaking too hard, and my head is pounding too loudly. I barely manage to get the window up a few inches before Vincent drags me backward by my hair once more. He shoves me to the ground and yanks my arms behind me. I cry out, straining against his grip, but it's no use. I am too weak.

He ties the wire around my wrists, and its edges slice deep into my skin. I grit my teeth as he pulls me upright and steers me to the wall where the four Harrises stare down at us from their portraits. As he slides the corner of the one of Will to the side, a small latch appears. He twists it and then pushes, and the whole panel with all four portraits recedes a few inches. With a grunt, he shoves the panel sideways, and it slides cleanly away, revealing a small, secondary room.

The smell of copper fills my nose as Vincent pushes me inside. The light from the window casts across crimson stains on the floor, a horrible continuation of the smear August and I found earlier. Dread bubbles into my throat, and I try not to choke on it as he maneuvers me to the opposite wall and attaches the wire around my hands to a hook. He then crouches, pulling out another length of wire and cinching it around my ankles until they're secure.

"There. That should keep you," he mutters, turning away and dusting his hands like he's rid himself of a nuisance.

"Please..." I rasp. "My sister..." Tears begin to roll down my cheeks again, and I do nothing to stop them. My nose drips down my upper lip, but my wrists are knotted so tight in the wire I cannot wipe it. All I can think of is Lucy and how she's going to die and how I'm not going to be there to hold her hand. Sobs choke through my mouth, tearing their way out of my chest and shredding my throat raw.

This is it. I have finally and truly failed my sister. Failed the magic Mother gave me. The only thing that made me special turned out to be my demise in the end.

And I'm not even going to get to say goodbye.

Vincent crosses to a closet against the opposite wall and retrieves a canvas, a bundle of paintbrushes, and some tubes of paint. Then he looks at me and shakes his head.

"It's like déjà vu seeing you there. You look almost exactly the way your mother did."

My head snaps up. "What?"

He shrugs as he sorts through his brushes until he finds the one he wants.

His simple statement screams in my ears, ripping through me, shredding my insides raw.

"She...she was here?" I lurch for him, and the wires dig deeper into my arms, slicing through my skin. Blood, hot and wet and sticky, slicks into my palms and drips from my fingers.

My thoughts stray to the journal August and I found here earlier and that sketch of the woman with her head splayed open.

I raise my gaze to meet Vincent's, the blood draining from my face.

"What did you do to her?" I whisper.

He looks at me, and the anger on his face cracks. "I'm so sorry, Myra," he whispers. "I always do this. Every time I care about someone, I find some way to destroy them."

My heart splinters. "Where is she?"

His Adam's apple bobs, and he turns away, digging his paintbrush a little too forcefully into a pile of yellow ochre paint on his palette. "I never meant to hurt her. That's the honest truth. When I first began to suspect she was a Prodigy, I only went to talk to her. I thought maybe she'd be willing to answer my questions without a fuss." He smears the paint onto the canvas with his teeth gritted. "But she made it difficult. Avoided me. Lied and said she didn't know what I was talking about. Had me removed from the studio and banned from returning." His forehead creases as he speaks, and his voice cracks. "I told her how desperate I was, how much I needed her help, but she was selfish. Uncaring."

I remember the terror in Mother's voice when she told Father that someone had been coming around the studio asking after her magic, and the pain in my chest intensifies.

"When I took her, I still didn't mean to harm her," he goes on. "I only wanted to show her how serious my situation was." His mouth twists, and he pauses painting to meet my eye. His gaze crawls through me, cold as ice. "She was cruel. No matter what I said, she wouldn't listen. If she'd only told me what I needed to know, done her part, she wouldn't have had to get hurt."

"What did you want from her?" I ask.

"First it was her knowledge," he replies. "Then, when she refused to give me that, it was her power."

I puzzle through his words, my whole body aching. Try as I might, I cannot put the pieces together. None of it makes sense.

"I'm sure you understand well the effects of healing other people with your magic," he goes on. "Taking on the pain of their injuries, the emotional turmoil, that kind of thing. It's impressive you were willing to absorb the agony of a fall from a fourth-story balcony in order to save your sister. She must be really special."

I squeeze my eyes shut, wishing I could block out his words. They rock through me like kicks to the gut.

"But did your mother ever teach you that that little aspect of our magic—that we take on the sevren we paint away from other people—works differently when you're painting a Prodigy?" He squirts a dollop of ladyrose gel onto his palette.

The journal I found here—Vincent's journal?—had said as much, but I don't respond.

"Don't feel bad if she kept that from you," he says. "She didn't seem particularly keen to tell me about it, either. I sort of discovered it on my own. When I tried to paint her the first time."

The paintings—the horrific, contorted people illustrated all over the room behind him—come into focus, and my head goes light. Horror chokes through every vein, every nerve. I jerk so hard that pain splits through my wrists, and more blood dribbles into my palms. "You painted her?" I feel like I'm screaming the words, but they come out the barest of breaths, like the daggered wind over an expanse of ice.

"Yes. I wanted to try a few of old Bertram Harris's tricks to get her to tell me what I needed to know. It seemed like that tactic would be cleaner. I wouldn't have to get my hands dirty."

I feel like I'm going to pass out.

"My first attempt was to paint her foot twisted. I did the portrait, and my body took on the sensation of how her foot felt before I changed it—apparently she stood a lot, because my foot developed this constant, dull pain, like I was wearing bad shoes or hadn't sat down in days. Only problem was, that ache never went away." His eyes glitter in the sunlight. "All of the sevren I'd painted away from her had become a part of me, and every sensation I felt in my foot was compounded by the doubled sevren. I waited a few hours for it to fade, but it never did. Even now, it throbs."

I gape at him, not quite comprehending, not sure I even want to.

"That's when I realized that it must be different with Prodigies. When your body takes away their sevren, you actually physically gain them yourself. Their sevren are compatible with your own because you are a Prodigy, as well." He purses his lips, mixing ladyrose gel into the colors with his palette knife. "So I got an idea. See, I'd been studying Prodigies for years, ever since I'd learned I was one. There's not a lot of information out there, but I did learn that Prodigy magic comes from a small nest of sevren in the brain called the fervora. The magic is quite literally tied to a physical part of the body. One that I could paint if I wanted. Or remove."

I stare at him. "You painted away her magic. You stole it from her."

"It took me several tries to do it, but I got it right in the end." He sets down his palette and approaches me, his shoulders hunched like he's almost afraid. Each step scrapes across the floor until he crouches in front of me. When he speaks again, his voice is barely a breath. "I'm afraid that was what killed her. Apparently, Prodigies cannot live without their fervorae. I didn't know it would do that." He lifts his gaze to mine, and his eyes glimmer with more tears. "Words can't express how sorry I am, Myra."

"No." I shake my head, my voice quavering. "No, she's not dead. She can't be."

He pinches the bridge of his nose, squeezing his eyes shut. "Please forgive me."

I scream, lurching for him. The wires on my wrists dig in deeper, and agony daggers up my arms. I arch my back, sinking to my knees as sobs tear through me.

Mother is not coming back.

I cave in. The feeble parts of my soul that have been keeping me upright, keeping me fighting, crumble.

I'm falling.

Everything hurts.

Mother.

"There's something else," Vincent whispers.

I hiccup, wheezing. "You killed him, too, didn't you? My father."

"He found me when I was disposing of her body," he says. "I swear to the Artist, Myra, I never meant to hurt either of them. But he was going to take me to the police. He would have had me locked up forever. And then your mother would have died for nothing."

I collapse, hanging by my bleeding wrists.

Vincent's fingers brush the hair away from my face. "Please know I never meant for anyone to get hurt. I just wanted to bring my son back."

I jerk out of his grasp, curling my knees up to my chest and burying my face in them.

"Myra?" he whispers.

They're gone.

Dead.

"Please," he says. "Say something."

Opening my eyes, I lift my chin slowly until my gaze is level with his. Tears course down my cheeks. I let them fall, let them soak into my collar with the blood and the paint. "Go to hell."

He recoils as though slapped and turns away from me, crossing on leaden feet back to his canvas and palette. With quaking hands, he picks up the brushes and takes his place behind the easel, gritting his teeth as he continues his portrait.

"If she had only been willing to help me, I wouldn't have had to take her fervora," he says. "Just like I wouldn't have to take yours now."

"All of those artists who disappeared…was that you, too?"

He nods once. "Even with your mother's power, I still wasn't able to create the baby. So I thought maybe there were more Prodigies I could take from. Or maybe if there weren't full-blown Prodigies, maybe some of the other painters in town would have trace amounts of magic or small fervorae I could use. But after I'd done portraits of several of them in an attempt to find out, I realized it wasn't helping. Your Ms. Moore had been the next one I planned to paint, but by that point I realized I was wasting my time."

"Did you kill Elsie, too?"

His frown deepens. "It was, again, an unfortunate turn of events that led to her death. Initially when you showed up here at the estate, I didn't pay attention to you. It wasn't until later when you and August came to my office that I finally looked at you and realized you had to be Lavinia's daughter. I decided to do some digging, so I paid Elsie a little visit. She was most uncooperative."

Every sentence bludgeons through me, skewering me to the wall. I can't move, can't breathe. I can't even blink. My eyes are fixed on his face, on the syllables of each word as they drop like daggers from his lips.

He killed Mother and Father. He killed Elsie. He is the reason Lucy and I were left alone to fend for ourselves in this world. The reason we ran out of funds and couldn't afford medicine or a doctor when Lucy's illness got bad. The reason I have no income to live on. The reason for all our pain.

And I trusted him, let him into my life, told him my secrets.

There's still one final piece of the puzzle I don't quite know what to do with. "Did you kill Will, too?" I ask.

"No, I didn't kill Will," he says, setting down his brush. "I killed Nigel."

"What?"

"Things got messy," he says slowly. "I've had to keep this forgery business a secret from my father, and I've been very careful with my disguises. But one morning before dawn, when I was sneaking back home, Nigel saw me changing out of my disguise. I had to kill him. He was too loyal to my father. He would have ratted me out in an instant, and that would have been the end of everything I'd spent so long building."

"Wait…" I stare at him. "You're not…?"

"You're finally catching on." He fishes in his collar, tugging out the silver chain with its three pendants. It matches exactly the necklace the cook wore that morning at breakfast when the governor scolded him. Pulling one of the small, cylindrical shapes out so it glimmers in the light, Vincent digs a thumbnail into some invisible seam, and it pops open, baring a small furled piece of parchment. He takes that out with careful fingers and flattens it, unfolding it and turning it over for me to see.

On it is a careful illustration of the man in front of me, complete with the perfectly styled beard, the dark hair, the thick lashes.

Then he opens another one of the pendants and pulls out another portrait. Instead of showing it to me, he settles his palm over its center and closes his eyes.

His skin ripples and begins to drip like linseed oil. The colors morph and twist, careful brushstrokes sliding, sweeping into new shapes, new colors. My heart skitters in my chest as the man before me grows taller, as his hair lightens, as his nose lengthens and his skin ages. Pale, wizened eyes gleam at me as his form solidifies. His dark, gold-trimmed clothing stretches taut over the taller, broader body.

"Recognize me, Myra?"

"Nigel," I whisper.

"This disguise has been quite useful the past two weeks," he says, shuffling on his chain to the third pendant. "But as for who I really am…" He unfurls his final painting, presses his palm to its surface, and his body liquefies once more. The white hair reddens. His wrinkled skin smooths and bleeds freckles. His cheekbones rise, and his eyes lighten as his body narrows.

When his features have settled, he gives me a slight tip of the head.

"Wilburt Harris Jr., at your service."

39

"You're not dead," I say, my breath leaving me in a rush.

"How observant of you to notice."

"Then the body was... Nigel?"

Will grimaces. "I actually liked that old man a lot. It was just a very unfortunate circumstance."

"Unfortunate circumstance..." I echo.

"It wasn't a premeditated thing. Like I said, he caught me in the middle of changing from Vincent back into my normal form, so I reacted. We were out by the kitchen exit. He'd come out to dump the remnants of a pig he'd just finished carving, and he had a knife right there on the platter. I grabbed it and..."

"So he *was* stabbed," I say.

"I figured it was the perfect way for me to disappear. I could finally leave that horrid life my parents had all planned out for me and be Vincent full-time. I was ready to step away from being Wilburt Harris Jr. Nigel delivered me his body to use to do so. I altered it to look like mine using my magic, added in the injuries to make it look like he'd fallen from the balcony, switched clothes with him, covered up the knife wound with some new skin…"

"The knife wound was still there."

He blinks. "What?"

I nod, my nerves zinging, my brain whirring. "Yeah, it was the oddest wound… It looked like he'd been stabbed, but there was no blood."

Will frowns. "Damn. I knew I should have been more thorough with it. See, I didn't bother to paint back together the wound internally—I just put new skin over the top of it. It must have split back open."

My thoughts stray to the faint black ink smears on the bottom of his shirt, the marks I thought had come from August's fingers when I'd believed he was the one who had done it. The ink must have come from Will's work as Vincent.

Then there was the clothing I found in the closet—the cook's uniform, ripped across the chest and covered in blood. He must have been wearing that when Will stabbed him. And then Will altered his body and, once he'd exchanged clothes with the dead body, stuffed the bloody uniform away to worry about later. Which explains how the chunk of the wax got into Nigel-turned-Will's pocket, as well.

"And then," I say, putting the final pieces together, "the governor called Vincent to cover up the death with a forgery."

He chuckles. "Ironic, right? Covering up my own cover-up with another lie." His smile fades into a scowl. "I should have expected behavior like that from my father—trying to make sure even his own son's death reflected as positively on him as possible—but it still hurt. Instead of mourning me, the first thing he did was figure out how to spin the story for his campaign. I loathe that man." He mops at his face and turns back to his painting. "Anyway. Enough of that. I've got a portrait to do."

I watch him work, watch the furrow in his brow, the clench of his jaw, the focus in his eyes. The fervor there, the hope, the desperation.

I know that feeling so well, the sensation of making something meaningful. Of imbuing life into something. It made me feel like a god, like I mattered. Like all of my failures and all of the ways I'd come up short could be painted away with a simple sweep of my paintbrush.

This is how I must have looked last night as I painted my sister, trying desperately to control what had become so out of control. Trying to take away the pain from the one I loved.

We are not too different from each other, Will and I. Both of us railing against the role our circumstances have forced us into. Both of us ashamed of the ways we come up short of the expectations placed upon us. Both of us turning to the magic of artistry as an escape, a release.

Both of us fighting, eternally fighting, to help someone we care about.

Yes, Will and I are the same.

The blood on my wrists slicks over my fingers. I rub my thumb and forefinger together, feeling the sticky wet between them, and ponder.

I could paint Wilburt. Here. Now. On the wall behind me with my own blood, I could paint away his fervora, take on his power as well as Mother's. With both of their magic added to mine, I might finally be strong enough, powerful enough, to heal Lucy's sepsis.

But even as the thought takes hold, as I press my fingers against the dusty plaster behind me, I pause.

If I did this, would I be so very different from the murderer sitting across from me now? He told me that taking my mother's fervora had killed her.

Am I so much like him that I would be willing to do that?

My sevren tingle as I look at Will.

I think of Mother. Of her kind eyes, soft face, gentle laugh. She, who always taught me to trust and love and hope for the good in others, would never want me to hurt him, no matter what he's done.

And I don't want to, either.

The words from her journal entry trickle through my mind.

I'm beginning to realize my magic isn't dependent upon how well I render an image or how thorough I am at getting all the details right. It seems like it could be more based on trusting my magic to know what it needs to do. Allowing my magic to be the one to control an outcome. Accepting it as part of me, an extension of my instincts.

Maybe that's what's been happening to me. Why the more I've used my magic, the more it hurts. Why I've failed time and time again. I have never viewed it as part of myself. Never trusted it.

I think of what August said that night on the balcony. *You and your sister don't have to bear everything alone.*

I've been fighting so hard for so long, clinging desperately to the things I can control.

Perhaps it's time to accept that there are things I cannot and never will be able to control. And maybe it's time to stop punishing myself for those things.

Maybe it's time to let my magic do its own work.

August proved to me I could trust him.

Maybe it's time to trust my magic, too.

I press my forefinger into the wrist of my other hand, coating it in more blood, and begin my painting of Will. This time, instead of tamping my magic back until I'm ready for it, I let it flow through me, let it guide my painting. I'm not quite sure what it wants me to do, but I choose to trust it. I hold my chin high, gazing at Will head-on, trying to keep the fear out of my eyes and the tears from spilling down my cheeks. I watch the way his brow furrows as he works, the way he pins his tongue carefully between his teeth.

I've never tried my magic with such a rudimentarily done painting, but if my mother was able to use hers drawing stick figures in a pile of flour, then this is worth a shot.

"Why did you hire me?" I ask, praying that keeping Will talking will slow down his progress on that portrait so I'll have enough time to complete my own. "As Vincent, I mean. If you wanted my fervora, and you already knew I was a Prodigy, why not do what you did to Mother and kidnap me?"

"I was well on my way to doing just that, actually. You climbed into my carriage willingly, and we were halfway here that first night. But then when you offered to do the portrait for me, it made me pause." He frowns. "I learned my lesson with your mother, didn't I? She never told me about you or your sister. It struck me that it was possible there were other things she hadn't let on even when I was being...persuasive. Besides, you know how our magic is. It does its best work when we know as much about the sevren we're working with as possible.

"I needed to be able to understand exactly how you likely associated with your magic, how you felt about it, the kinds of things you used it for. So when you said you could do the portrait for my office, I got the idea that perhaps I should try a different tactic with you. See how much I could get you to tell me if you believed I was your ally. And while we never discussed your magic outright, the things you told me about your sister, about your family, about yourself...well, with that information, I've been able to fill in the gaps and surmise enough."

I think of all of the intimate details about myself and Lucy I told him last night, and I feel faint.

"I'm afraid I did let myself get a bit carried away with the theatrics..." He smiles sadly, eyes flicking in my direction. "The people chasing you in the streets on those two different occasions? The man I hired to watch your apartment? I thought you'd trust me even more if I saved your life. If you considered me as a sort of protector."

Humiliation, shame, and anger fill me with fire, and I channel that into the bloody painting on the wall behind me. My fervora flickers to life as I finish the first layer.

A bubble of hope fills in my chest. That spark of magic means it's working so far.

I give the blood a few moments to dry, coating my fingers in more. As I begin the second layer, I draw on every ache, every frustration, every tear shed—all the things that have fueled me. All the things that have fueled Will.

I hardly know him, but I know precisely how he feels about his magic because it's how I feel about mine. Weak and worn, powerful and proud. I let my magic flow through every one of those emotions.

My heart gallops against my ribs, and fatigue and hunger drag me down. But I press on. This is my last chance, the only hope I have left. It has to work.

I can tell Will is getting close to finishing his own portrait. He keeps pausing to step back and survey it before adding in the last few details.

I'm close, too. Only a few more strokes of blood, and my portrait of Wilburt Harris Jr. should be complete.

Will throws down his paintbrush an instant later with a grimace. "All done." He rolls up his sleeves. And then his eyes catch on the awkward angle of my arms. "What are you doing?"

"Nothing." I sweep my thumb along the wall one last time as panic jolts through my limbs. Now I just need to—

He leaps across the space, yanking me away from the wall. I screech as the wire digs so deeply into my wrists that fresh blood spatters the floor.

"What is this?" he roars.

My rudimentary drawing glistens red in the sunlight. Because it was done in blood and not oils, it's difficult to tell exactly what it is, but I watch as Will's eyes pick out the image of a brain with a fervora nestled snugly at its base. Intact, but with its bonds to the sevren in the rest of his body sliced through, cutting his magic's power off from use.

It looks like a rose, unfurled and alizarin, dripping thorns like daggers beneath its petals.

Like Will has been. Hiding a killer beneath hypnotic eyes and a charming smile.

He lifts an arm to wipe the painting from the wall.

"No!" I cry, pulling the wire free of the hook and launching myself at him before he can. I loop my bound hands in front of his face and pull so the wire and my wrists are taut across his throat. Pain lances through my tendons, but I grit my teeth and pull harder. He stumbles, and I nearly topple sideways, but I dig my heels—one still missing its boot—into the ground. The wire on my ankles slices to the bone, but I hold my stance.

He claws at me, dragging his fingernails against my bare wrists and hands.

But I don't feel it.

Desperation and fury fill my body with flame. This boy will not destroy what's left of my family. I won't let him.

A flash of steel glints, and a searing pain slices along my forearm where I was cut last night, but much deeper this time. I cry out, and he wrenches my hands up over his head. I hit the ground hard, hissing as my blood streams everywhere. I make to scramble to my feet, but my bound ankles make me clumsy. His fist connects with the side of my head, and stars explode across my vision as my face slams into the crimson-stained floor.

He waits for me to move, but I cannot. My whole body seems to be made of lead. An ocean rushes in my ears, and it sounds like a thousand Lucys. *I love you, Myra*, they say over the top of one another, louder and louder until my mind is a cacophony of sound, of pain.

"Why couldn't you cooperate?" Will wheezes, getting to his feet and sheathing his dagger. "We could have been everything together."

I lift my head and spit at his feet.

He turns away as my vision swims. The sound of his boots on the floorboards pound in my head like a hammer as he returns across the room.

I force my eyes open, but flashes of white stab through everything. My mind is going foggy, fading to nothing. I cling desperately to consciousness with my fingernails.

Will's face swims before me. The shadow of his arm moves as he settles his hand into the center of his portrait.

With a scream, I wrench myself up.

"No!" Will cries as my palm connects with the blood painting on the wall.

Magic cascades up my arm in icy ripples. And I let it. Instead of forcing it back, I allow it to course through me, a frigid, electric current to fill my soul. My hand is fused to the wall as though it has frozen in place. I am a crystallized statue of blood and ice.

Rough hands wrap around my waist and yank me back, flinging me into the corner of the room.

But the magic is still ripping through me, thawing suddenly hot like a wildfire.

My head fills with a thunderous buzzing sound, and my fervora ignites.

It rises and rises until I am nothing but a snapping ball of power.

I yearn to control it, to tell it what to do and where to go.

But it already knows.

I have to trust it.

And so I let it build. I give it free rein of the painting in my mind's eye, of every sevren in my body.

My limbs quake. My ears roar. Magic burns through me, melting me like ladyrose petals.

And then it releases, and I collapse.

I squint through tears and black spots to see what has happened to Will.

"No," he breathes, tearing across the room to his portrait. "No!" He presses his hand to the canvas, squeezes his eyes shut. His jaw tenses. His fingers curl.

Then his eyes open and find mine. Despair and rage battle in them.

"What have you done?" he whispers.

"Now you…you can't hurt…anyone else," I wheeze.

"What have you done?" he screams, lunging for me. He wrenches me up by the throat and slams me against the wall. My body dangles uselessly in his grasp. I dig at his viselike grip, gasping for air, but none will come.

He glares hard at me, tears streaming down his cheeks.

"Why?" he sobs through his teeth. "I just wanted to bring Silas back. To give Ameline hope again."

I buck against him as smoke eats away my vision. Agony gnaws through my chest, but I grit my teeth and push it back.

My heartbeat thuds in my throat, a fluttering beat to the roar of a thousand Lucys screaming in my head.

But there's another voice, too. Shouting. Somewhere far away.

"Myra!"

"August," I rasp. Digging my fingernails so hard into Will's hands he hisses, I try again, louder this time. "August!"

40

Will grimaces, jamming his fingers harder into my wind-pipe, cutting off my cries. I cannot breathe. The room goes dark.

All I see is Lucy's tired face nestled in a knot of tangled brown hair, sunken in a pillow waiting for me.

Will weeps.

I stop kicking.

Too heavy.

Too much pain.

A banging sound punches through my skull, and Will's hand is wrenched away from my neck. I hit the floor, gasping, retching, coughing. My throat shreds itself raw sucking in air.

August and Will are a tangle of limbs, and then a sickening crunch fills the room, and Will hits the floor with a heavy thud.

August lets out a string of curses and dives for me.

"Artist, you're bleeding everywhere," he says, tearing a section from the bottom of his shirt and wrapping it tight around my forearm. Scarlet soaks through the cotton and stains his fingers. He gets to work untying the wires on my wrists and ankles. "How are you feeling?"

I try to form words, but everything is thick and fuzzy, and my throat is still convulsing. It's all I can do to keep my head upright. "Great…" I finally manage.

More voices echo from the hallways. Loud, angry voices.

"August Lloyd Harris, you have a hell of a lot of explaining to do. You know coming up here is strictly—" The governor rounds the corner and freezes, his mouth open. His eyes rove over the paints, the canvas, the blood, and me in August's arms.

But then Mrs. Harris comes up behind him. Her eyes light on the unmoving body on the floor, and she shrieks. "Wilburt!" Elbowing past her husband, she flings herself into the room, not even noticing as the hem of her skirt trails in puddles of blood. Tears fall noisily down her cheeks, and she hiccups as she presses her hand to his chest. "He's breathing," she sobs, gathering him in her arms and rocking back and forth. "My dear, sweet boy." She looks up at August and me. "But—but we buried him. How is this possible?"

Half a dozen servants trail into the room before either of us can respond, craning their necks and gasping behind their hands. They stop behind the governor and whisper among themselves, several of them pointing at Will, a few of them eyeing August and me.

Governor Harris is still standing there with his mouth open like some sort of fish. He glances at the painting Will had been doing of me, which has been knocked facedown onto the floor, and casts a look behind him, past the servants to the stacks of portraits filling the adjacent room.

When his eyes focus on mine, they are hard as stone, sharp like ice.

"Who are you really, 'Maeve of Avertine,' and what did you do to my son?"

I swallow, and the world drifts painfully out of focus for a breath. August's arms tighten on me, and everything rights itself. "My name is Myra Whitlock," I manage. "I am a Prodigy, and your wife hired me to bring your son back to life."

The governor barks a laugh. "You honestly expect me to believe that?"

Mrs. Harris doesn't speak. She listens with her mouth pursed and her arms wrapped protectively around Wilburt's head.

"Whether you…believe it…or not," I wheeze, "is entirely… up to you. But it's the truth." I continue, recounting a watered-down version of all that has transpired since Mrs. Harris showed up at Elsie's studio. Governor Harris's face goes purple as I speak, but he does not interrupt me. He stands there, unblinking, his scowl deepening. His arms tighten across his chest until the cuff links on his sleeves are ready to pop out.

The servants behind him listen silently, their eyebrows rising the further I get into my tale.

The longer I speak, the more fatigued I become. By the time I finish, it's all I can do to keep my head up.

As I trail off, Mrs. Harris speaks up. "Well, she's obviously lying, isn't she, darling? I would never deceive you like that, and our son could not possibly be to blame. He's not an artist. He's never been trained. How could he have done all of these portraits?" She gestures at the room and shakes her head. "No, this Prodigy most certainly has been up to something. She must have come up with all of this to blackmail you, dear. Tricked me into thinking she was my friend's daughter. Kidnapped our son. Tortured him, most likely. It's the only explanation that makes sense."

Her words are muffled, and my eyes keep drooping, but the panic and anger that whip through my system are sharp and clear. "I'm not lying," I rasp, and I hate how feeble and weak I sound. "Your son nearly just killed me. He knocked August out not an hour ago. You think I would have taken him on unless my life was at risk? He's twice my size."

"You're a Prodigy," the governor growls. "There's no telling what you're capable of."

"It wasn't—" I cough "—me." I turn to August. His face smears across my vision, quadrupling, fading. I cling to consciousness even as my body turns cold. "August can...tell you..."

The Harrises and all of the servants turn their eyes on August. He shrinks under the weight of their stares.

"Come on, Auggie," Mrs. Harris says. "She's lying, isn't she? It's all part of some plot to ruin our family or bring down your father or harm Will. Tell us she's the villain behind all of this."

August looks from his mother to his father and back, the color in his cheeks darkening. His grip on me pinches my skin.

"August," I whisper. "Please."

But his eyes are on his father, who takes several slow, measured steps toward us. "Let go of the demon, son." His voice is lethal. "Go on downstairs and call the police. We'll have this trespassing, kidnapping criminal thrown where she belongs."

"I'm not lying," I say, but my voice is so frail, I hardly even hear me. My limbs feel as though they are made of lead. I sag against August.

The room is full of shadows. Shadows that wait and watch.

August doesn't move, but he doesn't speak, either.

Something caves in my chest.

It's like last week when they cast me out into the snow. He's not going to be able to stop them from crushing him into submission again. They'll intimidate him until he has no choice but to say the words they want him to say, tell the story they want him to tell. He'll let me be the villain because his family needs their Wilburt Harris Jr.'s reputation to remain unmarred.

No matter how he may care for me, I will always be expendable to his family.

But August's fingers weave through mine and squeeze hard.

He inhales and exhales slowly, just like when he was giving his speech at that charity dinner, just like that day out in the hallway when he needed to talk to Felicity's father.

"No." The word comes out a squeak.

An audible gasp ripples through the room.

"Excuse me?" Governor Harris says sharply.

August clears his throat. "Myra's telling the truth. Mother did hire her. She even had me go pick her up myself." His words are shaky and timid and awkwardly high-pitched.

But he's saying them.

"Myra is not a kidnapper, and she's not a criminal," he continues, and his grip is so hard on my hand that I'm losing feeling in my fingers. "She's done nothing but try to help us. To help Will." He squeezes his eyes shut. "I won't let you hurt her."

His parents and their servants stare at him for several long moments, and the tension in the frigid air is so thick I can scarcely breathe.

August gathers me into his arms and stands up. "Now, if you'll excuse me, sir, I need to get her to a doctor before she bleeds out." He makes to stride past his father, but the governor's hand shoots out and wraps around his arm.

"What are you doing?" he growls.

"I'm taking her to the hospital." August stares straight ahead, not meeting his father's eye, not even turning toward him.

"We can't let her go around blabbing those kinds of stories about our family," he hisses so that the servants cannot hear. "The press would have a field day."

"So you want to let her die? To save your reputation?" Heat ripples off August in waves. He hardens his jaw. "You make me ashamed to be a Harris."

His father's glare intensifies. "What? So you think you're tough now? Look at you. You're shaking like a child afraid of the dark." He sneers, eyes roving over August's face. "You can try to pretend you're a man, but this anxiety of yours will always be a part of you." He steps in close and whispers, "You're broken, boy. Weak. And *I* am the one who's ashamed of *you*."

August clenches his jaw. "You're right," he says, his voice quiet but certain. "This anxiety *will* always be a part of me. It's not going anywhere, and I'm going to have to live with it for the rest of my life. But I am not broken because of it."

The governor opens his mouth to speak, but August goes on, his grip on me tight and solid.

"I've been apologizing to you for who I am for years, but I'm done believing the lie you've fed to me, the lie that says I'm less of a man because I'm not exactly like you. The lie that says I deserve less respect because I struggle." He lifts his chin. "I'm far stronger than you'll ever be. Because I've fought for every victory. Because those fights have taught me compassion and kindness. They've taught me to see the world for what it is, not for what I think it should be. So step aside, *Father*. I'm done minimizing my greatness so you can feel superior."

Yanking out of his father's grasp, August stalks past the servants and onto the landing. It isn't until we're out of sight that his facade of strength breaks and his whole body erupts in tremors. He gasps for air, clinging tightly to me like I'm a life raft in some turbulent, storm-tossed ocean.

My pulse pounds at the inside of my skull, and the light streaming in from the hall window fractures across my vision. I lift an unsteady hand and lay it against his cheek.

"You were incredible," I whisper as the world dissolves.

"Hang on, Myra." He's running now, and I jostle in his arms as he flies down the stairs. "Just hang on."

"Help… Lucy…" I manage before the thick sludge of unconsciousness pulls me under.

41

At first, all I am aware of is a quiet scratching sound, like a bird clawing against wood.

But as the sleep fades from my system, the heaviness of my heart drags me downward.

Mother and Father are gone.

Dead.

The word is heavy and final, and I hate it.

As my mind settles into consciousness slowly, gently, I begin to feel the aches in my bones. A gnawing pain in my arm, wrists, and ankles, a sharp throb in my throat, and a fatigue in my limbs that goes deeper than the soul.

I focus on my breathing. Quiet. In and out.

The air is fresh and smells faintly of cinnamon. Where do I know that smell from?

I think of Father's hands full of cinnamon buns with caramelized sugars dripping down his fingers. My mouth waters, and I lick my lips.

The scratching sound stops abruptly.

"Myra?"

It's a voice I recognize but cannot place. Familiar in its tentative quaver. Comforting in its deep, resonant timbre.

"Myra, it's me. August."

August.

I should know this name. It's on the very edge of my understanding, like if I tug on it, a whole slew of images and stories will unfurl and I will understand. But I cannot figure out how to pull that name forth.

Taking a deep lungful of air, I open my eyes. Light stabs across my vision, making me flinch, but after a moment, the pain subsides.

And there he is.

Floppy, fire hair. Splotchy freckles beneath aquamarine eyes. Broad shoulders, crooked smile.

"Oh, thank the Dear Lady and all Her daughters," he breathes, setting aside the notebook and pen in his hand and crossing from where he was sitting on a chair by the window to kneel at my bedside.

I try to push myself into a sitting position, but jolts of pain slice through my arm at the movement.

"Easy…" August's hands hover over me like he wants to help but he's too afraid to actually touch me. "You lost quite a lot of blood. The doctor said if we'd gotten here even a minute later, you would have died."

"Doctor?" That word carries upon it the weight of a thousand emotions. I wish I could dig it out of the muck in my head, make sense of why it's so significant to me.

"Yes. He's with Lucy now, but he'll be back to check on you any minute."

My eyes go wide.

"Lucy," I whisper.

And then it all comes rushing back with a painful vengeance. My sister, crumpled and dying. The hilt of a blade in my shaking hands, its tip pressed to August's throat. The cook, the forger, the governor's son. A portrait in blood.

I sit bolt upright, ignoring the pain and the way the world rocks violently with the movement. I throw the blankets off me and swing my legs around, not caring that all I'm wearing is a nightdress and August can see my bare calves.

"Myra, please," August says, his hands settling on my shoulders.

I try to shove him off, but his grip is firm.

"Let me go!" I say, squirming.

"You need to rest."

"Did you get there... Was it too... Is she...?" Tears sting my eyes as fear and panic pummel each other in my chest. I crane my neck to see past him to the door. "Where is Lucy?"

"Shhh," August says, his thumbs stroking small circles on my arms. "She's stable. The doctor performed emergency surgery a few days ago, and she's mending. They've got her on a new antimicrobial treatment that seems to be helping."

"I—" I rub the tears away from my eyes with my fists. "I want to see her."

"I'll take you there myself as soon as the doctor says you're fit to go," he says. "Please, just lie here and rest until he gets back and has a chance to look at you."

August's brows are knit with worry. A bandage is wrapped around his head, resting above his brows.

"She's not dead?" I choke on the ache, the longing, the Artist-damned hope in my chest.

He shakes his head. "Her state is still a bit precarious, but she's in better shape than she was when we found her. Please, Myra. If you'll lie back down, I'll tell you everything."

I purse my lips, my gaze straying toward the door once again. Swallowing a sudden wave of tears, I nod. "Okay. But as soon as the doctor says I'm all right, I want you to take me to her."

"Of course."

I settle against the pillows.

August pulls the chair closer to the bed. "Once we left the house, I sent one of our drivers over to your apartment to retrieve Lucy, and I brought you here to the hospital immediately. She arrived not long after we did, and she was…" He shakes his head. "She was in a bad way. They assessed her condition and took her straight into surgery."

"What kind of surgery?"

"It appeared that her bowel had perforated somehow and leaked waste into her abdominal cavity. That's what caused the infection and sepsis."

"Artist." I press my palm to my forehead.

"So they went in to remove the waste and repair the bowel. She's stable now, but she hasn't woken up yet. She'd gotten pretty bad. Her kidneys had started to shut down, she had clots in her bloodstream… Honestly it's a damned miracle she made it at all. They've done so many things to repair the damage, and they did say there's a possibility of lasting issues, but she's still here. Quite the fighter, isn't she?"

"She is," I whisper.

"I should have expected as much, given who she's related to." He gives me a gentle smile. "So they currently have her in intensive care where they check on her hourly for signs of more infection, but it's mostly a waiting game to see how her body will heal and whether their interventions were enough to save her."

My fault, my fault, my fault.

"Do they know what caused the bowel damage?" I ask.

He shakes his head. "Not yet. They told me they were going to take it one step at a time. Get her stable and healed from the surgery and sepsis, then proceed with a series of diagnostic tests to pinpoint what caused the issue in the first place."

I knot my hands together. "Thank you. For saving her. And me." I meet his gaze. "I owe you."

He frowns and mops a hand over his face. "After all that my brother has done to your family, it was the very least I could do."

"Where is he now?"

"A holding center up north."

My eyebrows rise. "Like a prison?"

"Of a sort." August's jaw tightens. "After I made sure you and Lucy were taken care of here, I went back to my parents and told them that if they didn't do something, I would go to the police. Father of course didn't want it to get out that his son was a killer, so he arranged for Will to be held at the containment facility instead of the local prison while the case is being investigated."

"Has he told them the truth?" I ask. "He killed Elsie, my parents, and all those artists who disappeared."

August winces. "Myra, I can't begin to tell you how sorry I am." He reaches out a hand toward mine but pauses, his fingertips centimeters away, and his cheeks go pink.

I twitch my hand into his, and he lets out a long, slow breath. The warmth of his touch trails up my arm and fills me all the way to my toes.

He's still the governor's son, and this probably means nothing. But for this moment, I let myself forget about propriety, forget about anything but the feeling of his skin against mine.

"I'm so, so sorry," he whispers.

"It's not your fault," I say, my voice a lot stronger than I feel.

"If I had paid more attention, if I'd had a better relationship with him, maybe I could have seen what was going on before it got so bad."

I squeeze his hand. "Maybe…but maybe not."

He purses his lips and nods, then drops his gaze to our intertwined fingers.

Every nerve in my body buzzes as he stares at them, and I try to decipher the unreadable emotion in the crease of his brow, in the tight corners of his eyes. Is he regretting having reached for my hand? Is he feeling guilty because he'll soon be promised to another girl?

Is he still afraid to choose me? After all we've been through?

Clearing my throat, I cast about for something to fill the silence. "So, uh…" I gesture around the room with my other hand. "Who's paying for all of this? Because I certainly can't afford it."

"My father is, actually."

"But your father thinks I'm a demon."

A shy grin steals across August's face. "It's true, but I also pointed out that unless he did something substantial to help, you might not be willing to keep quiet about what Will did to your family."

"You blackmailed him?" My brows rise.

"I did." He grins, almost bashful.

I squeeze his hand again. "Thank you. I can't imagine what a difficult conversation that must have been for you."

"I'll be completely honest, seeing you like that… You looked dead, Myra. I was so angry, it took all of my self-control not to throttle the man."

I snort. "I would pay good money to see that."

"Well, I, unlike some people, actually know how to use a broadsword."

"How hard is it to hack and stab? I mean, honestly."

A chortle escapes his lips, and we burst into laughter.

After a moment, he asks, "So what exactly did you do to Will?"

"I cut off his access to his power," I say.

"How?"

I launch into a short description of the realization I had while I was tied to the wall in Will's makeshift studio. When I realized that I needed to stop trying to command my magic and instead let it flow through me, let it heal the way it wanted to, cede control to something more powerful than myself.

"So the magic is still there inside of him, he just can't use it anymore?"

"That's right."

His eyes go somber. "How did painting that affect you, though?"

"I'm not sure yet. But nothing bad, I think. If anything, I've just adopted the pieces of the sevren I disconnected from his fervora, so my own connection to my magic might be a bit stronger."

He grimaces and nods. "That's a relief."

"Speaking of my magic, if you're going to take me to see Lucy, I'd very much appreciate if you could get me a canvas, some brushes, and some paints. I want to see if my magic can help speed along what the doctors have done to heal the damaged bowel."

The door swings open, and in walks a tall man with sparkling, expressive eyes. His coarse black curls coil tight against his head and glisten with strands of silver. A pair of round spectacles perch on a broad nose. "Oh, you're awake!" he says when he catches sight of me, his brown face brightening into a grin so fatherly it makes my heart ache. "I'm Dr. Amos."

"Hello," I say.

"I'll be back in a moment, sir." August gets to his feet and gives a slight bow of the head. "I need to get a few things." He casts me one last look before exiting the room.

42

August returns with his hands empty as the doctor finishes up his assessment. "How's she doing?" he asks as he comes through the door.

"She's still very weak. Severely anemic. I recommend that she rest for at least the next week. No exercise, nothing strenuous." Dr. Amos scrawls a few notes into his notebook before peering at me over the top of it. "You are lucky Mr. Harris was quick to get you here."

I nod, glancing at August, who has begun an intense staring match with the floor. "I am forever in his debt." As the doctor turns to head for the door, I ask, "Would it be all right if I visited my sister?"

He frowns. "I suppose, but I'd rather you didn't walk. Why don't I have one of my nurses fetch you a wheelchair?"

"That would be wonderful."

The doctor exits, and August smiles at me. "I stowed everything near Lucy's room. We can pick it up on the way."

A moment later, a nurse pushes a wheelchair in. She and August shoulder me carefully into the seat. I try to ignore the way my heart rate accelerates at the feel of August's hands on my waist again. The memory of that afternoon out on the ice in the garden maze fills my mind, bringing with it a rush of heat.

Far too soon, he releases me and circles behind the chair to push me through the door. I try not to let him see my disappointment.

The air is still and sterile in the hall. Sunlight shafts in through windows, cutting beams of gold across us as we make our way up a gently sloping ramp. Doctors and nurses in pressed, clean uniforms bustle past, and I can't help but stare at them. So long I have wanted desperately to be able to talk to just one, and now here are a dozen, shuffling around me as though my being here is the most normal thing in the world.

We round a corner and come to a stop in front of what has to be the isolation ward where Lucy's being kept. A bored-looking woman blocks the door.

"Hi," I say, swallowing my nerves. "My name is Myra Whitlock. My sister, Lucy, should be here?"

The woman frowns but seems to recognize my name and allows us through, nodding at August as though she's met him.

"Thank you," I say, breathless as anticipation and anxiety well in my stomach.

The nurse leads us down to a room at the end of the hallway. When I catch sight of Lucy, everything else falls away. She seems even smaller than I remember her—like she's being devoured by the pillows and blankets on her bed. All I can see are her stringy brown hair and the bandages twisted tight around her middle stained alizarin with blood. A doctor with a mask over her face and gloves on her hands nods a greeting to us as she checks the pulse in Lucy's neck and scribbles on a sheet of paper.

Tears sting my eyes, and I reach out to grasp Lucy's limp fingers. "I'm here, love," I whisper. "I'm here, and you're here.

We've both made it, somehow." I swallow through the tightness in my throat. "But you have to keep fighting. You're so close, Luce."

"Her coloring looks better than it did this morning," August says.

"You saw her this morning?"

He nods. "I've been switching between checking on her and sitting with you."

"But what about your mother? Your father? I can't imagine they approve."

His mouth draws into a tight line. "They don't."

"Did you talk to them about it?"

He chuckles, rubbing a hand along the back of his neck. "I... This is going to sound stupid. But I wrote them a letter."

"A letter?"

"Remember what you said in the cab on the way back from Vincent's? About how writing could be the way I use my voice? I haven't been able to get that out of my mind. So I decided to try it. I told them I wouldn't be leaving your side until you and your sister were healed and fit to leave the hospital."

"Oh, yes. It was brilliant of me to think of that."

He chuckles. "Don't let it go to your head."

I turn my attention back to Lucy, and my smile fades. I stroke circles on her palm with my thumb, drawing strength from the warmth of her skin. I feel like she and I have been running forever, pushing and pushing, fighting day in and day out, completely alone. And now, this bright, shy boy has come along and taken some of that weight from our backs. I'd forgotten what it felt like for us to not have to shoulder our fears on our own.

I feel like I can finally breathe.

Lucy's doctor turns to exit the room.

"Excuse me, could I ask you a few questions?" I say.

"Of course."

I spend the next half hour interrogating her about Lucy's condition, her surgery, and her current state. I ask her to detail the exact damage they found when they opened her up, to describe precisely what her bowel looked like and how they stitched it closed. I give her a paper and pencil from August's stash to sketch it out for me, and only once I truly feel like I've got an understanding of what I'm working with do I allow her to leave.

Once we are alone, August retrieves the armful of canvases, paints, and the easel from where he stashed them. "So what's the plan?"

"Can you set this all up for me? I want to help heal her surgical wounds so she doesn't run the risk of going septic again."

August obeys, situating the easel right in front of me and setting a canvas in place. Stealing a stool from a nearby desk, he slides it next to me. Then he lines up my paints and brushes on the stool. Handing me a small palette, he smiles. "I can't wait to see the master at work again."

Setting the doctor's sketch on the easel next to the canvas, I draw in a deep, steadying breath.

I still don't know what caused the bowel perforation, but getting her stable and healing from this surgery is paramount. I'll point my magic in that direction and then, for the first time, I will trust it completely with my sister's life.

With shaking hands, I pick up a paintbrush and turn to my canvas to begin what could finally be the painting that changes everything.

I work all afternoon and into the night. Luckily, August has memorized the doctor's rotation schedule, so he knows what time to hide my supplies and portrait before anyone comes in. When I finish the first painting and feel my fervora spark to life, I almost sob with relief. Picking my palette up, I get back to work mixing more colors for the healing layer.

As I go, I focus on the prickle in my fingertips, the icy flare of magic under my skin. I welcome the blush of cold in my hands and my mind. Instead of fighting it, trying to push it down into my chest until I'm ready for it, I allow it to twist its way through my hands.

The painting comes together differently.

At several points, I go to make one brushstroke here or a tiny modification there, and that itch in my fingers pulls me another way.

I let the magic guide me, let it flow along my sevren, and, no matter how it makes my stomach twist with anxiety to relinquish control over something so important, I follow its lead. As time passes, the chill in my hands and arms thaws, as though my magic is warming to me. Instead of prickles that I try to push away, it's like a trickle of soothing heat.

I'm not sure why, but I embrace the subtle change, leaning into the sensation, imagining Mother and Father are there with me, holding me up and guiding my brush.

Pinning my tongue between my teeth, I lean in close to the canvas, etching in alizarin crimson mixed with titanium white to create the pink, curving lines of a healed, uncut, un-perforated bowel. I drag in a touch of viridian to darken the alizarin for the shadows.

Once I finish the painting of her internal organs, I pull up a new canvas and begin a portrait of Lucy with the bottom of her shirt pulled up to her ribs so that her lower abdomen is exposed. This one will be for healing the external surgical site.

August lets me work in quiet, sitting off to the side scrawling away in his notebook and chewing on a cinnamon stick. His presence is soothing, and he makes himself useful by running out to pick up food for me every now and then.

It's nearly midnight by the time I finish the second portrait. The candles are burning low in their sconces on the walls.

Finally, I set my paintbrush down and stretch my fingers. "I'm done."

The scratching of August's pen ceases. He's at my side in an instant, peering past my shoulder at the painting.

"She's lovely," he whispers.

"She always has been." I study the painting in front of me. It's only a portrait of Lucy the way she appears in the bed in front of us now, but with her eyes open, her abdomen wound-free, and a pink-cheeked smile on her face. The smile she got from Father—the one I feel like I haven't seen in forever.

"Here goes nothing." I place my hands directly onto the center of both of the portraits. I've never done two at once before, but my magic tells me this is right, so I push aside my nerves and focus. Just like the other times, the wet paint slicks my skin, feeding into the building magic in my palm. A thousand tiny pinpricks spread into each finger, into my wrist, and up my arm. Threads of that new heat swirl through me along the sevren in my body, weaving together as they plunge past my shoulder and into my chest, where the sensation compounds until I'm gasping through the torrent of sparks and flame raging inside my rib cage.

I force myself to relax even as every instinct tells me to tense up and fight the mounting swell within. I let it flow through me, a tsunami of quinacridone reds and phthalo blues come to plunge me into their depths.

The diagram of Lucy's sevren unspools before me, and my magic latches on, sparking through every single one of her soul-threads.

The pressure inside of me builds until my skin vibrates at a frequency that could undo me, incinerate me to ash. Thinking of August and how he breathed through his fears, I force my shoulders loose, relax my jaw. The torrent does not subside, but my body seems to absorb it better, the warmth bleeding through me. I feel a strange sort of unfurling at my heart, and I instantly think of ladyroses catching flame. Alizarin crimson petals curling, smoldering, dripping magic through every inch of my body.

"A symbol of life," Mother whispered whenever the roses burned. "Beautiful, like birth."

She was right. My magic *is* beautiful. A raw, powerful part of me I've kept at arm's length for far too long.

I ride it, let it pull me along its riptide.

Please, I whisper. *Please be gentle with my Lucy.*

But it already knows. Because it's not this separate beast, rearing against my control. It is me, and I am it, and I don't have to fear myself.

It flows out for Lucy's heart, and I don't stop it.

The sensation swells, radiating through me like I've ignited. I hear Mother's lullabies, taste Father's butter sauces, feel Lucy's arms wrapped around my neck and August's fingers in mine. The many soul-threads of my life, bound together, holding me up, holding me together.

And then, all at once, it hushes.

A great pain slices into my lower abdomen, and I double over, gasping. My body goes weak, convulses, jolts so hard it's all I can do to stay in the wheelchair.

"Myra!" August grasps my arms to keep me from toppling. "What's wrong? Are you all right?"

"Yes," I gasp as tears trickle down my cheeks. I look up at him, barely able to contain the joy about to burst through me—a joy so strong it surges past the agony in my abdomen, past every thought, every fear, every sensation.

"We need a doctor." He gets to his feet and heads for the door.

I grasp his forearm and pull him back. "I'm...not hurt..." I wheeze.

"Like hell you're not."

"It's…my magic…" Sobs and tears choke over one another. "It worked."

"What?"

"I've taken…the pain…of her injuries. It means…her surgical wound…is healed." I look up at August, and his face warps in my tears. "It finally worked."

Wincing and grasping my stomach, I push aside the easel and squint hard to see Lucy, a tiny shadow in that mound of white sheets and pillows. I'm gasping for air, and August's hand is warm and solid on my arm. I grasp onto it, drawing strength, trying to keep my wits about me even as the pain in my gut threatens to make me pass out.

Lucy is still.

I grit my teeth, reaching out to hold her hand again. "Come on, Luce, I know you're in there."

Not a twitch.

"Please." I count my heartbeats.

One, two, three, four, five…

My stomach sinks.

"Lucy," I whisper.

Thirty-eight, thirty-nine, forty, forty-one…

Movement at the end of her bed draws my eye.

"Did you see that?" I yank back the blanket to expose Lucy's feet.

"See what?"

Her toes jerk again, and I shriek, "There! Tell me you saw that!"

"She moved!" August cries.

But still, I wait. Maybe it was an involuntary twitch. Maybe she's not—

Her eyelids flutter. "Myra?" she croaks.

I rise out of my wheelchair. "I'm here."

"Where's…" She licks her lips and tries again. "Where's Georgie?"

I let out a laugh, and then all at once I'm sobbing. Shaking so hard my teeth chatter. Snot runs down my lip as tears drip from my chin. I double over on the edge of her bed, grasping for her hand as my sobs intensify to the point where I'm barely able to breathe.

Lucy is okay.

She's still sick. Her illness hasn't gone anywhere, but the sepsis is gone. Her wounds have healed. *We are going to be all right,* Lucy said that night that feels like ages ago. *We will always have each other, and that is worth more than all the money in the world.*

I press my lips to her knuckles as pain streaks through my abdomen. My mind whirls. Stars whiten the edges of my vision. My knees buckle beneath me, and her hand slips out of my grasp as I slide down the side of the bed and curl into a ball on the floor, sobbing and sobbing and sobbing.

Lucy is awake.

My magic worked.

I may not have solved our financial issues or found a way to provide for us going forward, but I'll have time to worry about that later because my baby sister is going to live.

She is going to *live.*

43

The doctors come running soon after to witness the miracle recovery of their surgical patient, and they shoo us out of the room to assess her. August disappears down the hall to store all of my painting things in my room so that people won't find out how she was healed while I hover at the door, peering through the window for a glimpse of Lucy.

Nurses and doctors spend what feels like an eternity poking and prodding her, checking her vitals, and marveling over the smooth skin on her belly where the surgical wound was. I tell August to run home to pick up Lucy's pet frog, and he disappears as I press my face to the glass of Lucy's door for the hundredth time.

"Can I please go in?" I ask more times than I can count.

And finally, after a thousand nos, they let me inside. August carries in the frog's tank behind me and sets it on the end of the bed before ducking out into the hallway to give us privacy.

"Georgie!" Lucy pushes herself upright, pulling the squirming, slimy animal out and pressing him to her chest. Her voice is quiet, but it's fuller and more solid than I've heard in weeks. She turns stern eyes on me. "He's skinny. Have you been feeding him? You know he needs the fat crickets. He's a growing boy!"

"Hi, Luce." I climb up next to her, pulling her into my arms and pressing my face against the top of her head. Tears leak from my eyes all over again, dampening her hair. "Ava's been taking good care of him. I'm sure he was just worried about you."

"Why are you crying?" she asks, squirming in my grasp. "You're squeezing too hard and getting snot on my face. Also you reek. Have you bathed recently?"

"Good to see you, too," I say, laughing even as sharp jolts of pain continue to radiate from my abdomen into my hips. Smoothing my hands over her cheeks, I wipe away the residue of my tears. "I'm so happy you're all right."

"What happened to you?" Her eyes lock on the bandages on my arm and wrists before trailing up to the bruises at my throat.

I tug the sleeve of my nightdress down over my arm. "I'll be all right soon enough."

"Those doctors said we're in a hospital." Lucy nuzzles the frog's face with her cheek. "So tell me. Who did you rob?"

"It's—"

I'm interrupted by a soft knock. A moment later, the door opens, and Lucy's doctor enters. "Sorry to bother you."

"Oh, it's no bother," I say.

"I had something I wanted to speak about with the both of you." She perches on the end of the bed next to George's tank. "I've gotten some of your preliminary test results back, Lucy."

Lucy nods, still nuzzling her frog. Her eyes are sharp on the doctor.

"Of course, we can't say anything definitive yet, but I have had a few patients over the years with bowels that looked similar to yours."

"So you know how to help me?" Lucy asks, desperate hope cracking through her calm.

The doctor's smile fades ever so slightly. "I'm afraid that the studies on these particular conditions are still quite new, but if what you have is the same as what I've seen before, well... there's a possibility that you could have this illness for the rest of your life."

Lucy stills. "You mean there's nothing we can do?"

The doctor sets a comforting hand on Lucy's knee. "We've made lots of progress with some treatments that help alleviate the symptoms—medications and diet changes you can try—but I just wanted you to be mentally and emotionally prepared for a bit of a long haul."

Lucy asks questions, and the doctor answers as best she can, and finally, after what feels like an eternity, the doctor leaves, shutting the door with a gentle click.

Lucy and I sit in silence for several moments. I watch her face for any sign of emotion, but it's blank. She stares at the wall, cupping George stonily to her chest.

After a moment, I ask, "Do you want to talk about it?"

She sniffs. "I don't know what there is to say."

"What are you feeling?"

"Angry," she says, planting a fierce kiss on George's head and depositing him into his tank before turning back to me. "I mean...what the hell, Myra? Why does everything always have to be a fight?" Her eyes shine as she spits the words out. "For once, I thought I could be done with this. We're finally here, at a hospital. Doctors are everywhere. I guess I hoped they'd have more answers, and I'm angry that they don't."

"It's not fair at all." I nod. "And it makes me so mad I could break something."

She laughs, but it turns into a sob, and she draws her knees up against her chest. "I'm also scared. Of hurting forever. Of not being able to do the things I dream of doing. Of not getting to live the life I want to." She looks at me, tears dropping down her cheeks. "Of holding you back from the life *you* want."

My whole chest splinters. "No, Lucy," I say, gathering her into my arms. She shakes with sobs against my chest as I stroke her hair. "Don't you understand? *You* are my entire life. Fighting this by your side isn't holding me back. I wouldn't want to be anywhere else."

She hiccups against me as we cry together for several minutes, clinging to each other the way we always have. The two of us like a rock against the storm, a little huddled piece of security in a world set on tearing us down.

Finally, Lucy's sobs slow, and she sits back, rubbing the heels of her hands across her cheeks. "You know what else I feel?"

"Tell me."

"Determined. I am still Lucy. I still want the same things I've always wanted." She clenches her fists. "Yes, the path to my dreams may be harder and longer and far more painful than I want it to be. It may take me twice as much time and effort as someone else to attain my goals, but I *will* get there."

I brush the hair from her face. "And I'll be with you every step of that road, every doctor's appointment, every treatment. I will find another job to pay for the things you need, and we will do this together. The highs and the lows. The successes and the failures. You do not have to climb this mountain alone."

She gives me a quivering smile, and her voice warbles as she murmurs, "I love you, Myra."

"Artist, you have no idea how much I love you," I say, dragging her back into my arms and squeezing her tight.

★ ★ ★

An hour later, another knock sounds on the door. Lucy's now sitting at a table across the room feeding George some crickets with a pair of tweezers, and I'm reading a newspaper on her bed.

"Come in." I turn, expecting to see August. Instead, Mrs. Harris steps inside, her face smooth and stern. The traces of grief I saw in her eyes that first night when she stopped me in the street are gone, but the lines of fatigue around her mouth seem to have deepened.

"I'm sorry to interrupt," she says, "but may I have a word, Miss Whitlock?"

Nodding, I set the paper down and ease myself into the wheelchair, hanging on to the bed frame to steady myself until the room stops spinning. Then I follow Mrs. Harris out into the hallway, pushing the door shut behind me. Though Lucy's pain continues to carve its way along my insides, I keep it out of my expression, forcing a smile. "What can I help you with?"

"I've come to discuss the matter of your payment." Her words are tight and forced, like it pains her to say them.

"Payment?" I raise a brow.

"You did restore my son to me. As such, I'm willing to pay you the agreed-upon amount of five hundred thousand golds." She extracts a slip of paper from her breast pocket, but instead of handing it to me, she holds it between us like a warning. Her eyes dart from side to side, sizing up the nearby nurses and doctors as though assessing whether they're listening in. She lowers her voice to a whisper. "I'd like to make it absolutely clear how precarious your situation is."

"Excuse me?"

"Let's get one thing straight, Miss Whitlock. My son is locked up in a holding center. He's lost his whole future because of you."

I cross my arms. "Begging your pardon, ma'am, but he did those things himself. I committed no murders."

Her eyes blaze as she leans down to level my glare nose to nose. "Do not forget what I know about you. I could destroy you in an instant. You are nothing. *Nothing.* It is only out of the goodness of our hearts that my husband and I have kept our servants quiet about your little secret and haven't had you locked up ourselves."

I hold her gaze, setting my jaw, even as my insides squirm. "Are you threatening me again, Mrs. Harris?"

Slowly, ever so slowly, she hands over the check. "I'd be very, *very* careful if I were you, Miss Whitlock."

"Funny," I say, taking the check and inspecting it, keeping my voice level and my expression unperturbed. "I was going to say the same thing to you."

Mrs. Harris raises a brow as I meet her eye and give her a devil's smile.

"With the election coming soon, it would be quite the scandal for people to find out Wilburt Harris Jr. murdered a dozen Lalverton citizens this year, wouldn't it?"

"If we have you locked up, you won't be able to blab about it," she hisses.

But I cock my head. "People in prisons have ears, too, don't they? Would you really want to take that risk?"

Her eyes bulge. "You wouldn't dare."

"Wouldn't I?"

She steps back, pasting on a pained smile. "Fine. But take it from an older and wiser woman—I would be very careful of who you make your enemy, child."

"Thank you for the advice," I say.

She hisses, straightening the scarf around her neck and turning to leave.

"Before you go, Mrs. Harris," I call after her, seizing what might be my only opportunity to fill in the one missing piece of the puzzle. "I do have one last question for you. If it's not too bold."

She stops and faces me again, crossing her arms with a great, irritated sigh. "Yes?"

"Why did you come to Elsie's studio that day?"

She purses her lips, sizing me up, before deciding to answer. "I knew Will had been researching Prodigies. I didn't know why, but I'd noticed books about them popping up in his room for weeks. When he died, I found a list he'd drawn up of portrait artists in town. All of their names were crossed off but for Elsie, so I thought maybe he'd been looking for a Prodigy and discovered she was one. I wanted to know if it was true, and if it were, why my son cared. It wasn't until I met you and noticed you'd healed my dog that I realized maybe you'd be able to bring my son back to me."

I nod slowly.

The lines around her mouth tighten. "Good day, Miss Whitlock."

"Pleasure doing business with you, Mrs. Harris."

Her mouth thins as she turns on her heel and stalks up the hall, her shoulders rigid and her head held high.

44

A few days later, the doctor says I'm well enough to leave the hospital. Lucy will have to stay for a while longer as they try to learn more about the illness still wreaking havoc on her system, but she's brighter and healthier than I've seen her in months. They've moved her into a children's ward with puzzles and books, and they've said I can visit her anytime I like.

I bustle about her hospital room as she scribbles notes in her Lawrence River initiative files at the table in the corner. Pulling back the curtains around her bed, I busy myself cleaning up the papers we were using earlier as Lucy tried to teach me how to fold a paper frog.

Morning sunlight streams into the room, and I try not to think of how it would turn August's hair to fire if he were here. After Lucy's miraculous recovery three days ago, he said he had some things he needed to take care of, and I haven't seen him since.

I try to tell myself it doesn't matter, that of course he couldn't stay here with me forever. He has a life and a betrothal waiting for him out there that have nothing to do with me. I was a mess that needed cleaning, and now that I'm all tidied up, he can return to what matters.

Yet every time someone stops in, my heart leaps into my throat. Each time it's not him, another part of me wilts.

So when a soft rap sounds on the door, I don't turn, don't even allow the hope in my chest to soar.

"Come in," I say in a tone much brighter than I feel.

The knob squeaks when it twists, and footsteps shuffle into the room.

"Myra."

I freeze, one of Lucy's pillows gripped in my hands. The heart I'd been doing so well at taming goes berserk, thrashing against my ribs, up into my throat, down to my feet.

"Hello, Mr. Harris," I say.

"Wait, is this him?" Lucy asks, gaping. "Like *him*-him?"

My cheeks burn. "Lucy, this is August Harris. August, meet my sister, Lucy."

"How do you do?" He takes her hand and kisses the air above her knuckles.

She giggles. "How do *you* do?" Then she cups her hand around her mouth and says in a loud, fake whisper, "You didn't tell me he was this handsome!"

"All right, I think it's time for you to get some rest," I say, leaping between them and dragging her to the bed. "Why don't you lie down?"

She sticks out her tongue at me and climbs into the sheets.

I turn back to August, still clutching the pillow like a fool. "Mr. Harris. To what do we owe the honor?"

"Come on." His smile fades. "Don't do that."

"Do what?"

"Act like I'm no more than the son of the governor."

"But you *are* the son of the governor."

He stares at me for a long moment, his lips pursing into a tight line. "I wrote another letter to my parents."

"About?"

"Felicity."

Her name slaps me across the face, and I wind my hands into the pillowcase, focusing on the pinch of the fabric against my knuckles so I don't have to pay attention to the ache in my stomach. "Oh? What did it say?"

He keeps his eyes intent on mine. "I told them I wouldn't agree to the betrothal."

Lucy lets out an excited squeak.

I blink at him. "You *what*?"

"You were right. Everything I've been doing has been all for the wrong reasons. Solely to make my parents happy. To do what was expected of me, what would make me look like less of a failure." He lets out a slow breath. "I'm done pretending to be what they want me to be. I'm ready to live my life the way I want it."

I search my mind for something to say, but nothing comes. "Oh…"

We stare at each other, and the minutes stretch out for eternity. The tether of eye contact between us pulses like an invisible braid of sevren, impossible to untangle.

"That's not all I came to say," August goes on.

"Oh?" Is that the only response I can come up with now? Have I completely forgotten how to use words?

He tugs off his cap and drags a hand through his hair as his face turns a deep shade of scarlet. "I was actually wondering if… That is, I was hoping you'd… See, I've been thinking about it, and… Oh, sweet Artist." He mops at his face with his cap, scrunches his eyes closed, and forces out, "I'd like to invite you to accompany me to the literary symposium next week."

"What?"

He buries his face in his hands. "Please don't make me say it again. That was exhausting."

I laugh. "No need. I was just surprised. Are you going to present your work?"

"Don't be ludicrous, Myra." He snorts. "I'll not be making any more public presentations for the rest of my days if I can help it. But I am going to see if they'll accept my work for consideration without one. It's like you said, I can be me and still live my life. I need to stop apologizing for who I am."

"August, that's...that's wonderful."

He peeks at me between his fingers. "So would you like to go?"

"I—" I run a hand over the material of my hospital gown, and my stomach twists. Even this frock is nicer than anything I have back at home. The thought fills me with shame. "I don't know."

"What?" Lucy flings her arms out, appalled. "Of course you do! You were just telling me last night you wished he'd—"

I throw the pillow at her. "That's quite enough out of you!" I drag the curtain hanging from the ceiling closed around her bed and turn back to face August, embarrassment making me sweat. "I'm sorry about her. She can be..."

"I can still hear you!" Lucy calls.

"No, you can't," I retort, crossing my arms.

August tries not to smile, but his lips twitch. "So would you like to go with me?"

I twist my fingers. "It's just that...you've seen what I am. Where I come from. We live in different worlds, August. What would people think if they saw us together in public?"

"I don't care what they think. Isn't that the whole point? Not worrying about appearances anymore?"

"*Is* that the point?" My voice is small.

"Of course it is, Myra."

I remember being in Rose Manor, buttoning pearls on a dress to go to breakfast. I think of the way his parents always looked down their noses at me, how their servants whispered behind their hands to each other when they found us on the fifth floor together.

How long will this new indifference about his appearance last?

He's still standing there, waiting for me to say something, his hands turning his hat around and around in a way that's making me dizzy.

"I just don't think it could work between us," I say quietly.

His face falls.

"Only because—" I rush on "—I don't know how to be with someone as important as you. I didn't grow up in the public eye. You say you don't care about appearances anymore, but it's ingrained into your life, bred into you with the same genes that gave you those adorable ears." My voice breaks, and I dig my bare toes into the cold tile. "Maybe it would be harmless for me to attend the symposium with you, but what would happen after that?"

"We could go to another one. Attend a poetry reading together. Visit a museum. So many things." He takes a step forward. "Anything. Everything. Nothing. I don't care what we do, Myra, as long as I'm doing it with you."

"Please don't say that unless you mean it," I whisper as tears gather in my eyes. "I know how difficult things are for you with your parents, and having me around will surely only contribute to that."

He reaches toward me, his hand hovering mere inches from my cheek. "Some things are worth that kind of fight, Myra, and you are worth *every* fight."

"Are you sure?" My voice warbles dangerously close to sobs.

He tosses his hat aside and gathers my fingers in both of his hands. "You make me happier being me than I've ever been in my life. I can't tell you how freeing it is to be *seen*." He pauses, offering me a tentative smile. "I can't promise you I won't mess up. I can't promise that there won't be hard times, times where the battle might seem too much to bear. There will be many anxious moments to come, because that's part of who I am and the reality of what going against my parents will be like, but I'm willing to take the harder road if that means I get to keep you in my life."

His voice drops to a near whisper. "I'll be honest, there are so many unknowns, so many things about the future I'm choosing here that I can't bank on, and that terrifies the hell out of me. But there is one thing I can promise you." He brings my hands up to his mouth and brushes his lips along my fingertips one by one. "You never have to face anything alone again. I will do whatever it takes to be the person you can count on when everyone and everything else fail you." Warm tingles trail under my skin, and I shiver.

"Please," he says, dropping one of my hands so he can tuck one of his into my hair and tilt my head up to him. "Come with me to the symposium. And then come with me to the pub and the museum, to the park, to the sunset, to the sky."

His cinnamon breath is warm on my lips, and I remember that night on the balcony under the stars when I wanted so badly for him to close the distance between us.

"You speak like a poet," I whisper.

When he laughs, I feel the rumble of it where my hands rest against his chest, and my whole body trembles.

"Just say yes!" Lucy cries from behind the curtain. "For Artist's sake, Myra!"

"Go to sleep!" I shout back, not taking my eyes from August's.

"So?" he breathes, his nose brushing mine softly. "Will you go with me?"

My breath hitches as his other hand releases mine to slip around my waist.

"You're very persuasive," I say, and when I wet my lips, my tongue grazes against his lower one.

He sucks in a breath, and then all of a sudden his mouth is on mine. I wrap my arms around his neck and press against him. His hands are shaky, tentative at first. His kiss is soft, reserved, full of questions.

So I pull him in deeper, show him with my body that I want him closer, closer, always closer. His grip on my lower back solidifies, and his fingers knot themselves in my hair.

And suddenly the quiver in his movements vanishes, replaced by a need, a want. We crush ourselves against each other, gasping for air between kisses.

I am full of hope and light, power and fight. Viridians and alizarins and ultramarines swirl within me, and I weave my hands through his hair, feel those light lashes butterfly across my cheeks, taste the cinnamon in his breath.

"Ew, are you two kissing? I'm *right here*," Lucy says.

August and I laugh and continue without pause.

This kiss is not the passionate tryst that I always imagined a kiss would be. Our noses knock against each other, and I can't quite figure out how to breathe. We break apart to laugh and then dive back in for more. I feel his smile against my own, and it sets my heart galloping.

This is a kiss of light. Of hope. Of trust.

I've spent my whole life striving for perfection, running myself into the ground searching for how to make things right, how to control every outcome, every moment. But maybe perfection does not mean there aren't things we wish were different. Maybe perfection comes from leaning into the things that we have to fight for because those are the things that bind us to the people worth keeping.

Maybe that's what the answer really is to the aches and the toils of this cruel world. Finding people we can lean on and love.

Because no matter how many paintbrushes I might use or which colors I might blend, I could never capture this moment. This moment that a past me might have found flawed. This moment that is so unutterably flawless.

When we finally break apart, I press my forehead against his, drinking in his breath, grasping his lapel in my fists like I never want to let go. "All right, you've convinced me. I'll go with you to the symposium."

"*Thank you!*" Lucy says exasperatedly.

I giggle as August's nose brushes along the length of mine. "Are you sure you don't need more convincing?" he breathes, his thumbs trailing across my cheeks.

"Actually, now that you mention it..."

He pulls me in once more, but pauses just before his lips touch mine. "There's only one condition to this outing."

"Oh, *you* asked *me*, and now you're saying it's conditional?" I raise a brow. "What kind of gentleman are you anyway?"

"I'm charming."

"Is that what they're calling 'incorrigible' these days?" I drop my gaze to his lips. "Tell me, charming Mr. Harris. What's your condition?"

He dips his head to meet my eye and grins. "How about you try *not* to decorate the cab door with your knickers this time?"

I stick out my tongue at him. "Oh, ha ha. Very funny. We're all laughing here."

He snorts, obviously pleased with himself. "Does that mean you accept my condition?"

"I make no guarantees."

He laughs and kisses me again, and as the sun dances through the window, I bury myself in him, spread my imperfections bare, and let vulnerability fill me with warmth and hope.

EPILOGUE

glance out the window of the coach as it slows to a stop. The sun glitters a brilliant titanium white, skipping across the snowdrifts clumped on the stone wall that surrounds the holding center where Wilburt Harris Jr. is being held.

I gather the paintings and sketches in my lap, stacking them carefully and easing them back into the bag I brought them in. My portfolio for the Lalverton Conservatory of Art and Music, finally complete and ready to be delivered on our way home this afternoon. It seems that accepting my magic was a crucial step to being able to paint without distraction, without stress, without fear. Since I got home from the hospital a month ago, I haven't been able to stop painting.

I also haven't been able to stop thinking about Will.

August climbs out of the carriage and extends a hand to help me down. I leave my portfolio on the seat behind me and grasp onto him as I step lightly into the snow. We face the outer gate of the holding center side by side, my arm firmly locked around August's elbow and my heart driving a frantic beat through my rib cage.

"Are you sure you want to do this?" August asks, his breath puffing like mist in front of our faces. "I can go in and talk to him for you."

I shake my head. "No. It should be me."

We approach the entrance and pull on the bell rope. A gong sounds somewhere inside, and soon, guards have appeared, questioned us, verified identification papers, and allowed us through.

The holding center is quiet and stale. I try not to peer down hallways or through doors as we are led down one flight of stairs and then another, plunging into the gray, frozen earth.

"He's in the cell at the very end on your right," our guide tells us.

I glance up at August. "I think I'd like to speak to him alone, if that's all right."

August's lips thin, but he nods, pressing a kiss to my forehead.

And then I'm walking through the dim, candlelit corridor on my own. My shadow flickers alongside me on the walls, tall and eerie and long. My footsteps echo, scrape across the stone, rattle the hairs standing upright on my arms.

I ball my fists in my skirt as I reach the end of the hallway.

A shadow sits in the far corner of the last cell.

Will.

I clear my throat, stepping up to the bars.

The shadow raises his head, and the firelight glints off a half smile.

"Myra Whitlock," he says, his voice husky from disuse. "You couldn't stay away, could you?"

"I've come to ask you something important." I hold my chin high even as his words raise gooseflesh on my arms.

Slowly, he pushes to his feet and shuffles closer. It takes everything in me not to step back.

Lantern light illuminates his face, which, in spite of the drab clothing and unkempt hair, looks as handsome as ever. He grins lazily at me, draping his freckled arms through the bars.

"Lovely dress," he says with a wink. "I always did think red was a becoming color on you."

"Where are my parents?" I ask. "What did you do with their bodies? I'd like to have them moved to the family plot in the cemetery. Give them a proper burial."

His smile fades. "You'll never forgive me for what happened to them, will you?"

"'Happened to them'? Your word choice is very telling, Mr. Harris."

"I didn't know you then," he says, eyelashes shuttering.

"Would it have changed anything if you had?" I snap.

His brows rise. "Of course it would have. Do you think I revel in the fact that I've ruined the lives of the only two girls I've ever cared for?"

His words ring sharp in the stale air, and he lifts a hand to run a finger along my jaw.

The breath catches in my throat, but I don't jerk away. "You don't know what it means to care. You knew me for only a week."

"One can learn a lot about a person in a week. Especially a person so similar to oneself."

"I'm nothing like you," I spit.

His smile deepens. "Lie to yourself all you want, love. It doesn't change what you know to be true."

I meet his gaze head-on. "Where are their bodies?"

He drops his hand. "We could have been unstoppable together, you and I. Our combined power—it would have changed everything."

"No, Will."

"Yes. You can't tell me you don't wonder about it. What it would have been like—you and me, painting the world the way we wanted it. Building it into something wondrous. Something worthy of us. Worthy of you."

"I don't," I say, curt and short. "I don't think of you at all."

"Liar." He winds his fingers around the bars and glares at me. "You've destroyed everything. Taken my magic, ruined my life… Does it make you happy to see me in here like this? Does it bring you joy?"

"Where are my parents?" I ask, my voice ringing a bit too loud as I try to keep my grip on the nerves bubbling like acid in my throat.

"You think you've won, don't you?" he continues, his eyes lethal in the dank light. "The villain is locked away, and you're the heroine who's saved the day, restored peace to the ailing city of Lalverton." He leans in close and hisses, "This is far from over, Miss Whitlock. These walls cannot hold me, not forever. And when I get out of here—and I *will* get out of here—rest assured that I will come for you. What you've done will not go unanswered. You have my word on that."

The air in my chest is thin, and my head spins, but I force my eyes to remain on his, unblinking, unflinching.

"Tell me where they are."

His mouth curls into a grin as he backs into the shadows, eyes glinting yellow.

"Will!" I pound on the bars. "Please!"

But he does not speak again.

Tears burn in my eyes when I finally turn away and stalk up the hall. All I wanted was to say goodbye properly to my parents, to have a place where I could put flowers on their birthdays and visit when I missed them.

August catches sight of my expression, and his own darkens. "He wouldn't tell you?"

"Let's go." I grasp his arm and pull him toward the stairs. "Maybe I can—"

"He's not going to help us."

We mount the stairs, return to the glowing white of the sunlight, let the gate close and lock behind us.

But as we climb into the carriage that will take us back downtown, I can't stop Will's words from repeating in my head.

What you've done will not go unanswered.

You have my word on that.

★ ★ ★ ★ ★

ACKNOWLEDGMENTS

This book. In some ways, it was the easiest I've ever written. It's the only book I've done yet that didn't require an entire from-scratch rewrite. The outline only took me a week to pull together. The characters leapt to life as soon as I thought of them. Myra's story—her desperation to help her sister, her fierce loyalty, her unyielding desire to control the uncontrollable—seemed to come from somewhere deep inside, fully formed and ready to write.

But in many ways, this book was also one of the hardest I've ever written. Delving deep into the anxious, broken parts of me to build August. Harnessing the fears I've felt for the ones I love and the very harsh reality of their mortality. And, all the while, *knowing* from the start that readers *would* read this one. This story was never just mine, the way the ones that came before it were at certain points. Throughout the entire process, I had its future readers in the back of my mind. Waiting and watching and interpreting, and that was far more difficult than I anticipated.

I quite simply could not have built this story into what it has become without the support of several people. People who helped me shoulder the weight of this new Reader Expectation aspect of writing I'd never dealt with before. People who reminded me I could when I was afraid I couldn't. People who held me up when the fear of failure nearly crushed me.

So, to start things off, the first thank you will always go to Jon, who ceaselessly supports me pursuing this wild dream even when it requires late nights and early mornings and lots of solo dad time for him. Who reminds me why I love this every day. Who never lets me quit. Thank you for being my rock, my comfort, my inspiration. "I love you" is never enough to communicate the depth of my appreciation for you, all you are, and all you do.

Thank you to Mom and Dad. Thank you for pushing me to pursue my dreams and cheering me on from the sidelines. For telling everyone you meet about my books and passing out bookmarks like Christmas cards. For supporting me, even when my stories give you heartburn. I couldn't have asked for better parents.

Thank you to Kim Chance, Megan LaCroix, Jessica Froberg, and J. Elle, without whom this story could never have come to fruition. Thank you for the critical reads and the honest feedback, for prodding me to make the story better, for reminding me that I was capable of greatness. Thank you for the Marco Polos and the pep talks and the gifs and the late-night text messages. I will forever be grateful for you.

Thank you to Rose Erickson. You took on a full beta in a quick turnaround and gave me feedback that helped more than you know. And your enthusiasm made a fundamental difference in my confidence in this story in a way I could never put into words.

Thank you to the many authenticity readers who read early

drafts and shared their experiences with me, who helped me learn and grow through the course of developing this book. Your insight and feedback were truly invaluable.

To Julie Lochridge, who helped me develop the details of the oil painting scenes in this book. Thank you for your suggestions, for your careful read, and for sharing your knowledge and expertise with me. Myra couldn't have become the artist she is without you.

Thank you to Christa Heschke, my amazing agent, who is always only an email or phone call away. Thank you for having my back and championing my stories in the way I always hoped my agent would. Thank you for being a friend and a business partner, for believing in my characters and my books, for fighting for them. I am so beyond lucky to have you in my corner.

To Daniele Hunter. You helped me so much. I will forever be grateful for the insight you've given me, for the advice and encouragement, and for the brainstorming sessions. Thank you for everything!

To Connolly Bottum, whose editorial expertise never ceases to blow my mind. Every time I get an edit letter from you, I find myself awed, inspired, and empowered. I'll never be able to explain just how wonderful it is to work with an editor who not only understands my vision for my work and my stories, but who also has such a keen eye as to help push me to grow in ways I didn't even realize I needed to grow. This book simply would not be what it has become without you. Thank you, thank you, thank you.

To the entire Inkyard Press team. Thank you for all of your ceaseless hours spent on my book's behalf. Thank you for your expertise, your kindness, and your tenacity. You've made my dreams come true, and I'll be forever grateful for that. And thank you especially to the art team for a cover that made me almost drop my phone when I first saw it. I don't deserve you!

To the author friends who have supported me in DMs and Instagram comments. You all are what makes this publishing journey survivable! Shelby Mahurin, Shannon Dittemore, Diana Urban, Ashley Schumacher, Rachel Griffin, Allison Saft, Ava Reid, Lyndall Clipstone, Adalyn Grace, Ashley Shuttlesworth, Candice Connor, Courtney Gould, Cyla Panin, Jessica Rubinkowski, Lauren Blackwood, Kylie Lee Baker, Margie Fuston, Nicole Bross, Sam Taylor, Tori Bovalino, Vanessa Len, Laura Rueckert, and soooo many more (you know who you are). Thank you for grounding me, commiserating with me, and celebrating with me.

To my children. You won't read my books for many years, but I hope that when you do, you find hope and power and fight in these stories. That you look for real magic in your lives. That you understand that almost everything I know about love and sacrifice and hope is because of you. You four are everything to me.

And to you, reader. Thank you, always, for giving my characters and their journeys space in your mind and in your heart. None of this would ever be possible without you.

Don't miss another thrilling fantasy
from Jessica S. Olson:

Sing Me Forgotten

Turn the page for a sneak peek!

I am a shadow. A shimmer of black satin. A wraith in the dark.

Music soars above the audience to where I hide behind a marble cherub near the Channe Opera House's domed ceiling. The lead soprano's vibrato trembles in the air, and my eyes fall shut as her music sends her memories rippling across the inside of my eyelids in shades of gray. The images are fuzzy and the emotions distant, but if I surrender myself to them, I can almost forget what I am for a moment.

Every night when the curtains rise and lights engulf the stage, when the seats fill with whispering patrons and the air shivers with the strum of strings, I glimpse the world outside—a world I've never seen with my eyes but know better than the beat of my heart because I've experienced it through a thousand different pasts.

The lead soprano's memories pull me in, and for a moment I am her, dashing out onto a stage bathed in golden light and sending my voice to fill the theater. The audience watches me dance, and though I cannot see their expressions from the soprano's vantage point, I imagine their eyes glassy with tears as my song plunges into their souls and strums along their heartstrings with slow, practiced grace. Their faces shine, their gazes riveted on my beauty. I raise my hand to my own cheek where I can all but feel the warmth of the spotlight.

But instead of smooth skin, my fingertips slip against my mask. I jolt my hand away, hissing, and relinquish my hold on her past.

My attention flicks to the premium box where Cyril Bardin meets my gaze. *You're too visible, Isda*, his eyes say.

I shrink into the shadows as applause smatters like raindrops below, not nearly enthusiastic enough to ensure adequate ticket sales. It seems the soprano, though nearly flawless in her performance, was not enough to make up for the rest of the abysmal cast.

Luckily, I'm very good at my job.

The clapping peters out as Cyril strides onto the stage. The performers line up behind him, tugging at their costumes and adjusting their wigs as discreetly as they can. Where their smiles pull across lips tight with too much makeup and wrinkle in tired, powdery lines around their eyes, Cyril's is charming, as always, accentuated by a regal, high forehead, paper-white hair, and a clean-shaven jaw. He gestures to the crowd with twinkling eyes. "Merci, my illustrious guests." His voice booms out to bounce back from the far walls. "It has been truly a pleasure to entertain you tonight."

Without thinking, I reach for the pendant at my throat and twist its chain around my fingers as anticipation bubbles like champagne in my stomach.

"Now before I bid you au revoir, it is time once again for the Channe Opera House's age-old tradition of having the audience join our performers in a special rendition of the Vaureillean classic, 'La Chanson des Rêves.'" Cyril turns to the orchestra at his feet and nods. "Maestro."

The conductor cues up the strings, then climbs onto the stage at Cyril's side and raises his baton. As one, the audience launches into the familiar tune.

The skin on my left ankle bone prickles—the place where I once carved the Manipulation Mark that enables me to harness my magic. The scar has since faded and been scraped away by clumsy tumbles down the stairs, but the ability that carving it gave me is still just as strong any time voices fill the air with music. My power purrs to life in my chest, reaching out toward each voice, yearning for the memories that live in them. I scan the faces quickly, letting images and emotions trickle through me one after the other, a burbling current of sights and sounds and smells.

When people sing, I see their memories, starting with the newest. If I want to, I can comb backward through time, sifting through the liquid swirl of moments in their minds as though rippling my fingers through water in a creek.

It is only in these moments that I truly feel alive. Where the world has forced me to hide, hated me for my power, tried to kill me for what I am, I have found my purpose in surrounding myself with its music and holding the memories of its people in my hands. They don't know I'm there, churning through their minds among their secrets and darkest moments, but I know. And no matter how many nights I've spent up here tucked away in the shadows, the thrill of finally having some measure of power over them sends tingles straight through every nerve of my body.

This is my performance, the only one I am allowed.

Copyright © 2021 by Jessica Olson